Patricia Scanlan was born in Dublin, where she still lives. Her previous bestsellers are *Apartment 3B*; *Finishing Touches*; *Foreign Affairs*; *Promises, Promises*; *Mirror, Mirror*; *City Girl*; *City Woman*; *City Lives*; *Francesca's Party*; *Two For Joy*; *Double Wedding* and *Winter Blessings*, a collection of quotes, blessings, poems and reminiscences. Patricia is the series editor and a contributing author to the Open Door series. She also teaches creative writing to second-level students and is involved in Adult Literacy.

www.**booksattransworld**.co.uk

DIVIDED LOYALTIES

Patricia Scanlan

BANTAM PRESS

LONDON · TORONTO · SYDNEY · AUCKLAND · JOHANNESBURG

TRANSWORLD PUBLISHERS
61–63 Uxbridge Road, London W5 5SA
a division of The Random House Group Ltd

RANDOM HOUSE AUSTRALIA (PTY) LTD
20 Alfred Street, Milsons Point, Sydney,
New South Wales 2061, Australia

RANDOM HOUSE NEW ZEALAND LTD
18 Poland Road, Glenfield, Auckland 10, New Zealand

RANDOM HOUSE SOUTH AFRICA (PTY) LTD
Isle of Houghton, Corner of Boundary Road & Carse O'Gowrie,
Houghton 2198, South Africa

Published 2006 by Bantam Press
a division of Transworld Publishers

A catalogue record for this book is available from the British Library.
ISBN 9780593048726 (cased) (from Jan 07)
ISBN 0593048725 (cased)
ISBN 9780593055991 (tpb) (from Jan 07)
ISBN 0593055993 (tpb)

Typeset in 12/15½pt Ehrhardt by
Kestrel Data, Exeter, Devon.

Printed in Great Britain.
Clays Ltd, St Ives plc

3 5 7 9 10 8 6 4

Papers used by Transworld Publishers are natural, recyclable products made
from wood grown in sustainable forests. The manufacturing processes conform
to the environmental regulations of the country of origin.

One of the most precious things a friend can give is time.

To dear Alil and Aidan who gave me so much of their time and help when I was moving house last summer.

This book is dedicated to both of you with much love and gratitude.

ACKNOWLEDGEMENTS

I myself do nothing. The Holy Spirit accomplishes all through me.
Robert Blake

Dear Holy Spirit, thank you so much for *Divided Loyalties* and for all my other books.

With great gratitude I give thanks:

To Jesus, Our Lady, St Joseph, Mother Meera, St Anthony, St Michael, White Eagle and all my Angels, Saints and Guides. My most wonderful inspirations.

To my parents and family: we are so lucky. For all the love and cherishing: thank you. Without you it would all mean nothing.

To all my friends who are such a support, and I especially have to mention Sheila O'Flanagan, computer whizz and dear friend, who has dragged me screeching and protesting into updated Macs, broadband, and all those computery bits that terrify me. Dear friends, you know who you are and you know how much I value you.

To Evelyn and Ruth Shern, who always get the first read and give me honest opinions. Dear Evelyn, I hope you enjoy this one.

To Sarah, Felicity, Susannah and Olivia, my champions as well as my agents. Thank you so much.

To Francesca Liversidge, my editor and protector in the hard world of publishing. Dear Francesca, you're my rock and always have been.

To all in Transworld, and Gill Hess and Co – a great team to have behind you. Onwards and upwards!

To my colleagues in HHI who make work fun.

Thanks also to my colleagues at New Island – looking forward to Series Five. And then . . . To Fintan Ardagh and all at Ergonomics Ltd for The Chair of chairs! It's mega! Thanks to Kim, David and all at Witherspoon Associates. I really appreciate what you do on my behalf.

To Professor Ciaran Bolger, thank you. My life has changed completely.

To all in the Bon Secours Hospital, Glasnevin, for their consistent kindness. Not only to me, but also to my family.

To KC. My God! What are you trying to do to me? I saw you in your leathers and thought this is as good as it gets. Now I've seen you in your tux . . . What next!

To John and Pat in Rathwood Homes and Garden who were very helpful.

To all who helped me move house but especially to: Brian Hennessy and all at Sherry Fitzgerald in Killester. Your kindness and patience were unbelievable. It was a joy to do business with you.

To Fiona, Anne Marie and Jenny in Mason's Estates who have always been so helpful and professional.

To Garrett Fitzpatrick and Dorothy in O'Reilly Doherty & Co, and to Frank Furlong in AIB Finglas. Always only a phone call away.

To Dave Stapleton, who painted my house as if it was his own and who gave me so much advice, as well as hanging up dozens of paintings.

To Keith Rooney, who is a fabulous carpenter.

To all, a big and heartfelt thanks.

And especially thanks to you, my dear readers, who consistently go and buy my books and send me lovely letters. May your lives be full of Love and Blessings. Enjoy!

WINTER

1

'LET'S TRY FOR ANOTHER BABY?' SHAUNA CASSIDY FINGERED THE flat, full pack of her contraceptive pill and scowled resentfully. Her husband, Greg, groaned from his side of the bed.

'Aw, Shauna, I don't know. Chloe's been such a handful since she was born, and besides, she's only two.'

'Don't say that,' Shauna flared indignantly, her heart sinking at his negativity. This wasn't the first time that she'd broached the subject of trying for another baby. For the last couple of months she'd become increasingly broody. She wanted Chloe to have a brother or sister close in age to her but, so far, Greg wasn't having any of it.

'Come on, Shauna.' He yawned and nearly gave himself lock-jaw. 'She had colic for the first year. And that bloody reflux. Not to talk about the temperatures every time she's getting a tooth. She rarely sleeps a full night, we've only just started to have a social life again and we're moving to the Emirates in January. Your timing is lousy.'

As if on cue, a fretful squawk from the room across the landing turned into a heart-rending howl. 'And you want another one?' Greg muttered, turning on his side and pulling the duvet up over his ears. Shauna glared down at him.

'Come on, Greg! I don't want to start another month on

11

the Pill; we need to talk about this sooner rather than later.'

'Not tonight. I'm knackered. For God's sake go in to her or we'll never get to sleep,' he growled.

'Ah you're always knackered,' she said exasperatedly as she threw back the duvet and hurried into the next room to comfort their little daughter.

Greg felt the tension begin to seep out of his body as he stretched his limbs and heard Chloe's sobs peter out as his wife's soft crooning soothed her. Was the woman mad? he wondered drowsily. Imagine two babies in the house, screeching and yelling. He loved his daughter but she'd completely disrupted their lives. Even Shauna couldn't deny that. They rarely had a night out together. Everything had to be arranged around feeding times and nap times. It was a pain in the butt. There were times he even felt that Shauna was so completely focused on Chloe and her needs that she'd hardly notice if he wasn't around any more. He remembered how she'd always made a fuss of him and danced attendance on him before she'd got pregnant. Those days were a distant memory.

Perhaps it would all change when they went back out to the Gulf. He was really looking forward to going to work in the Emirates, despite the instability in the region. He'd kept in contact with people he'd known and they all assured him that life went on very much as normal in spite of the volatile political situation. Shauna felt a little jittery sometimes, especially when the bombs had gone off in the residential compounds, but Greg had pointed out that Abu Dhabi was much more stable than Saudi and far more cosmopolitan. The war in Iraq wasn't having such an impact there. Look at all the people going out on holidays and buying property in Dubai, which was only a couple of hours' drive down the highway, he'd pointed out reassuringly.

If they didn't go now they'd never go, he urged. His wife had reluctantly agreed, knowing that he was right, at least about the timing.

They'd met at a party in Riyadh ten years ago. He was an architect in a big construction company. Shauna had worked in the personnel department. They were both in their early twenties, making lots of money and having a ball. They'd clicked and started dating. Greg sighed, remembering those carefree days. They'd had a great, relatively stress-free couple of years and then come home to get married.

The money they'd made in Saudi had bought them a four-bedroom house in Malahide; they hadn't even needed a mortgage. They'd bought it in Shauna's name so they wouldn't have to pay stamp duty as they were still paying off the mortgage on the place that Greg had bought when he was single. The apartment was now let, and the rent more than covered the mortgage repayments.

Greg wanted to increase his property portfolio and get into the property business in a big way. He'd bought and renovated two small redbrick houses in Cabra and made a relatively good profit on them. It had given him the taste for property speculation. Another stint in the Gulf would boost the bank balance enough to get him on the next rung of the property ladder.

It had all been going swimmingly until Shauna had got broody. He'd managed to put her off for a few years but she'd said that she didn't want to be too old having her first child and that thirty was considered quite old for a first-time mother. Reluctantly, he'd agreed to try for a baby. Chloe had been conceived a couple of months after they'd stopped using contraception and Shauna had been over the moon.

Greg scowled under the duvet. It seemed she was getting broody again. As he'd told her, her timing was lousy. Well, she could forget it. When they moved back to the Gulf they'd have an au pair to help out with Chloe and they were going to start having fun and socializing again. Life in Abu Dhabi would be far less restricted than their life had been in Saudi. It was just what they needed. Once they were out there, she'd forget all this baby stuff. His eyelids drooped and within minutes he was asleep.

Shauna could hear her husband's snores rumbling across the landing. Selfish lump, she thought sourly. Greg rarely got up to attend to Chloe. *You wanted her, you deal with her* was the unspoken reproach that had permeated their marriage since she'd had the baby.

What was wrong with him? Why couldn't he enjoy their child? Why couldn't he see that it would be good for them to have another baby, sooner rather than later, so that the children would be companions for each other? It made sense. They'd be around the same stage getting through all the childhood and teenage stuff. They'd be close to each other, there for each other in times of trouble, just like her siblings were there for her.

She looked down at Chloe's blond head nestled into her shoulder and her heart contracted with love. Her daughter's curls were the colour of spun gold and framed her head like an angelic halo. Her two little cheeks were fire-engine red and her chin was damp from dribbles. Shauna wiped her mouth tenderly with a soft bib. Chloe whimpered.

'It's all right, darling. Let's give you a drop of Calpol and you'll be as right as rain,' she murmured, stifling a yawn. It looked as if it could be a bumpy night. If she was up with one child she might as well be up with two, she thought resentfully. If she didn't get pregnant soon Chloe would be too old for her sibling. She'd love to have another little girl. It would be wonderful for her daughter to have a sister. Shauna smiled, thinking of her own sister, Carrie. She was really going to miss her when she went back out to the Gulf. Not only was Carrie her sister, she was her best friend. She'd understand Shauna's desire for another baby better than anyone would.

2

CARRIE MORGAN HATED MATHS, ALWAYS HAD AND ALWAYS would. She'd thought she'd finished with the damn thing for good when she'd left school. She hadn't reckoned she'd be battling with it again in her thirties. And losing badly, at that.

If she was having problems with subtraction how on earth was she going to manage when her children were doing isosceles triangles and all that gobbledegook? She tried again, as patiently as she could.

'Eight from seven you cannot take. Borrow one and cross off the—'

'No, Mom! That's not the way Teacher does it,' Olivia wailed. Carrie stared at her daughter in exasperation.

'Well that's the way we did it at school. I don't understand the way your teacher does it.' This new way of doing maths was doing her head in.

'That's 'cos you're stupid, Mom,' Olivia yelled as she stomped out of the kitchen in high dudgeon.

'Olivia Morgan!' Carrie roared. 'Come back here and don't be so cheeky. How *dare* you?' At precisely that moment the pot of homemade vegetable soup bubbled over, the creamy froth foaming across the top of the cooker.

'Lord Almighty give me patience,' she muttered, lifting

the pot off the heat. She could hear Olivia sobbing her way upstairs.

'Mom, it's just not your day.' Her son, Davey, chewed his pen at the other end of the kitchen table as he struggled with his English spellings.

'I guess not.' She managed a smile as she wiped away the mess. Davey, thank God, was placid and easy-going compared to his younger sister, who was definitely going to end up on the stage, she thought ruefully. High drama and Olivia went hand in hand.

'Do you know how to do the subtraction the way Miss Kenny does it?' she asked him hopefully.

'I think so, Mom. Will I try and explain it to Olivia?' he offered.

'We'll let her calm down for a minute. You finish your spellings and we'll have another go.'

The shrill jangle of the phone made her sigh. 'Hello.' She tried to hide her irritation.

'Carrie, I'm not feeling very well. Could you drop my dinner over instead of me having to come over to you?' her father, Noel, said in his martyr voice. He usually ate dinner with them in the evening.

'What's the matter with you?' She tried to inject a note of concern into her voice. This was all she needed.

'I've a pain in my arm. I'm sure it's nothing,' he said mournfully.

Carrie's heart sank. As sure as eggs were eggs she'd end up bringing him to the doctor who'd arrange blood tests and ECGs, all of which he'd had done before.

'Right. I'll be over later. I'll have to bring the kids with me; Dan's working late.'

'Thanks, love,' her father said gratefully. 'See you later.'

As if I haven't enough to be doing, she thought grumpily as she added a slab of butter and a sprinkling of salt to the potatoes and wielded her masher with a vengeance.

Noel lived in a bungalow at the other end of the large seaside village of Whiteshells Bay, in North County Dublin, where she had grown up. It was convenient that he lived so close, but tonight was not a good night for one of his hypochondriac episodes.

Tonight was Boy Scouts night. She'd been hoping Dan would be home to bring Davey to the club, but the sprinkler system in one of his glasshouses had gone on the blink and it had to be sorted. He'd sounded pissed off when he'd phoned her, so she'd bitten back her grumbling reproach and told him she'd keep his dinner for him. Dan worked hard for his family. He'd built up a sizeable market gardening business on the farm his father had left him but he had to spend long hours at work sometimes, to Carrie's intense frustration.

'You'll be dead before you're fifty!' she had exploded in exasperation one wet, windy Sunday morning a few weeks ago, when he'd got out of bed while it was still dark to get dressed to go and inspect his glasshouses.

'Forty-five, even,' he teased as he towelled his chestnut hair dry after his shower.

'I'm serious,' she retorted, thinking how fit he looked as he stood, all six foot one of him, bare-chested, lean and rangy, in front of her, with a towel tied at his waist.

'Ah don't be grumpy,' he chided, bending down to kiss her. She'd kissed him back, unable to stay mad at him.

'Come back to bed,' she urged, wanting him, running her fingers through his damp hair.

'I've a date with a hot tomato,' he murmured, nibbling her ear. 'When I get back.'

She'd watched him leave, half exasperated, half amused. She caught a glimpse of herself in the mirror, auburn layers sticking up wildly, a dusting of freckles across her nose, green eyes, fringed with dark lashes, a tad puffy. No wonder he preferred his tomatoes, she thought ruefully as she burrowed back down in the bed and fell asleep almost instantly.

Imagine having to compete with a tomato for your husband's affections, she'd complained to Shauna, who'd called over to visit later that day.

'Tell me about it,' her sister said dryly. 'I've to compete with drawing boards and T-squares.'

'And you're the good-looking one in our family,' Carrie remarked, wondering how her younger sister always managed to look so groomed and elegant. Her naturally blond hair fell over her shoulders in a silky curtain. Her eyes, as blue as cornflowers, sparkled over high cheekbones and she had a gorgeous snub nose that Carrie had always envied. Shauna was slender and petite. Carrie always felt like an Amazon beside her.

'You have curves where women are meant to have curves,' Dan constantly assured her, with an appreciative glint in his blue eyes that always made her feel good about herself.

'I was dying for a shag last night and Greg fell asleep on me. I went to brush my teeth and go to the loo and when I came back into the bedroom he was snoring,' Shauna moaned.

'So much for our sex appeal.' Carrie grinned. Shauna had giggled in spite of herself and they'd comforted themselves with a slice of coffee cake.

Carrie spooned carrot and parsnip mash onto the heated plates, and gave a wry smile as she remembered that particular Sunday. Shauna had taken Chloe, Davey and Olivia to the zoo and she and Dan had spent the afternoon in bed making the most of a child-free Sunday afternoon.

'I ended it with the Tomato,' Dan had whispered mischievously as he slid his fingers up under her T-shirt, making her shiver with anticipation.

It had been a loving, lusty afternoon and she had reason to remember it now, she thought ruefully, as her breasts ached with soreness. Her period was late and she didn't need a test to know that she was pregnant. Maybe that was why she was so crotchety lately. Poor Olivia. If she thought life was tough now, wait until her nose was put out of joint by the new arrival.

'Olivia, come down and have your dinner, pet, and we'll have another go at the sums,' she called placatingly.

'Don't want any dinner,' Olivia shouted huffily.

'OK, I'll give an extra portion to Dad and Davey,' Carrie challenged.

Silence.

Then, sulkily, 'I'm coming.'

Carrie smiled as she plated up Dan's and her father's dinner. Was that child psychology, emotional blackmail or what? At least it had worked for today. Now if she could only get a handle on those bloody sums she'd be doing OK.

She was glad to flop onto the sofa once the children were in bed. She'd seemed to spend the evening getting in and out of the car. She'd dropped off Davey at his Scouts. Then she'd bought a pregnancy test kit, delivered her father's dinner, brought in his washing off the line, and gone shopping for cat food for him.

Her father had eaten all his dinner, and told her that he felt a little better. He'd looked fine to her. He didn't look pale or flushed, but he had confided that he'd been talking to a neighbour who'd told him that one of the neighbours down the road had suffered a heart attack. Carrie could see his medical encyclopedia beside his armchair and guessed that he'd been reading up on the symptoms. One day she was going to burn that damn book, she thought irritably. Next to the Bible, it was the most well-thumbed volume in her father's house.

Afterwards she brought Olivia into Seashells Café for hot chocolate, as a treat to make up for their earlier tiff. Seashells Café was one of their favourite haunts. It was right in the middle of the village, beside Fisherman's Lane, and its big bay windows had panoramic views of the coast and sea. In summer it was always packed with day-trippers to the beach, but at this time of year it wasn't so busy and she and Olivia had settled at one of the round pine tables in the bay window. It was a bright, airy place, decorated in nautical blues and creams, and the walls were hung with a selection of framed sepia photos of the village in the 'olden days', as her daughter called them. They'd sipped their hot chocolate companionably and made their peace with each other, before collecting Davey, who proudly showed them his collection of nautical knots.

Dan had arrived home around nine, yawning his head off, and wolfed his dinner.

'You look whacked,' he observed as he handed her a mug of tea and a chocolate Kimberly a little later.

'I am.' She snuggled in beside him on the sofa in the den. A fire blazed up the chimney and she felt pleasantly relaxed. 'And it's going to get worse.'

'Why?' He eyed her quizzically.

'Remember the Sunday afternoon that you shagged me senseless?'

'Yessss . . .' he said slowly, his blue eyes widening as comprehension began to dawn.

'I think I'm pregnant.' Carrie studied him warily. They hadn't actually discussed having a third child.

'You *think* . . .'

21

'Well, I'm more or less sure. I just have to do a test to confirm it and I wanted us to do it together.'

'Do you want to do it now?' Dan asked. Stoically.

'Will we?'

'Come on, so.' He pulled her to her feet and dropped an arm round her shoulder.

'Do you mind if I am?' she asked hesitantly. If Dan wasn't happy about her being pregnant she'd be gutted.

'Of course I don't if you're OK with it.' He smiled down at her and she felt inexplicably happy. Dan Morgan was the best thing that had ever happened to her. She was still as crazy about him as she'd been when they'd first married.

'So it looks like we're pregnant,' he said ten minutes later as they studied the wand she held, which showed two unmistakable blue lines. His arms tightened around her and they kissed until she drew away breathless.

'By the way,' he murmured as his hands slid down to her waist and over the curve of her hips. 'I just want to clarify one thing. It was *you* that shagged *me* senseless that Sunday afternoon.'

'Whatever you say, darling. Let's do it again. Just be gentle with the boobs, they're ready to explode!' Carrie whispered, tiredness forgotten as her hormones ran rampant at the touch of his fingers.

Later as she lay drowsily in the crook of his arm she thought of Shauna. This new baby would be a playmate for Chloe in years to come. As it was, Olivia and Davey were very protective of their little cousin. Carrie was looking forward to telling her sister her news. She'd ring Shauna first thing in the morning and arrange for them to have lunch or coffee. She was glad Shauna was still at home to share her good news. It would be much nicer to tell her face to face than to say it down a phone line when she was thousands of miles away. She was going to miss Shauna like hell. Why she wanted to up sticks and head out to live in a war zone was unfathomable. But that didn't seem to bother her or Greg unduly. As needles of rain began to hurl themselves against the bedroom window and the east wind blew in from the sea, Carrie mused that if it were her, she wouldn't bring her kids to live in a place as unstable as the Gulf.

She was dreading her sister's departure to the Emirates. Their father was getting more demanding and they'd always shared the responsibility of him since their mother had died three years ago. Now, with another baby on the way, and Shauna leaving for God knows how long, Carrie couldn't help feeling more than a little daunted.

Shauna led such a charmed life, she always had. Sometimes Carrie couldn't help feeling the tiniest bit envious. Wouldn't it be lovely to go to an exotic country and have maids and nannies to help you manage? It would be fabulous to spend your time partying and socializing. Even though Whiteshells Bay was a picturesque little seaside village, and Carrie liked living in it, exotic was hardly the adjective to describe it.

She sighed, and then smiled as Dan gave a low rumbling snore. She might live in a sleepy seaside village, and she might be pregnant and have an ageing, demanding father to take care of, but she had a kind, witty, supportive, sexy husband and two good little children. She wasn't doing too badly at all.

The phone rang, jerking her into wakefulness tinged with dread. Phone calls at this hour of the night weren't good news.

'Hello, Carrie, it's Dad. I think I need a doctor. The pain's gone into my chest. I think I'm having a heart attack.' She could hear the panic in her father's voice.

'You're not having a heart attack. Stop getting yourself into a tizzy. I'll be there in a minute,' she assured him.

23

'I didn't like to bother Shauna. I know the baby's teething,' her father said feebly. 'And besides, you're nearer.'

'That's OK. I'll be over as soon as I get dressed.' Carrie tried not to feel resentful. It wouldn't have mattered if Shauna lived next door to him; their father would always call Carrie in an emergency. He and his younger daughter didn't get on too well. Their personalities had always clashed, but since his wife's death the hostility between them had deepened. And as for Bobby, the youngest in their family, he had washed his hands of his father just as Noel had washed his hands of him. Carrie would be wasting her time expecting any help from him. Not that he could help anyway right this minute, seeing as he lived in London, she thought glumly. She yawned as she pulled on a pair of jeans and a sweatshirt. She couldn't honestly blame Bobby after the way their father had treated him. Her only brother was gay and that was anathema to their father, an affront to his religious beliefs. Once their mother had died, Bobby had gone to London, unable to deal with his father's hostility. Understandable, but it didn't change the fact that she was the one getting up in the middle of the night to go and look after Noel. She was the eldest; she was the responsible one. And she was getting fed up of it.

3

'WHY DIDN'T YOU RING ME EARLIER? I'D HAVE COME UP.' SHAUNA frowned as she untangled the phone cord that Chloe had twisted into a knot.

'What was the point in the two of us being up all night hanging around a hospital?' Carrie said tiredly.

'I was up anyway with Chloe. She's got a big bruiser of a back tooth coming,' Shauna responded glumly.

'So Dad told me,' Carrie said dryly. 'He said that was why he didn't want to ring you.'

'That's not very fair on you, though.'

Shauna knew she should feel guilty, but part of her was mightily relieved that her father hadn't phoned. Greg would have been far from pleased if she'd woken him up to tell him to take care of Chloe because she had to drive up to Whiteshells Bay in the middle of the night.

'What did the doctors say?'

'They're keeping him in; they're hoping to have a bed for him later on today. He's on a trolley in A and E.'

'Look, why don't you go to bed for a couple of hours? I'll come over later and we can go and visit him this afternoon,' Shauna suggested, anxious to offer some support.

'Would you, Shauna? I'm whacked. I could do with a few hours' shut-eye.'

'Take the phone off the hook and I'll be over in time to pick up Olivia from school,' her sister instructed briskly.

'She'll be thrilled to see Chloe.' Carrie sounded more cheerful. 'See you later . . . and thanks.'

'No problem,' Shauna assured her, twirling her finger in one of Chloe's soft corkscrew curls. She had planned to spend a few hours working on a wedding dress she was making to order. She had to hand-sew dozens of sequins and beading onto an ornate fur-trimmed jacket that was being worn over a very simple, elegant, satin sheath dress. Chloe's nap time would have allowed her a few precious uninterrupted hours to get on with the job. It was the last dress she had been commissioned to make before she left for the Emirates and she was anxious to get it finished on time.

Typical of her father to muck up her plans. Shauna's lips tightened in annoyance. She didn't know how Carrie could keep her patience with their dad; she certainly didn't have the tolerance for him that her older sister had. She was far more likely to argue the toss with him about his deeply conservative beliefs than Carrie was.

She had railed at their restrictive upbringing and there had been many rows in their teenage years as their father issued edicts about where they could go and whom they could socialize with. Boys were definitely off limits! Noel McCarthy was a street angel and a house devil as far as his younger daughter was concerned. Well respected in the community, he was a pillar of the Church, involved in all its fundraising and parish activities. Many times she'd been roped in to deliver the parish dues envelopes or the Easter and Christmas information cards, and she'd had to do the church collection every week.

She had argued bitterly that it was her father who had offered to do such work, so why should she have to do it? It was no joke trudging round all the houses in the large village on a wet, windy evening with an easterly gale blowing in off the sea. Her friends would be snug and warm in their houses, watching TV, while she'd be standing, resentfully, on doorsteps waiting for people to put their few coins into the collection envelope.

Carrie had just got on with it. She did the houses north of the church, Shauna the ones south of it. Bobby had managed to get out of all parish duties by once stuffing his ration of parish dues envelopes into the bin outside the chipper. Unfortunately he didn't stuff them in far enough and a gust of wind had whipped a few of them out onto the street later that evening and they'd been discovered by Mrs Foley, one of the ladies of the parish committee of which Noel was chairman. There'd been consternation as Noel was informed of this outrage.

The three of them had been summoned to the small room off the garage that Noel used as an office and interrogations had begun. Bobby had confessed to his crime after Noel had accused Shauna of the transgression, knowing of her oft-stated objections to delivering the envelopes.

Bobby was good like that; he couldn't let his sister take the blame for something that he'd done. Their father, red with fury, had banned Bobby from watching TV for a year and had assured him that such a crime against God's good work would require much repentance and good deeds.

Bobby had later whispered to Shauna that it was worth it not to have to deliver those hated envelopes. But as the days turned into weeks, and he was ordered from the sitting room when the TV was turned on, his bravado slipped and he confessed that he really missed *Star Trek* and *Top of the Pops*.

Their mother, Anna, who had a soft, kind heart, had allowed

him to turn on the TV as soon as he had finished his homework, but it was switched off at five thirty before their father arrived home from work. Noel worked as a bank clerk in the town of Swords, just north of Dublin, and Bobby prayed that he would never get moved to a bank nearer home.

Shauna shook her head impatiently as she lifted her tired little daughter in her arms, revelling in the way she snuggled in close against her neck. Why was she swamped with all these unhappy memories? She wanted to forget those times. She was grown up now, an independent woman, free of Noel and his authority; she shouldn't hark back to the past.

She was determined that Chloe would never grow up with the hang-ups that were a legacy of her own childhood even to this day. A lack of self-esteem, a lack of self-worth, would not be traits that her daughter would grow up with. Noel might see himself as a good-living, God-fearing, upright member of the community, but Shauna knew otherwise, and she had the emotional scars to prove it. If it weren't for Carrie she'd let him fend for himself. He was a small-minded bully who used emotional blackmail on his daughters and son with varying degrees of success.

Well, no success, it seemed, in Bobby's case, Shauna acknowledged, smiling as she remembered her brother's last phone call to her.

'How's the old buzzard doing? Still saying decades of the rosary in the hope that I'll discover that I'm not gay after all and it was only a temporary aberration? And my immortal soul isn't damned for eternity?' Although the words were joky and light-hearted, Shauna knew that behind them lay a deep, wounding hurt that might never be healed.

Bobby was the baby of the family. Four years older, she felt fiercely protective of him. When their mother had died suddenly of a heart attack, they'd all been devastated. But Shauna would

28

never forget her father saying, in his deceptively mild-mannered voice, 'You know, Bobby, all the worry about you and this attention-seeking of yours worried your mother dreadfully. It must have put a terrible strain on her heart. Your greatest gift to her now would be for you to sort yourself out and find a nice girl and go and get married like a normal young man.'

Shauna would never forget how her brother had paled at his father's cruel, damaging words, turned on his heel and walked out of the house.

'That was a terrible thing to say, Dad. How dare you call yourself a Christian,' she'd exploded, hating him. 'Bobby was born the way he is. God doesn't judge him. God made him, God knows him. He is as beloved of God as any other soul of His creation. What sort of warped belief have you got? Where is God's compassion and mercy in your religion? Your God is horrible. I'm glad I don't believe in *Him*.'

Noel had risen to his feet, ashen-faced at this unbelievable attack on his authority and beliefs. 'That's enough from you, miss, you who ignore the Church's rulings in spite of our best efforts. God weeps to hear your ignorance of His teachings, and if you don't like what I have to say, the door is—'

'Stop it! Mam's not cold in the grave and look at the pair of you!' Carrie's disgust had silenced them, and they had argued no more, but that was the day when her father had sundered the very tenuous tie of love or loyalty that had existed between him and his youngest children. It was only out of a sense of obligation and guilt and not wanting to let Carrie have to carry the burden alone that Shauna mucked in and did as much as she felt she had to.

One of the big pluses of going back out to the Gulf would be the distance it would put between her and her father. It would be a relief not to have to listen to his moaning, self-pitying whinges and his opinionated dictates. Carrie really should put her foot down and tell him to get on with it. Dan was very patient with Noel; Greg wasn't half as accommodating and rarely visited with Shauna. On the rare occasions that Noel called to their house, her husband would have a short conversation with him and then disappear up to his office. When she was younger, years ago during their engagement, she'd always been on edge that Greg would blow his top about her father's pointed jibes about 'living in sin' and tell him to get lost. Noel had never forgiven her for refusing to even consider letting Greg ask him for his permission to marry her.

'I'm not your chattel, Dad. You don't own me,' she informed him tartly, much to his disgust.

'Couldn't you just do it to keep the peace?' her mother urged, to no avail. It was only for her mother's sake that she had allowed him to walk her up the aisle. And that too had been a source of conflict, because of her father's insistence that she go to confession to make sure she had no stain of mortal sin on her soul as a result of living with Greg before marriage.

He really had so much to answer for, she thought bitterly, remembering the rows and trauma that her father's beliefs had inflicted on the family. How her mother had lived with him and put up with him she would never fathom, because if he had been her husband she would have surely murdered him.

That conflict would not happen in her little family, she vowed as she laid her sleepy toddler in her car seat and covered her with a soft, woolly blanket. She raced back into the house, grabbed one of her daughter's bottles from the fridge, shrugged into her own coat and was about to set the alarm when the phone rang. She was tempted not to answer it but was afraid it might be her client checking on the progress of her wedding dress.

'Hi,' she answered crisply, standing at the door so she could keep an eye on Chloe.

'Shauna, how's it going? You haven't been in touch lately so I said I'd better give you a ring. We don't want you disappearing out of the country without getting a chance to say goodbye.' The breezy tones of her sister-in-law, Della, floated down the line. Shauna's heart sank. *She* was definitely the last person Shauna needed to hear from today.

'Della, I can't stop to talk. Chloe's in the car, Dad's in hospital, and I've got to rush and pick up Olivia, so I'll give you a buzz later in the week, OK?'

'But—'

'Della, I really have to go. Greg's at work if you want a chat with him,' she said hastily. 'Talk to you soon, 'bye.' Without even giving her sister-in-law a chance to respond she hung up, set the alarm and locked the door behind her.

4

'AND HOW *ARE* THE FREELOADERS?' CARRIE ENQUIRED ACIDLY AS they walked along the beach a couple of hours later.

Shauna giggled. Carrie was not one to mince her words. 'Don't even go there,' she groaned. 'I didn't engage in any conversation. I used Dad shamelessly, said he was in hospital and that I had to go, and hung up.'

'I bet she's looking to stay for a weekend before Christmas.' Carrie skimmed a stone across the white-crested waves.

'Well she can look all she wants. It's not going to happen and I *mean* it this time,' Shauna said with uncharacteristic steeliness. Her in-laws, Della Keegan, Greg's only sister, and her husband, Eddie, were the bane of Shauna's life. They lived near Cavan and on their frequent weekend trips to Dublin would often end up on her doorstep, unannounced, with plans to stay overnight. It hadn't been so bad when neither couple had children but once Della had had Kathryn and a year later Shauna had Chloe it got much more awkward and gradually she'd begun to resent her in-laws' unwelcome intrusions.

Greg and Eddie would head off to the pub and she'd be left with Della and the babies. Della was a great one for one-upmanship and was always boasting about this acquisition or that. Frankly, Shauna couldn't give a hoot and wished her sister-in-law would shut up wittering and give her some peace. The Keegans' casual assumption that they could just drop in and stay over any time it suited them didn't seem to bother Greg, and when she'd complained he'd informed her that he liked seeing his family and that she was lucky to have hers living just a couple of miles away. She couldn't very well argue with that, and his comments made her seem churlish and inhospitable.

Carrie understood her frustration. She'd seen Della and Eddie at their freeloading best after they'd gatecrashed a barbecue she and Dan were holding for Shauna's birthday.

They'd arrived empty-handed, eaten and drunk all round them, made no effort to help with the wash-up, and ended up too pissed to drive and sleeping on the couch. That was the weekend she'd christened them the Freeloaders.

'I bet they'll wangle an overnighter no matter what you say.' Carrie grinned as she picked up a shiny, translucent shell for Olivia's collection.

'Nope! It's not going to happen. I've a dress to finish, I've to make a start on my Christmas shopping and besides, I just don't *want* them staying. I end up exhausted from running around after them. Della's as lazy as sin and she lets Kathryn do what she likes. That child is getting spoilt rotten.' She scowled, kicking a piece of driftwood out of her way impatiently. 'She's pregnant again, so of course that's an even bigger excuse to put her feet up and do nothing.'

'I hope you won't be saying that about me,' Carrie teased, smiling at her sister.

'Why would I say that about you?' Shauna asked, puzzled. Comprehension dawned. 'You're pregnant! Oh, Carrie, are you delighted?' she asked wistfully, trying to ignore the little jolt of envy that shot through her.

'Yeah, I am. I'd like Olivia to have a sister, or Davey a brother.

Actually, I'd like twins so I could have one of each.' She laughed, her green eyes sparkling as she confided her joyful news.

'Congratulations. Is Dan pleased?' Shauna hugged her sister tightly, ashamed of herself.

'Yep. He's great. He did the test with me. If I could only drag him away from his bloody glasshouses and tunnels he'd be perfect,' Carrie said ruefully.

'Men and their work.' Shauna shook her head. 'You'll never believe it,' she added slowly, 'but last night I asked Greg if *we* could try for another baby.'

'And?' Carrie arched an eyebrow at her expectantly.

Shauna wrinkled her nose. 'He wasn't too keen. He more or less said we're only just getting back to something like normal after having Chloe. I just think now's the time to go for it, so that they'll be company for each other. I'd really love Chloe to have a sister or brother. I don't want her to be an only child. It must be lonely. If I didn't have you I don't know what I'd do.' Her voice wobbled and to her dismay she burst into tears.

'Hey, hey, what's wrong?' Carrie looked at her in concern before putting her arms round her and giving her a comforting squeeze.

'I don't know.' Shauna sniffled. 'I suppose Greg's attitude doesn't help, and then bloody Della on the phone, and Dad being in hospital and me feeling guilty about you being up all night, especially now, knowing that you're pregnant. Sorry, I know it all sounds very me, me, me, and you've enough on your plate too. It must be my hormones,' she wept, her words almost incoherent.

She knew why she was crying but she couldn't say it to her sister. She couldn't say that when she had measured Greg's attitude to having children against Dan's, her husband had fallen far short and it hurt. Desperately. She wanted to be loyal to Greg but all she felt was resentment surging through her.

'Don't worry about last night. Didn't you collect Olivia for me today and let me get some shut-eye? Aren't we going in to see Dad together? Don't beat yourself up about it, Shauna.'

'It's just that you're so kind to him and I'm such a bitch to him. I don't feel any love for him, I'm just angry at him.'

'We're different, Shauna. You stood up to him. I don't have your pluck, I tried to deal with it in other ways, more passively, I suppose. It doesn't mean that I agree with him all the time or like the way he behaves,' Carrie said wearily.

Shauna wiped her eyes. 'You're just a kind person, Carrie, and, let's face it, I'm a wagon.'

'No you're not,' her sister said stoutly. 'Stop crying, now. Here's Olivia.'

'Mammy, look what I found.' Olivia danced across the sand waving a small crab. Her cheeks were bright from the fresh air and the bracing breeze whipped her copper pigtails around her face.

'Ah the poor little thing. Is he alive or dead?' Carrie asked, peering at the crab.

'Dead as a dodo,' Davey assured her. 'Couldn't have him for tea.'

'You're not going to eat my crab,' Olivia protested.

'Don't start,' warned Carrie as the pair squared up for a row.

'But Mom,' her son objected. 'I only said—'

'Enough. You've got five minutes left and then we've to go and see Grandpa.'

'I'm going to have a funeral for my crab,' Olivia announced mournfully. 'You can all come.'

'A funeral for a *crab*!' Davey scoffed.

Carrie quelled him with a look as Shauna stifled a giggle, amused at their carry-on. Chloe gurgled happily, adding her tuppence-worth, kicking her little wellington-clad feet happily over the edge of her buggy, delighted to be with her cousins. 'Out, out,' she entreated, arms outstretched, straining at the straps that held her prisoner.

'Come on then,' Shauna relented, opening the clasp and releasing her daughter from her captivity. Chloe, ecstatic at her freedom, legged it for the sea. She was in much better form today and her cheeks weren't as red. The tooth was finally through. At last, Shauna thought gratefully as she called on her daughter to be careful.

'Don't worry, I'll mind her,' Davey assured his aunt as he followed his little cousin to the water's frothy edge. Olivia joined them, having carefully wrapped her deceased crab in a tissue and given it to Carrie to mind. The trio squealed and danced in the foam, Chloe completely unafraid. It gave Shauna enormous pleasure to see how protective Olivia and Davey were of her.

She was really going to miss Carrie and the kids. When all was said and done, family was more important than anything.

'Will you come out and visit? You'd still be able to fly,' she asked, suddenly lonely.

'It would be a bit of an adventure, wouldn't it? I don't know if Dan could manage it. I don't think he'd leave his precious crops for two weeks and there wouldn't be much point in going all that way for less, would there?' Carrie said doubtfully.

'He could come for a week and you could come for two,' Shauna urged. 'Come out at Easter when the kids are off school.'

'We'll see. And we'll see how I'm feeling. If I was waddling around like a big whale it wouldn't be very comfortable.'

'No, probably not,' Shauna conceded.

'I suppose we'd better get a move on if we're going to see Dad,' Carrie said reluctantly.

'Pity we have to go, it's lovely here. I could stay all afternoon,'

Shauna sighed, inhaling the salty air, turning her face to the buttery November sun. The sky was azure, dotted with little cottonbuds of clouds, and the sea whispered against the shore, its lullaby peaceful and soothing. Miles of white sand unfurled on either side of her and the Mountains of Mourne were hazy in the distance, a backdrop to the beacon in Mornington at the end of the pier, which stretched like a long finger into the sea.

'Look at the capers of them. Chloe's having a ball.' She turned her gaze on the children.

'I know. It's nice, isn't it? In another couple of years the age difference between Olivia and Chloe won't mean a thing. They'll be like sisters,' Carrie observed.

'Yeah, they will, won't they?' The thought comforted Shauna. 'Let's make sure they're always close.'

'God, Shauna, you're terribly maudlin today. Have you got PMT?' Carrie eyed her quizzically.

'No, I'm just over them. Started a new Pill pack last night, unfortunately.' She smiled ruefully. 'I guess I hadn't factored in how much harder it would be to go abroad this time. I suppose it's because of Chloe and the kids.'

'Don't go then,' Carrie retorted.

'If we don't go before Chloe starts school, we won't go at all. It's a good opportunity for Greg. He's got a great new job out there. There's loads of building and development going on at the moment. It's too good an opportunity to miss.'

'But what about the Iraq war? Does that not worry you?' Carrie asked bluntly.

'Will you stop going on about it?' Shauna said tetchily. 'Of course it concerns me. But everyone we've spoken to out there maintains that it's making no difference to their lives, except at the airports, and that's affecting us all.'

'True,' Carrie agreed, backing off.

'Look, the first hint of danger and Chloe and I will be home, and Greg can stay if he likes,' Shauna said reassuringly.

'Don't mind me. I was always a worrier.' Carrie grinned.

'Don't I know it. I shared a bedroom with you for long enough. Remember the time there was a small earthquake in Wales and you were afraid to go asleep in case we had one and the ceiling collapsed on top of us? You kept me awake all frigging night!'

Carrie giggled. 'It's probably where Olivia gets her dramatics from, although she's much more of a drama queen than I was.'

'You had your moments,' Shauna teased.

'We better get our asses in gear. Don't forget we've a funeral to go to as well as a hospital visit,' Carrie said.

'She'll forget all about that,' Shauna assured her as she manoeuvred the buggy towards the shore.

'Are you kidding? And miss an occasion of *high* drama? It's Olivia we're talking about here.' Carrie smiled at her sister. 'If you have tears to shed, prepare to shed them.'

An hour later, Shauna sat at her father's hospital bedside and tried not to fidget. 'I've had an ECG and a stress test and blood tests. They're waiting for the results,' Noel informed her self-importantly. 'I wonder have my arteries narrowed. I heard them talking about an angiogram. It's possible I might have to have a bypass. Poor Tom Cowen had a bypass and died on the table, never even woke up from the anaesthetic. It would make you think twice about going under the knife, wouldn't it?' He focused his watery, grey-eyed gaze on her.

'Don't be worrying about these things until they happen,' Shauna murmured, trying not to be sharp. Why did he always have to turn everything into a drama?

'Sure you won't have to be worrying about it. You'll be on the other side of the world, deserting us all,' her father said tartly.

'Were you waiting long for a bed?' She ignored the jibe.

'Long enough. Your sister was very kind to me.'

'Yeah, Carrie's great.' Shauna knew he was getting at her but wouldn't give him the satisfaction of rising to his bait.

'Why didn't you bring the little one up to see me?' he asked petulantly. 'I'd like to see as much of her as I can. She won't know me when you finally get sense and come home to live for good.'

'Carrie's minding her in the car – that's why I'm only staying a few minutes. A hospital ward's no place for a toddler; it's not fair on the other patients. If you want to come down with me, I'll bring her into the reception area,' she responded coolly.

'The world and his mother comes in here. That's nonsense,' Noel contradicted, unimpressed with her argument. A young trainee nurse walked by and smiled at them.

'Ah it's Nurse Carey, the prettiest nurse on the ward and the best at giving injections.' He smiled with saccharine sweetness that had Shauna gritting her teeth in irritation. 'You're a great girl,' he went on, looking around at the other patients to make sure they agreed with him.

The nurse gave a self-conscious smile and hurried on. Shauna bit her lip. She wanted to tell him to stop acting like an old fool, embarrassing young girls with his nonsense. What a notice-box he was. If they only knew what he was really like, she thought irritably.

'A grand little girl and respectful with it,' he added pointedly, a scowl replacing the honeyed smile.

'Right, I'm going to let Carrie and the kids up. If you want to come down with me, come on. If not I'll say goodbye,' Shauna said crisply, standing up.

Noel put on a weak, plaintive voice. 'I don't think I'd be able for it,' he murmured, lying back against his pillows.

Tough, Shauna said silently. 'Do you need anything?'

'I'll get Carrie to fetch my few bits and pieces. I don't want to be putting you to trouble.' He sighed deeply.

'Grand,' she replied airily. 'Sleep well tonight.'

'You might want to tell your brother that I'm in hospital in case anything untoward happens.'

'Well that's unlikely, but if I'm talking to Bobby I'll tell him.'

'Not that he'll be that worried, I'm sure,' sniffed her father.

Probably not, she wanted to say, but she felt she'd been bitchy enough. 'I'll send Carrie up,' she said in a kinder tone of voice. ''Bye, Dad.' She made no effort to kiss him.

''Bye, Shauna,' Noel said tiredly and turned his head away.

'How is he?' Carrie asked, handing Chloe to her a few minutes later at the car.

'Martyr mode. I've to let Bobby know he's in hospital in case anything "untoward" happens.' She threw her eyes up to heaven. 'I asked him if he needed anything but he said he'd ask you to get his bits and pieces. I did try to help out,' she added defensively.

'Right, I'll go on up. Come on, you two,' Carrie said to Davey and Olivia, but there was a slight edge to her tone.

'How about if I go on back to your place and rustle up a bit of dinner for us? We can eat together before I head off home. I don't know about you but I'm hungry, and Chloe's due a bottle.'

'Are you sure?' Carrie hedged. 'I know you're busy.'

'Yeah, it's no problem. Besides, haven't we a funeral to attend?'

Carrie relaxed and grinned. 'Forgot about that. Root around the fridge and do pasta or whatever's handy.'

'No problem. See you later.'

As she surveyed the contents of Carrie's fridge, she knew why she'd offered to make dinner. Guilt, pure and simple. She knew Carrie carried most of the burden of their father's care and part of her was very glad to let her do it, but she also knew it wasn't fair. Unfortunately for Carrie and fortunately for her it was clear Noel preferred it that way and there was nothing she could do to change that.

There is. You could be a bit nicer to him.

But I don't want to be nice. He made our childhoods miserable.

Let go of the past. There's no point in hanging on to it.

He's a judgemental bastard. Why should I be nice to him?

What are you doing now? Judging. When you point a finger three fingers point back at you.

'Oh, for God's sake,' she muttered, irritated by her internal dialogue.

'Baw ba, baw, ba.' Chloe tugged at her fleece.

'OK, darling,' she soothed, glad to banish her guilt to the back of her mind. She heated up a bottle for her daughter, chopped bacon, onions and mushrooms and sautéed them, lined a pie dish with thinly sliced potato, covered it with the sautéed mixture, added a handful of grated cheese and kept layering the pie until the dish was full. It would be cooked by the time Carrie got home and she hoped her sister would enjoy it. She chopped and sliced peppers, aubergines and tomatoes, drizzled olive oil over them and added seasoning. They'd roast in the oven with the pie. It would be a tasty dinner, she thought with satisfaction as she cleaned her utensils.

Chloe curled up on the soft, well-worn sofa under the window and drank her bottle with hungry appreciation. Dusk began to creep across the sky and the lights along the coast started to twinkle in the encroaching twilight. Shauna switched on the lamp and set the table as the aromatic smell of cooking filled the big homely kitchen.

41

5

CARRIE YAWNED AS SHE STARTED THE IGNITION. SHE WAS DEAD tired. There was homework to be done; she needed to collect her father's prayer book and novenas, to bring in to him later. At least she didn't have to do dinner. It had been kind of Shauna to offer to cook. She just wished that her younger sister and their father could resolve their differences and get over themselves so that everything wouldn't be left to her. If Noel was going to be in hospital for a while, she was going to suggest alternating the hospital visits, so that she wouldn't end up having to drive over to Drogheda twice a day.

'Mom, we've to bury my crab,' Olivia piped up from the back of the car.

'Olivia, you've got homework to do when we get home. We can do it tomorrow. It's getting dark.'

'He'll be stinking,' Davey observed laconically.

Her son was right. She could already get the whiff of smelly crab through his tissue shroud. Decomposition was setting in. It was probably best to get it over and done with.

'Right, funeral, lickety-split, and then dinner and then home-work with no arguments,' she decided.

'Can we watch—'

'Not until homework's done,' Carrie warned, wishing they weren't such TV addicts.

'I'm starving,' Davey grumbled.

'Shauna's got the dinner on. We won't be long,' she said wearily, hoping her sister had made enough for Dan as well. If not she'd ask him to get a chippie just this once.

'Of course there's enough,' her sister assured her twenty minutes later, as she dished up the steaming, mouth-watering pie that she had just taken out of the oven. She placed the dish of roasted vegetables on the table and proceeded to fill their plates. They all tucked in with hearty appetites.

'That was gorgeous, Shauna. Thanks,' Carrie said gratefully, smiling as she watched Davey scrape his plate. He had already scraped the side of the pie dish, which he assured his aunt was always the best part because of the crispy bits that stuck to the dish.

'Pity we couldn't imbibe. I feel like getting tiddly,' Shauna said regretfully as she cleared the dishes from the table.

'You've to drive home and I've to drive back to the hospital, unfortunately.' Carrie yawned.

'Are you going back in?' Shauna jerked round in amazement.

'He wants his prayer books and novenas.'

'Oh, for God's sake, you've already been in there once. What does he expect? Does he not realize you've got children to take care of?' she burst out.

'Aw, it doesn't matter. I'll do it tonight when Dan gets home. If he's going to be in for a while we'll sort something out about alternating our visiting. OK?'

'OK,' Shauna agreed crossly. 'He won't be kept in, anyway. There's nothing wrong with him. He's just taking up a bed.'

'Not in front of the kids, Shauna,' Carrie said sharply.

'Oh . . . sorry.'

'Mom, I'm going to put my crab in a big matchbox, and cover him up with kitchen roll before he goes into his coffin.' Olivia had clearly been giving the funeral arrangements some thought.

'Let's do it now, then,' Carrie said crisply.

'Will you help me?' Olivia looked entreatingly at her older brother.

'OK,' he agreed kindly and Carrie felt a wave of affection for her son. Good old Davey. He really was Olivia's champion when all was said and done.

Poor Little Crabby Crab, as he was now known, was laid to rest under the damson trees at the end of the garden. A small bouquet of long past their best busy Lizzies lay ready to be placed on the freshly dug grave. A cross, made out of ice pop sticks, would mark Crabby Crab's final resting place. Olivia led the mourners to their assigned positions and tenderly knelt down and placed the large matchbox in the grave.

'May he rest in peace,' Davey intoned solemnly.

'Amen,' echoed Carrie and Shauna, trying to keep their faces straight.

'Will he go straight to heaven?' Olivia pondered as she arranged her posy this way and that until she was satisfied.

'Of course he will.' Shauna assured her.

'Granny's there.'

'Yes, she is.'

'Will Grandpa go if he dies?'

The sisters looked at each other.

'Yes, he will, Olivia. Everyone always goes back to God, eventually. Because He made them and they're part of Him,' Carrie said matter-of-factly.

Shauna chewed her lip and remained silent. Carrie knew it probably wasn't what her sister wanted to hear, but it was a thought that brought comfort to her and if Shauna didn't like it she could make up her own mind about the issue.

The breeze soughed through the branches of the trees. A shower of crispy, russet leaves floated down over their heads and a new fingernail moon peeped between the clouds.

Carrie shivered, suddenly chilly. 'Let's go in,' she suggested. She didn't want to be thinking of death and funerals. It brought back sad memories of their mother, and fears of deaths to come. It reminded her more than she cared to remember of just how deeply divided her sister, her brother and her father were.

Was this the way it was always going to be? Continuous dissension and disunity? It was too depressing to think about and as she waved Shauna and Chloe off ten minutes later, she felt uncharacteristically angry with her sister that she wouldn't try to make more of an effort to forget the past and get on with life.

Greg was sprawled in front of the TV sipping a beer when Shauna got home, his briefcase flung in the hall, his coat draped over the banisters. Her lips tightened. It didn't take two seconds to hang up his coat under the stairs, and put away his briefcase. And why hadn't he started to cook his dinner?

'Da, da,' Chloe said delightedly, tripping into the sitting room, arms out to be lifted up. He looked tired. His brown eyes were red-rimmed from long hours at the computer. He was handsome, though, Shauna reflected. His eyes, fringed with silky black lashes, were heavy-lidded and sexy. His mouth, firm and sensual, and his sallow skin gave him a faintly Mediterranean appearance. His mother, Joanna, maintained that the family had Moorish blood in their veins. She felt she had been a slave in Morocco in a past life. Greg's mother was very much into past lives and mystical experiences, but not so great at keeping in touch with her family in the present one. Widowed, she travelled a lot and they rarely saw her.

Moorish blood or not, Greg was a good-looking man, and women flocked to him at the parties they attended. His thick black hair could do with a cut, Shauna noted as her husband reached to lift up his daughter.

'Hello, babs.' Greg smiled at her but wasn't too happy moments later as she grabbed his beer glass and splashed the pair of them. '*Chloe!*' he snapped, plonking her onto the floor. She began to howl.

'Oh, for God's sake, Greg.' Shauna sighed in exasperation. 'I'm going to get her ready for bed, she's had a long day. There's steak in the fridge if you want it. I've had dinner over at Carrie's.'

'That was nice for you,' he said peevishly.

'We went in to see Dad. If you want to put Chloe to bed, I'll cook a steak for you,' she offered.

'I'll get a Chinese.' He scowled.

'Suit yourself,' Shauna said tightly. If he was too lazy to stick a steak on the pan and a potato in the microwave, that was his tough luck. She'd given him the option of cooking or putting their daughter to bed and he'd taken neither, so he could bugger off.

She decided she'd better give Chloe a bath as she had sand in her hair and in her ears. The toddler was not best pleased and screeched loudly as Shauna attempted to wash her hair. All she wanted to do was fall asleep. The fresh air and exercise at the beach had knocked her for six.

Another tussle ensued as Shauna struggled to towel her hair, but eventually, exhausted, Chloe gave up wriggling and sat tiredly in the crook of her mother's shoulder as she dried her silky golden curls. She was asleep before Shauna slipped her into her romper suit, and she couldn't resist one last loving cuddle, inhaling the clean, talcy baby smell of her before she laid her in her cot.

She tidied up the bathroom, and stood at the top of the stairs debating whether to go down and join her husband, have a bath herself, or spend an hour or two working on the wedding dress. The sooner she got it finished the better. It would free her up to make a start on her sorting and packing. Greg's new company were shipping out their belongings to the Gulf so at least Chloe would have familiar toys and possessions to help her acclimatize in her new home. She wanted to start doing some Christmas shopping early, too. The more organized she was in that direction the better. She didn't want to be in a big rush with everything a last-minute drama.

'Come on, you can do it,' she muttered, forcing herself to go into the small boxroom that she used as a workroom. The dress hung in all its glory, smothered in white tissue on the back of the door, and the jacket lay where she'd left it, draped on her sewing table. A box of crystal beading awaited and with a sigh Shauna made herself comfortable and began the time-consuming, delicate task of applying the beading along the back panel. She worked steadily and with care and was only vaguely conscious of a ring at the doorbell and Greg's deep voice murmuring a few words. The smell of spare ribs and barbecue sauce being heated in the microwave wafted up the stairs. She supposed she could have made more of an effort to get Greg his dinner but it was unfortunate that she'd been so late getting home. Anyway, it wouldn't kill him for once, she thought crossly as she snipped at a piece of thread. Life wasn't all about him.

Greg cursed as he burnt his finger on a rib. He'd left the bloody things in the microwave for too long and they were too hot to eat.

His stomach rumbled. He was starving. Was it too much for a man to ask for his dinner to be ready when he came home from a hard day's work? Shauna had been off gadding all day with Carrie; the least she could have done was have a meal prepared.

It was all so different from when they'd first married. He sighed, remembering how Shauna couldn't wait for him to come home from work and how she would feed him tasty dishes she'd cooked specially for him. Sometimes they hadn't even paused to eat before making love the minute he was in the door. Why couldn't she have been content with that for a few more years? Now it was all babies' bottles and bath times and crotchety snapping at him and bloody Chinese takeouts that left you feeling hungry an hour later.

At least in Abu Dhabi they'd have a maid to do all this stuff and he and Shauna could get back to having some sort of normal relationship again. He comforted himself with the thought.

It was very quiet upstairs. He'd heard his wife going into her workroom. She was probably in a huff with him. He took another bite of his spare rib and flicked over to Sky Sports. He should make the most of the chance to watch a match in peace and quiet. How often did that happen? Greg took a slug of his beer and settled himself onto the sofa. He should mention to Shauna that Della had called him earlier in the day, wondering if they were having a going-away party. That was something they should organize, for sure. It would be a hell of a night. The thought of it cheered him up greatly. If there was one thing he really enjoyed it was a good boozy bash, especially when he was the guest of honour.

'Well, Della's right, Shauna,' Greg said exasperatedly the following evening, as he uncorked a bottle of red wine for them. 'We'll have to have a going-away party. You didn't think we were going to fly off and not say goodbye to people, did you?'

'Of course not, Greg, but we've to get over Christmas first. I suppose I was just thinking of going out for a couple of drinks, maybe. I wasn't planning a going-away party as such,' Shauna retorted as she served him up a plate of steaming carbonara.

'We'll get caterers in and do it properly,' he suggested.

'You want to have it here, at home?' Shauna couldn't hide her dismay.

'Yeah, why not?' Greg looked surprised, a forkful of pasta suspended halfway to his mouth.

'What about Chloe, if she wakes up?'

'Put her to sleep again,' he said exasperatedly.

'Well, that won't be much fun for me,' Shauna declared. 'And there'll be all the clearing up afterwards.'

'Come on, lighten up, Shauna. We'll be saying goodbye to our friends and family, so let's enjoy it. We used to do great parties.' He grinned at her, and her heart softened. Greg was such a party animal. He had a great capacity for enjoying himself and he was a terrific host. It was one of the things that had drawn her to him. His ability to take pleasure in things was infectious; he had been a breath of fresh air to her . . . so different from her father.

'You're right, hon. Let's have a humdinger of a party.' She leaned across and gave him a kiss. Greg *was* right. She needed to lighten up. The last few days had been far too intense and serious and gloomy and doomy.

Carrie had phoned her earlier that morning to say that their father was being discharged from hospital with a clean bill of health, much to his disgust, she'd added wryly.

I could have told you that, she was tempted to say, but she refrained, knowing that it wouldn't be appreciated.

So that was one problem sorted. She'd spent a good three

hours on the wedding jacket and the end was in sight for her last commission at home. She planned to drum up business abroad by networking with all the women's groups that were part and parcel of expat life. Shauna was glad she'd had the experience of living in the Gulf before. She knew what to expect. It wouldn't be such a culture shock this time.

She might as well enjoy the next few weeks at home and look forward to their going-away party and then, perhaps, when they were settled in the Emirates, she'd bring up the subject of getting pregnant again. Her timing hadn't been great, she conceded. They had enough on their plates emigrating, without her being in the throes of early pregnancy. No wonder Greg hadn't been too enthusiastic. In another six months' time they would be well settled and it would be a much better time to consider another baby.

Feeling a lot happier, Shauna took a sip of her wine and listened to Greg as he began planning their party.

6

'SURPRISE SURPRISE! WE'RE ON THE WAY HOME AFTER DOING SOME Christmas shopping in the big smoke and we thought we'd call by and say hello.' Della stood grinning on Shauna's doorstep a few weeks later. Her three-year-old daughter, Kathryn, kicked one of the big terracotta pots of polyanthus and pansies that stood beside the porch door.

'Don't want to go in there.' She scowled.

'Howaya, Shauna,' Eddie muttered, standing behind his wife.

Oh, bloody hell, cursed Shauna silently as she gave a frozen smile and stood aside to let her in-laws into the hall.

'Hate this house,' Kathryn announced loudly as she followed her parents.

'Oh, darling, don't be naughty,' Della reproached. 'Come in and say hello to your baby cousin.'

'Don't want to.' Kathryn stuck out her tongue. She raced into the lounge and made a beeline for Chloe's toys.

'So how's life? Any chance of a cup of tea? I'm gasping.' Della plonked herself into an armchair and patted her bump. 'Pregnancy and Christmas shopping are definitely not compatible,' she moaned. Eddie sprawled on the sofa and began flicking through the TV stations, ignoring the fact that Chloe had been watching a Disney video. *The cheek of him*, Shauna thought indignantly as Chloe looked at Shauna, unsure about these strangers invading her little world, and hurried across the room to hide behind her.

'Hasn't she got so big! Come here, darling, and give Auntie Della a big kiss,' Della invited. Chloe clung stubbornly to Shauna's leg.

'She'll come out of herself if you just ignore her,' Shauna advised, giving her daughter a sympathetic cuddle.

'So! What's new? All sorted for Christmas?' Della settled back comfortably in her chair. 'Are you going to Carrie's?'

'Not this year, no—'

'Really! I thought you would be; you usually do. That's interesting.' Della sat upright. 'Well maybe we should sort something, seeing as it's your last Christmas for God knows how long. We could come down to you, you know the way we muck in anyway, and it wouldn't be any hassle. Even better, we could let the two men do Christmas dinner and we could totally flop. We deserve it,' she added a tad caustically, glancing in her husband's direction.

'No problem,' Eddie drawled, not even looking in their direction, pretending to be engrossed in a darts match on the sports channel.

Holy divinity! Shauna thought in horror. What a nightmare scenario. It was time to nip that idea smartly in the bud. Thank God she had an excuse.

'Well actually, *I'm* doing Christmas this year.' She could barely hide her relief. 'Carrie, Dan and the kids are coming and Dad and Bobby will—'

'Hey, you guys?' Greg walked in from the hall. Shauna hadn't even heard his key in the lock.

'Yo, bro!' Della grinned at her brother. 'Shauna and I were just making plans for Christmas. She tells me you're having her gang, so how about we come too and all muck in and have a real Christmas hooley, seeing as it might be your last one here for a while?' she suggested enthusiastically.

'Don't worry about its being our last one. I'm hoping to get home for Christmases.' Shauna shot a look of entreaty at her husband and tried to keep the panic out of her voice.

'Well we'll hardly be home next year, seeing as we won't even be a year there and you'll be home for the whole summer,' Greg pointed out unhelpfully. She could have thumped him.

'That's settled then.' Della rubbed her hands gleefully. 'A big family get-together. It will be a blast.'

'Sounds good to me.' Greg grinned, planting a kiss on Shauna's cheek. 'Eddie, do you want to pop down to the pub for a beer and we'll let the women make their plans?'

'You're on.' The other man unfurled himself from the sofa with alacrity and followed his brother-in-law into the hall.

'What about your dinner?' Shauna said tightly. Was she having a nightmare, she wondered distractedly, or had Della just inveigled an invite for the Keegan gang for Christmas, aided and abetted by Greg? How could this be happening? She felt totally out of control. Greg was smiling at her as if everything was normal. Had he no idea of her dismay?

'I'll bung it in the microwave when I get home,' he said offhandedly. 'Right now a cool beer sounds good to me. Why don't you call the babysitter and then you and Della could come with us?' he suggested, seeing that she wasn't too impressed with him. 'We could make a night out of it.'

'Sounds like a terrific idea,' Della approved. 'I have pyjamas in the car for Kathryn, you could lend me a nightshirt tonight and we could stay and not worry about driving home late.'

'It's a bit short notice for Gemma,' Shauna protested, feeling totally manipulated by her sister-in-law. That fucking bitch

Della had marched into her house, invited herself and her family for Christmas, and was now all prepared for a sleepover. Shauna knew that she was in a really awkward position. And Della was playing on it.

She had offered to do Christmas this year out of a sense of guilt because she wasn't sure when she'd be home for Christmas again, and she wanted to give Carrie a break. Greg had been fine with it and had made no protest; he was very good that way. She could hardly turn round and say that she didn't want *his* family.

It was just that Della was so slyly manipulative. She was *such* a cow. Shauna knew well that she'd sit on her ass like Lady Muck and expect to be waited on hand and foot. After all, she was *pregnant*. Not that that made any difference: in all the time Shauna had known her, pregnant or not, she was a lazy wagon. It was going to be exhausting. Eight adults and four children. Her heart sank at the prospect.

'Give Gemma a call,' Greg urged. 'She could probably do with some extra spending money for Christmas.'

'Look, it's Friday night, it's two weeks to Christmas, she'll be out partying,' Shauna retorted as she went to the phone to call her babysitter.

Gemma's mother answered the phone and informed Shauna that Gemma was indeed out at a college party.

'I guessed that. It was very short notice.' Shauna wasn't in the slightest bit surprised. She wished the woman a Happy Christmas and hung up. 'Out partying,' she informed her husband shortly.

'Would Carrie babysit?' Della suggested brightly.

'I'm not dragging Carrie all the way in from Whiteshells Bay,' Shauna retorted curtly, unable to conceal her annoyance.

'I suppose not,' Della said disappointedly.

Shauna took a deep breath. It was obvious that they were here for the night and there was nothing she could do about it. 'Why don't you go with the lads and I'll babysit,' she offered grudgingly. At least she wouldn't have to sit listening to her sister-in-law jabbering on, because the way she was feeling about Della at the moment she could cheerfully have knifed her.

'I *could* do with a night out.' Della beamed. 'Are you sure? Thanks a million. I'll just go and get Kathryn's jimjams. She might be a little bit hungry; we had a meal in town around four. She likes brown bread and tuna, or fruit salad and yoghurt, for tea.' Della hauled herself out of the chair and went out to the car. Shauna stood speechless at her cheek.

Greg avoided her glare. He knew that she was hopping mad now.

'Don't want Mommy to go out,' Kathryn screeched, throwing a Care Bear at Eddie.

'Stop that, Kathryn,' her father growled.

'Won't!' Kathryn yelled, throwing a dolly.

Chloe watched, thumb in her mouth . . . fascinated.

Shauna marched out to the kitchen. She was damned if she was going to deal with it. Let Eddie and Della sort out their brat!

'She'll get over it.' Della ignored her daughter's tantrum, dumping pyjamas and a bottle onto the island in the kitchen. 'I'll just go and have a pee and we'll be off. I'm really looking forward to this. I haven't been out in ages.' She headed for the downstairs loo.

'Is there anyone else you could try? How about that girl Noeleen we used a couple of times? We could have a good night out, Shauna. We could do with it.' Greg appeared at the door pretending nothing was amiss.

'Noeleen doesn't know Kathryn. I'm not going to inflict that little brat on a babysitter,' Shauna retorted.

'It's not *my* fault,' Greg muttered.

'Nothing's ever your fault,' Shauna hissed. 'You suggested going to the pub, you didn't mind leaving me here on my own with bloody Della.'

'Oh, for God's sake!' He scowled exasperatedly as Della clattered back into the kitchen.

'Ready?' she enquired, squirting some perfume onto her wrist.

'Mommy, Mommy, Mommy,' squealed Kathryn, grabbing her arm.

'Stop that nonsense, Kathryn.' Della shook her off irritably. 'Look, Auntie Shauna has something nice for you, haven't you, Auntie Shauna?' She winked at Shauna.

'Me, me,' Chloe demanded, determined not to be left out.

Shauna stared at her sister-in-law. 'Are you talking about biscuits?' She couldn't hide her surprise. Della was generally very strict about what Kathryn ate. Sweets and biscuits were a rare treat.

'Whatever. Or ice pops, if you have them. Just this one time,' Della said magnanimously.

'Pops, pops.' Chloe got in on the act.

'We'll leave you to it, Shauna.' Eddie grinned at her, knowing she was annoyed. Shauna didn't like Eddie Keegan. He was a sneery, jeery, spineless freeloader who hadn't an ounce of sensitivity, she fumed silently.

'Biscuits, biscuits,' Kathryn demanded. Raging, Shauna opened the biscuit jar and handed her niece a Jaffa cake.

'Me, me,' demanded Chloe, little hand out.

'Say please,' Shauna snapped.

'That's right, teach them their manners,' Eddie jibed as he followed Della and Greg to the door.

Kathryn stuffed the biscuit into her mouth and held out her hand for another. 'More.'

'Say please, Kathryn,' Shauna said sharply, as the front door closed behind the others.

'No!' Kathryn said rudely.

'Fine, no more biscuits then.' Shauna put the biscuit jar back in the press.

'Want more,' Kathryn screeched.

'Tough,' Shauna retorted as her niece threw herself on the floor and howled.

'Nautee.' Chloe looked at Shauna, her big blue eyes like saucers at this display.

'Very. Let's go and watch Winnie-the-Pooh,' she suggested, lifting her daughter in her arms and kissing her as she walked into the sitting room.

Kathryn continued to screech, but as far as Shauna was concerned she could get on with it. She'd had more than enough for one day.

Chloe settled down to watch her favourite Winnie-the-Pooh, and laughed delightedly as Piglet went sailing and bailing during a very blustery day. Kathryn, hearing her cousin's giggles, edged her way into the room, thumb in her mouth. In spite of herself Shauna felt sorry for her. Della had brushed her off and made no effort to comfort her. She *was* only three, after all.

'Come in and sit down and watch the video,' she invited kindly.

'Want Mommy.'

'Mommy will be home later. Come and sit down and relax. Are you tired?'

Kathryn nodded.

'Are you hungry?'

Another nod.

'Would you like sausages for tea?'

'Can I have three?' Kathryn perked up. Biscuits and sausages in one day? She couldn't believe her luck.

'Please,' Shauna said firmly.

'Please,' Kathryn echoed.

'Me, me too.' Chloe was not to be left out.

'Yes, you too. Stay and watch the video and I'll go and make your tea.' Chloe should have been getting ready for bed with a bottle, not watching videos and eating sausages, she thought ruefully. Still, it was nice for her to have some company, even if it was her spoilt cousin. She wondered how Kathryn would cope with the new arrival. Badly, she predicted, as she heated the frying pan and opened a packet of sausages.

At least she'd be well away from the Keegans out in the Emirates. That in itself was worth living abroad for. The sausages started to sizzle and her thoughts turned to the bed in the guest room. Gemma, her babysitter, had been the last to sleep in it but Shauna was damned if she was going to change the sheets. She had enough to be doing. Ten minutes later, as the children sat eating sausages and bread and butter, she ran upstairs with the iron, plugged it in beside the double bed in the guest room, poured a drop of lavender oil into the steamer and, throwing back the duvet, began to iron the creased bottom sheet. There was a mascara mark on one of the pillowcases so she simply took off the pillowcase, ironed it, and put it back on with the marked side facing down. 'That will do the pair of you,' she muttered resentfully as she tucked in the sheet and shook out the duvet.

She was damned if she was going to go to any more trouble for the bloody freeloaders. As soon as the kids were in bed she'd ring Carrie to tell her the latest.

Della sipped her white wine spritzer, enjoying the hum of chat and laughter that permeated the bar. It was good to relax. It had been tiring shopping and Kathryn's whinging was very wearing. Still, life was good, she reflected. She was enjoying her drink. They were having an Indian takeaway later, something she only allowed herself as a rare special treat when she came to Dublin. All those additives were a nightmare, but tasty. She'd get a lie-in in the morning and allow herself a slice or two of bacon for brekkie. She never cooked a fry-up at home, much to Eddie's dismay. He loved coming to his in-laws for the food alone. Fat lump, she thought, glancing over at him. He was guzzling a pint like there was no tomorrow. He was *so* unhealthy! At least she took care of her body.

They'd have a walk on the beach and inhale all those healthy ions and then have lunch. They'd probably have to leave after lunch. Shauna would hardly extend an invitation for another night's stay-over. Pity.

Best of all, Christmas was sorted. The relief of not having to worry about turkey and stuffing, and all the palaver that went with Christmas dinner, was tremendous. It would be a most relaxing Christmas, actually, she decided. They'd arrive on Christmas Eve and have mulled wine, one of Greg's specialities. Carrie would help Shauna in the kitchen on Christmas Day. Della would offer her assistance, of course, but she knew it would only be for form's sake. They wouldn't let a guest help out. Especially a pregnant one, she thought happily. They'd stay for Stephen's Day as well, and meander home late the following afternoon. A nice little mini-break, and why not? Shauna was dead lucky, heading off to a warm, sunny country with maids to wait upon her hand and foot. She really fell on her feet marrying Greg. He'd provided her with a big house and a fabulous lifestyle. She had gorgeous clothes, and Chloe wore nothing but the best.

Della and Eddie lived in a dormer bungalow near Virginia in Cavan, where he worked as a systems analyst for a large IT company. It was a nice bungalow, tastefully decorated, but not nearly as big as the Cassidys' house. Della didn't have an en suite in the guest room, nor a utility room, nor an island in her kitchen, which was on the small side.

She worked part time in a local health store, the Organics Experience. Her salary paid for their second car and a foreign holiday each year, but it couldn't quite bring her up to the level of her sister-in-law's lifestyle. It was hard not to be jealous sometimes. Shauna always wore expensive clothes and her accessories were perfectly co-ordinated. Even in a tracksuit, the other woman looked effortlessly elegant, and when she'd been pregnant with Chloe, she'd had only the tiniest bump.

Della caught sight of her reflection in a mirror behind the bar, and scowled. She was birdlike and wiry when she wasn't pregnant, but now she was puffed and bloated. She had a problem retaining fluid, just as she'd had in her previous pregnancy. It was annoying because she was very careful about her nutrition. Her fine, mousy hair fell down to her shoulders and she had a high forehead, a dumpling of a nose, and thin lips. Her brown eyes looked bulgy, rather than heavy-lidded and sexy like her brother's. Greg had inherited the good looks gene in the family, she reflected discontentedly. She looked down at her swelling bulge and felt like an elephant. It was very disheartening. She turned away from the mirror and took another sip of her spritzer. It wouldn't take long to get her figure back after the birth, she assured herself.

Greg and Shauna were going out to the Gulf for a few years and she was determined to make the most of it. Holidays in the sun, lazing around turquoise pools, swimming in the Arabian Sea. Maids to wait on her and mind the children. Trips to the desert, shopping in the designer malls. Jewellery shopping in the souk. Barbecues and picnics. Bliss. She might be jealous of Shauna, but she had her uses, for sure.

7

'SHE'S INVITED HERSELF FOR CHRISTMAS. OH, *SHAUNA*!' CARRIE yelped down the line. 'Look, we won't come. I'll do Christmas here for Dad and Bobby.'

'You will not, and leave me all alone with that cow, and lardy Eddie?' Shauna exclaimed. 'Don't be so mean.'

Carrie laughed. 'No, honestly, Shauna, I don't mind.'

'Well, *I* do. I asked you all for Christmas and you're coming and that's that. You can eat and run if you want to. Far be it from me to inflict the Keegans on you.'

'Did you tell her that we were coming? Why didn't you just say no to her?' her sister asked, clearly taken aback at the news.

'Listen, it all happened so fast, I'm still gobsmacked *myself*,' Shauna retorted. 'Della was just so devious about it, though. She didn't ask me directly, she sort of suggested it in front of Greg and put me in a bloody awkward position. If I'd have said no it would have looked so churlish, especially as I was having my family.' Her voice trailed off.

'That was low, the sneaky witch. I can just see her doing it, too. It's so much her style. I told you she'd wangle a stay-over before Christmas too, didn't I?' Carrie couldn't hide her I-told-you-so tone.

'Well it's a pity you didn't foresee the Christmas catastrophe, Madam Psychic,' Shauna said glumly.

'Look, we'll make the best of it. We'll get pissed, and it will wash over us like water off a duck's back,' Carrie comforted her.

'You can't get pissed, you're pregnant,' Shauna pointed out.

'Oh!' There was silence at the other end of the phone. Shauna grinned.

'Got you there!'

'Forgot about that,' Carrie said ruefully. 'Just means you'll have to drink for the two of us.'

Shauna giggled. 'I might just do that.'

'No might about it,' her sister retorted.

'It's going to be bad enough trying to keep Dad from having a go at Bobby, without having to deal with that lot. If he and Bobby manage to get through Christmas under the same roof without having a bust-up, it will be a miracle.' Shauna sighed.

'I know,' Carrie agreed gloomily. 'Put Della sitting beside Dad for dinner.'

'Oh, Carrie, you're wicked.' Shauna guffawed.

'See, it's not going to be so bad after all,' Carrie teased.

'I did something awful,' Shauna confessed.

'What did you do?' Carrie was still laughing.

'Della told me that Kathryn likes brown bread and tuna or fruit salad and yoghurt for tea, so I gave her sausages. Honest to God, even though she can be such a brat, the poor little mite thought all her Christmases had come together. I hope to God she doesn't get sick, or at least, if she does, that she waits until they get home. She's sleeping with them tonight.'

'Were they organic sausages?' Carrie asked dryly.

'My ass,' drawled Shauna.

'Well at least you'll have organic potatoes and veg for

Christmas, so that should suit Madam. I'll tell Dan to get you the cream of the crop.'

'Thanks. I love Dan's vegetables.' Shauna yawned. 'I'm knackered. I opened a bottle of wine when the kids went to bed and I've had three glasses. I don't care if it's rude. I think I'll go to bed.'

'You go, girl,' Carrie encouraged her. 'I'll talk to you tomorrow. What time are they going at?'

'The sooner the better, but knowing them it will be evening time.'

'I'd suggest you come up to us for lunch, but knowing Della and Eddie, they'd say they were coming too,' Carrie said.

'We won't risk it. Thanks for the offer, though. 'Night, Carrie. I'm going to leg it up to bed before they get home. Greg can entertain his family on his own tonight.'

'Sleep well,' Carrie told her and hung up.

'I will.' Shauna yawned again as she switched off the TV and turned off two of the lamps. She left one on so that the others would have some light and slipped upstairs to check on the toddlers. Kathryn lay sprawled across the double bed in the guest room, thumb in her mouth. Shauna's heart softened as she looked at the sleeping child. She couldn't help her parents; in fact she was very unfortunate in the pair she had, she thought caustically as she gently pulled the duvet over her niece. Fortunately, she'd been worn out after her long day and had gone asleep almost as soon as her head hit the pillow, so there had been no more whining for 'Mommy'.

Shauna went into her bedroom and rooted out one of Greg's T-shirts for Della. She was so big now one of Shauna's night-dresses wouldn't fit her. She left it on the dressing table along with some bath towels. More washing that she didn't need, she thought crossly. She'd hardly get away with leaving the same sheets on the bed for Christmas.

Chloe was fast asleep, her hand under her cheek, looking adorable, and it took all her willpower not to sweep her up in her arms and kiss and cuddle her. A wave of longing swept through her. She'd *love* another baby. Chloe and Kathryn had bonded over their sausages and played happily for an hour before she'd put them to bed. Chloe loved playing with other children. She needed company, she needed a sibling. Shauna sighed. Perhaps this time next year she'd be pregnant, she thought optimistically as she closed the door and slipped into the sanctuary of her own room. It was a horrible night out, the weather had broken and she was glad to lie in bed snug and cosy, hoping that she'd be asleep before Greg and the Freeloaders got home.

Noel made himself a cup of cocoa, took a goldgrain biscuit from the packet and sat down at his kitchen table. He allowed himself one biscuit every night. It was his little treat. His knee ached and he rubbed it as he sipped his hot drink. He was starting to show his age, he thought, a little depressed. Sixty-five sounded so much older than sixty. He didn't like being old. He hated becoming dependent on people. He was finding his parish work taxing but didn't want to say it to poor Father Doyle, who, although a few years younger than himself, was crippled with arthritis.

It was bad enough that Theresa Clarke had taken over as chair of the parish committee. Noel hadn't liked giving up the prestigious position, but he couldn't be seen to be ungracious. He'd had a couple of stints as chairman over the years. He wasn't even treasurer, either, which carried some power and responsibility. No, he was reduced to being the secretary, taking orders from Madam Theresa, and she was relishing her power. It was all very upsetting. He wasn't looking forward to Christmas either. Since Anna had died, life hadn't been the same. He was terribly lonely without his wife. The house was empty, a shell since she'd gone. Bobby had taken off to London to live a degenerate life, and Noel could only hand him up to the good Lord and hope that he would come to his senses and change his ways. His son was coming home for a few days at Christmas and he didn't know whether he was glad or sorry. He didn't like to think of Theresa and her ilk whispering and gossiping about his family's business. If only Bobby would make the effort to tone it down. He was so flamboyant in his clothes and manner, almost inviting people to look at him and see how different he was.

And then there was Shauna, always ready to argue the toss. They were going to her house for Christmas this year. He would have preferred to go to Carrie's. He felt more comfortable there and Davey was a grand little fellow. A real little man, just like his father. He smiled, thinking of his grandson. He wanted to teach him the Stations of the Cross this year. Carrie was a little lax in that regard, but he'd say nothing. He'd just bring him round the church himself and explain each station.

Twiskers, his little black and white cat, rubbed her head lovingly against his leg. Noel bent down and lifted her onto his lap. She'd originally been called Whiskers as a kitten but Olivia hadn't been able to pronounce it and her best effort had been 'Twiskers'. It had stuck.

He supposed he should make out a list for his Christmas shopping. He wanted to get some presents for a few of his committee members. Not Theresa, or Vera Donoghue; he didn't like them. But Mrs O'Neill, his next-door neighbour, and Harriet Kelly were nice women and kind with it. He'd need gifts for Shauna and Bobby as well as Carrie, and presents for the grand-children. He'd do out a list for Carrie and she could look after it. He'd start it now, and write some Christmas cards. That would keep him occupied for an hour or so and then he'd say his rosary and go to bed.

Christmas was a busy time in the parish. He'd been organizing the setting up of the crib and the delivery of the Christmas Mass notices. He stood up to get a pen and paper from the mantelpiece and winced as a dart of pain shot through his knee. He hoped it was only arthritis and nothing more sinister. He must check his medical encyclopedia when he had finished his chores, he decided. At his age anything was to be expected and Shauna might not be so dismissive of his health problems if it was discovered that he had something serious! In fact, she might even stay in the country and not take his grandchild away to foreign parts that were dangerous to live in, exposing her to cultures and beliefs that were far from what her mother was reared to.

He doubted that Shauna and Greg would be practising their religion and that could only be detrimental to little Chloe. It was bad enough calling the child Chloe. What was wrong with a good Irish name, or, even more apt, a lovely saint's name like Anne, or Bridget?

With a heavy heart, Noel sat back down to his task, Twiskers at his feet purring contentedly.

Bobby stroked the pale lavender cashmere scarf that he'd bought for Shauna. He hoped that she'd like it. He thought it was gorgeous. He'd bought a pale apple green one for Carrie. He laid them on the edge of the sofa, pleased with his purchases. He was tired. He'd gone Christmas shopping after work and it had been crazy. Harrods was a mass of heaving, stressed humanity, and his feet and arms ached from all the walking and bag-carrying. By the time he'd struggled up the steps of Swiss Cottage Tube station he was fit for nothing. It was a pity it was so late. He could have gone for a swim in the Swiss Cottage Marriott and then gone for a pint in the Washington. That would have revived him.

He took a sip of chilled Chardonnay and nibbled a Tuc cracker smeared with duck liver pâté and sat down in front of the electric fire that, in the dim lamplight of his flat, looked almost real. He missed a real fire, with the smell of logs and peat briquettes burning and crackling, but at least his fire was welcoming to look at. His mate, Bazzer, had to make do with an antique gas monstrosity and his flat was a real kip. Bobby was lucky with his gaff on Fellows Road. His landlord had let him paint it in a creamy yellow throughout. His bedroom, though small, was clean and at least separate from his living room, unlike Bazzer's large but draughty bedsit.

Bobby liked living so close to Hampstead. He liked its chic cosmopolitan buzz and the fact that he was only a walk away from the green open spaces of Primrose Hill, where he liked to sit and look down over London and write the poetry that was so dear to his heart. He worked as a receptionist in the Willows, a small, compact hotel that catered to businessmen and women, just off Hampstead Heath. It was hard work, and the hours were often unsociable to say the least, but he liked the job, his breezy, outgoing personality well suited to dealing with the public.

After the stresses of living with Noel, struggling not to suppress who and what he was, life in London was in complete contrast to the life he'd lived at home. He wasn't judged. He wasn't under pressure to conform to anyone's idea of who or what he should be. He was free to be himself. He had a great circle of friends, and although he missed his sisters and their children, and grieved for his mother, he could say in all honesty that he was happier than he had ever been in his life.

It would be nice to see the girls again for Christmas and he could endure Noel and his pious exhortations in the knowledge that it was only for a few days and his life in London was there waiting for him.

'I don't know, Dan, maybe I *should* do Christmas again this year. Shauna will have enough on her hands with that shower.' Carrie lay snuggled against her husband's shoulder sipping a mug of hot chocolate. A sudden squall had blown up and sheets of sleety rain battered the windows. The wind keened around the house like a howling banshee wailing her grief and anger to the world. The sound of the pounding waves surging and ebbing along the shore added their own symphony to the night. Carrie was glad that Dan was home from work and that the children were in bed and they had these precious moments to themselves. The fire crackled in the hearth, the flames casting dancing shadows around the walls. An Enya CD played soft music. Two big cream candles were burning on the coffee table and she was enjoying their relaxing evening together. Well, it had been relaxing until Shauna had phoned with her news.

'I just can't believe the cheek of Della. She's so pushy and sly. There was no way Shauna could say no to her. Greg can be very casual the way he treats her sometimes.' Carrie was upset for her sister.

'Whatever you want to do, Carrie, is fine with me. I don't mind,' Dan said easily. 'We can have Christmas here and I'll cook.'

'She said she wanted us to come. That she didn't want to be left alone with them,' Carrie said doubtfully.

'She has a point,' her husband observed as he took a long, satisfying draught of his beer.

'It's a bummer. They really are the meanest people I've ever met. They take advantage of Greg and Shauna like nobody's business. I bet they'll be hotfooting it out to the Gulf before they even have time to settle in.'

69

'You can take that as a given.' He smiled down at her.

'You know what I suggested?' Carrie grinned.

'What?'

'I suggested she put Della sitting beside Dad for dinner.'

'And put Bobby sitting beside Eddie,' Dan said mischievously.

Carrie burst out laughing. Eddie was always wary of Bobby, much to her brother's amusement.

'Do they not have gays in his part of the country? Is he afraid I'll jump on him? He'd be *so* lucky,' Bobby had whispered to Carrie at one of Shauna's parties, making her snort with laughter. Sometimes she wondered how her brother could stay so unruffled by the continual underlying homophobia displayed by the likes of Eddie and their father that was part and parcel of his life. She really admired his guts and courage in staying true to himself. She was longing to see him for Christmas.

'We should go. We'll get Shauna pissed and she'll be fine,' Dan murmured, interrupting her musings and leaning down to kiss her. Carrie forgot the Keegans, Bobby, Christmas, and everything else, as she wrapped her arms round Dan and kissed him back.

8

SHAUNA STRETCHED AND GLANCED AT THE CLOCK AND COULDN'T believe that it was eight fifteen and Chloe was *still* asleep. This was as close to a miracle as she could get. Beside her, Greg was totally conked out.

Surprisingly, she felt refreshed. She couldn't remember going asleep. She remembered lying, tense and resentful, hearing Greg, Eddie and Della clattering dishes around the kitchen without making any effort to keep the noise down. If they woke Chloe up they could look after her, she'd thought, feeling the anger surge through her with every rattle of cup and plate and saucer. She could hear Della giggling and Eddie's and Greg's deeper voices bantering back and forth.

She must have drifted off to sleep, for she hadn't heard Greg coming to bed, and as the sunlight slanted in through a gap in the curtains she felt a lot less pressurized. A decent night's sleep was a lifesaver. The conversation with Carrie had helped enormously. She promised herself that she wasn't going to get stressed out for Christmas. There was no point. Even before Della had invited herself and her family, Shauna had been fretting about having her father and Bobby together. She was afraid she'd let fly if Noel started getting at her brother. Now she had Della to get on her nerves as well. They'd all better pray that she didn't have PMT. That would be nicely explosive. She grinned and stretched. Carrie and Dan and Bobby would be there. They'd get her through it, and she wanted her sister especially to have a decent Christmas. She deserved it.

Greg stirred beside her. 'Morning,' she said brightly, determined to hang on to her good mood.

'What's good about it?' he groaned.

'Sun's shining, weather's cleared up. Chloe's still asleep and I don't have a hangover and you're cooking brekkie,' she said smugly.

'Not before I do this.' Greg pressed himself against her and cupped her breasts in his hands.

'What about Della and Eddie?' she murmured, enjoying the dart of desire that shot through her as she felt him getting aroused against her.

'What about them?' Greg murmured before turning her over to him and kissing her hotly. Shauna gave herself up to the pleasure of the moment, hoping against hope that Chloe wouldn't wake up until they were finished. They'd been interrupted so many times since she'd been born that Greg had said irritably one night that she might as well save her money on the Pill, since she didn't need it. They had a method of contraception all their own called Chloe.

The gods were kind. They even had time for a cuddle afterwards before Shauna heard her daughter call hopefully across the landing, 'Mama? Mama?'

'Perfect timing,' she said with satisfaction.

Greg leaned up on one arm and looked down at her. 'You're in a very good humour this morning,' he said suspiciously.

'Why not?' she said lightly.

'I didn't think you were too happy last night. You gave me a few glares.'

'I just wish Della and Eddie would give me a little notice when they're staying. I could have organized a babysitter and gone out with you,' she said mildly. She wasn't going to start a row about her in-laws. Soon enough they'd be far away from them and they'd no longer be a source of friction between her and her husband.

'Fair point, I suppose,' Greg conceded. 'What about them coming for Christmas?'

She saw the wary look in his eyes and knew he was expecting an earbashing. She had him off balance. Maybe she was a bit off balance herself, she thought ruefully, remembering her anger of the previous night.

'Mama?' Chloe called.

'Look at it this way, we won't have to do Christmas for a while. We'll be owed three, one with Eddie and Della, one with Carrie and Dan and one with Bobby, if he ever moves back to Ireland,' she said smoothly and slipped her nightdress back over her head.

'Good way of looking at it,' Greg agreed, running his hand over his stubbly jaw. 'I thought you wouldn't be too happy about it.'

Oh, I wasn't, trust me. And I would have liked you to back me up on it but that never happens, she thought silently as she tied the belt of her dressing gown round her waist.

'What's three more mouths to feed?' She shrugged and left her husband staring after her, not sure at all about what he was hearing.

It's only for one day, Shauna comforted herself as she pushed open the door of her cherished daughter's room and saw Chloe, blond curls in glorious disarray, her two cheeks rosy red, standing up in her cot, arms out to be lifted.

'Hello, my darling. How are you this morning?' she asked, joy

73

suffusing her as Chloe wrapped her two little arms round her neck and snuggled in for her morning cuddle.

''Allo.' Kathryn padded in and Chloe completely lost interest in Shauna and tried to clamber out of her mother's arms. Shauna laughed and put her down. The two cousins smiled at each other and went immediately to the toys in the toy box. What an irony, she thought with wry amusement. Kathryn and Chloe were getting on like a house on fire.

There was no sign of Della or Eddie so after she had changed Chloe's nappy, with much protesting from her daughter who wanted to continue playing, she brought the two of them downstairs and made their porridge and plopped a spoonful of honey in each dish. Greg was cooking the fry-up and Shauna inhaled the aroma of sizzling bacon and sausages hungrily. Kathryn was able to feed herself and Shauna fed Chloe, who was watching her cousin intently, ready to go when Kathryn did. 'Come on, eat up. You can go in and play when you're finished,' she said firmly as Chloe wriggled in her baby chair, demanding to be let out.

'Oi, you two, get yourselves down here,' Greg yelled up at Della and Eddie ten minutes later, pouring orange juice into glasses.

Shauna heard them moving around the bedroom and Della ambled downstairs five minutes later wearing Shauna's dressing gown, which barely fastened over her bulge. 'I didn't feel like getting dressed so I borrowed your dressing gown,' she said casually as she sat down at the table. Shauna felt her blood pressure rise. Della had no qualms about going into her room, borrowing dressing gowns, perfume, make-up, whatever. There were no boundaries where she was concerned.

Stop being petty, she told herself crossly, not wanting to get into a bad humour.

'Just bacon for me, no sausages or fried bread. That's laden with cholesterol,' Della said self-righteously.

'Ah get a life,' Greg jeered and Eddie laughed. 'Lash it on here, boyo,' he urged Greg greedily.

Shauna tried to ignore her feelings of distaste as she watched her brother-in-law shovel egg, sausage, bacon and mushrooms into his mouth.

'Did Kathryn have some breakfast?' Della asked idly.

'Porridge,' Shauna said dryly. 'I fed the two of them.'

'Excellent.' Her sister-in-law ignored the pointed barb and buttered some toast. 'Are we going for a walk on the beach?' she asked. 'The weather's picked up.'

'You go if you're that energetic.' Her husband shook his head.

'Will we bring the kids?' Della turned to Shauna.

'OK,' Shauna agreed. It was a gorgeous day, cold and clear, perfect for a bracing walk on the beach, and she wanted Chloe to get some fresh air.

Three hours later she and Della were strolling back along the strand to the car while the children ran and skipped gaily ahead of them.

'This is a great amenity to have on your doorstep, and to be so near the city,' Della remarked.

'Yeah, it is. Having been brought up by the sea, I always wanted to live by the sea.'

'And you're so near town, lucky thing.' Della's little hazelnut eyes gleamed enviously.

'Cavan is nice too. You have that lovely lake close to you, and gorgeous countryside.'

'Um,' Della said unenthusiastically.

'And all that organic meat and veg you can get,' Shauna wittered on, wondering whether she would get a chance to do some more Christmas shopping. She was almost finished but she had a few last-minute stocking fillers to get and she was trying to be as organized as possible.

'Will I get you an organic turkey? I can order it from the butcher I get *all* my organic meat from. I couldn't *bear* a frozen turkey.' Della sniffed.

'I wouldn't *dream* of serving a frozen turkey.' Shauna was stung by her sister-in-law's smug superiority. 'I've got an organic turkey on order already and I'll be getting veg and potatoes fresh from Dan. So you needn't worry about the quality of food you'll be eating,' she added tartly.

'Oh, I didn't mean anything. Your food is always delicious.' Della backtracked rapidly.

Smug bitch. Shauna was hopping mad. *Don't let her get to you*, she told herself, trying to regain her equilibrium. This was what she hated about Della: her sister-in-law could press her buttons so easily. Was she just extra prickly or was she justified in feeling mad? Her dad pushed her buttons, Della pushed her buttons, Eddie pushed her buttons. She was a disaster, she thought glumly.

Carrie got on great with her sisters-in-law; they were very nice girls. Could Della be described as 'nice' in any circumstances? Shauna didn't honestly think so.

'I wonder will we have a white Christmas?' She wrapped her scarf tighter round her and changed the subject. It was bitterly cold and the tops of the Dublin Mountains were covered in snow.

'The kids would love it. Maybe we should come early on Christmas Eve in case the roads are icy,' the other woman said offhandedly.

Shauna's jaw dropped. Della was planning to come on *Christmas Eve*! She could get lost. Shauna would have enough on her plate without having the three of them in the house the

76

day before Christmas. She took a deep breath. This was too much. She'd been manipulated enough; it was time to put her foot down.

'If you don't mind, Della, I'd prefer if you did Christmas Eve in your own house with Kathryn. We'll be up to our eyes and Chloe doesn't really understand about Santa so she'll be going to bed at the usual time with no fuss. We always go to Mam's grave on Christmas morning and Carrie and Dan go visiting his family in the morning as well, so I hope to have the dinner around three thirty or so to give everybody time. OK? If you leave between one thirty and two you'll be in plenty of time. It just makes life that much easier all round,' she said very, very firmly.

'But we can come and help,' Della protested. 'You shouldn't have to do it all on your own,' she added with sugary insincerity.

'I won't be on my own, don't worry. I'll have Greg,' Shauna said resolutely. 'We'll see you Christmas Day.'

'Oh! OK, if that's what you want,' Della said sulkily.

'Great. We should get home. You'll probably want to be heading off so you won't be driving in the dark. The traffic was very heavy today, wasn't it?' If she was putting the boot in she might as well do it properly, Shauna decided. For Della's presumption, she was damned if she was going to ask them to stay to lunch. They'd had such a feast at breakfast time they couldn't possibly be hungry anyway, she thought nastily.

'I might give Kathryn something to eat before we go. She'll be hungry after the walk,' Della said coldly, thoroughly miffed.

'I have brown bread and tuna. Just what she likes.' Shauna smiled brightly, ignoring her sister-in-law's tone. It was rare to get the better of Della, and it felt good. If Greg wanted to cook lunch for his sister he could go right ahead.

Her husband didn't seem so inclined. He was working in his office and Eddie was watching sport on the TV.

'I'm just going to get Chloe ready for her nap. There's brown bread in the bread bin and tuna in the press. Help yourself.' Shauna waved in the direction of the kitchen.

'Want sausages and biscuits,' Kathryn demanded.

'There's sausages in the fridge.' Shauna smiled sweetly as she popped a bottle in the microwave for Chloe.

'I don't give Kathryn sausages,' Della said crossly.

'Whatever. Come on, sprite.' Shauna tucked Chloe under her arm and headed upstairs. Della could just get over herself. Shauna wasn't putting herself out over her any more this day.

It was with some satisfaction that Shauna watched the Keegans drive off an hour later, lunchless. By putting her foot down about Christmas Eve she felt she'd regained some control over the situation. But when she thought about it later, she wondered whether Della would do as she was asked or whether she would, as she had done often in the past, ignore Shauna's wishes completely and appear on their doorstep on Christmas Eve, one arm as long as the other, ready for another freeloading episode. They hadn't even left so much as a bottle of wine this time, she thought indignantly as she closed the door behind them.

'They'd better not arrive on my doorstep on Christmas Eve after what I've said to her,' Shauna told Carrie grimly, later on, 'or, by God, there'll be a row to beat all rows, I can promise you that. She had the nerve to say that she couldn't bear to eat a frozen turkey, as if I'd buy one. She offered to get one at *her* butcher's, as if we can't get organic here.'

'You big eejit, you should have let her get it and pay for it. You can bet your ass you won't be getting anything else from Les Misérables,' Carrie chided.

Shauna guffawed. 'Les Misérables! Carrie, you're downright nasty, but I love it. You're right, I suppose. Bad thinking on my part, but she'd only have arrived with an oversized hen. And she'd have arrived with it on Christmas Eve, so no thanks. It wouldn't be worth it. I've ordered a twenty-two pounder so there'll be enough meat for you to take some home with you. I know Dan likes his turkey sandwiches on Stephen's Day.'

Thanks, Shauna. I was half thinking of getting one to cook on Stephen's Day myself.'

'Don't bother! What's the point of coming to me for dinner if you've to cook a friggin' turkey? Take as much as you want of mine and for God's sake relax. That's the whole point of not having to do Christmas.'

'OK, I surrender,' Carrie assured her. 'How about if I ring Della nearer Christmas and ask her what beer does Eddie prefer as we'll be bringing over a few cans and say something like "See you for lunch on Christmas Day"? Then she'll know that I know she's coming on Christmas Day and she mightn't be so inclined to pull a "surprise surprise" stunt!'

'Oh, good thinking, Carrie. That might put a halt to her gallop.'

'It better,' Carrie said firmly before hanging up. Shauna smiled. Della would think twice about landing on her doorstep on Christmas Eve after Carrie had sorted her.

'Honestly, Eddie, imagine expecting us to drive to Dublin on Christmas *Day*. You could have knocked me down with a feather. Shauna can be so thoughtless sometimes. I even offered to help with the dinner preparations on Christmas Eve. She can be very ungracious, that girl.' Della was livid. 'And you'd think they would have given us some lunch before we left. I hope she doesn't expect us to drive home on Christmas night. I wouldn't put it past her.'

'Don't be daft, Della. They won't expect us to go home

Christmas night, I'm telling you,' Eddie assured her. He patted his rotund belly. He was a big stocky man, with double chins, fat fingers, and ruddy cheeks. He loved his grub. 'I intend to have a big feed, and a good few scoops so I won't be able to drive and you just say you're too tired because you're pregnant. They won't expect us to drive home late Christmas night.'

'Carrie and Dan and the rest of them will have to,' Della snapped.

'They only live up the road. We live in the country,' he pointed out.

'I'm pissed off about it, anyway. Imagine inviting people to come for Christmas and expecting them to drive on Christmas Day. The day will be practically over by the time we sit down to dinner. Some hosts they are,' Della grumbled, conveniently forgetting that it was she who'd invited herself to Shauna and Greg's in the first place.

9

'ANY SIGN?' CARRIE'S VOICE FLOATED DOWN THE TELEPHONE wires around midday on Christmas Eve.

'Not so far. My nerves are in shreds.' Shauna sighed.

'I'll be over in under an hour and then we'll go and pick Bobby up, OK? Stay calm, little sister. I'll bring the potatoes and veg with me.'

'OK, see you soon.' Shauna smiled, glad of Carrie's support. She hung up and continued wrapping the last of her presents, a set of warm pyjamas and a big Barney cuddly toy for Kathryn. She'd left them until the last minute, afraid that Chloe would somehow manage to get her hands on the Barney and want him for herself. Her daughter was fast asleep in her cot, but Shauna was a little concerned that she was cutting another tooth. She was doing an awful lot of dribbling. Shauna didn't want her to be fractious on Christmas Day. There was nothing more wearing on company than a cranky toddler.

The house was spotless; she'd had the mini-maids in the previous day. The linen was changed on the beds in the guest room and the smaller bedroom just in case Bobby decided to stay a night. She hoped that he would; she was longing to spend time with him. He'd promised that he would come out to visit her in the Gulf. That would be a treat to look forward to.

It would be nice having sun to heat up her bones, and to go swimming in the warm sapphire waters that lapped the Emirates. She was looking forward to some decent shopping too. January was actually an excellent time to be going out there, she acknowledged. The contrast between sunny, bright, balmy Abu Dhabi and grey, freezing, wintry Ireland would be enough to put a smile on anyone's face.

In the circumstances she felt quite cheerful. She was reasonably organized. She had sorted all the clothes that she was bringing to the Gulf. All summer stuff, fortunately, which didn't make life too difficult. She'd packed books, CDs and about five copies of *Vanity Fair* that she had being trying to catch up on for the past few months. She had her sewing machine and accessories all ready and the van was coming to collect everything on the 28th. Greg had his packing sorted too. Once their stuff was gone, she'd know there was no going back.

She looked around the lounge, pleased with her Christmas decorations. She'd gone for gold, green and red, and her tree was a sight to behold, sparkling and shimmering in the bay window. The red and white lights of the tree reflected in the polished wood of the floor, giving a very satisfying effect and showing up the gleaming sheen the mini-maids had achieved.

The mantelpiece was draped with a bough of pine, holly and ivy and the scent of the pine, mixed with the scent of the satsumas studded with cloves and dusted with cinnamon, was a treat for the senses. Two red candles in gold candlesticks stood at either end of the mantelpiece. She'd have them lighting on Christmas Day. Sprays of frosted gold and red-berried dried branches in a Louise Kennedy glass vase in the alcove beside the chimney breast was her only other decoration. Shauna liked the idea of less is more. She'd had the sofas and chairs steam-cleaned and the gold fabric had come up wonderfully clean. She was very pleased with it. The rich, dark green colour of the walls lent a warm, cosy air to the room and the gold curtains, which matched the fabric on her sofa and chairs, were draped elegantly over the wooden poles framing the window, finishing off the room. Shining rosewood units shone under their polishing and the crystal in the drinks cabinet sparkled. The lounge ran the width of the house and was ideal for entertaining. It was her favourite room.

Across the hall in the dining room, her mahogany table, polished within an inch of its life, was dressed with her best linen, crystal and cutlery. Chunky red and gold crackers decorated every place setting. The adults would enjoy them as much as the kids. She'd make a fresh centrepiece of holly, ivy and red roses in the morning and that was all she had to do there. She'd been determined to set the table while Chloe was asleep. It was a time-consuming job and the last thing she needed to be doing on Christmas Day.

Greg had gone out to get the car washed and fill it with petrol and do a few other little 'chores', he'd told her, and she guessed that he was buying her Christmas present. It irritated her. He'd had weeks to do that and yet he'd left it to the last minute. He'd better be back in time so that she could go to the airport with Carrie to collect Bobby.

The doorbell rang and she nearly jumped out of her skin. Was it Della and co.? she wondered with a sinking heart. She edged behind the Christmas tree and tried to peer out the window. She couldn't see their car in the drive. Relief flooded her as she hurried out to the hall. It was her neighbour, Hilary, with a bottle of champagne and a gift-wrapped present for Chloe.

'Hi, honey. I'm dropping this in now because we're heading over to Galway. Have a great Christmas and we'll see you when we get back.' She gave Shauna a warm hug.

'Come in and have a drink while I get yours,' Shauna invited.

'Can't stay for long, hon, John has the car packed. And we want to head off as early as we can. It's the pits driving in the dark.'

'I know. I won't delay you, then. Thanks a million for the presents, Hilary,' Shauna said, bending down to get her neighbour's Christmas gifts from under the tree.

They chatted for a few minutes, and as she was standing at the front door waving Hilary off, Shauna heard Chloe stir. She'd hoped that her daughter would sleep longer, but maybe it was a blessing in disguise and she'd sleep longer in the morning.

She was feeding her some mashed potato and chicken when Carrie arrived, laden. 'I've brought everything over today, veg, potatoes, beer, wine and goodies.' She unpacked deep shopping bags and went back out to the car to bring in a crate of beer just as Greg was turning into the drive.

'Great timing,' she grinned. 'Will you carry this in?'

'Sure,' he said equably. 'Did you rob an off-licence? You're too kind, Carrie. There's no need for all of this.'

'There is need,' Carrie said firmly. 'Fair is fair.' She often wondered how her brother-in-law felt about Della and Eddie's meanness, but of course she wouldn't dream of commenting on it.

'We'd better head off. I'd say the airport will be pandemonium,' Shauna suggested after she'd packed away Carrie's shopping.

'Yeah, and the traffic is dire. We'll see you God knows when, Greg.' Carrie smiled.

'We'll take my car so you won't have to drive. It's bad enough having to come in from Whiteshells Bay,' Shauna offered.

'Fine with me,' Carrie agreed.

'This is great, isn't it?' Shauna remarked cheerfully as

she reversed out the drive. 'I feel like a schoolgirl skipping school.'

'Me too. Davey and Olivia are up to ninety and bickering to beat the band, they're so excited. And if I hadn't put my foot down and said I was going to collect Bobby from the airport, Dan would still be in his blinking glasshouses.'

'Let's make the most of it. If we have time we'll even have a coffee.'

'No arguments from me.' Carrie stretched her legs and relaxed her head against the headrest. She hadn't exaggerated about the traffic. It was very heavy and as they neared the airport it became slower-moving and then bumper to bumper.

'Might as well park in car park C. We won't get parking any closer. Sorry about the walk.' Shauna pulled her ticket from the machine and the barrier went up.

She had to circle for fifteen frustrating minutes looking for a space before she finally found one. It was awkward to get into because one of the drivers had parked over the white line and Shauna was fit to be tied as she manoeuvred into the tight spot. As the pair of them eventually hurried through the draughty, fume-filled car park towards Arrivals, Carrie remarked that they'd hardly have time for coffee, unfortunately for her, because she was craving something sweet and had been going to treat herself to a chocolate biscuit.

They battled their way through the hordes to the monitors and saw that Bobby's flight was on time and had landed.

'Just in time. Honestly, I could have flattened Greg. He decides to go and do his bits and pieces with the car this morning and I know that he was getting my present as well. Typical of him to leave it to the last minute when I could have done with him in the house. I was half afraid that he wouldn't be back in time for me to come to the airport. He drives me mad sometimes,' Shauna confessed as they edged their way towards the arrivals barrier. The airport was chock-a-block and Shauna was already the victim of a trolley bash as harassed travellers headed for the exits.

'Well you have the house looking great,' Carrie commented, battling through the throngs at the barrier.

'Thanks to the mini-maids,' Shauna said dryly, elbowing a busty blonde out of the way.

'Excuse me!' snapped the blonde.

'Sorry,' apologized Shauna and kept going, dragging Carrie behind her until they were at the front of the barrier.

'You're something else,' giggled Carrie as the doors parted and a river of people spilled out into the arrivals hall.

'Can you see him?'

'No, can you?'

They craned and stretched for at least ten minutes before their first welcome sighting. 'There he is, there he is!' Carrie exclaimed, waving madly.

'Crikey, look at his highlights. Wait until Dad gets a load of that. It's the Killer Queen himself.' Shauna's smile went from ear to ear as she pushed her way towards the barrier opening and reached out her arms to embrace her brother, tears in her eyes.

'My turn,' Carrie exclaimed, launching herself at Bobby.

'Don't you cry too,' he remonstrated, but his own eyes were suspiciously bright as he hugged the both of them. They held each other, their gladness at being reunited tinged with sadness at the knowledge of how much their mother would have enjoyed such a reunion.

'Come on, let's get out of here. It's worse than Heathrow.' Bobby gave them a little nudge and pushed his trolley towards the exit.

'Can we go for a coffee or a beer somewhere and have a little catch up, just the three of us?' Carrie asked eagerly, holding on to Bobby for dear life. 'Or are you in a desperate hurry to get home, Shauna?'

'Not in the slightest.' Shauna laughed. 'Greg can take care of Chloe for another hour or two. It won't do him a bit of harm, he gets away with murder as it is,' she added with a slight edge to her voice.

Bobby arched an eyebrow. 'Everything not OK in Paradise?' he queried.

'Everything's fine . . . well, apart from the Freeloaders inviting themselves for Christmas.'

'You're joking! Bloody hell.' Bobby pulled a face. 'Della and slobby Eddie. I've changed my mind. I'm going back this second.' He halted dramatically.

'Give over.' Shauna grimaced. 'I feel bad enough about it as it is.'

'Oh, OK, then just for you. But Eddie better watch out. I might jump on him.'

'It's OK, Carrie's got everything under control. She's told me to put Dad sitting beside Della.'

'You're evil,' Bobby grinned.

'You don't know the half of it. Come on, guys, there's a little coffee shop in Swords that might be open. They do coffee cake to die for.'

'Sounds good to me,' Bobby agreed. 'Lead the way.'

Thirty-five minutes later they were tucking into a thick wedge of creamy coffee and walnut cake and drinking hot sweet tea.

'This is the life. Cake and no argumentative kids,' Carrie said dreamily, licking her fingers.

'I never knew you had such a sweet tooth. You're usually more into savouries.' Bobby looked at her suspiciously. 'Are your boobs a bit fuller? Is your hair straighter? Have you something to tell me?'

'You're *so* gay,' Carrie teased affectionately. 'A straight bloke would never notice.'

'I have empathy, me, from my difficult childhood, you know. I'm very sensitive,' Bobby mocked himself. 'You're preggers, aren't you?'

'You bet I am.' Carrie smiled.

'Are you pleased? Is Dan?'

'Yeah, delighted.'

'He's a good bloke. I'm glad for you, Carrie.' He leaned across and kissed her. 'How are all my darlings? I am dying to see the kids.'

'Believe me, they're dying to see you. We had a row because they wanted to come to the airport,' Carrie assured him.

'You should have brought them.'

'Are you mad? This is my sane time. As soon as I go back to that house I'll be a fishwife after five minutes.'

'And how is my godchild?' He turned to Shauna.

'Gorgeous. Wait until you see her. She's a real little sprite. Isn't she, Carrie?'

'She's adorable. I'm really going to miss her.' Carrie's lip wobbled.

'Carrie, stop!' Shauna exclaimed. 'You can't do that to me.'

'Sorry.' Carrie swallowed. 'It's my hormones.'

'And how's Dad? Has he got the red carpet out? Do you think he'll like the hair?' Bobby gave a dramatic toss of his blond locks, lightening the mood immediately. His sisters laughed.

'Dad's himself.' Carrie threw her eyes up to heaven. 'He wants me to go to Midnight Mass with him tonight. He had me doing all his Christmas shopping, and I could have throttled him because he was so pernickety. Oh, he's himself all right.'

'I'll go to Mass with him. Just think of it as my contribution to the Christmas effort,' Bobby volunteered.

'You're on.' Carrie jumped at the offer. 'Thanks, lovey. I want to go to bed as early as I can because my two are so excited, I bet they'll be awake in the middle of the bloody night, but I didn't like the idea of him going on his own. It's too lonely. Needless to say he wouldn't miss it even though he's coming with us in the morning as well.'

'You get your beauty sleep and don't worry, I'll accompany Papa to Mass. I've got a gorgeous maroon mandarin style jacket, very seasonal. I'll wear it, and a green silk scarf. Whiteshells Bay, prepare to be dazzled.' Bobby grinned.

'I'd nearly drive all the way up just to see you.' Shauna couldn't hide her amusement. Noel would be horrified. He'd far prefer to see his son dressed in a 'proper' suit. It really irritated him that Bobby wasn't prepared to tone it down. Christmas certainly wouldn't be boring, she mused, as she signalled the waitress for the bill.

'I'll wear it tomorrow, weather permitting,' Bobby promised. 'We'll be going to the grave, won't we?'

'Yep.' Shauna nodded.

Bobby sighed. 'It doesn't get any easier, sure it doesn't. Part of me is dreading going home because it just hits me all over again that Mam's not there. I keep expecting to see her sitting in her chair doing her crossword.'

'It's easier for us, I suppose,' Carrie reflected. 'We're here all the time. It's not that we've got used to it, you never get used to it, but you just don't expect to see her.'

'Until it's happened to you, you don't really understand what people go through, sure you don't.' Shauna sighed. 'You say all the platitudes and feel sorry for people who've had a bereavement and after a while you forget that they're still sorrowing.

Life goes on, you think. It goes on for sure but the missing of them never goes away. I never really realized that until Mam died.'

'I know it's awful, but lots of times I wish it had been Dad that went, not Mam,' Bobby said quietly.

'Me too,' Shauna murmured.

'Ah guys, please don't. He's getting old. He's lonely. His life isn't easy either,' Carrie chided.

'Oh, listen to us,' Bobby exclaimed. 'Maudlin talk and we're not even drunk.'

'No, it's good to talk like this. At least we've always been able to talk and share. We're lucky.' Shauna patted Carrie's arm. 'I didn't mean to upset you.'

'Me neither,' Bobby assured her.

'That's OK. You know, we should be getting a move on. It gets dark so early these afternoons, doesn't it? It's just gone half three.' The grey, gloomy dusk had descended, the Christmas tree in the corner of the small coffee shop coming into its own in the twilight.

'I love Christmas trees at this time of the day. At dusk they always look so magical,' Shauna said as she wrapped her scarf round her neck.

'Me too. I hate sunny Christmas Days when you can't see the lights properly.' Bobby shrugged into his leather jacket.

'And I hate mild Christmas Days too,' Carrie interjected. 'I love frosty, crisp, cold Christmas mornings when you can see your breath going to Mass.'

'You might have your wish. It's bloody freezing now.' Shauna shivered as the three of them walked back to the car. It was a light-hearted drive back to Malahide to collect Carrie's car. They were glad to be in each other's company, catching up on all the news, just the three of them.

Bobby was gobsmacked when he saw Chloe, who hid shyly for a little while before gaining confidence and coming to stand at his knee.

'You are a stunner, young lady. Look at how big you are. The last time I saw you, you were crawling around the floor, and now look at you, practically ready for the catwalk,' he teased, making outrageous faces at her, causing her to burst into hearty guffaws. 'Shauna, she's amazing. I'm so glad I came home. I'm dying to see Olivia and Davey as well. We'll have fun tomorrow, no matter what.' He hugged his younger sister. 'I'll spike Della's drink for her and get her blotto—'

'You can't. She's pregnant, unfortunately,' Carrie informed him as she slipped her jacket back on. 'Come on. I need to get home.'

'Nuts! Well, I'll think of something, never fear. Chin up, sugarplum. We'll see you tomorrow.' He winked at Shauna.

'Welcome home, Bobby. It's great to see you.' She hugged the daylights out of him and was hugged tightly in return.

Noel buttered some of the fresh bread he'd bought earlier and laid a slice of cooked ham down on the first piece, with thin slices of tomato on top. The kettle had boiled, and some fruitcake already cut and buttered sat in the middle of the table. Carrie had told him that she'd made a lamb shank casserole for their dinner, which he and Bobby could eat later in the evening. He wanted to have something prepared for when they arrived; he wanted his son to feel that he had gone to some trouble. He dropped a small piece of ham down to Twiskers, who pounced on it delightedly. Bobby had always liked cooked ham sandwiches as a child. Noel hoped he still liked them.

He shook his head as he made the sandwiches. Theirs was such a fraught relationship and always had been. His son was the most stubborn character he'd ever met. From when he was a youngster, he'd pitted himself against Noel, and poor dear Anna had been stuck in the middle, trying to keep the peace. His late wife had been misguided. If she'd let Noel take a firmer stance with their youngest child he might not have turned out the way he had. Anna had mollycoddled him, Noel thought sorrowfully. Not only had she mollycoddled him, she'd pandered to his every whim.

It had infuriated Noel. Even to this day the memory of it made him bitter and cross. Bobby had come between him and his dear wife on many occasions and although forgiveness was the aim of every Christian, it was difficult sometimes. He was quite convinced that poor Anna's end had been hastened prematurely because of the behaviour of their son.

Noel sighed deeply. He must try hard to let go of the anger and resentment he felt towards his youngest child. Fortunately he was going to confession later tonight. He would pray hard to be absolved of all his sins and he would pray even harder that Bobby would sort himself out.

It seemed to him that Bobby went out of his way to be girlish and outrageous. Why couldn't he be more . . . Noel struggled to find a word . . . more . . . more manly. He had tried to get him interested in hurling and football, he'd made him join the Boy Scouts to toughen him up, insisting that he go camping and hiking, but all Bobby was interested in was playing his guitar and writing poetry.

Noel hadn't wanted him to get a guitar; he'd been vehemently opposed to it. But Anna had got him a job in the local greengrocer's and out of his wages he'd saved enough to buy that damn instrument, and once he'd started working he'd refused to play hurling and football any more. Noel had been extremely angry. To his remembered shame, he hadn't spoken to his wife for two weeks, God forgive him. And God forgive Bobby, he thought bitterly. He had a lot to answer for.

His behaviour was an affectation, a looking for notice, that had always afflicted his son. Noel was sure he could behave normally if he made the effort. And as for the other unmentionable thing . . . the liking of other men . . . that was too distressing to contemplate. The Bible was very clear on it, as he'd told his son and indeed his daughters over and over again. It was too painful to think about. The sigh came from the depths of his being. He dropped more ham on the floor for Twiskers, who devoured it and rubbed her head against his leg, and pressed the top slice of bread onto the last of the sandwiches.

Maybe he'd get a pleasant surprise when Bobby arrived home. Maybe he'd got all that nonsense out of his system and was now 'normal'. Noel fervently hoped so. He cut the sandwiches in half and arranged them on the plate, then went into the sitting room to put another few logs on the fire. It was good to come home to a blazing fire. By making the effort he was acting in a forgiving manner, he comforted himself. God would surely be pleased with him. He heard the crunch of tyres outside the window and saw Carrie's car pull to a stop in the drive. Noel peered out eagerly, hoping to see a smartly dressed, 'normal'-looking young man get out of the car.

An apparition dressed in a brown leather jacket and a beige floaty silk scarf got out. Noel stared at Bobby's hair. The last time he'd seen his son his hair was its ordinary brown colour. Now it was different shades of blond. Just like a woman, Noel thought in dismay.

'O Mother of God give me patience and strength,' he prayed as he heard Carrie's key in the door. 'This is a hard cross to bear.' Bobby had become even more outrageous. He hadn't straightened himself out one bit. If anything, he was a thousand times worse.

'Hello, son,' he said heavily as Bobby came through the door. He didn't even bother to shake hands. What was the point? If his only son wouldn't even try to make an effort on his visit home, why should he bother?

'I've made sandwiches, they're in the kitchen. Help yourself; Carrie will make you a cup of tea. I've to go and see Father Doyle about something. I'll see you later.'

Just for an instant, Bobby looked crestfallen as Noel went into the hall to get his coat. 'See,' he whispered to Carrie. 'He can't even bear to be in the same house as me.'

'Don't forget it's Christmas Eve. There's always a lot of things to do in the church,' Carrie said lamely, hurting for him.

'Nah.' He shrugged despondently. 'Some things never change.'

10

'MAMMY, DADDY! HE'S COME, SANTA'S COME!' THE SHRIEKS OF excitement penetrated the fog of sleep that shrouded her, and Carrie struggled to come to consciousness. Beside her Dan snored contentedly.

'Wake up.' She gave him a dig in the ribs as Olivia and Davey danced into their bedroom, light from the landing shining onto their faces, which were radiant with excitement.

'Daddy, I got a chopper bike!' Davey could hardly get the words out he was so excited.

'Mammy, Mammy, I got a bike too and a Barbie Bride. Look, she's got a veil and everything.' Olivia was in ecstasy as she waved her doll under her mother's nose.

'And we got sweets in our stockings, real chewy toffees.' Davey's cheeks were bulging.

'Give us one,' Dan said groggily, hauling himself up into a sitting position. 'What time is it, Carrie?'

Carrie squinted at her alarm clock. 'Four thirty-five. Ten minutes later than last year.'

'Dad, watch me cycle up the hall,' Davey urged.

'Come on so,' Dan agreed, flinging back the duvet. 'If you give me another one of those sweets.' He smiled at Carrie and she smiled back at him as she lay against the pillows with Olivia snuggled in beside her. This is happiness, she realized. That rare fleeting moment when everything is just perfect.

Della gazed with dismay at the heap of puke-stained sheets and clothes strewn in her bath. She ran the shower hose over them then piled them all into a basket and headed for the kitchen and washing machine. This was the third time that Kathryn had puked. The girl in the crèche had told her that there was a bug going around when she'd gone to collect her at midday.

When she'd taken her to the doctor he'd just given her Dioralite and told her to keep Kathryn hydrated and not to let her mix with other children for a couple of days. Her daughter was sleeping fitfully now, after her last bout. She was flushed and hot in the bed in the spare room. Eddie had come in from the pub well pissed and was snoring, oblivious. It was five a.m.

Della was utterly browned off. They could hardly go to Dublin if Kathryn was puking. The doctor had said not to have her around other children, as the bug was highly contagious even if it was only a twenty-four-hour thing. She felt like crying. Such rotten luck. Christmas ruined. She supposed she should soak some aduki beans and take a leg of lamb or a joint of beef out of the freezer, seeing as she had no turkey. She went to open the door and paused. She'd give it another hour or two. If Kathryn didn't puke any more she'd take her chances. She wasn't going to let a bloody bug spoil her Christmas jaunt to Dublin.

Bobby stirred in the bed, conscious that he was cold. His feet were like two ice blocks. He was sleeping in his childhood divan and the duvet had slid off him. Noel, parsimonious at heart, did not believe in keeping the heating running all night and the house had grown chill. He shivered and pulled the duvet back over him, burrowing down into the warm spot his body had created. He had slept badly, his body tense and restless. He wanted to go back asleep but his mind was racing.

He knew Noel had been dismayed when he'd made his offer to go to Midnight Mass. 'Carrie's coming with me,' his father had assured him hastily.

'No, I told her to go to bed early. She's tired from her pregnancy. I told her I'd go with you,' he'd said firmly.

'You're grand. I can go myself; you go to bed. I'm sure that you're tired after travelling. Go to Mass in the morning with the family,' Noel urged.

'I promised Carrie that I'd go with you and besides, I like Midnight Mass. I love the carols.' Bobby dug his heels in.

'Have you a proper coat? It's cold,' Noel said gruffly. The silence hung between them. Bobby knew well that his being cold was not the issue. The younger Bobby would have stood his ground and resisted; the older, more mature young man that he now was let it pass.

Bobby had gone to Mass wearing an old green parka over his maroon jacket. He knew it was a compromise, but for Carrie's sake he'd made a decision to try to get through the few days at home with as little hassle as possible. If Shauna hadn't been going abroad in the New Year, he might not have bothered coming home this year. But it might be their last time together as a family for a while. He wanted to make the most of it.

'Tanta Plause.' Chloe stroked the cuddly miniature Santa at the end of her Christmas stocking and listened with delight to the musical chimes emanating from the little xylophone Shauna was playing for her. It was seven forty-five a.m., the turkey was stuffed and in the oven, Greg was asleep and Shauna was playing with her daughter and sipping a welcome cup of tea.

The aroma of roasting turkey was beginning to fill the kitchen and she inhaled it appreciatively. She wanted everyone to enjoy their Christmas dinner. The caterers that she used had delivered several dozen tasty canapés, starters, soup, pudding and a selection of desserts, but she'd prepared the potatoes and vegetables that Carrie had brought. The ham was cooked and the marrowfat peas were steeping. She and Greg had done as much preparation as they could the previous evening but had managed to get to bed before midnight so she wasn't too exhausted.

She wouldn't have minded some help stuffing the turkey and lifting it into the oven. It was very heavy and just about fitted, but Greg had rolled over when the alarm clock had shrilled earlier and made no offer to help. Sometimes her husband could be decidedly selfish. His family was coming as well as hers; it wouldn't have killed him to muck in a bit more.

Once the Christmas dinner was cooked and served she was downing tools, she decided. They could all help themselves to whatever they wanted afterwards and if Della and Eddie imagined for one second that they were getting a cooked dinner on St Stephen's Day, *she* wouldn't be cooking it!

Greg could drive up to Mass in Whiteshells Bay and back, today, she decided. If he thought she was going to drive and he was going to drink he could think again. If he had helped out with the turkey she would have driven with a good heart, but he could go shag himself, she thought grumpily. Della and co. were coming and she was going to be nice and relaxed and just the slightest bit tipsy when they arrived.

11

CARRIE WATCHED WITH PRIDE AS DAVEY STOOD AT THE ALTAR holding his staff and dressed in long red and white robes, playing his part as St Joseph with great gravitas. She saw him bend down under the small manger and whisk out the little doll wrapped in swaddling clothes, and hand it to Ciara Clarke who was playing Mary. Ciara tenderly placed the doll in the manger, smoothing its blanket as the shepherds began to crowd around.

'And so the infant Jesus was born,' intoned the small narrator breathlessly as the children's choir began to sing 'Angels We Have Heard On High', their young, enthusiastic voices filling the church.

'I bet you wish it was that easy,' Bobby murmured, highly entertained. 'Oh, look. One of the angels is having a row with another one. This is better than the Abbey.' Two little angels were engaged in a silent struggle over ownership of a scroll that bore the legend *Baby Jesus*. Fraught, the junior infants teacher hastened to settle the argument.

'It was never like this in our day. It's great, isn't it?' Bobby approved as Olivia in her role as Balthazar made her dramatic entrance carrying her jewellery box, which, much to her disappointment, did not contain gold, frankincense or even myrrh.

'Couldn't you at least get *one* of them?' she'd demanded of her mother, when she'd been given the part.

After the last carol had been sung and the crib had been visited, the family set off for the graveyard that adjoined the church grounds. It was a chilly, bracing day. Banks of gunmetal cloud lay to the east on the horizon, a portent of the bad weather that was forecast for later in the day. The sea was choppy, with big white-frosted waves rolling in to shore. Birds chirruped in the bare-branched trees. Two red-berried pyracanthas on either side of the old green iron gates blazed their glory against the surrounding stone walls. Graves were festooned with flowers and wreaths, seasonal offerings for loved ones. Here and there, in small groups or singly, people stood at the graves. Carrie had always felt sorry for her friends and neighbours who had to go and visit graves on Christmas Day. Now they were part of that sad circle and it had become one of their Christmas rituals.

'That's a lovely wreath,' Carrie said appreciatively as Shauna laid the arrangement of holly, ivy, skimmia, evergreen foliage and snowberries on their mother's grave.

'I made it up myself. I like doing things like that rather than buying ready-made stuff. I always feel Mam would like it better. Daft, I know.' Shauna straightened up and brushed two holly berries off her gloves.

Carrie laid her arrangement of red roses and carnations nestled in frothy wisps of gypsophila beside Shauna's wreath. 'I got these because I used to always buy her red roses and red carnations for her flower arrangements on Christmas Day. It was our little tradition.'

Bobby knelt down and put a lovely outdoor candle arrangement in front of the headstone. He lit it before slipping the open-topped glass cover over it to keep it from blowing out.

Noel knelt and tenderly placed his offering of yellow and pink roses from the bushes in their own garden. Gardening had been a great bond between Anna and himself and he nurtured his roses especially carefully so that he would have fresh flowers to place on his wife's grave on Christmas Day. A tear trickled down his cheek and Carrie's heart contracted when she saw him brush it hastily away. She placed an arm round his shoulder and stood silently beside him.

Bobby saw it too and bowed his head, struggling with the myriad emotions that consumed him. His father's harsh words came back to haunt him. It was because of worrying about him that his mother had suffered her heart attack and died, Noel had accused cruelly. Although Bobby's reasoning mind argued that this was nonsense there was that small, dark, fretful place in him that wondered if his father was right and it *was* all his fault.

'Bim bam bom, bim bam bom.' Chloe's carefree song broke the sad, subdued silence around the grave. 'Bim bam bom, bim bam bom,' she sang gaily to the sky, her curls dancing exuberantly in the breeze.

'What are you singing, darling? That's a lovely song,' Carrie exclaimed, glad of the diversion.

'That's "Jingle Bells" to me and you, if you listen carefully,' Shauna explained, grinning. Davey laughed uproariously.

'Bim bam bom!' he echoed. 'She's *really* funny.'

'I like that version.' Dan chuckled, lifting Chloe in his arms and singing 'Bim bam bom' back at her.

'I bet Granny would like that too,' Olivia said thoughtfully. 'She liked Christmas songs. She used to sing them to me when I was small.'

'Do you remember that?' Carrie looked at her daughter in surprise. 'Yes, Mom,' Olivia assured her. 'I used to sit on her knee and she used to sing me the songs. Will I sing her a song?'

101

'Yes, love, you do that,' Noel said, his eyes lighting up. 'Granny would love that.'

'I'm going to sing "Little Donkey",' Olivia decided. 'This is especially for you, Granny. I hope you're having a great Christmas in heaven. Santa brought me a Barbie Bride. I just thought I'd tell you before I start,' she said matter-of-factly as she gazed up at the sky, earnest and intent.

> *'Little donkey, little donkey,*
> *On a dusty road,*
> *Got to keep on plodding onwards,*
> *With your precious load.'*

Her pure childish voice rang out in the cold, clear air, her breath little curlicues of frosty white.

'*Ring out those bells tonight* . . .' Bobby added his contribution.

'*Bethlehem, Bethlehem.*' Dan's deep baritone joined in.

'BIM BAM BOM. BIM BAM BOM.' Chloe was not to be outsung.

Carrie and Shauna started to giggle. And soon they were all laughing, even Noel, as they stood at the grave, singing to Anna, all except Greg, who shuffled, mortified, from one leg to the other, wishing they'd hurry up and get on with it. He hated visiting graves. He thought it was morbid. His own father had died years ago and he never visited the grave. His mother and a friend had gone to Egypt for Christmas, anxious to do a past-life regression at the pyramids, so he wouldn't be seeing her again for a while.

'Children are great, aren't they?' Shauna remarked to Carrie as they walked back down the narrow path towards the iron gates. 'I just loved the way Olivia spoke to Mam as if she was there. I love the way she sang for her with no inhibitions, as if it was the most natural thing in the world.'

102

'We should learn from our kids. It would be nice to believe Mam is here in spirit. It makes it more bearable to think so, doesn't it?' Carrie sighed.

'I think she *is* here. I feel very close to her sometimes,' Shauna said quietly. 'Sometimes I sit and light a candle and play soft music and just think of her and I swear I can feel her around me.'

'That's a nice thing to do. I must try it sometime,' Carrie said thoughtfully.

'I do it when Chloe's having a nap. You could do it when the kids are at school. It's like switching off from the world and going to a different place.'

'I could do with switching off from the world.' Carrie grinned. 'Come on, let's go back to my house and have a cup of tea and a bite to eat before you get on the road. I'll bring Dad and Bobby to Malahide in my car and Dan can bring the kids in his after we've finished our visiting.'

Shauna frowned. 'That would mean Dan couldn't have a few drinks. I know that you're not drinking, but I'd like Dan to be able to and he won't be able to if he's driving.'

'We're not all going to fit in one car,' Carrie pointed out.

'Dad and Bobby can come back with us after we've had a cup of tea with you,' Shauna said firmly. 'I'll sit in the back with Chloe and Bobby. Dad can sit in the front. He can stay the night or go back with you if he wants to. Bobby's staying.' Shauna pulled her scarf tighter round her neck.

'Thanks, Shauna, that's a good idea. I'd say Dad will come home with us, but we'll see how it's going. I'd like Dan to have a couple of drinks and relax. He's been working his ass off coming up to Christmas,' Carrie said gratefully.

'No problem. Try and not be too late getting over, won't you? It would be nice if we could have some time together before the Freeloaders arrive.'

'I'll do my best. Dan's parents are going to his aunt's so they'll be anxious to get going. We won't have to stay as long as we usually do,' Carrie assured her. 'With any luck we'll have an hour or so before Della and co. arrive.'

Della shook a travel tablet into her hand and held it out to her daughter. 'This will make you feel better, chicken. Now when we get to Shauna's don't say anything about being sick. Sure you won't?'

'No, Mommy,' Kathryn said wearily, swallowing the tablet down with a sip of 7-Up. The best thing about being sick was getting lemonade, she decided. 7-Up tasted lovely.

Della glanced at her watch. Just gone half ten. The tablet would work within an hour and hopefully Kathryn would sleep her way to Dublin. She knew Shauna had said to come in the afternoon, but she could take a running jump. Della had no intention of hanging around a minute longer than necessary. Once that tablet was absorbed into Kathryn's system they were hitting the road and if Shauna didn't like it, she could lump it.

'You'd want to mind that chap on the bike there, Greg. He's not very steady. I suspect that he's drunk,' Noel declared as Greg drove out of Whiteshells Bay and headed for the M1.

Shauna gave Bobby a dig in the ribs and grinned. Bobby elbowed back. They were sitting in the back of the car and Noel had a running commentary on everything from his front seat position. Chloe, flakers in her seat after all the excitement of being with her cousins, was fast asleep. Shauna tucked a blanket round her daughter. 'It's great that she's having a nap now; she won't be cranky at dinner,' she remarked cheerfully. She was surprised at how stress-free she felt, but she was actually enjoying her Christmas Day so far. The dinner was under control,

Chloe was in good form, and Greg hadn't protested too much when she'd told him that he was driving to and from Whiteshells Bay. She'd very much enjoyed her two glasses of champagne at Carrie and Dan's and it had been fun watching the kids, giddy with excitement, play with their toys as they tucked into smoked salmon and delicious home-made brown bread.

She was looking forward to spending time with Bobby. She figured he could do with some rescuing. He'd been subdued at the grave and Shauna knew instinctively that he was remembering his father's cruel assertions about the reason for their mother's death. He was going to stay the night in her house and Carrie was bringing their father home. Her brother would have some respite from Noel.

'Ah what speed are you doing there, Greg? I think it's fifty on this stretch,' Noel interjected.

'Don't worry about it, Mr McCarthy,' Greg said tightly, trying to hide his irritation.

'You don't want to be stopped for speeding,' Noel warned self-righteously.

'The crib was lovely,' Shauna remarked diplomatically, her nice buzz of relaxation beginning to fray. She could see by the taut line of Greg's jaw that he was getting annoyed.

'The new committee decided on using artificial greenery. I don't think it worked as well as when myself and Mrs Murphy were in charge of it,' Noel said petulantly. He had always looked after the decorating of the crib but this year the responsibility had gone to Mrs Hall and Miss Carter, much to his dismay. Father Doyle had told him that after his last hospital stay, he should not be doing strenuous duties such as putting up the crib. Noel had protested, but Father Doyle had suggested giving 'the women' a chance to show their mettle.

They had gone way overboard in Noel's estimation, using

poinsettias along the base of the crib. He couldn't be sure, but he didn't think poinsettias were indigenous to the Holy Land, a fact he was going to research and point out at the next committee meeting. He'd mentioned it to Mrs Hall but she'd just brushed him off and told him she was in charge this year. Noel had been raging. She wasn't even from the parish. She'd moved from Dundalk a year ago and had muscled in on the parish committee. He detested her.

'I thought it looked good. I liked the poinsettias,' Shauna remarked, unaware of his feelings about the showy plants.

'Not at all realistic,' Noel said dismissively. 'Cactus would have been more appropriate if they wanted authenticity.'

'Oh.' Shauna had no answer to that.

'Traffic is heavy enough, isn't it?' Bobby observed.

'I suppose everyone is out and about visiting,' Greg replied as he put the boot down to overtake a red van. Shauna saw her father's gaze flicker towards the speedometer and hoped that he'd keep his mouth shut. Greg would only take so much and then he'd tell Noel to mind his own business. She didn't want a bad atmosphere to taint the day. Fortunately Noel, apart from a deep inhalation of breath, said nothing and Greg slowed down a little as he came onto the stretch leading to the turn-off for Malahide.

It was with relief, ten minutes later, that she saw the house ahead of them. She intended plonking her father in front of the TV with a cup of tea the minute she went in. That would keep him out of harm's way. The smell of roasting turkey that wafted out of the kitchen, filling the hallway, made them all sniff appreciatively.

'Smells good,' Greg approved.

'Will you just lift it out to baste it?'

'Sure,' her husband agreed. 'I'll just put Chloe into her cot.

Bobby, help yourself to a drink; you can pour me a beer. And whatever your dad would like.'

'Would you like a cup of tea, Dad?' Shauna took her father's coat.

'Lovely, Shauna. That would go down nicely.' Noel rubbed his hands.

'Why don't you come in and sit by the fire? There might be something you'd like to watch on TV.' She led him into the lounge and switched on the TV and the coal-effect gas fire. She handed him the remote control, showed him how to use it and then went to the kitchen where Bobby was opening two bottles of beer.

'What are you going to have?' he asked.

'I think I'll have a white wine spritzer. I need to keep my wits about me for a little while longer, regretfully.' She made a face. The doorbell rang.

'I'll get it,' Greg called. It was Maria and Colin: neighbours from down the road. Five minutes later another couple called in and a jolly buzz filled the house as Greg poured drinks for them and they nibbled on the selection of canapés Shauna had ordered from the caterers. The turkey, basted and turned, was cooking satisfactorily and Shauna had time to have a quick drink before she started the rest of the dinner. She made Noel's tea and brought it in to him. She was determined to make the effort to see that he enjoyed his day. Carrie's kindness was something to aspire to, she thought a little guiltily, remembering how sharp she often was with him.

'Are you all right there, Dad? Will you have another canapé?'

'No, this is grand. I don't want to spoil my dinner,' Noel assured her. He was watching a service of carols and Bible readings and was quite happy as he was. Shauna, her daughterly duty done, felt free to mingle with her guests. She hoped Carrie and Dan and the kids wouldn't be too long. If only Della and Eddie weren't coming it would have been great. Still, they wouldn't be here for another hour and a half or so, she comforted herself as she took a long drink of her Chardonnay spritzer.

She was in the kitchen with Bobby putting more canapés on a tray when the doorbell pealed again. 'Great, Carrie and Dan are here,' she said happily.

'I think not,' Bobby murmured as Della's gay tones rippled through the hall.

'The sneaky tart!' Shauna raged. 'She never listens to what I say. I'm sick of her. Why does she always have to push it?'

'Here.' Bobby handed her a full glass of champagne. 'Get that down you and you'll be flying and you won't give a hoot about her.'

'It would take more than a glass of champagne to sort out how I feel about that cow.' She scowled.

'Come on now, come on, don't let her spoil your Christmas,' her brother urged, handing her the champagne flute. 'Drink up.' He took a generous slug from his own glass. 'Take a leaf out of my book,' he advised as Della breezed into the kitchen.

'Well, aren't you blooming, Della. Is it triplets you're expecting?' he schmoozed insincerely, winking at Shauna when he got behind the other woman.

'Oh!' Della was momentarily taken aback. She didn't think she'd put on *that* much weight.

'Quite a party,' she said, kissing Shauna on the cheek. 'I'm glad we came early, it would have been a shame to miss it,' she added acidly, placing two bottles of wine on the table.

'Oh, you'll make sure you never miss *anything*, Della. Thank you *so* much for the wine.' Shauna glanced at the two bottles and wasn't the slightest bit surprised to see that they were cheap supermarket wines. Probably on a special offer, she thought nastily. 'Bobby, get a drink for Della and Eddie, will you?' she said dryly.

'Delighted to,' Bobby said cheerfully. 'Some Amé for yourself, I expect. Pity you're preggers – the champers is just *gorgeous*! But I know you're into the health kick, and I think it's great not to drink when you're pregnant. Poor Carrie's in the same boat.' He had no intention of pouring Della a glass of expensive champagne.

'Well, one glass wouldn't make—' The doorbell pealed again, interrupting her as both Bobby and Shauna hurried to the front door, assuring each other that 'I'll get it'.

'She's not getting any of my good champers,' Bobby vowed as he opened the door to Carrie's gang.

'I thought the Keegans weren't coming until later,' Carrie murmured as Shauna stepped back to let her in.

'Well, that was the plan.' Shauna made a face as she took her sister's coat.

'Typical,' muttered Carrie as she helped Olivia remove her hat and scarf.

'Happy Christmas,' Della said unctuously, beaming as she emerged into the hall and threw her arms round Carrie.

'Same to you.' Carrie fought the urge to shrug her off.

'And to you, Dan.' Della launched herself on Dan, who had just come into the hall.

'Kids, go on down to the playroom. Chloe and Kathryn are there,' Shauna said. 'Dan, a pint?' She smiled at her brother-in-law.

'I'd love one, thanks,' he agreed, strolling into the lounge to join the others.

'I'll get it,' Bobby offered and the women followed him back into the kitchen.

'Mommy, Olivia won't let me get on Chloe's new rocking

horse.' Kathryn raced in to her mother, furious, a few minutes later.

'Tell her she's got to share,' Della ordered.

'You can have a go when Olivia's finished, Kathryn.' Davey had come to see that Olivia's name was not being blackened. 'We all have to take our turns,' he pointed out firmly, arms crossed in his I-won't-take-any-nonsense pose. Shauna struggled not to laugh at Della's nonplussed expression.

'Not fair.' Kathryn sulked.

'Very fair,' Shauna said firmly.

'Well, she is that bit younger than they are. She doesn't understand,' Della said, a tad annoyed.

'A good time to start, Della. Davey will sort it; he's very good at playing fair,' Bobby said firmly. 'You forget about it and go and join the party and I'll be in with your drink.' He ushered her out of the kitchen before she had a chance to protest.

'If you want to play with us you have to take turns.' Davey eyeballed Kathryn.

'He's right.' Shauna backed him up. Kathryn realized she wasn't getting anywhere fast.

'OK,' she capitulated.

'Well done, Davey. Thanks for that.' Shauna gave her nephew a hug. 'How about some more 7-Up and a biscuit to keep you going until dinnertime?'

'Thanks, Shauna.' Davey basked in her praise.

'Me, me,' Kathryn insisted.

'And you. We couldn't forget *you*,' Shauna said caustically as she poured the 7-Up and gave them a few biscuits to take with them.

'See.' Bobby smiled at his sister as he came back into the kitchen five minutes later. 'Easy peasy. Now drink up, kiddo, and let me worry about darling Della.'

'Did you see the look on her face when you suggested the Amé? She was gagging for a glass of champagne.'

'Well, she's not getting any of my Moët, I told you. Imagine arriving with two bottles of plonk for Christmas. How mean is that? Spawn of Scrooge,' he exclaimed indignantly.

'I love you, Bobby.' Shauna burst out laughing.

'Right back at ya.' Bobby held up his glass to her and they clinked together, united against the enemy as they always had been, ever since they were kids.

12

'THE ARSE IS GOING TO FALL OUT OF IT,' SHAUNA FRETTED AS SHE and Greg struggled to lift the huge, steaming bird out of the roasting tray.

'Hold on. Let me get the fish slice under the leg. That's where it's sticking,' Greg muttered, perspiration forming on his forehead as he bent over his task. 'Quick, slide the plate underneath.'

Shauna did as she was bid, sliding the big platter under the turkey, which was dripping juices and stuffing all over the roasting dish. 'It's definitely cooked, isn't it?' She blew her hair out of her eye as she placed the heavy-laden platter on the island.

'It looks fine, really golden, and the stuffing is gorgeous,' Greg assured her, licking his fingers.

'You mash and cream the potatoes and I'll slice the ham. We'll let the juices settle before we carve the turkey,' Shauna said.

The sprouts and the mushy peas were cooked and the roast potatoes and roast parsnips needed just another few minutes.

'Need any help?' Carrie stuck her head through the doorway.

'You're fine, go and relax,' Greg told her.

'I can't. I feel guilty,' she confessed, grinning. 'Here, let me mash them and you do something else.'

'Bring the cranberry sauce and the bread sauce into the dining

112

room and bring Chloe's high chair in to the table. You can put her beside me,' Shauna told him.

'OK.' Greg handed the masher to Carrie, who wielded it with gusto.

When he had gone out of the kitchen with the sauce dishes Carrie whispered, 'I just had to get away from the Mother of Perpetual Sorrows. I've had every ache and pain of her pregnancy. God, she never stops. I couldn't believe they were here before us.'

'I should have known. I suppose we were lucky they didn't land on us yesterday. Is Dad OK in there?'

'He's watching *Indiana Jones* and enjoying it, giving Eddie a running commentary the whole way through.' Carrie mashed vigorously and added a cholesterol-laden dollop of cream and butter.

Shauna grinned. One of Noel's more irritating habits was to comment to all and sundry on whatever he was watching on the TV. It drove all his children mad, especially when they were trying to concentrate on whatever news or film they were watching.

'Just give Kathryn the smallest piece of turkey and mash, Shauna.' Della appeared at the door.

'No problem,' Shauna said brightly.

'Are the kids eating in the playroom?' She perched on a stool at the island, much to Shauna's irritation.

'No, they're eating with us.' Shauna looked at her in surprise.

'Oh . . . I see. I thought you'd want some peace and quiet.' Della sniffed.

'Della, it's Christmas. Family time. I wouldn't dream of them eating separately from us. Christmas dinner with the kids is fun. I love watching Chloe with her cousins.' Shauna tried to keep the edge out of her voice. She wished Della would buzz off back into the lounge. She wanted to be able to dish out in comfort, using her fingers if she had to without having her sister-in-law looking over her shoulder. Thank God she hadn't been in the kitchen when the ass had threatened to fall out of the turkey.

'Any chance of a streaky rasher?' Bobby appeared and whisked a crunchy bit of bacon off the turkey breast. 'Della, what's a woman in your condition doing in the kitchen? Go in and put your feet up for goodness' sake and make the most of it.'

'Do you think?' she simpered.

'Absolutely.'

'It's not very fair having Shauna do all the work,' she said sanctimoniously.

'Never fear. I'm here. Would you like a cushion for your back?'

'That would be great,' she agreed as she followed him back to the lounge.

'Well done Bobby.' Shauna gave Carrie the thumbs up as she prepared to carve the bird. 'Did you hear her? *It's not fair having Shauna do all the work.*' She mimicked her sister-in-law. 'What a hypocrite!'

'There! Am I good or what?' Bobby reappeared and demolished another rasher.

'You're such a lick,' Carrie accused, grinning.

'I got rid of her, didn't I, and she thinks I'm the bee's knees,' he said smugly. 'Have you ever seen anything like Eddie? The guy hasn't stopped eating since he got here.' Bobby helped himself to a spoonful of stuffing.

'Look who's talking!' Shauna jeered.

'No, I mean really going to town on the grub. He's eating peanuts, crisps, canapés and chocolates. He'll never eat his dinner.'

'Oh, never you fear, Eddie will eat his dinner and so will Della and they'll have tea *and* supper. They give locusts a bad name,' Shauna retorted as she finished slicing the breast.

'Miaow.' Bobby grinned.

'Wait until you have in-laws,' she teased. 'Any sign of anyone special?'

'Naw, I'm not looking. I've got a few good mates. I like being single. I like my freedom, and being my own boss. A reaction to being bossed around at home, I suppose.'

'We were all bossed around, Bobby. You shouldn't let it stop you from having a relationship,' Carrie murmured.

'If I could find a gay Dan I'd have a relationship quick enough, I can assure you. How come all the good ones are straight?' Bobby moaned. 'Look at Eddie, he's to die for!'

They all laughed as Greg walked into the kitchen.

'What's the joke?'

'Aw, nothing, we were talking about the kids. Honey, will you carve a couple of slices off the other side of the breast?' Shauna handed him the carving knife. 'I want to start plating up.'

'Mom. That Kathryn one won't get off Chloe's new rocking horse and no-one else can get a go. She's really mean.' Olivia burst into the kitchen indignantly, followed by a red-faced Chloe who had been up playing with her cousins for the last hour.

'Well it's almost time for dinner anyway, so go and tell Davey to wash his hands and you do the same and we'll sort out the rocking horse after dinner, OK?'

'Oh, OK. Can I have loads of turkey?'

'Loads,' Greg assured her, cutting a piece of the breast and giving it to her on the end of the carving fork.

'Oh, yummy,' Olivia drooled, and blew on it. Chewing happily, she went back to the playroom to boast of having the first piece of turkey.

115

Ten minutes later, they were seated at the beautifully dressed table and Noel was saying grace.

'Amen,' Olivia and Davey said hastily, anxious to tuck in.

'You know, I've waited three hundred and sixty-four days for this,' Davey said eagerly as he dug his fork into his starter.

'Well, enjoy it,' Shauna encouraged him, relieved that they were all sitting down and the meal was under way.

'You'd think you never got a bite, Davey,' his mother chided, laughing.

'Ah, you know what I mean, Mam. Christmas Day dinner only happens once every year.'

'And very lucky we are, Davey, that Our Lord chose to be made man on this day,' his grandfather said piously.

'I suppose it's really His birthday party,' Davey observed. 'We should put a candle on the Christmas cake.'

'Brilliant idea,' Olivia agreed.

'I'm blowing it out,' Kathryn decreed.

'Everyone can blow it out,' Shauna said firmly, as she swallowed some lobster mousse. The starter seemed to be going down well; Eddie had finished his already.

Greg helped her clear away the plates and stack them into the dishwasher, while Bobby brought in the children's main course.

'This is scrumptious,' Davey enthused, pronging a crispy roast potato with his fork as Shauna served the others.

'High praise. If Davey's happy, I'm happy.' She smiled affectionately at her nephew as she sat down herself.

'When is your baby due?' Noel turned to Della who was seated on his right.

'Early March,' Della informed him, hoping he'd shut up and let her eat her dinner in peace.

'That's great. And Carrie's expecting too. I take my hat off to the pair of you, for following the ideals of Christian marriage. So many couples plan their families to suit themselves. This modern world is so selfish.' He glanced down the table at Shauna. 'Chloe could do with a brother or sister,' he observed.

'If you don't mind, Mr McCarthy, that's actually none of your business, and it's not a topic for discussion at the table in front of the children – or in front of anybody.' Greg glared at his father-in-law, furious.

Noel turned a deep puce. 'Umm . . . er . . . I didn't mean to offend.' An awkward silence descended on the table. Shauna could have kicked her father hard on the shins. The cheek of him. She didn't mind Greg's taking him to task one bit. It was just unfortunate it was at the Christmas dinner.

'Gorgeous sprouts,' Bobby babbled. Carrie looked at him and he had to hide a grin.

'They're tasty all right,' she murmured. 'Perhaps gorgeous might be a little OTT.'

'No, the roast potatoes are best,' Davey argued, completely unaware of the tension. Shauna started to relax again. The first hiccup sorted.

'Nice turkey,' Della observed.

'Are you still working in the health shop?' Noel enquired, clearing his throat and veering to a safer topic.

'Oh, indeed I am.' She turned to him. 'We've expanded, you know.'

'Dan, have more stuffing,' Greg offered.

'Don't mind if I do. Lovely meal, you guys.'

'I'll have some of that.' Eddie held out his plate.

'It's a real treat sitting down to a dinner that's cooked for you.' Carrie smiled at Bobby. 'Do you cook proper dinners or do you eat out of packets?'

Shauna let the waves of conversation drift over her. She

117

looked at the steaming plate of food in front of her but didn't feel that hungry. A tiredness enveloped her. Adrenalin had kept her going but now that the dinner was served and she could relax, she felt like going asleep. It must have been the wine and champagne she'd drunk.

'We've built on a small extension to the shop and Marla rents it out to an acupuncturist and a reflexologist. And on Saturday mornings a fortune-teller does readings. She's brilliant,' Della informed Noel. Shauna hid a grin. Della was in for a lecture although she didn't know it.

'Well now, you know, Della, that type of thing, fortune-tellers and palm-readers, and tarot cards, goes against the teachings of the Church. The Bible says that . . .'

Shauna caught Carrie's eye across the table and gave her the tiniest wink. Putting Della and Noel together was an inspired piece of table seating.

'I don't want my dinner. I feel sick,' Kathryn announced.

'Oh, dear,' Della murmured. 'Don't eat it then. It's probably all the rubbish you've been eating.'

'She didn't get any rubbish here.' Shauna bristled.

'I didn't mean that,' Della said distractedly. 'Eddie, bring Kathryn into the playroom until I've had my dinner, and then you can come and finish yours.'

'I'll bring mine with me. I hope she doesn't puke,' Eddie grumbled. 'You'd think that doctor would have given her something yesterday.'

'You had Kathryn at the doctor? You never said. What's wrong with her?' Shauna asked politely.

'Nothing at all.'

'A tummy bug.'

Della and Eddie spoke simultaneously.

'She has a tummy bug?' Shauna eyeballed Della.

'She's just a little off colour.' Della couldn't meet her sister-in-law's eye.

'Great,' Shauna said coldly. 'Let's hope it's not infectious.'

'Want to go to the playroom, Daddy,' Kathryn whined.

'Come on, you,' Eddie said grumpily, taking his plate with him.

'More wine, anyone?' Greg asked smoothly.

'Why not?' Dan agreed and Greg topped him up.

'Bobby?'

'No argument from me.' Bobby held out his glass.

'I wonder is it this winter vomiting bug they talk about in the hospitals?' Noel murmured.

Oh, shut up, you old idiot. Della was fit to be tied. The old codger was doing her head in.

'We should all take some apple cider vinegar. Do you sell that in your shop, Della?' Noel queried.

'Oh yes, we do indeed. Very effective,' Della said crossly. When she got her hands on Eddie she was going to kill him. Him and his big mouth.

'Shauna, more wine?' Greg eyed his wife warily.

'Thanks,' she said, taking pity on him. It wasn't his fault he had a self-centred, selfish wagon for a sister.

'Good girl,' he murmured, filling her glass, relieved that she hadn't got into a snit about the bug and the way he'd put her father in his place.

'I don't think I'm going to fit Christmas pudding. I'm bursting,' Davey announced cheerfully.

'Well, if you can't fit it in now, you can have some later,' Carrie assured him.

'I'll be hard put to it to fit pudding myself, Shauna. This is a delicious dinner.' Dan smiled at his sister-in-law. 'Thanks to the both of you for going to so much trouble. A toast to our hosts.' He raised his glass.

119

'To our hosts,' echoed Bobby. 'The hosts with the most.'

Davey guffawed, amused by his uncle, as they all clinked glasses, Olivia insisting on getting out of her chair and clinking everyone's glass. Chloe waved her plastic mug in the air until kind-hearted Davey clinked with her, and then Dan, and then Bobby.

'Cheers,' Olivia explained. 'Say cheers.'

''Eers,' Chloe echoed, delighted with herself.

Why would Della want to miss moments like this with her child? She would have been perfectly happy to let the kids eat on their own. She's an idiot, Shauna thought scornfully, watching the fun the trio were having with their toasts.

'I suppose this time next year you'll be in the Gulf,' Della observed.

'Oh, let's not talk about that now,' Shauna said crisply, seeing the sadness cloud Carrie's eyes. 'Who's for pudding?'

'Maybe I could fit a teeny piece,' Davey said seriously.

'Go for it, Davey,' Greg encouraged him as he began to clear the plates.

'Can we pull the crackers?' Olivia asked, her eyes dancing with excitement.

'Go right ahead.' Shauna held out her cracker to her niece, who pulled vigorously. Soon the table resounded with bangs and laughter and silly jokes.

'Della, Kathryn says she feels sick. You better deal with it.' Eddie appeared at the door.

'Oh, for God's sake!' his wife exclaimed in exasperation as she stood up from the table. 'Why can't you do it?'

'Well, she's calling for you,' Eddie muttered.

'I'll get you a basin,' Shauna said hastily, hurrying out to the kitchen.

'Is she going to go blagh?' Olivia asked. 'Remember when I went blagh and there was carrots in it?'

'Stop it, you horrible child. We haven't finished eating.' Bobby made a face and Olivia giggled.

'And sweetcorn,' she added.

'Ugh!' Bobby grimaced even more wildly.

'I'll have some pudding if it's going,' Eddie declared.

'With custard and brandy butter?' Carrie asked coolly.

'Anything that's going. You wouldn't get that in our house, so don't be delicate with the helpings.' Eddie didn't even notice Carrie's hint of sarcasm.

She went out to the kitchen to salvage some pudding for him, and looked up as her sister came back into the room after bringing Della the basin. 'What a pair they are,' she fumed. 'That Eddie is something else.'

'Imagine bringing a child with a tummy bug into someone's house. If Chloe gets that I'll swing for her. Can you just believe it, Carrie?' Shauna was hopping mad.

'No. She sure takes the biscuit, and as for greedy-guts at the table, what a slob. He hasn't an ounce of manners.'

'Well, Kathryn is sleeping in their bed and if she pukes all over them, tough luck,' Shauna raged as she slashed a slice of pudding for her brother-in-law and poured custard over it. 'Give him a tiny little bit of brandy butter, the big walrus, and make sure he doesn't sneak any more.'

'Yes sir!' Carrie teased. 'You know, if I were you I'd suggest they go home. I bet Eddie doesn't want to be puked on all night.'

Shauna's eyes brightened. 'That's an idea. I'd better run it by Greg, though. I don't want him to think I'm getting rid of them.'

'Here he comes now. I'll make myself scarce,' Carrie murmured, picking up the tray of desserts and smiling at her brother-in-law as he held the door open for her.

'Will I see if anyone wants trifle?' Greg asked, bending to put dirty cutlery into the dishwasher.

'I bet Eddie will,' Shauna retorted.

'Umm.'

'They shouldn't have brought Kathryn, knowing she had a bug,' she burst out.

'I know. That was a bit much,' Greg admitted.

'She's going to be sleeping in the same bed as them. If she's puking that's going to be very awkward. I think they'd be better off bringing her home,' Shauna said bluntly.

'I suppose. Unless we bring Chloe into bed with us and give them her cot.'

'No, Greg. I don't want her puking all over Chloe's cot,' Shauna exclaimed indignantly.

'Oh! Right.'

'Will you say it, then?'

'No, you do. It's awkward.'

'Well, do you want them to stay the night?' she demanded. 'I don't mind. It's up to you.'

Della hurried into the kitchen. 'Do you have any kitchen towel and Dettol?' They could hear Kathryn howling in the play-room.

'Greg, will you get it,' Shauna said tautly. Why could he never back her up when she needed it?

'Kathryn's covered in puke, Della. I think you'll have to give her a bath,' Davey said helpfully. He'd gone to investigate the howls, and come to the kitchen to report. 'What will you do if she pukes in the bath?'

'Davey, go in and eat your dessert like a good boy,' Shauna instructed. She was beginning to feel somewhat queasy at his questions. Greg followed his sister out of the kitchen armed with Dettol, kitchen towel and a mop.

'Ah, shag it,' Shauna muttered and went back in to the table to eat her dessert.

'Everything OK?' Eddie mumbled.

'No, Kathryn's sick. Maybe you should go and give Della a hand,' Shauna suggested grimly.

'Ah, she'll manage fine.' Eddie smirked. 'That's what women are for. I'll have another helping of pudding if you have one.'

'I'll go and give Della a hand.' Carrie stood up, disgusted.

'Sit down, Carrie. Greg's with her,' Shauna ordered. 'The last thing you need to get is a tummy bug,' she said pointedly, but it was wasted on her brother-in-law, who was helping himself to a chocolate biscuit. She took a deep breath. 'You know, Eddie, maybe it would be a good idea to take Kathryn home to her own bed. Because she'll be sleeping with you and she could have an accident—'

'And go blagh all over you,' Davey added helpfully.

'Exactly,' Shauna said firmly.

'Well now, I can't drive,' Eddie said slowly.

'Della can,' Bobby interjected. 'She only drank minerals.'

'It's entirely up to yourself,' Shauna said silkily. 'I'm just pointing out what could happen. I wouldn't fancy getting puked on myself, if it was me . . .'

'Couldn't we borrow a cot?' Della suggested when her husband reluctantly suggested going home to her a while later. He did not like the idea of Kathryn up-chucking on him one whit. 'What about your friends next door? Would they have one?'

'They're spending Christmas in Galway.' Shauna couldn't believe that she was still angling to spend the night.

'Could Chloe sleep with you and—'

'No, that's not an option. If you knew she had a bug you really shouldn't have come. It wasn't fair on the child.'

'I wanted to spend Christmas with my brother before he goes away,' Della snapped.

'Nevertheless it wasn't a good idea, Della.' Shauna didn't care any more. She'd had enough.

An hour later, after Kathryn had been sick again, a sulky Della, a pissed Eddie and a sleeping Kathryn were sitting in their car.

'I think it's the best thing all round. At least she'll be in her own bed and you'll both get a chance to sleep,' Shauna said crisply.

Della ignored her. 'Thanks for having us, Greg,' she said pointedly as she started the engine. 'I hope the roads won't be icy.'

'You'll be fine,' Dan said kindly. 'It's a cloudy night; it won't freeze. Safe journey.'

''Bye.' Carrie waved cheerfully, delighted for Shauna's sake that they were going.

'You'll be home in no time. There won't be a soul on the road, they'll be all nodding beside the fire, smashed. Weren't you the wise one not to drink?' Bobby smiled innocently.

Della was furious; Eddie was already practically snoring. If Kathryn got sick on the journey home she was on her own.

'I better get going,' she snapped. ''Night.'

'Thanks for the wine,' Shauna said insincerely, feeling not the slightest bit of sympathy for her sister-in-law.

'I'll say a prayer for you,' Noel said earnestly.

That was the last straw. Della gunned the engine and roared out of the drive, tyres screeching.

'And it's only six fifteen,' Shauna murmured to Carrie, trying to hide her delight until Greg had gone in.

'Yippee!' Bobby punched the air when they were on their own.

'That was a stroke of luck.' Carrie tucked her arm into Shauna's. 'If you could call it that!'

124

'Yeah, well, it's her own fault for being so mean as to invade someone's house when her child had a bug. I wouldn't do that to my worst enemy. Now let's really party,' she whispered as they hurried back into the warm house and closed the door on the cold, grey night.

13

'THAT LAST VODKA WAS A VODKA TOO MANY,' BOBBY GROANED as they walked along the beach in the watery, hazy sunlight that threw lemon glints onto the glittering sea, making him wince. It was mid-morning on St Stephen's Day and he, Carrie and Shauna were taking some badly needed fresh air. Ahead of them, Greg, Dan and the kids were skimming stones across the water.

There were plenty of people out and about walking their pets or striding briskly across the strand in an effort to walk off the excesses of the previous day.

'It was great that you could stay, Carrie. Thanks for sleeping on the sofa, Bobby,' Shauna said gratefully.

'I didn't think Dad would be up for it, but once he said he'd stay so that Carrie wouldn't have to drive home, it was no problem,' Bobby assured her.

'It was a good night, wasn't it?' Carrie grinned. 'Davey and Olivia couldn't believe their luck when Greg suggested we should stay.'

'It couldn't have worked out better. They'll always remember this Christmas. You should have seen Chloe's face when she saw them this morning. She *danced* with excitement. Did they sleep OK, Carrie?'

'Like logs. That blow-up bed Colin and Maria lent us was perfect.'

'It was a good job I thought of it *after* Della and Eddie were gone.' Shauna burst out laughing. 'Colin and Maria are good fun, aren't they? It was great they came back with me when I went to borrow the bed. All in all, not the worst Christmas ever,' she said with satisfaction. 'Well, apart from Dad's remarks on "Christian marriage" at the table,' she added wryly. 'I thought Greg was going to blow a gasket. I wouldn't mind, but I'm *desperate* to have another baby. The irony of it.'

'Are you?' Bobby looked at her in surprise.

'I'd love one.' She sighed. 'Chloe needs a sister or brother, but unfortunately Greg's not on for another child at the moment. I'm hoping that he'll change his mind when we're settled in Abu Dhabi.'

'I suppose this isn't the ideal time to be pregnant. It'll happen when it's meant to happen,' Bobby said comfortingly.

'I hope so,' Shauna said longingly, watching with pleasure as Chloe galloped along the beach in her red wellington boots, as fast as her little legs would carry her, chasing Davey with a clump of seaweed.

'Hello?' Noel answered the phone after its third ring, looking for a pen in case he had to take a message.

'Oh! Who's that?' a vaguely familiar voice asked.

'It's Noel, Shauna's dad. Who am I speaking to?'

'Oh!' There was a pause. 'It's Della.'

'Ah. How is the little one?'

'Much better. Actually, we were thinking we might even take a trip down again.'

'Well now, Greg and Shauna are gone for a walk with Dan and

Carrie and the children so I'll get them to give you a call when they come back.'

'Dan and Carrie? Did they stay the night?' Della's voice rose an octave. 'Where did everyone sleep?'

'Well, I slept in the small guest room, Bobby slept on the sofa and Dan and Carrie slept in the double room and the children slept on the floor—'

'On the floor? That wasn't very comfortable.'

'Ah no, they were in a pump-up bed type of thing,' Noel explained patiently. 'Their friends brought it over. They stayed and had a couple of drinks. A very nice couple,' he carried on, oblivious.

'I see,' Della said coolly. 'Well, tell them I rang.'

'Indeed I will,' promised Noel affably. 'Take care now.'

He put the phone down and went out to the kitchen to make himself a cup of tea. He'd been asked if he'd like to go for a walk, but he hadn't been in the mood for it. He hadn't slept very well in the strange bed. He'd like to be at home, but he didn't want to spoil Carrie's day. She'd been delighted when Greg had suggested they stay the night. She'd suggested he ask his neighbour, Mrs O'Neill, to feed Twiskers, which the kind woman had done willingly.

As he waited for the kettle to boil his gaze fell on a white envelope that contained what looked like a bank statement. Shauna and Greg certainly weren't short of a bob or two, he conceded as he flicked open the envelope and took a peek. It was a Visa bill. Noel didn't possess such an item. That was for rich, posh people.

He studied the statement, noting the expenditure on frivolities like catering companies, beauty salons and off-licences. More money than sense, he sighed as he stuffed the bill back in the envelope. Another bill, an ESB one, made his eyes widen. It was three times the amount of his bill. Such waste! He tutted as he peered along the bottles of wine in the large wine rack under the island. It was far from Chablis and Sauvignons and Chardonnays and Merlots that Shauna was raised. Where had she got her notions? He wasn't too fond of Greg; he far preferred Dan. Dan had much more respect for his elders. Dan would never have spoken to him with such disrespect. Noel's lips tightened at the memory of Greg's snub. Shauna hadn't even spoken in his defence; none of them had. It was hard being a father. They'd learn that someday and then they'd understand what he'd been trying to teach them.

Noel made himself a cup of tea, cut a slice of Christmas cake and went to see if there was anything worth watching on the TV. The house was lovely and warm and after a while his chin drooped onto his chest and he fell asleep.

'That Shauna is a two-faced bitch,' Della muttered as she slapped a piece of goat's cheese onto a rice cake, poured herself a cup of peppermint tea and sat down at her kitchen table. A pump-up bed would have suited Kathryn fine last night. She hadn't been sick any more and it was obvious she had passed the worst stage of her tummy bug. They could have stayed last night if Shauna hadn't got into a tizzy. And to think Carrie and Dan had jumped into their bed. Would they be as quick to jump into their coffins? So much for family loyalty. Greg had shown none.

The only good thing was that she hadn't had to put up with that irritating old bore, Noel. She'd make sure never to sit beside him at anything again. He'd wittered and waffled until she'd wanted to clobber him. She was going to ring Greg and try to wangle another invitation to Dublin today or tomorrow, or at the very least New Year. Shauna needn't think that she'd pulled a fast one on her!

*   *   *

'Della was hoping to drive back down!' Shauna couldn't believe her ears. She, Carrie and Noel were in the kitchen making coffee while Dan and Greg were watching horse racing on TV. Bobby was playing football with Davey out the back and Olivia and Chloe were playing with their dolls.

'Hmm. She said something like that. Give her a ring, and she can tell you what she wants to do,' Noel suggested.

'Can you believe her nerve?' Shauna muttered to Carrie, then returned her attention to her father. 'Did she know that Carrie and Dan and the kids stayed the night?' she asked with pretended offhandedness.

'Yes. She was worried about the children sleeping on the floor but I told her you'd got the loan of a pump bed.' Noel looked quite pleased with himself.

'Oh, no. I'm sunk,' Shauna groaned.

'No you're not. You and Greg and Chloe are coming to stay with us tonight.' Carrie grinned.

'And we're going to Colin and Maria's for New Year, so we're covered there in case she tries to muscle in next week. Oh, you're a lifesaver, Carrie. Thanks.' Shauna gave Carrie a quick hug. 'I'm going in to tell Greg we're off to your house tonight. Are you sure now? We'll have dinner here before we go.'

'I'm certain. I'd love it. We'll have a good night for ourselves and a lazy day tomorrow. Will it be OK with Greg?'

'If he doesn't want to come he needn't bother,' Shauna retorted. 'I'm coming with Chloe.'

'Sounds good to me,' Greg agreed when she put it to him.

'Great. You can have a few beers and a drink at dinner and I'll drive, if you like?' Shauna offered magnanimously.

'What a wife!' He patted her ass as she stood beside him and he pulled her onto his lap. Shauna laughed and kissed him.

'Ditto for you, Dan.' Carrie had followed Shauna into the lounge. 'But it's only because I'm pregnant.'

'You're such a tough nut,' Dan teased, squeezing her hand.

'You bet I am.' Carrie traced a finger down the side of his jaw, thinking how much she loved the way his eyes crinkled up when he smiled.

They spent a lazy afternoon playing card games with the kids, and sprawled in front of the TV. Around three fifteen, Shauna murmured, 'Oh, gosh, we were supposed to ring Della. Dad said that she phoned when we were out. Do you want to give her a call, Greg?'

'You do it,' he said lazily.

'OK. I'll do it in the kitchen; it's quiet out there.' She smiled at Davey and Olivia who were playing a rambunctious game of snap with Bobby and Dan.

'Della, hi!' she said cheerily when her sister in-law answered the phone. 'How's Kathryn?'

'Kathryn's fine,' Della said snootily and Shauna could hear the sharpness in her tone. 'She never got sick any more. We could have stayed after all.'

'Oh dear. Pity.' Shauna made a face as she twirled the cord of the phone between her fingers.

'I believe Carrie, Dan and the kids stayed afterwards and that you managed to get a pump-up bed,' Della added acerbically.

'Would you believe, I remembered that Colin and Maria had one,' Shauna said smoothly.

'Great. Well, now that Kathryn's OK again we were thinking we'd drive down this evening and stay the night. It was such a shame to cut our visit short yesterday. She could sleep on that bed; she'd love it,' Della said airily.

'Oh dear, we're actually going to Carrie's in an hour or so. We

131

might even stay a couple of nights there,' Shauna said, covering herself for the next night as well.

'Oh!' Her sister-in-law's disappointment was palpable. 'Well, how about New Year?'

'We're going to a party for New Year. We won't be here,' Shauna explained cheerfully.

'Well then, we'll have to come and stay for your going-away bash,' Della snapped.

'I'm trying to get over Christmas first. That's another day's work, Della. I'm delighted Kathryn's on the mend. We'll talk soon. Have to go – we're heading off to Whiteshells Bay shortly and I need to get organized. See you.'

She didn't even give Della time to answer but hung up, flipping her sister-in-law a triumphant two fingers as she did so. That girl had such a neck, she thought, feeling she'd been dragged through the wringer. She simply couldn't take no for an answer. Now she was making plans for the going-away do. Shauna shook her head wearily. There was only so much she could deal with. That argument was for another day. Pity she was driving, she could have done with a drink, she thought longingly as she went back to the others. She'd have to be patient and wait until they were in Carrie's.

Around four, she and Bobby prepared a cold meat and salads buffet that everyone helped themselves to. 'King crisps and Branston pickle are the perfect accompaniment to cold turkey and ham,' Bobby said dreamily, licking his fingers after stuffing a handful of crisps into his mouth.

'I love chutney,' Carrie confessed. 'I've gone mad on tomato chutney. It's one of my cravings.'

'She's eating all our profits. I can't keep her in tomatoes,' Dan moaned. They all laughed, enjoying the banter. By the time they had tidied up and packed some night clothes it was almost seven

132

and within five minutes of starting their journey Chloe and Olivia were asleep. It had got bitterly cold again and sleety snow showers swirled around the cars as they drove north.

Shauna dropped Noel home; he wanted to go to bed early, he said. He was tired. The house was cold and she insisted on putting the heating on for him, knowing that he'd probably turn it off after an hour.

'Do you need anything?' she asked kindly.

'Just a good night's sleep.' He yawned. 'I'll see you tomorrow.'

She felt almost sorry for him as she let herself out of the house. It must be lonely living on his own, even if he was an interfering old busybody. Still, it was a relief to close his front door behind her. She hated visiting her childhood home. Most of her memories were unhappy. The only joy in their house had been of their mother's making and now that Anna was no longer there, it wouldn't bother her if she never saw the place again. Sad but true, she thought dolefully as she got into the car and tried to shrug off the vague mantle of depression that always descended on her when she went home. The house was getting shabby. It needed doing up. Maybe she would say something to Carrie about getting it painted. She and Greg would pay for it, their contribution to Noel's quality of life since they were going to be away for a couple of years. Suddenly the thought of lazing on the beach, warmed by the sun, far, far away from this cold, grey place seemed delightful and she wished that the move had all been sorted and that she was there.

Carrie had put the kids to bed by the time she got back and the fire was roaring up the chimney, the flames dancing, yellow and orange, casting flickering shadows in the lamplight. The Christmas tree lights twinkled like multicoloured stars, a beautiful sight that never lost its magic. The family room that opened off the kitchen was such a cosy, welcoming room, she thought as she sank into one of the comfortable armchairs and took the gin and tonic Dan handed her.

'Gorgeous,' she murmured as the tart, refreshing cold liquid slid down her throat. 'You make the best G and T of anyone I know.'

'One of my many attributes,' Dan said smugly. 'Carrie's a lucky woman.'

'Huh! No-one else would put up with you and your glass-houses.' Carrie threw a cushion at him.

'I see Davey got Monopoly. I haven't played that in years. Anyone fancy a game?' Bobby invited.

'Will we, for a bit of a laugh?' Shauna said eagerly. She loved board games.

'First out makes supper,' Carrie decreed.

'You're on,' Dan agreed.

They played an uproarious game of Monopoly, cursing roundly as they landed in jail or had to pay a fortune in utilities. Dan was the first out and he busied himself in the kitchen making a feast of crackers, pâté, cheeses and savoury vol-au-vents.

'How can we be hungry?' Shauna wondered, inhaling the aromas that were wafting out of the kitchen.

'I don't know, but I'm really peckish.' Carrie stretched luxuriously, thoroughly enjoying her evening.

'It was all that naked aggression you were displaying. I never played such a vicious game of Monopoly in my life, and I know a bit about the property business. You're a barracuda,' Greg slagged, feeling totally laid back.

'OK, you lot, do you want me to set the table posh, or do you want it in on your knees?' the chef demanded.

'Knees,' everyone chorused as Bobby went to help Dan carry the food in.

They ate and chatted and laughed, sprawled around the fire, comfortable in each other's company.

'Thanks for this, Dan, Carrie, I'm really enjoying it. It's been a lovely day and night,' Shauna said as she snuggled into Greg and he kissed the top of her head. She had a rare feeling of well-being and she was looking forward to Chloe's waking up in the morning to have fun with her cousins.

'I'm glad I came home,' Bobby confessed. 'I was having second thoughts once I'd booked the flight, but now that I'm here, I'm having a great time. It's very relaxing. Much more than I thought it would be. I can't say Dad hasn't got to me; he's as bad as ever he was, and it was hard at the grave yesterday, but I can deal with it better. Maybe it's because I'm older.'

'He's himself,' Carrie murmured.

'Indeed he is. At least your marriage is living up to the requirements of the Church!' Shauna smiled at her husband. 'We're failing dismally.'

'He went a step too far, Shauna.' Greg frowned.

'Yes he did, I agree. You were right. I'd no problem with what you said.' She bit into a Tuc cracker smothered with duck pâté.

'At least there's *hope* for you pair. I'm a lost cause.' Bobby grinned.

The phone rang and Carrie stretched out to answer it, wondering who was ringing at that hour of the night.

'Oh, oh, OK. I'll be over,' they heard her say.

'What's up?' Dan asked.

'It's Dad. He's sick, he thinks he's got that bloody tummy bug.' She stood up wearily. 'I'd better go over.'

Dan stood up and put a hand on her shoulder. 'Sit down, Carrie. You don't have to go tonight. It would be different if he was on his own, but Bobby's here. You'll take care of him,

Bobby, won't you? Carrie could do with a little break,' he said firmly, eyes fixed on his brother-in-law.

'Oh, yeah, sure, of course,' Bobby said hastily, hauling himself off the floor. 'Stay where you are, Carrie. It won't take me five minutes to get home. Thanks for a great evening.'

'Are you sure?' Carrie felt bad.

'No problem. Dan's right. You and Shauna do it all the time. My turn.'

'I feel mean.' Carrie turned to Dan after Bobby had left.

'Don't,' Dan retorted. 'Bobby's perfectly capable of looking after your dad for a night. There'll be plenty of nights when you'll be on call, so make the most of it.'

Carrie knew he was right but her evening was spoilt. She knew Noel would be disappointed that she hadn't gone to take care of him and she knew, too, that Bobby was only going because Dan had made it impossible to refuse.

Shauna chewed her lower lip; Dan's remark had been a little pointed. Was he letting her and Greg know, subtly, that he felt they were leaving Carrie in the lurch?

Bloody Della and her selfishness. If it wasn't for her and that damned bug they would have been sitting happily getting quietly tipsy, relaxed with the world. Now the evening was ruined. She hadn't offered to go, she thought guiltily. Irritation swamped her. Why couldn't they be like a normal family instead of having all this angst and stress? It was at times like this that she felt she couldn't get to the Gulf soon enough.

14

BOBBY PULLED UP THE HOOD OF HIS PARKA, SHIVERING AGAINST the biting wind that sliced in off the sea. What a pain in the ass! He'd been enjoying the relaxed, easy fun they'd been having and he'd felt pleasantly woozy after the wine and beer he'd drunk. Carrie's house was warm and comfortable. He could have gone asleep sitting beside the fire. Now he had to go home and look after his dad and the house would probably be bloody freezing.

Dan had given him no option. He supposed he would have been perfectly happy to let Carrie go. Which wasn't very fair, he acknowledged dolefully. Dan had certainly thought so. Bobby respected the way he'd looked out for Carrie. Dan was a real man. Strong and solid. Greg was much more mercurial and selfish. Carrie was far happier in her marriage than Shauna was. Just watching the two couples it was obvious that Carrie and Dan were a team who pulled together, whereas Shauna and Greg sometimes had an edge about them that hinted at strain.

He hadn't realized how much Shauna wanted another baby. But when he'd seen Chloe playing with her cousins, he knew his sister was right to try for one. He would have hated to be an only child. He had a great bond with the girls. He was lucky, he knew that. They had been his protectors and supporters when he was a child and that had carried on into adulthood. The two of them mothered him faithfully and he had to admit he enjoyed it.

An empty beer can skittered across the street as a gust of wind swirled down Fisherman's Lane, the smell of the salty, sandy seaweed and the creaking of the boats bringing back childhood memories. The air was fresh and rich after the fume-laden fug that he'd grown used to. He'd slept like a log on Shauna's sofa; he wasn't too sure how he'd fare tonight.

The village was deserted. Glimmers of light, fizzing from the Christmas trees that decorated cottage windows, shone out onto the quiet street. Splashes of orange from the sodium street lamps illuminated his way home. He hurried past the butcher's shop and remembered how as a child he'd hated having to go to the butcher with his mother. The smell of blood and sawdust and the sound of Jim Ryan chopping meat with his big carver had frightened him. He'd been a real little wimp, he thought wryly as he passed the church and the graveyard. The wind whistled through the stripped branches of the swaying trees, lamenting and keening, the old gates rattling in the breeze. He tried not to think of his mother in that dark cold place. The cemetery was peaceful and restful in daylight, but at night it was lonely and sad.

'Fuck you, Dad,' he cursed as he passed the big redbrick house belonging to the priest, and saw the lights of his father's bungalow in the distance. If it wasn't for Noel he'd be relaxed and warm and pissed in Carrie's, instead of cold and stressed and filled with unhappy thoughts. Resentment surged through him; Noel had never treated him with kindness, so why should he have to show him any? he thought sourly.

'Is Carrie with you?' Noel asked weakly when he let himself in and found his father hunched over the fire in the kitchen.

'There was no need for her to come. I'm here.' He tried to keep the annoyance out of his tone.

'She said she was coming,' Noel said petulantly. 'I've been very sick, you know.'

'You'll be fine. It's just a tummy bug.' Bobby injected a false hearty note into his voice.

'As long as it doesn't affect my hiatus hernia. That can flare up something terrible,' Noel moaned.

'Have you any magnesia?' Bobby sighed.

'I took some.'

'Why don't you go to bed and I'll bring you some hot milk,' Bobby suggested.

'Put some pepper into it. Your mother always put pepper into hot milk when anyone was sick,' Noel said.

'I know, I remember.' Bobby went to the fridge and took out a carton of milk as his father rose feebly from the chair and headed for his bedroom. 'And the Oscar goes to . . .' he muttered as he filled a saucepan and turned on the gas. Noel wouldn't entertain having a microwave.

His father hadn't turned off the heating before he went to bed and Bobby decided he was damned if he was going to spend another cold night in the house, so he wasn't going to turn it off either. He threw a few logs and a shovelful of coal onto the fire to build it up. He'd finish the thriller he was reading in front of it. A real fire was a treat. Listening to it hiss and spark and flame brought him back to when he was a little boy on wintry afternoons when it was getting dark and his father was still at work. His mother would be cooking their dinner and he'd be sitting by the fire reading, safe for a while from the hassle of the school yard and his father's disapproval.

He brought Noel in his hot milk. It was disconcerting to see his father in his brown pyjamas looking vulnerable and washed out. For the first time Bobby could see that Noel was starting to age. His hair was thinning, he had liver spots on his hands, and tonight his face had a greyish hue.

'Do you need anything else?' he asked gruffly.

'No. Thanks for the milk.' Noel too was clearly feeling awkward.

'Right, call me if you need me. I'll leave my bedroom door open.'

Noel hunched down under the bedclothes with a deep sigh. Bobby left the door ajar and headed for the welcome respite of the fire-brightened kitchen.

Noel huddled under his bedclothes feeling queasy and annoyed. He was only a nuisance to his children, he thought sorrowfully. Carrie couldn't even be bothered to come and make sure that he was all right. And Bobby was only here because he had to be. As for Shauna, he could be dead in his bed for all she'd really care. She'd been antagonistic towards him from when she was a little girl and even to this day he could still sense it from her.

Carrie had been his pet, his favourite. Kind Carrie who had always tried to please him and her mother. But tonight she'd let him down and left him to his son's tender mercies.

A stomach spasm gripped him and waves of nausea swept over him. He could be dying for all they knew. If he was found dead in his bed in the morning it would serve them all right, he thought vengefully as he made his shaky way to the bathroom.

'Mammy, I feel sick.'

Carrie woke out of a deep sleep to see Olivia, pale and shivering, standing beside the bed. 'Oh, no,' she groaned. If she could get her hands on Della Keegan she'd break her damned neck, she swore, as she swung out of bed and brought her daughter to the bathroom. Dan snored peacefully. Carrie knew

140

that if she woke him he'd take care of Olivia, but she was awake now. What was the point of two of them being up?

He'd really stood up for her this evening, she thought, remembering the heart-warming feeling of knowing that she was loved and cherished that had enveloped her when he'd put his hand on her shoulder and told her to sit down. Dan was the greatest gift the universe had ever given her. He had a kind and steady heart that had her and the children at its core. She was a very lucky woman, she acknowledged, remembering how gentle his hand had been.

Bobby had been taken aback when her husband had more or less told him to go home and look after Noel. He'd hidden it well and been agreeable but Carrie had caught the initial look of dismay on her brother's face. It might be good for Bobby to realize that Noel was getting old. Maybe some of the old wounds might heal, she thought wistfully, ever the optimist.

'How's Dad? Olivia puked all night and Shauna's feeling queasy.' Bobby could hear the weary tone in his sister's voice at the other end of the phone.

'He was sick twice. He wanted to call the doctor at five a.m. but I managed to persuade him to wait. I phoned him an hour ago so we're waiting for him.' Bobby yawned.

'Oh, crikey. The house could do with a hoover—'

'Don't panic. I've hoovered and polished and changed his bed. I'm a regular Mrs Mop,' he assured her.

'Don't forget the bathroom. The doctor might go in to wash his hands.'

'Good thinking. I'll do that now. I don't want Mam haunting me. She was always very particular when the doctor was coming.'

'I'll try and get over later on,' she promised him.

'Don't worry, I'll manage fine. I'll do something light for

141

dinner; I'm sure Dad won't be eating, anyway. I'll talk to you later.' Bobby hung up and went into the bathroom to give it a clean.

His father had refused an offer of tea and toast, and was anxiously looking out his bedroom window to see if there was any sign of the doctor's car. He was convinced he was dying.

'Would you get me the priest?' he said weakly to his son when he poked his head round the door to see if he was all right.

'If the doctor thinks you need the priest I'll get him when he's gone,' Bobby said firmly.

Noel's lips tightened. He wasn't used to being disobeyed, or, even worse, treated like a child.

'I want Father Doyle, now,' he ordered.

'Here's the doctor.' Bobby indicated the car pulling into the drive, relieved beyond measure that he wasn't going to have to go on a wild goose chase looking for the priest. He hadn't realized what a hypochondriac Noel had become. Poor Carrie, she had a hell of a lot to put up with, he thought as he hurried to open the door.

Twenty-five minutes later he was on his way to the pharmacy to get a prescription. The doctor had given Noel an injection that had made him drowsy, much to Bobby's relief. Dr Reid had assured Noel that he had a twenty-four-hour stomach virus and that he was in no danger of death.

'Bit of a worrier,' he'd murmured to Bobby on his way out. 'He'll be fine tomorrow. No solids, some boiled 7-Up, perhaps a slice of toast later.'

Noel had stayed in bed all day and Bobby had busied himself around the house, giving it a good cleaning. He knew Carrie wanted to get a woman in once a week to polish and hoover but Noel wasn't having any of it. He really ought to start thinking about her well-being, Bobby scowled, as he washed the kitchen floor. She was pregnant and had enough to do looking after her own house without having to hoover and polish and clean her father's.

He was cleaning the windows when his sister drove up with a tureen of chicken soup and a chicken and mushroom pie for him.

'My God, you should come and stay more often. The place is gleaming,' she said, following him into the kitchen.

'I'm going to say to him about getting someone in,' Bobby said firmly, as he plugged in the kettle to make her a cup of tea.

'I've been trying to get him to do that for the last year. I know the very woman, too, but he won't have it. He thinks she might steal things on him. He's very distrustful sometimes, not to mention judgemental,' Carrie said ruefully as she ladled the soup into a saucepan to heat it up.

'I know,' Bobby agreed, not at all surprised. 'He'll just have to get over his sad lack of faith in human nature. I'll work on him,' he assured her.

'I can do my own cleaning,' Noel said crossly the following morning. He was nibbling on a slice of toast and drinking a cup of hot, sweet tea when Bobby brought up the subject.

'Dad, be realistic. You're getting on, Carrie's pregnant and has got her hands full with her own family. It's not easy trying to look after two houses—'

'She doesn't have to look after my house. I told you I'm perfectly capable of looking after this place by myself,' he said testily. 'Don't worry, I won't be a nuisance to anyone, least of all you.'

'Don't be like that!' Bobby flared at his father's ungraciousness.

'Well who do you think you are, coming here and telling me what to do and what not to do in my own house? And trying to make me feel guilty about Carrie doing a bit of hoovering. She's never complained to me and she's well able for it. She's a young woman. It would match you better if you'd straighten yourself out and go and concentrate on finding a nice girl for yourself and settling down!' He glared at his son, all his anger coming to the surface.

Bobby stared at him, furious. 'Listen, you selfish, ignorant, sanctimonious hypocrite. I won't ever be settling down with a girl and you *know* it. You know I'm gay and always have been and always will be. It's the way I was born, however much you want to deny it, so deal with it. And I won't say it to you again. So cut the crap, Dad. And stop treating Carrie like a drudge—'

Noel's face mottled puce, his veins standing out purple against his temple as rage permeated every fibre of his being. 'How *dare* you! You have a nerve to speak to me like that. Get out of here, get out of my sight, and may God forgive you because I wo—'

'No, you won't, Dad, because you're a judgemental hypocrite! Well one thing I know that it says in the Bible is judge not lest ye be judged. But you've spent your life judging even though you think you're so bloody saintly, spending all your time in church. You think you're going to go to heaven and I'm not, don't you? Well let me tell you, you have a lot to learn about compassion and mercy and you won't learn that on your knees at the altar rails. You would have made a great Pharisee. Jesus had a great name for your sort. Whited sepulchres. I remember *that* from the Bible, too. It suits you down to the ground. Everyone thinks you're a good, churchgoing Christian; well, *I* know better,' Bobby said heatedly, his voice shaking. He turned on his heel and slammed the bedroom door good and hard.

He was relieved that he was going back to London today. He'd never set foot in this bloody house again, he vowed as he packed his rucksack and waited for Carrie to collect him to bring him to the airport.

Noel lay shaken and agitated as he heard the front door close and the slam of car doors before the grind of tyres told him that Bobby was driving away, possibly for good. He didn't care! He was livid. How dare that young pup speak to him the way he had? How dare he accuse him of being a whited sepulchre, quoting the Bible at him? It was surprising that he even knew a quote from the Bible, Noel thought bitterly, still stung by his son's harsh accusatory slurs. He took a sip of the tea Carrie had brought him and saw that his hands were shaking. It had been a most distressing incident. His heart was beating far too fast. Noel drank the tea and tried to calm himself.

Bobby was never setting foot in this house again and as soon as he was feeling any way better, he was going to go to his solicitor and change his will, Noel decided, feeling a little more in control. Bobby was not going to get one penny of his money. He'd gone too far this time. Noel had put up with enough. He had a good mind to leave it all to Carrie and Dan. Greg and Shauna didn't need his money. As far as he could see, they were loaded. He heard the car engine getting fainter in the distance and had never felt so lonely in his life.

15

'YOU ONLY HAD ANOTHER COUPLE OF HOURS TO GO AND YOU WERE doing so well. Could you not have risen above whatever he said to you and ignored it?' Carrie couldn't hide her exasperation. 'He's sick, he's getting old—'

'Don't *start*, Carrie. He had it coming. And don't try and make me feel guilty. He's made me feel guilty about everything, all my life,' Bobby raged. 'He never tried to understand. His way of understanding was to bring me to a fucking psychiatrist when I was ten. Do you remember *that*, Carrie? He was trying to make out that I was a nutcase, and I think he would have preferred it if I had been,' he added bitterly.

'Yes, I remember,' she said wearily. 'He thought he was doing his best.'

'Why do you always stand up for him? Why do you never stand up for me? You *always* take his side,' he cried.

'Oh, for God's sake, Bobby, stop it. You sound like Olivia. What age are you?' Carrie snapped. 'I'm sick of the whole bloody lot of you. You'll be gone, Shauna'll be gone and I'll be left to pick up the pieces. He'll probably get chest pains tonight or something and I'll end up spending the night in A and E in Our Lady of Lourdes.'

'Sorry,' Bobby muttered.

They sat in resentful, angry silence, Bobby casting a lingering look at the graveyard as they drove past. He'd planned to visit before leaving Whiteshells Bay but with all the upset of the morning he hadn't got round to it. He didn't want to ask Carrie to stop; she was probably dying to see the back of him, he thought self-pityingly as he stared out the window.

He saw his old teacher, Mrs Crosby – or rather Florence Dympna as everyone in the village called her, as far back as he could remember – crossing the road at the traffic lights. She was wearing a green hat with a jaunty feather. The teacher had always adored hats and had a big collection of them and he'd always admired them when he was small. She hadn't lost her sense of style, he noted with approval. The lights turned green and they drove on. He smiled as she waved at him. Florence Dympna was a very sprightly eighty-year-old. She'd encouraged his love of poetry and reading when she'd taught him all those years ago. He would have liked to stop and say hello but Carrie's jaw was set and he didn't feel he could ask for any favours.

The houses started to thin out and soon they were driving past Dan's rows of shining glasshouses, and his neatly kept fields that would soon be tilled for spring planting. The sea sparkled in the sunlight, shimmering and glossy, the sky sapphire. Mediterranean blue almost. A black Labrador bounded exuberantly along the beach, ecstatic with life as his owner threw sticks for him to catch. Bobby sighed deeply. He was torn between missing the beauty of the place he had grown up in and the desire never to set foot in his village again.

'Shauna's not coming to the airport. Chloe's running a temperature, so we'll just call for five minutes.' Carrie broke the silence.

'OK.' He shrugged. They didn't speak again until they got to Malahide.

'I need to get petrol. I'll drop you off and get it so we won't be delayed,' she said distractedly as they drove into the town.

'I'll pay for the petrol,' he offered hastily.

'Don't be daft,' she retorted but her tone was softer and for that he was relieved.

'You look the worse for wear, or are you getting the damned bug?' Shauna said when she opened the door to him. 'Where's Carrie going?'

'To get petrol,' Bobby said forlornly.

'What's wrong with you?'

'Had a humdinger of a row with Dad. Called him a whited sepulchre and told him he'd make a great Pharisee and got kicked out of the house for good.' He grimaced. 'I think telling him that he'll never learn compassion kneeling at the altar rails was probably the straw that broke the camel's back, but at that stage I didn't care. I wanted to hurt him for the way he's hurt me.'

'Way to go, Bobby,' Shauna said dryly. 'What was a Pharisee again, remind me?'

'They were the self-righteous geeks in the Bible who were always thumping their chests and boasting about how much they gave to charity and saying how wonderful they were and how much they knew of the word of God.'

'Oh, Bobby, I bet *that* hit a sore point.' Shauna grinned.

'He went ballistic, absolutely ballistic. I thought he was going to croak there and then.' He shook his head as if trying to get rid of the memory.

'Does Carrie know?'

'Yeah. She had to make him a cup of tea, he was allegedly so upset. I say allegedly because I know that he was just mad because I answered him back. He's not upset, he hasn't a heart to be upset.' Bobby followed his sister into the kitchen. 'Carrie's pretty mad with me herself. She said both you and I'd be gone and she'd be left to clean up the mess. It's so ironic. That's what started the bloody row. I was trying to persuade him to get someone in to do his cleaning so Carrie wouldn't have to,' he said plaintively as he lifted Chloe into his arms and cuddled her to him.

'She's right and I feel bad about going out to the Gulf, but only because of her. It won't cause me too much grief to be leaving Dad behind and that's an awful thing to say,' Shauna confessed glumly.

'He's reaping what he's sowed, Shauna, and I feel just like you so either the two of us are horrible people or what we're feeling is OK because of the way he treated us when we were growing up.' Bobby sighed.

'We're not horrible people,' Shauna said stoutly. 'We're just trying to deal with . . . with stuff. Will you come out to visit us in the Gulf?' She hugged him.

'You bet I'll come. I'll want to bond with this gorgeous scamp.' He kissed Chloe on top of her head as she lay curled against him, her eyes bright and watery.

'I don't know if it's the bloody bug or a new tooth. I could swing for that Della one. Even Greg's pissed off about it. He went to a meeting with his accountant feeling decidedly queasy.'

'A Christmas to remember.' Bobby arched an eyebrow.

'Or one best forgotten, more like it,' she said caustically as she went to open the door for Carrie who had just rung the doorbell. 'Sorry about the mess, the van is coming to take our stuff. Have we time for a drink?' she asked as her older sister stepped inside.

'I need to get Bobby dropped off and get back to Olivia and let Dan get to the glasshouses for an hour or so. And I've to do a dinner for Dad.' Carrie glanced at her watch.

'It's the last time we'll be together for a while. How about sharing a split of champagne? We'll only get a mouthful each,' Shauna urged, anxious that they not part in such a gloomy fashion.

'OK,' Carrie agreed, stroking Chloe's cheek.

Shauna poured the golden bubbly liquid into three champagne flutes and poured some apple juice into Chloe's little cup. 'To better times,' she toasted.

'To better times,' her siblings echoed dutifully but Shauna knew their hearts weren't in it and she felt like crying as she hugged Bobby goodbye.

'Don't!' he warned as he saw the tell-tale glitter in her eyes.

'Right, go on,' she said hastily. 'I'll phone you.'

'And don't come to the door,' Bobby said, wishing this part was over.

Shauna bit her lip as she heard the door close behind them. What a horrible way to part. Thanks to Della and to her dad, the family's last Christmas together for the foreseeable future had been ruined.

'Don't get out of the car, drive up to the set-down area and I'll get out there,' Bobby said as Carrie indicated left off the roundabout and drove into the airport.

'Ah no! I'll park and come in and see you off properly,' she protested.

'No, don't, Carrie. I hate saying goodbye. I'm much better going in on my own, please.' He turned to her.

'Are you sure?'

'Positive.'

'Sorry about getting mad.'

'Sorry about leaving you to pick up the pieces,' he reciprocated as she pulled into a space and cut the engine.

They flung their arms round each other and hugged tightly and then Bobby got out of the car, opened the back door to grab his rucksack and was gone with a quick wave.

Tears welled up in her eyes as she headed for the exit. What a dreadful way to say goodbye. Their family was even more fractured than before and all she wanted to do was go home to Dan and lay her head on his chest and feel his strong arms round her. If it wasn't for Dan she'd be sunk, she reflected as she drove out onto the M1 and headed back home.

Bobby wandered into Hughes & Hughes and stared unseeingly at the rows of books adorning the bookshelves. He'd checked in and had half an hour to spare before boarding. The best thing to do was to not think about it at all, he told himself firmly as a raft of titles made him focus on his reading requirements . . . He needed to concentrate and find a good thriller to take his mind off everything. He might as well forget about home. London was his home now. There was no going back.

'The things he said to me, Carrie. They were scurrilous. He has no respect at all. I'm his father. Well I'll tell you one thing, I'm going to my solicitor and I'm cutting him out of my will,' Noel fumed as Carrie set a plate of steamed fish and creamy mashed potatoes in front of him.

'Oh, Dad, you can't do that.' She was horrified.

'I can and I will,' he said forcefully. 'I don't want ever to set eyes on him again. He's gone too far this time.'

'That's a very unforgiving thing to do, Dad. You might regret it. And you know Mam would be very upset to think that you'd do that to Bobby or to any of us,' Carrie said firmly. 'It's vengeful and spiteful, Dad, and beneath you,' she added, trying to appeal to his better nature.

'I don't want a lecture from you,' he retorted, stung by her remarks.

'Fine. I'm going home to my family; thank God *we* love each other. If you need me, ring me,' Carrie said pointedly.

Her father maintained a stubborn silence and she let herself out of the house and wished that she, and not Shauna, was heading to foreign parts.

'That's it, Mrs Cassidy, just sign this document, please. Good luck in the Gulf.' The freight van had come to take the clothing, personal possessions and few belongings they intended bringing to their new home. The young man handed her a pen and indicated where she should sign her name. She did so with a flourish and felt a wave of anticipation. After the past couple of days she was delighted to be going abroad. Away from her father, away from Della and her manipulative behaviour, away from painful memories, away from *everything*. Greg was right, they were young, and they should make the most of life. It was her and Greg's choice to try another lifestyle. There was nothing to stop Dan and Carrie from doing likewise should they ever want to.

She'd had enough guilt trips laid on her, she told herself fiercely. She wasn't going to let another one ruin her future.

16

'GREAT PARTY, SHAUNA,' LIZ DELAHUNTY, AN OLD FRIEND FROM her Saudi days, congratulated her. 'I wish I was going back,' she said wistfully. 'I can't persuade Mick, he says the political situation's too unstable.'

'It seems to be OK in the Emirates. If it ever gets really dicey we'll just come home,' Shauna said lightly. A few people had brought up the political situation but she wasn't too concerned. Greg had friends all over the Gulf and they were keeping him up to date.

It was almost eleven thirty and the house was jam-packed with friends and neighbours. The caterers had done a great job and a huge buffet was laid out on the table in the dining room.

Not even Della and Eddie could ruin her evening. She'd phoned them a few days before the party and told them that they had to find a babysitter for Kathryn if they wanted to come. The house was to be a baby-free zone. Carrie's sister-in-law was going to mind Olivia, Davey and Chloe in Whiteshells Bay so that they could party the night through.

Della hadn't been too happy, but for once Shauna had been adamant. If they were coming they had to leave Kathryn at home. Shauna hoped against hope that they wouldn't come, but she knew in her heart and soul that they'd be there.

She'd borrowed the pump-up bed again and made it up and put it in the smaller bedroom. There was a divan in there as well. Della and Eddie could decide whether they wanted to share the pump-up or Della could have the divan. Carrie and Dan were having the double bed in the guest room with the en suite.

It had given her a small sense of victory to move Eddie and Della into the other room. It was pathetic, she knew, but they made assumptions that the en suite was *their* room to come and stay in whenever *they* felt like it. Della had been decidedly miffed when they arrived to find that Dan and Carrie were already installed in *their* room. 'I've borrowed the pump-up bed and it's made up. If you feel it's too low for you and your bump you can hop into the divan,' Shauna said airily to Della and then ordered Eddie to bring their overnight bag up to the small bedroom.

'Oh!' We've been *demoted*!' Della's gay laugh was forced, her little cold eyes hard and unsmiling.

'Go in and mingle and I'll get Greg to fetch you a drink.' Shauna completely ignored the sly jibe and ushered her sister-in-law into the crowded lounge. 'Greg?' she called to her husband, who was pouring a glass of wine for their solicitor. 'Della and Eddie are here. Will you organize a drink for them? Greg will get you a drink, Della. Feel free to help yourself to the buffet,' she said politely and left the other woman to her own devices. Della and Eddie knew some of their friends, and Shauna was damned if she was going to spend her precious party entertaining the in-laws from hell!

For form's sake she'd invited her father but warned him that it would be crowded and noisy and that Dan and Carrie would be staying over so he'd have to stay over too, unless he drove himself. Noel had declined the invitation, much to her relief.

'You young people go and enjoy yourselves. It's not for the

likes of me,' he assured her and she hadn't tried to make him change his mind.

The atmosphere was buzzing, and she was enjoying mingling with her friends. Once she'd made the decision to get the caterers in, she'd determined to be a guest at her own party and it was fun.

'I think Della's nose is out of joint. She's been very cool with me,' Carrie murmured an hour or so later as they stood side by side at the buffet.

'Tough.' Shauna grinned. 'Try one of these marinated prawns, they're gorgeous, and make sure to taste a few scallops. Eddie, true to form, has been raiding the buffet all evening and I swear to God I was getting panicky that there'd be nothing left.'

'Did they bring anything?'

Shauna gave a dry laugh. 'Are you mad? Not a sausage.'

'They're the pits, aren't they?' Carrie always found their meanness incredible.

'At least they'll be out of my hair,' Shauna said cheerfully. No-one was going to spoil her good humour tonight.

It was after five when she got woozily into bed. She was tight, she thought giddily as Greg handed her a pint glass of water and two Solpadeine.

'Great party, wasn't it?' he remarked as he sat down heavily on the bed to take his own tablets. 'At least neither of us will have to get up too early in the morning. I'm bunched.' He got into bed beside her. The bedsprings in Dan and Carrie's room creaked rhythmically.

Greg grinned. 'That pair next door are having a ride. I wouldn't be able to if I tried. Sorry 'bout that, Shauna.'

'Me neither,' she yawned. 'This is their night out. They don't get away without the kids that often.'

'Sad bastards,' Greg muttered and fell asleep instantly.

155

Lucky, I'd call them, Shauna thought drowsily, remembering how she'd caught them snogging in the kitchen earlier. The passion was still in their marriage, even after all these years. She wondered whether her and Greg's relationship would be so enduring, then fell asleep.

'We're the only two without hangovers, Carrie,' Della twittered irritatingly as they all sat round the kitchen table around midday the following morning.

'Be quiet, Della,' growled Eddie as he shovelled sausage and bacon into his gob.

'Well I told you you were drinking too much,' nagged his wife.

'Oh, shut up,' he snapped.

'Good enough for you,' she said smugly. Shauna wished she'd put a zip in it. Her head was throbbing. Dan winked at her as he poured her another cup of freshly percolated coffee.

'This will sort you. I made it good and strong.'

'Lovely,' Shauna said appreciatively. She was surprisingly hungry in spite of her dodgy head.

'We'll get a move on soon if you don't mind, Shauna.' Carrie buttered a slice of toast and smeared it with marmalade. 'I don't want to take advantage of Sadie's kindness. It's great having a sister-in-law living so near us.'

'I'm sure she won't mind,' Della said. 'I told my babysitter that I wouldn't be home until this evening.'

Surprise surprise! thought Shauna, unimpressed. 'I'll head off with you. I want to bring Chloe to say goodbye to Dad.' She turned to Greg. 'Are you going to come or do you want to stay here and tidy up?'

He squinted at her. 'I'll stay here. I'll phone your dad later to say goodbye. I'm going to have to go back to bed for an hour. I'm dying.'

'Well don't stay in bed all day, I don't want to come home to a mess,' she warned, knowing that Della and Eddie would do nothing to clear up if Greg went back to bed.

'I'll fill the dishwasher for you,' Dan offered.

'Thanks, Dan,' Shauna said gratefully. 'Even if you just collected the glasses and we gave them a wash so they'll be ready for the caterers.'

Between them, Dan, Carrie and Shauna had the place reasonably shipshape before they left for Whiteshells Bay. Carrie had filled a black sack with rubbish and leftover scraps and Shauna had stacked the glasses into boxes. The dishwasher was on its second load and she didn't feel too bad about going. She had organized for the mini-maids to come and give the house a thorough clean when she was gone. Their next-door neighbours had a key and were going to keep an eye on the place and Greg had organized for a gardener to come once a month to keep the front and back gardens in order.

'Well, see you, Della. You'll probably be gone by the time I get back,' Shauna said pointedly as the other woman stood up to embrace her. 'The best of luck with the birth.'

'Thanks.' Della kissed her on the cheek. 'Safe journey. We'll be out to visit. It will be fantastic to have somewhere warm to go on our holidays.' She turned to Carrie. 'Keep in touch, Carrie. We'll pop down sometime to show off the baby.'

Carrie's eyes widened as she shot a look at Shauna. 'Umm,' she murmured non-committally.

'Right, let's go, girls,' Dan said briskly as he held out his hand to Greg. 'Good luck, mate. Enjoy yourself.'

'You bet, Dan. Hope to see you out for a visit.' Greg shook his brother-in-law's hand.

'See you, Eddie.' Shauna backed out the kitchen door. She was damned if she was going to give that big slob a kiss.

157

'G'luck, Shauna,' he mumbled. 'See ya sometime. Can ya drink out there?'

'Yeah.'

'Good. We'll be over for a party. A nice big barbie would hit the spot. Is that the place where they have the belly dancers?' He guffawed.

'Ignore him.' Della glared at her husband.

'With pleasure,' muttered Shauna as she followed Dan and Carrie out to the cars.

It was strange to know that this was the last time she'd drive out to Whiteshells Bay for a while, she reflected, as she drove northwards behind Dan and Carrie. She'd come home in the summer with Chloe, to escape the unbearable temperatures. Greg wasn't going to come home this summer so it would be eighteen months before he'd set foot on home soil again.

Chloe launched herself upon her when she followed Carrie into the house and wrapped her little arms round her. 'Sadie, thanks a million.' Shauna smiled at Carrie's sister-in-law as she cuddled her daughter tight. 'Was she OK for you?'

'She was great, not a bother,' Sadie assured her.

'You wouldn't say otherwise,' Shauna said gratefully.

'She didn't cry at all,' Olivia said. 'She slept in my bed and we had great fun. I wish you weren't going away far.'

'We'll be home in the summer, pet. Sure we'll hardly be gone before we're home again, and you and Davey and Mam and Dad will come out to visit and we'll have a great time.'

'Will the new baby be able to come?'

'Of course. You lucky thing, getting a new baby.'

'Why don't you get one for Chloe?' Olivia fixed her with a blue-eyed stare.

'I'm going to do my best to get one,' Shauna said patiently.

'You just have to ask Holy God. That's what I did.'

'You ask Him for me, darling,' Shauna said with a pang. She was going to miss Olivia and Davey desperately.

'OK,' Olivia said matter-of-factly.

'I'm going to bring Chloe up to say goodbye to Grandpa. Do you want to come?' she asked, strapping her daughter into the buggy.

'Yes please. Can I push the buggy?'

'Sure.' Shauna smiled. She was glad her niece was going to come with her. She wasn't looking forward to the visit. Noel had made enough disparaging comments about bringing Chloe abroad and depriving him of his grandchild. He'd have to tone it down if Olivia was there. How sad it was that she was dreading visiting her own father, she thought despondently as she and Olivia strolled down the village with Chloe.

'Would you like an ice cream?' she asked her niece as they came to Nolan's, the small corner shop opposite the church. It had hardly changed from when she was a child, even to the bell ringing when the old-fashioned door handle was depressed, and the glass-panelled green door opened into the dark, wooden-floored little shop that sold everything from wellington boots to knitting needles as well as basic groceries. Olivia headed straight for the deep freeze and dived down to locate a Magnum. Shauna treated herself and Chloe to a brunch, and, remembering how her father had a soft spot for Maltesers, she bought a large box for him.

'Grandpa will love them. I wonder will he open them?' Olivia eyed the chocolates longingly.

'I'd say he might,' Shauna said as they walked along the footpath towards her father's house.

'Hello, Dad.' She put on her cheeriest voice as she poked her head into the kitchen.

'Ah you brought the little one to see me?' Noel's face lit up when he saw Chloe. 'And my other little treasure,' he said, smiling at Olivia, who was patting the cat.

Shauna opened Chloe's clasps and the toddler struggled out of her buggy and hurried to join her cousin and Twiskers. 'Say hello to Grandpa and give him his present,' Shauna instructed, giving her the chocolates.

Chloe beamed and held the chocolates out to her grandfather. 'Gocklat,' she said.

'That's a very good effort. She's not bad at talking,' Noel said and Shauna's heart softened towards him.

'Will I make us a cup of tea?' she suggested.

'Lovely. And we'll have some gocklat.' Noel twinkled at Olivia, knowing full well that she loved Maltesers.

'So you're off the day after tomorrow,' he said as Shauna filled the kettle and switched it on.

'Crack of dawn. We fly from Dublin to Schiphol and then transfer to a KLM flight to Abu Dhabi.'

'And is it direct then?' Noel queried, as he watched his grand-daughters play with the cat.

'We stop in Dhahran in Saudi but we don't get off the plane,' Shauna explained, as she heated the pot and rooted for tea bags.

'Very strict country,' he mused.

'It's much more liberal where we're going,' she assured him.

'Can you practise your religion if you want to?' Noel knew his priorities.

'Indeed you can, there's a mosque and a church almost side by side according to Julia, a friend of ours out there. So I'll be able to go in and say a prayer for you and light a candle.'

'Say one for your brother while you're at it,' Noel said morosely as the kettle whistled and she poured the boiling water into the teapot. It was an old brown ceramic pot that had been there since her mother's time and Shauna felt a terrible pang of loneliness sweep over her as she placed the worn tea cosy over the pot once she'd poured the tea. How wonderful it would have been to have brought her mother to the Emirates for a holiday. She would have thoroughly enjoyed the adventure of it, being a far more outgoing person than her husband.

Noel tore the cellophane wrapping off the chocolates as Olivia and Chloe stood patiently at his knee awaiting the goodies.

'Only a few, now. They're for Grandpa,' Shauna warned.

'Have one yourself.' He offered her the box and for a moment there was peace between them and they smiled at each other. Shauna popped the round chocolate delight into her mouth and took a drink of tea. The taste of the hot tea melting the chocolate was delicious and she and her father savoured their little treat.

They drank their tea and he enjoyed the company of his granddaughters. 'I'll miss that little one, I can see your mother in her,' he said sadly when she slipped Chloe's coat on her.

'I'll send you photos every few weeks,' she promised. 'We'll be home in the summer. That's only a few months.' She straightened up and pulled on her own coat. She swallowed hard. Saying goodbye was a lot harder than she'd imagined and she couldn't understand why. Maybe it was seeing her father's joy in Chloe. He was very tender with her and Olivia. If only he could have been like that with his own children.

'Take care of yourself,' she said quietly.

'You too, Shauna.' Noel patted Chloe on the head and smiled down at Olivia, who had thrown her arms round him in a hug. She was such an affectionate child, Shauna thought, marvelling at how natural and unaffected and loving her niece's embrace was. She couldn't ever remember hugging her father or being hugged in return. She leaned over and kissed his cheek, noting

161

how grey and tired he looked. He patted her arm awkwardly. 'Safe journey. We'll see you in the summer.' He went to move out to the hall but she stopped him.

'Don't come to the door, Dad.' Her voice faltered and a lump the size of a golf ball stuck in her throat.

'I'll see you off,' he protested and then caught the sheen of tears in her eye.

'Oh. Oh, right. Lead on, Macduff,' he said to Olivia, who laughed delightedly.

'That's my nickname from Grandpa,' she said cheerfully as she reached up and opened the front door. Shauna busied herself wheeling the buggy into the hall. When she reached the door she turned and looked back. Noel was standing in the kitchen looking after them, and she saw an ageing, stooped man holding his black and white cat for comfort, and couldn't bring herself to hate him any more.

He nodded at her and she managed a little wave, knowing that if she tried to speak she'd burst out crying. She closed the door behind her and struggled to compose herself as they walked back along the village. They came to the graveyard and she paused. 'Are you going in to see Granny?' Olivia asked, bringing the buggy to a halt.

'Will you stay here with Chloe? The path looks a bit mucky at the gate.'

'OK,' Olivia agreed. 'Tell Granny I was asking for her.'

'I will, darling,' Shauna assured her. She hurried up the path and turned left to reach her mother's grave. The wreaths and flowers they'd laid on Christmas Day looked the worse for wear but she didn't touch them. Carrie would take care of that as she took care of everything, she thought guiltily.

'See you, Mam. I'll be home in the summer. Come with me to Abu Dhabi,' she murmured, touching the headstone. The

162

breeze whispered in the trees and for a moment she felt a great peace and knew her mother's spirit was with her and would be wherever she was in the world. Comforted, she hurried back to Olivia and smiled. 'Granny sends her love,' she said.

'I bet she's having a great time up there. You can eat as much chocolate as you like and *never* feel sick,' her niece informed her with the utmost confidence.

'That sounds like a great place.' Shauna smiled as they continued on their journey.

'How did it go?' Carrie enquired when they got home.

'Much better than I thought. Dad's good with the kids, isn't he?' She took off her coat and hung it up and followed her sister into the den.

'Surprisingly.' Carrie nodded.

'How could anyone not be crazy about Davey and Olivia? I'm going to miss them like hell.' She sighed as she took Chloe's hat and gloves off and unbuttoned her coat.

'We're going to miss you. Let's not talk about it. Let's just pretend that you're not going away, that you're just going back home to Malahide as normal,' Carrie said tightly.

'OK,' Shauna agreed. She was dreading their goodbye and had refused Carrie's offer to bring her to the airport.

'We've a present for you,' Davey announced. 'Can we show it, Mam, can we show it?' he begged.

'OK,' Carrie agreed.

'Sit down and close your eyes,' Davey instructed. 'Now open,' he said a few minutes later after some fumbling. The TV was on and she heard Chloe, Olivia and Davey singing 'BimBamBom' at the top of their voices, laughing hilariously as they did so. She saw them playing and running along the beach and vaguely remembered Dan messing with the video on St Stephen's Day.

'Me and my dad had it planned to do this video for Chloe so

that she won't forget us,' Davey said earnestly, and this time Shauna couldn't stop the tears. Neither could Carrie.

'Dad, the two of them are crying,' Davey exclaimed in exasperation to his father, who had just walked into the room.

'Women do that all the time, son. You just have to get used to it,' Dan drawled, throwing his eyes up to heaven as he saw the two sisters sniffling on the sofa. 'Shauna, I'm off to the glasshouses for an hour. I'll see you in the summer,' he said, enveloping her in a bear hug as she stood up to say goodbye to him.

'You're the best, Dan,' she murmured against his chest.

'So Carrie says.' He grinned down at her. 'Mind yourself, kiddo.' He kissed the top of her head, squeezed Carrie's hand and was gone.

'I suppose I'd better get a move on myself.' Shauna gulped. 'Do you think that other shower will be gone home to Cavan?'

'I don't know. Did you hear Della saying to keep in touch and that she'd be coming for a visit with the baby? What a neck she has. If she thinks she's going to start her freeloading jaunts to Whiteshells Bay she has another think coming,' Carrie exclaimed, remembering the dismay she'd felt when Della had dropped her bombshell.

'I'll await developments with bated breath.' Shauna grinned. 'Maybe I'll have a cup of coffee before I go just to give myself another hour. You'd notice the stretch in the evenings, wouldn't you? In the Gulf there's hardly any dusk. It gets dark once the sun has set. I'll miss the dusk.' She filled the kettle and spooned coffee into two mugs, in no hurry to go.

It was after four when she left. As with her father, she asked Carrie not to come to the door. She didn't even kiss her sister. She couldn't. It had been hard enough saying goodbye to Davey and Olivia. Just as well that Chloe was too young to understand. She was falling asleep.

'I'll ring you tomorrow,' Carrie said heartily as Shauna buttoned her daughter's coat yet again.

'Great. Talk to you then,' Shauna said briskly. 'See you, kids.'

''Bye, Shauna. Sure you won't forget to buy me the plane?' Davey reminded her of her promise to buy him a KLM model aircraft.

'Sure thing, Davey, and a Barbie for Olivia.' She smiled at her niece. She didn't even look at Carrie as she went out to the hall and let herself out of the house.

'I will not cry. I will not cry,' she muttered as she drove through the village in the gathering dusk. 'Concentrate, concentrate,' she ordered herself as her eyes blurred with tears. Swallowing hard, she brushed them away. The worst was over now – well, apart from the hassle of airports and the flights. Soon she'd be in her new apartment on the Corniche overlooking the Arabian Gulf. And her new life would have started.

17

IT WAS LASHING RAIN AS SHAUNA HURRIED OUT TO THE TAXI. SHE yawned hugely; she'd been up since four thirty. It was now five forty-five and they were finally on their way. Greg locked the door and hurried out to join them.

'That's it. We're off.' He smiled at her, excited as a little boy. 'Look what we're leaving, Shauna. What a horrible morning, so dark and wet and gloomy. We're going to be waking up to sunny skies and temperatures in the eighties in the middle of winter. Yippee!' he yelled and Chloe laughed delightedly.

Her own excitement was mounting. Now that they were on their way and there was no going back, she was looking forward to seeing their new home. An apartment on the Corniche sounded lovely. Right beside the sea. It had three bedrooms, two en suite, a maid's room, two reception rooms, a utility room and a fully fitted kitchen. And it was on the third floor with a large wrap-around balcony. It sounded fabulous.

The company had lined up several candidates for the job of au pair and she'd be interviewing them a few days after their arrival. Their shipment had arrived safely. All they had to do was get there themselves.

The airport was bustling with early morning commuters to London and Europe and they joined the queue for their flight to Holland. Chloe gazed around her with interest from the safety of her buggy; she seemed to sense her parents' excitement and was in high spirits for the unearthly hour of the morning.

She wasn't so happy an hour later as the Aer Lingus jet roared down the runway, and she howled in terror until Shauna eventually managed to calm her down with a bottle of apple juice and a rusk. As the flight levelled out and she got used to the steady thrum of the engines, her eyes drooped and she fell asleep in Shauna's arms. Shauna felt like sleeping herself and eventually nodded off for about twenty minutes, waking with a jerk as the plane banked over the North Sea.

At least Schiphol was an easy airport to push a buggy around, she thought gratefully as they headed for the transfer lounge via one of the huge moving walkways. They had time to shop and she would have thoroughly enjoyed browsing if she hadn't had to entertain Chloe, who was restless in her buggy.

'I want to get something,' Greg said, pointing towards a cluster of shops and leading her into a diamond shop. Her eyes widened.

'What are you doing?' she asked.

'Buying my wife a diamond or two. You can have them set in earrings? Ring? Bracelet? Pendant?' He smiled at her, his brown eyes glittering as brightly as the diamonds that surrounded them.

'Oh, Greg. I don't know.' She was completely overwhelmed.

'I really appreciate you giving me the chance to do this, Shauna. I love you,' he said quietly.

'I love you too.' She kissed him. 'We're going to have a great time.'

'I know. We deserve it. Both of us have worked hard for it. Now go and see what you'd like, to mark this moment in our lives.' He hugged her tightly and she felt a rare sense of contentment.

Eventually, she selected three fabulous sparklers to be set in a ring when they got to Abu Dhabi.

After their purchase they still had three-quarters of an hour before boarding so they sat in one of the little coffee stops and drank hot chocolate and ate a muffin and let Chloe run around to stretch her legs. Shauna had given her a travel tablet when they landed in Schiphol and she was hoping that it would make her drowsy for the long flight ahead as well as preventing any sickness.

The flight was boarding when they got to the gate and Shauna could see that it was practically full. She'd bought a couple of magazines and Greg had chosen a Bill Bryson travel book. If Chloe slept they'd get a chance to relax and read.

Again the take-off frightened Chloe and Shauna held her close, soothing her and calming her, hearing another child at the rear of the plane howling loudly as well. They were seated in the middle section of the huge Airbus, and eventually Chloe calmed down as Shauna read her a Wibbly Pig story.

After an hour she fell asleep, sucking her thumb, and Shauna flicked through *Hello!* until her own eyelids drooped and she too fell asleep. Hours later, the plane descended into Dhahran airport and the majority of the passengers disembarked. It was dark outside: the time difference had kicked in and the stars twinkled above them. They sat on the tarmac for about an hour while the Saudi religious police came on board to do their checks. Shauna was glad they were going to the Emirates, which was much more relaxed and cosmopolitan.

She was immensely relieved an hour later when the flight finally touched down at Abu Dhabi airport. In spite of her tiredness the beauty of the arrivals hall, with its stunning mosaics of greens and turquoise, awed her. 'Isn't this lovely, Chloe?' She smiled down at her daughter, who was toddling along beside her, delighted to be able to move around after the long flight.

A company representative with their name on a card was there to meet them at the high perspex partitions where they had to collect their visas. He threw the white form over to Greg and twenty minutes later, formalities completed and luggage collected, they walked through the airport doors to a blast of hot, humid air.

Abdullah, their driver, led them to where the car was parked. It was velvety dark and the stars sparkled brighter than her diamonds. A crescent moon hung over the sea. A ripple of heat, the scents of jasmine and frangipani, the chirruping of the cicadas, assaulted her senses and she felt exhilarated. They were here at last. The car was air-conditioned and they settled back for the thirty-kilometre drive on the long straight road to the capital.

'Why have we come to the Sheraton?' she asked as the car eventually pulled up outside the foyer of the massive hotel.

'Because, darling, we're staying here for a few days until we have the apartment organized the way we want it. I thought it would be nice to have a mini-holiday.' Greg was like a schoolboy.

'Oh, Greg, what a great idea!' she exclaimed, touched at his thoughtfulness. Sometimes he really could come up trumps.

Their room was cool and luxurious, and the pink marble bathroom was the height of luxury. Shauna filled the bath, undressed herself and Chloe, and stepped with her into the foamy water, Chloe almost dancing with excitement at this treat. It was incredibly relaxing to sink back into the soft suds and feel all the aches and stresses of that long day float away. Chloe was almost asleep as Shauna dried her hair, and she snuggled into the cot, pulled her knees up under her tummy and conked out.

While Greg had a shower, Shauna ordered room service and half an hour later they were eating a tasty supper, and toasting each other with champagne. Before they went to bed they stood at the French doors gazing out at a dhow, all lit up, as it sailed serenely along the moonlit waters of the Arabian Gulf.

'It's hard to believe that we're here, isn't it?' Greg murmured into her ear.

'I know. I feel I'm in a dream.' Shauna yawned against him.

'Well it's not a dream,' he said firmly. 'It's the start of the best time of our lives.'

Shauna gazed up at her husband, his brown eyes dark with desire as he pulled her to him. She ran her fingers through his silky black hair and whispered, 'We're going to have to be really quiet. No moaning and groaning.'

'I will if you will. Isn't this the best possible start to our new life?'

'Mmm,' she murmured, kissing him. Soon, she promised herself, soon she was going to come off the Pill and get pregnant and that truly would be the best time of her life. Happier than she had been in a long, long time, Shauna switched off the light and led her husband to the enormous bed that awaited them.

SPRING
(three years later)

18

Hi Shauna

We're coming!!!!!! All of us! This day six weeks. Flights booked. KLM 421 departing Amsterdam 1350, arr Abu Dhabi 0020. And I just can't wait. It's freezing over here, howling gales. Spring my ass. I can't believe that I'm finally getting out to see you in the Gulf. Della was really rubbing my nose in it at Christmas that I hadn't been out yet. But you know how I wanted to wait until Hannah was that bit older. Can you believe that she'll be three in the summer? There are times she reminds me so much of Chloe. I'm longing to see them all playing together again. Needless to say I'm not saying a word to Davey and Olivia until nearer the time. I'd be plagued. And I'm not saying anything to Dad either for a while. I don't want him getting agitated. He won't be too happy but he'll have to get over it. I still can't get over Della and Eddie going out to you at Christmas again this year. You'll have to nip it in the bud or it will become a habit! I suppose I'll have to give her a ring to say that we're going out in case she has any presents for you . . . ha ha!

I can't believe that Dan has taken two weeks off. It's unheard of but he has great faith in his farm manager and for the first time ever he feels he can put his precious glasshouses in someone else's hands.

Dad's got bronchitis, a really bad dose. He's on a second course of antibiotics so he's feeling very sorry for himself. I've been up and down to the house three and four times a day. I wanted him to come and stay for a few days but he wouldn't. Let's hope he's sorted in six weeks' time because come hell or high water I'm coming.

Was talking to Bobby at the weekend. He's going skiing in St Moritz. Great for some.

Dying to see you. Give Chloe a big kiss for me. I'll get Dan to email the photos of Hannah. You know me . . . computer illiterate. It's a miracle I've mastered email.

C xxx

Carrie read over her email to Shauna and pressed the send button. Moments later she heard the satisfying ping indicating that it had been sent and she scrolled down to disconnect her access.

She was bubbling with excitement. At last she was going to see Shauna's home for herself. True, she'd seen videos of the beautiful apartment on the Corniche, but it wasn't the same as being there. It was hard to believe Shauna had been in the Gulf just over three years. And there was no sign of her coming home. It looked as though Chloe would be starting school out there. Greg was making a fortune, working on countless new developments and in no hurry to come back to Ireland. As far as she could see he was there for the long haul.

She supposed she really would have to give Della a ring to see if she wanted anything brought out. Carrie sighed. She knew what that meant. Della would come down from Cavan with her two kids and spend the day with her and sit back and do nothing.

She'd arrived just before Christmas to collect Carrie's Christmas presents for Shauna and really made the most of it. Kathryn and her young brother, Ashley, had fought like cat and dog. Della had ignored them and sat in the den, drinking tea, and eating anything that was going. Carrie would have been as well posting the gifts, she'd thought ruefully, listening to the racket Della's kids were making.

'Imagine, you haven't been out to the Gulf yet and it will be our *third* visit. You don't know what you're missing. A fabulous holiday on the cheap. You don't have to lift a finger. The jewellery is great value; you wouldn't buy less than eighteen carat. You've just got to go.'

'I didn't think it was fair on Hannah, a long journey like that, and Dan was tied up with work. It's only in the last year that he's managed to make it all work without him being there twenty-four seven,' Carrie'd explained evenly, trying to quell the urge to tell her to piss off.

'I wouldn't be waiting for Eddie if he couldn't come. That would be his tough luck.' Della snorted. 'I'd be off like a shot.'

'I guess that's the difference between us,' Carrie drawled.

Della reddened at the implied rebuke. 'Otherwise I'd hardly see Greg at all. It's different for you, you see Shauna for the whole summer every year,' she protested.

Huh! Carrie wasn't impressed. Della wasn't *that* close to her brother. If he were working in the back of beyond somewhere she wouldn't be half as eager to spend her holidays with him.

It *was* great that Carrie was able to spend the whole summer with her sister. Shauna came home in June and stayed until early September. Greg hadn't come home the first year; he was too busy settling in and working on projects. He'd come home for three weeks the second year, and they'd all gone back to the Gulf

175

together. Carrie had enjoyed her time on her own with Shauna and Chloe and maybe, she reflected, absence was making the heart grow fonder because her sister and her father seemed to have made some sort of effort to set aside their differences. Noel loved Chloe. He often said she reminded him of Anna and he was always delighted to see her. Shauna made the effort to bring her to see him regularly during the summer.

Carrie sighed as she went into the kitchen to prepare the dinner. The same unfortunately could not be said for Noel and Bobby. Since that disastrous Christmas three years ago, there had been no contact between father and son. Bobby had not been home since.

It saddened and worried her. What if they never reconciled their differences? What a terrible burden for Bobby to have to carry when their father died.

'It's none of our business, Carrie. It's between Bobby and your father. They're grown-ups and they have to sort it themselves,' Dan told her matter-of-factly when she fretted about it. She knew he wasn't being offhand. He was looking at it from a detached, mature point of view whereas she was deeply involved. 'Stop being their mother all the time. You're not their mother. That's not your role, so stop taking it on,' he'd said to her once and she'd been furious with him. It was rare for her to be angry with Dan, but she hadn't spoken to him for a day until an old saying of her father's, 'The truth often hurts', came to mind. She had to admit that her husband was right whether she liked it or not.

What made her want to mother them all? she wondered as she peeled the potatoes at the sink, looking out at the daffodils and snowdrops being battered by an easterly gale. Was it because she was the eldest? If Shauna had been the eldest, would she have taken on that role? Carrie gave a wry grin. Somehow she didn't think so. Shauna had a great way of drawing her boundaries and she didn't let family matters encroach upon her freedom. Her attitude to Bobby and Noel's estrangement was one of indifference. She completely understood Bobby's point of view and didn't feel a rapprochement was going to make any difference one way or the other.

She was too much of a worrier, that's what her problem was, Carrie told herself crossly as she diced carrots and turnips. She was going to take a leaf out of Shauna's and Della's books and forget about family problems and concentrate on *herself* and have the holiday of a lifetime.

She heard her daughter call from the bedroom and a smile lighted her face. Hannah was awake after her nap. She hurried down the hall into the small bedroom that had been decorated in warm yellows and terracotta to complement the Winnie-the-Pooh curtains and quilt cover.

'Hello, my precious?' She leaned down and lifted her daughter into her arms.

'Mamee.' Hannah snuggled in to her, her head of copper curls tangled and delightfully awry after her sleep. What joy this child had brought them, she thought gratefully, pushing aside all thoughts of family feuds as she tickled her daughter, who squealed with glee and begged for more.

Shauna had cried when she'd held her for the first time and Carrie had felt a pang of pity for her younger sister. So far there was no sign of her getting pregnant and it was a huge source of grief and angst to her. Greg was being totally selfish as far as Carrie was concerned and she was losing any respect and affection she had had for him. What was it about the Cassidy siblings? Their self-centredness was incredible. She'd often felt sorry for Greg having a sister like Della, but as far as she could see he was getting as bad as she was.

'Don't tell me it's not our business, I know it's not. I'm just saying it to you,' she'd told Dan. 'I need to get it off my chest. I think he's being a bit of a bollox,' she'd burst out after the Cassidys had gone back to Abu Dhabi at the end of the previous summer.

'You won't get any argument from me there,' Dan had said quietly and she'd felt relieved that she wasn't alone in her thinking.

She was really looking forward to seeing Shauna and Chloe, Greg she could take or leave. According to Shauna he'd turned into an even bigger workaholic than he'd been at home so she probably wouldn't see that much of him, which would suit her fine.

'Filomena, will you take these videos back to Spinneys and bring Chloe with you while I'm having my coffee morning? You can take her to the Pizza Hut for a treat. Will you set out the coffee cups and plates before you go? I still have a box of florentines; I'll serve them with the biscuits.' Shauna peeled and sliced a couple of juicy mangoes and put them in a dish for Chloe. She had just come from her early morning workout and she needed to change and get herself organized fast.

'Don't want to go for a walk with Filomena,' Chloe said sulkily. 'I want to stay here.'

'Don't you want to go to the Pizza Hut? You can have Diet Coke if you're very, very good.'

'Why don't you come, Mom? You said you'd come,' Chloe entreated.

'Not today, darling. I have to have my Newcomers' Coffee Morning,' she explained patiently. 'How about tomorrow after-noon you and I go to the beach with Jenna and Carly?'

'OK,' Chloe muttered and Shauna bit her lip. She had her rug appreciation group this afternoon and tonight she and Greg were invited to an art exhibition in the Cultural Centre. Greg was anxious to go as he had spent the last year working on designs for a chain of new hotels across the UAE. The one in Dubai was almost completed and he and the manager were looking for just the right piece of artwork to hang in the foyer. He wanted something different, something out of the ordinary. He was hoping he might find something that would suit tonight.

Chloe always got very cross when Shauna was busy with her activities. It would be good for her to start school in September. This summer, she was going to devote all her time to her daughter, Shauna promised herself as she hurried down the marble-floored hall to her bedroom. Filomena had made the bed and cleaned the en suite. Shauna had showered in the gym but her hair was damp and she plugged in the hair dryer and began to dry it, sitting on the edge of the huge bed that dominated the bedroom.

Della had nearly got lockjaw when she'd seen the bedroom, Shauna remembered with a grin. It *was* luxurious. A emperor-size bed dominated the room. Dressed in oyster and cream, with big plump cushions and pillows, it was sumptuous. Cool swathes of cream muslin and slatted cream blinds shaded the room from the brilliant sunlight. Cream and gold pieces of furniture – drawers, dressing table and bedside lockers – were attractive as well as functional. Richly woven rugs lent warmth to the cool marble floor. A huge painting of a red-gold poppy decorated the wall facing the floor-to-ceiling sliding doors that led out onto a wide, terracotta-tiled balcony. A walk-in wardrobe and a tiled en suite completed the room.

Her bedroom at home always seemed so small after this room, she mused as she dried her highlighted blond hair. Greg loved this room. He loved the apartment and he loved living in the

Gulf. Their lifestyle was the envy of many, she was well aware of that, but deep down she harboured a resentment that was hard to ignore sometimes. She still wasn't pregnant despite several very upsetting rows.

He'd asked her to give him time to settle into the job and get established and she had tried to explain that time was passing. She was thirty-six next birthday, and even if they did have a baby it would be no company for Chloe, who was five now and would soon be going to school.

'Soon,' he kept saying. 'Soon.' She'd noticed that whenever she started getting on to him about it he'd stay later and later in the office, or else go off on inspection trips to Bahrain, Dubai and Doha, but once she let the subject drop and played the dutiful wife he was cheerful and exuberant and full of the joys of life. The life and soul of the party.

And there were plenty of parties and functions to attend. Life in the Gulf was one hectic social whirl and while she enjoyed it and had plenty of friends, she enjoyed going home in the summer to escape from the intense heat and humidity, to recharge her batteries and flop for the weeks until Greg came home. Once he was home, they entertained for most of the time and her lazy days of lounging out on Carrie's deck while the kids played together were over.

She made up her face carefully. She'd bought some expensive Sisley make-up the day before and she enjoyed trying out the new green and brown shades that she'd selected. They brought out the gold flecks in her blue eyes and she expertly applied some liquid eyeliner to emphasize them even more.

She strolled into her walk-in closet and flicked through the rails of clothes before selecting an ice pink pair of beautifully tailored Capri pants and a white broderie anglaise off-the-shoulder top. That would do fine for her coffee morning. The top was a little too revealing to be out and about in. She'd wear a dress to her rug appreciation group.

Filomena had laid out the coffee cups in the lounge, on the large low coffee table that stood in front of the cream leather sofas. The lounge too was decorated in cool cream and gold, modern luxurious sofas mixing with antique pieces that she'd picked up here and there. Her favourite piece was a sideboard carved out of highly polished wood with delicate filigree work and tiny little drawers. She'd seen it in the souk in Oman and bought it and some hand-carved wooden bowls on a shopping trip that a crowd of them had taken.

A silk triptych in golds, reds and yellows adorned one of the magnolia walls. It drew the eye with its large bright splashes of colour, in contrast to the muted pastel shades that were predominant in the big room. Sliding doors led to the balcony and the curtains rippled in the light, warm breeze that whispered in off the sea. Shauna stood looking out at the sparkling aquamarine waters of the Arabian Gulf, which dazzled the newly arrived expatriate or visitor but sometimes left her longing for the turbulent, grey, choppy whitecap waves of the Irish Sea.

'We're going now, ma'am,' Filomena called from the hallway. Shauna walked out to say goodbye. Her au pair, round-faced and cuddly, with a head of black curls and eyes as dark as melting chocolate, stood in the hall with her hand in Chloe's. Filomena was twenty-five and from the Philippines. She was a hard worker, conscientious and extremely trustworthy. Shauna knew that she was very lucky with her.

She also knew that Filomena was equally lucky with her and Greg. Some maids were treated like dirt and worked to the bone. Shauna made sure that her employee had good time off and was paid a decent wage. Filomena was very good with Chloe, although sometimes Shauna felt she gave in to her too much.

Chloe was in danger of being spoilt and Shauna tried her best to guard against it.

There had been more than a few rows with her cousins at Christmas. Shauna hid a grin, remembering Chloe stomping off to her bedroom shouting 'I don't care if caring is sharing, I'm not sharing with Ashley. He's breaking all my toys!' The holiday had been fraught, to say the least, especially as the weather had been uncharacteristically bad and they'd been stuck in a lot.

'See you later, darling.' She bent down to kiss Chloe who turned her head away, her gorgeous little mouth pursed in a thin line. 'Why are you being cross with me?' Shauna knelt down. 'Isn't Filomena going to bring you to Pizza Hut as a treat?'

'I want to go with you.'

'Oh, poor Filomena. That's not nice,' Shauna chided. 'I have to meet some ladies who are new out here and have no friends, not like me and you who have loads of friends. Come on, give me a kiss and a hug.'

Reluctantly her daughter planted a kiss on her cheek and took her nanny's hand. ''Bye,' she said glumly and marched stoically out the door.

Shauna sighed deeply. This lifestyle was hard on kids, she acknowledged. Chloe saw little of her father. Greg was gone at the crack of dawn and often home after she'd gone to bed. She'd make friends and then they'd be gone, their parents moving to another position in the peripatetic life of the permanent expat. She was lucky she'd had Filomena since they had come to Abu Dhabi. Some of her friends changed nannies every couple of months and seemed to have no continuity in their childcare.

It would be wonderful to have Carrie and Dan and the kids out for Easter. That would give Chloe a sense of family. And then it would be no time until the summer and they'd be home again.

The doorbell rang and the first of her guests announced their arrival at the intercom. Taking a deep breath, Shauna prepared to greet two newcomers to Abu Dhabi, just as three years ago she too had been welcomed into the expat community and made to feel at home.

19

'YOU'RE *ALL* GOING TO VISIT SHAUNA. AT EASTER! OH!' NOEL couldn't hide his dismay at Carrie's news. 'I suppose I'll have to fend for myself so.'

'I'll cook dinners and put them in the freezer for you; you won't have to fend for yourself. You know we haven't been out at all to see Shauna and she's there three years, Dad. In fact we haven't been on a holiday together for a long time and it's good timing for the kids. They won't miss much school at all, just a day or two,' Carrie explained patiently.

'So I'll have nobody here in case anything goes wrong?' he exclaimed mournfully.

'What's going to go wrong?' She tried to hide her exasperation.

'Well I'm hardly over this dose. It could come back. It could even develop into pneumonia or pleurisy.' Her father sank down onto his chair at the kitchen table.

'You're not going to get pneumonia or pleurisy. Sure your cough is gone.'

'Ah it kept me awake a bit last night.' He scowled. 'And I'll have nobody to come to the Easter ceremonies with me either. It will be a lonely Easter for me.'

'Do you think that you could make me feel any worse, Dad?'

Carrie snapped. 'I haven't had a decent holiday in years. Dan has worked all the hours God sends. We're going away for two bloody weeks, not a lifetime, and you're taking all the good out of it. I've asked the nurse to keep an eye on you and Mrs O'Neill is next door if you're stuck, and if anything awful happens you can ring Bobby.' She was so angry she didn't care what she said.

'As if I'd ring *him*,' Noel was affronted. 'After the way he spoke to me.'

'Well that's your problem, not mine. And you'd want to sort it. I'm disgusted that you've taken all the good out of my holiday. That was really, really selfish, Dad. I'm going. I'll see you with your dinner tomorrow.' She grabbed her coat and burst into tears.

'Ah don't be like that now!' Noel exclaimed in dismay, but Carrie had had enough. Years of suppressed resentment at the way he took her for granted filled her and she slammed the front door good and hard, tears streaming down her cheeks as she got into the car.

She reversed onto the road and drove towards the small car park further down the road that overlooked the beach. There was no other car there and she drove in and cut the engine. She needed a tissue. Her face was dripping with salty tears and great shuddering sobs shook her body.

Her father was *utterly* unfair. He took so much for granted. The cooking and cleaning she did for him, the running of errands, the trips to the doctor with him. She wasn't a bloody skivvy, but she might as well be, the way he treated her, she thought sorrowfully as she looked out at the turbulent, leaden sea pounding the shore. The truth was, she did feel more than a little guilty. She'd worried about leaving Noel alone but Dan had said quite firmly that it was only for two weeks. He was well able to look after himself. He could drive around and get his own shopping and it might be very good for him to be more independent. It would also be very good for him to see just how much Carrie did for him, her husband had added.

Noel really was lucky. Poor Mrs O'Neill next door was a widow. Her son lived in Canada and her daughter lived in Australia and she had to take care of herself with little family support. And she did it very well. Carrie sighed, wiping her eyes. Mrs O'Neill played bridge three nights a week. She was in the local ladies' club, she played bowls, and she lived life to the full. Noel could do well to emulate her.

If only Bobby were talking to him it wouldn't be so bad going away. Should anything serious befall their father he could fly over from London. It would be a safety net of sorts. She blew her nose and took a few deep breaths. She'd better get home. It was homework time. Noel normally ate his dinner with them but he'd been keeping inside after his bronchitis and she'd been dropping his dinner over to him. It had become a habit. It was a habit he'd want to get out of quickly. He could start coming back to the house for his dinner, she thought crossly as she started the ignition and headed for home.

'Are you OK?' Dan gave her a quizzical look when she walked into the kitchen. He had filled the dishwasher and the table was cleared. Davey and Olivia were sitting doing their homework and Hannah was playing on the sofa with her dolls.

'Mam, can you spell Sicily?' Davey asked.

'Yeah, S-i-c-i-l-y,' she said. 'What do you want to know that for?'

'We're doing a project about volcanoes and there's a big one called Mount Etna in Sicily,' he explained.

'Right.' She smiled down at him and felt a wave of affection for him as he sat there with his chestnut cow's lick sticking up, and the smattering of freckles over his nose making him look endearingly childlike.

'We're doing a project on nature,' Olivia piped up, never one to be outdone. 'I've to collect some snowdrops and daffodils and primroses, Mam.'

'We have daffodils and snowdrops in the garden and there's primroses on the bank of Dad's field, so we can collect them tomorrow.' She ruffled her daughter's hair.

'Cup of tea?' Dan offered.

'I'd love one,' she said wearily.

'How's your dad?' he asked casually as he filled the kettle.

'Don't ask!' she said sourly.

'I take it you told him about the trip,' he murmured, conscious of the children at the table. They hadn't been told about the forthcoming holiday. Carrie had planned to surprise them the following day during Saturday's family breakfast. It was the only time in the week that they all sat down for breakfast together.

'Hmm.' She nodded. 'Not impressed.'

Dan's jaw tightened and a frown crossed his handsome face. 'Come on into the sitting room and we'll watch the news,' he suggested. 'You go in and I'll bring your tea.'

'OK,' she agreed.

She went into their sitting room, and flung herself down on the big squishy sofa. It was a serene room, decorated in shades of lemon and blue, and the big bay window to the front had a window seat, which was delightful to sit in in the afternoon, when the sun shone through. One of her favourite things to do was to have a cup of coffee and a read of the paper sitting in the window seat, if she got the chance when Hannah was having her nap.

French doors to the back led out to her deck and she could see the snowdrops and daffodils weaving backwards and forwards under the damson trees. There'd be plenty for Olivia to bring to school. The grey skies had a tint of pink as the sun began to set. It was after six, and it was still bright. There was a great stretch in the evenings. Even that would normally be enough to cheer her up but she felt flat and despondent after her row with her father.

'So what happened?' Dan walked in and handed her a cup of tea and a Club Milk.

Carrie took a sip of her tea and unwrapped her biscuit. 'He laid a huge guilt trip on me, said he'd have to fend for himself. Wondered what he'd do if he developed pneumonia or pleurisy. Wouldn't have anyone to go with him to the Easter ceremonies; it would be a lonely Easter, blah, blah, blah.'

'Don't take it on board, Carrie.' Dan scowled. 'That's very unfair of him.'

'I know. It's bloody emotional blackmail, that's what it is.' She grimaced. 'And I let him have it. Totally lost it. And banged the door on my way out.'

'That's no harm. You're too soft. It's good for him to realize that he can't take you for granted.'

'He found that out today. I guess the worm turned.' She bit into her Club Milk and felt quite miserable.

'You deserve this holiday, Carrie, we all do.' Dan leaned over and stared into her face, concern mirrored in his blue eyes.

'I know we do, I just wish I didn't feel as guilty as hell,' she said disconsolately.

'Stop feeling guilty. You've no need to; you do more than enough for your father. Come on now, forget it. We're going to have a great holiday and your dad will be fine. I'll get Sadie to look in on him now and again.'

'Would you? Do you think she'd mind?' Carrie brightened, knowing that someone from the family would be there for Noel. Dan's older sister had a heart of gold. She lived a couple of miles outside the village. If she checked up on Noel now and again, Carrie would be able to go away with a much lighter heart.

'That's a great idea, Dan, if Sadie wouldn't mind. I'll have all his dinners cooked so she won't have to worry about anything like that.'

'I'll say it to her tomorrow. Now relax,' he said as the door opened and Hannah toddled in.

'Daddee.' She beamed, arms stretched out to him.

'Here's the best little girl in the whole wide world,' Dan exclaimed, scooping her into his arms and nuzzling his chin in her hair. Carrie watched them and marvelled at how loving a father he was. Noel had never been able to show much affection to his children; it was only with his grandchildren that his crusty exterior had softened somewhat. He had missed out on a lot in his relationship with his children. Dan would never need to use emotional blackmail; there was far too much love and affection between him and the kids to have to resort to that sad tactic. He was right. They deserved that holiday. If she was going around fretting, it would spoil his holiday and that would be most unfair. This time she needed to put her own family first. And there was no harm in that. Noel would just have to get on with it.

Noel knelt in the church, his rosary beads slipping through his fingers. There was a novena on that he hadn't wanted to miss and he'd wrapped himself up well and walked through the dusky village, catching up with his neighbour, Mrs O'Neill, at Malone's pub.

'How are you, Noel?'

'Ah not the best,' he said glumly.

'Have you still got that dose on you? I thought Carrie said you were over it.' She was surprised.

'I'm still coughing at night.' He fell into step beside her.

'Still, it's good to see you out and about again. Carrie was telling me she's off out to see Shauna. Isn't it great for her?'

'I suppose it is. I'll be left here on my own.' He gave a deep sigh.

'Oh, for goodness' sake, Noel, the girl's only going for two weeks. What would you do if you were like me with no family around me? You're very lucky. Me, I have to get on with it,' she snorted as they walked through the gates of the church. 'I'll see you later,' she said as she blessed herself with holy water. He watched her march up the aisle. She was older than he was. She'd been seventy last year. No-one would guess it; she was a very vigorous woman for her age, he thought admiringly.

The candlelight flickered against the walls of the church. Only the sidelights were on, casting a subdued peachy glow. It was silent and peaceful, just a handful of parishioners dotted here and there. Noel genuflected and slipped into his favourite seat at the end of the third row from the top. Mrs O'Neill was in the front seat ahead of him.

He supposed that she was right. He was lucky to have Carrie so near him. If he were like his neighbour, he'd have to look after himself and get on with it. He'd been shocked when Carrie had lost her temper and let go at him. She'd never done that before. He hadn't liked to see her go off crying. Carrie was the kindest of his children, and he hadn't meant to upset her. Maybe he'd been a bit whingy, he thought guiltily. He shouldn't have made her feel bad. The girl deserved a good holiday. He'd say nothing else about it, he decided as the full lights came on and Father Doyle emerged by the altar. If Mrs O'Neill could live by herself and look after herself year in year out, he could surely manage it for two weeks. He'd show them all, he vowed. He was well able to shop and do his own cooking if he had to.

His heart sank at the thought. He'd never been completely on his own before. A flicker of apprehension licked through him. He was afraid of being on his own. Not that he'd admit it to a sinner, but Carrie had always been his safety net. The knowledge shocked him and made him feel extremely vulnerable. He hadn't realized how much he depended on her. For two weeks, he was going to have to walk the tightrope alone.

'I'd like you to come to the islands with Pierre tomorrow, Shauna. He especially asked if you were coming. It will be a good day.' Greg yawned and stretched. They were sitting on the balcony watching the dhows sailing up and down on the silver sea, over which hung a glorious full moon. In the distance the call to prayer echoed around the city and below them white-robed figures hurried to their mosques.

'Aw, Greg,' she groaned. 'I hate going out with that man; he's such a bore. He thinks he's God's gift and he never stops bragging.'

'He's the managing director. He's influential. He wants us to go on a picnic with him, so we go.'

'You go. I'm not bringing Chloe on his speedboat again. He's so ignorant. He went so fast the last time we were bouncing up and down and we were drenched sitting in the back. It was a really uncomfortable trip. When we go to the islands with Kareem he drives slowly so that we can enjoy the scenery and the kids don't get drenched. And Kareem makes everyone wear lifejackets. I feel much safer with him. Pierre is such an arrogant prat, he's too much of a show-off to wear a lifejacket.'

'Oh, don't give me a hard time, Shauna. Jenna and Brett are coming and Carly will be with them.'

'It's our day off, Greg. It would be nice just to spend the day together as a family,' she moaned, taking a slug of her Chardonnay.

'We *will* be together. We'll be on a picnic.'

'With half the bloody company.' Shauna scowled.

'Don't exaggerate,' Greg retorted. 'Look, there's a huge project coming up in Dubai and I want to be involved. Pierre can put in a good word for me.'

'You didn't tell me this,' she said slowly. 'Are you thinking of moving?'

'It could be on the cards in a year or so.'

'So we just up sticks and head for Dubai.'

'Yup.' He grinned at her. 'Or I could commute, stay there three days a week.'

'Well thanks for discussing it with me.'

He leaned forward eagerly. 'It's a great opportunity, Shauna; there's all kinds of development going on out there. It's the place to be. Their tourist trade is booming and the biggest and best hotels are being built there. Not to talk of apartment blocks.'

'And what about Chloe? She's starting school this year. It's not fair uprooting her.'

'Shauna, kids are adaptable. Look at the majority of them out here – they've all lived in other states in the Gulf. It's no big deal.'

'That shows how much you know. Look at poor little Saladin Sharrif. He's moved three times: from Saudi to Kuwait, then Bahrain and now here. And he's only seven and he's the most nervous, unconfident little scrap you could ever meet. He told Chloe he doesn't make friends any more because he always has to say goodbye to them. That's the saddest thing I ever heard.'

'We're not going to move three times,' Greg said dismissively. The phone rang. 'Get that, will you?' He yawned.

'Yes, your majesty,' Shauna drawled as she stood up to go inside. He was something else. Making plans without even discussing it with her. He'd want to cop on to himself.

'Hello?' She picked up the phone.

'Shauna, hi, it's Jenna. Are you going on this damn picnic tomorrow?'

Shauna laughed. 'Hi, Jenna. I was just arguing with Greg about it. I don't want to go. I can't stand that fat little toad.'

Jenna giggled. 'He's horrible, isn't he?' she agreed.

Shauna really liked Jenna Williams, a sporty, witty American whom she'd met and clicked with at a company function soon after arriving in Abu Dhabi. She'd had a toddler the same age as Chloe and the pair had become the best of friends. Brett, her husband, a laid-back six-footer, got on well with Greg and the four of them socialized a lot together. She and Jenna shared a dislike of their husbands' boss.

'I don't want to bounce out to the islands at a hundred miles an hour on his bloody speedboat. My ass was really sore after the last trip, and Chloe and I were drenched, but Greg thinks we should go. There's some big project coming up in Dubai and he wants to be in the running,' Shauna moaned.

'Brett too.' Jenna sighed. Her husband was a surveyor in the same company. 'What I was ringing to say was that we're going to take Kareem's boat. He's offered it to Brett for the month that he's in South Africa, so if you and Chloe wanted to come with us we'd be free to come and go when we please and we wouldn't be trying to break any speed records. The last time I was out with that jerk I nearly threw up. I was nauseous for a day afterwards.'

'That would be great, Jenna. Thanks for thinking of us. We could go and brown-nose but at least we wouldn't be stuck waiting for his nibs to decide when it's time to come home.'

'Right. I'll prepare a couple of dishes; will you bring your delicious dip?'

'Sure.'

'I'm so glad you're coming,' Jenna said fervently.

'I'm so glad *you're* coming. It won't be such an ordeal. It's terrible, isn't it? Here we are, two grown women, and we can't put our foot down and refuse to go. We need our heads examined,' Shauna exclaimed.

'They'll just owe us big time after this one. See you at the boat.'

''Night, Jenna.' Shauna smiled and hung up.

'Who was it?' Greg topped up her wine.

'Jenna. Kareem has loaned them his boat so they're taking that and she's offered us a lift. You can go with Pierre, Chloe and I can go with Jenna,' Shauna informed him.

'That's a bit rude,' Greg protested. 'Pierre invited you. It would look bad you going off with Jenna and Brett.'

'They won't be going at a hundred miles an hour,' Shauna retorted.

'Look, I need all the help I can get here. Be reasonable, Shauna.' He glowered at her.

'No, *you* be reasonable, Greg. It's always all about you. Pierre's a speed merchant. He's dangerous. I don't want Chloe in his boat,' Shauna said angrily. 'How dare you tell me to be reasonable. You sit there and calmly tell me you're thinking of moving to Dubai. You never even discussed it with me. You've been promising me for the last three years that we could try for a baby and you keep putting it off, and I'm sick of it, Greg. You're being a real bastard about it. Why are you so against having another child? Why?'

'For God's sake, keep your voice down,' he growled. 'You don't want everybody in the building to know our business.'

'I don't give a hoot who knows our business,' she snapped, but she lowered her voice. 'Why don't you want another child? I want to know.'

'I just don't want one now,' he said sulkily. 'We're starting to have a life again, Shauna. You've enjoyed the past few years. Admit it. We've a great life here. We're doing things we'd never do if we were at home. If you have a baby, we're going to be tied.'

'Yes, I've had a good time, I agree, but I want a family. Look how happy Dan and Carrie are with their family,' she said hotly. 'Why can't we be like that?'

'I don't mean to be rude, Shauna, but look at their lifestyle.' Greg looked at her as if she was mad. 'Dan works in his market garden morning noon and night, Carrie's a housewife. Boring, boring, boring.'

'But I always assumed that you'd want a family once we started having children. I—'

'Well that's what you get for assuming, Shauna,' he said coldly. 'You know what they say? Don't ever assume because it makes an ass out of you and me. Get it? Ass u me!'

'That's a horrible thing to say, Greg Cassidy. Chloe needs company. She never sees you,' Shauna said in disgust.

'I'm providing for her, aren't I?' Greg said hotly. 'She's going to inherit a very healthy property portfolio. She's going to be a very wealthy woman when we bite the dust.'

'Yes, she'll be wealthy, but she'll have no family to turn to, she'll be on her own.' Shauna couldn't hide her bitterness.

'Oh don't be so dramatic, Shauna,' he said derisively. 'She'll have all her cousins.'

'It's not the same,' she protested. 'I want her to have a sister or brother. I'll be thirty-six soon, Greg. I'm not getting younger. It might not be as easy to get pregnant after coming off the Pill. It could take a year, which means I'll be thirty-seven getting pregnant and nearly thirty-eight when I have the baby. I don't want to start another packet of the Pill. It's been three years since you said we could try for a baby and I'm just sick of it.' She burst into tears.

'Oh, for God's sake. I'm going for a walk on the Corniche. You're doing my head in, Shauna.' Greg jumped to his feet and headed for the front door, leaving her sobbing on the balcony.

After a little while, her crying eased and a measure of calm returned. It didn't help that she had PMT, she supposed, as she poured herself another glass of wine. How could she have got it so wrong with Greg? She'd always assumed they'd have children; he'd never said anything to the contrary during their early years together. Had she been a fool to make the assumption? Had their free and easy lifestyle turned him away from the idea of having a family? What an irony.

All she'd ever wanted was to have a family of her own, a happy family, just like Carrie and Dan. She wanted Greg to be a father who loved and cherished his children, not like her own rigid father. She'd married Greg because she'd thought he was everything Noel was not – outgoing, fun to be with, liberal, good-humoured – but behind it all he was controlling her as much as Noel had. The realization hit her like a ton of bricks. She wanted another child and he was stopping her from having one.

She could always just stop taking the Pill and pretend she'd had an accident, she supposed, but what joy would there be in conceiving like that? Greg's resentment of the baby would be too damaging. She wouldn't have a child under those conditions. It would be very wrong.

Wearily she closed the doors and switched out the balcony lights. She didn't finish her wine. She didn't want to be travelling on a speedboat under the glare of the sun suffering from a hangover. It was just as well Filomena was on her night off; it would have been awkward having a row like that knowing that she was in her room, listening to their raised voices.

She left a light on in the lounge for when Greg came back and went into the bedroom and undressed. She could almost taste the bitterness she felt as she poked her Pill out of the foil, and took it with a sip of water. More unhappy than she remembered being in a long time, she slid into bed, grateful at least that it was big and wide and she didn't have to have any contact with her husband.

Greg walked along the Corniche listening to the sea lap gently against the rocks. He felt totally harassed and pressurized. He didn't want another child. What was so wrong with that? Why couldn't Shauna be happy with what they had? They had a lifestyle that was the envy of their Irish friends. And if he got the job in Dubai it was going to get better. He was building up a strong property base at home. They were in their prime. They were affluent. It was enough for him. Why couldn't it be enough for her? He glanced across the street and admired the shiny, glass-fronted building that housed an international bank. Good piece of architecture, he noted. When the sun shone on it, it gleamed copper and gold. He slowed his footsteps and decided to head for the Sheraton, solid and imposing in the distance. He'd have a beer to cool himself down. He wouldn't mind going on the piss but he needed to have his wits about him tomorrow. If he could impress Pierre Laportaire enough he'd be well on his way. Dubai was where it was all happening. Exciting as Abu Dhabi was, Dubai had the edge, internationally. Another rung on the ladder of his already very successful career. If only his wife would come to her damn senses. He just didn't need this right now.

As he sat nursing his pint in one of the cool, air-conditioned bars, mulling over his problem with Shauna, a thought struck him. The tension seeped out of his body; there was a course of action he could follow which would result in a win-win situation for them. He should have thought of it years ago and saved himself a lot of grief, he chided himself. He finished his pint and walked through the huge marbled foyer and headed for home.

The light was on in the lounge but it was empty and he guessed that Shauna was in bed. He switched it off and took his shoes off and padded into the bedroom. 'Are you awake, Shauna? I want to talk to you,' he said softly. He could see her curled up on the edge of her own side of the bed. 'Come on. Let's talk.' He went round and sat beside her. 'Listen, how about if you come off the Pill when you go home for the summer and we start trying when I come home in August?' he said softly.

Shauna sat up in bed, her hair tousled, her face tear-streaked. 'Do you mean it this time, Greg? You're not just trying to pacify me?' she asked quietly.

'Yes, darling, I mean it. You're right, I've been a selfish bastard putting you off all this time. I forgot it's different for women. That old biological clock ticking. So how about it? August we go for it?'

'Why wait until August?' she whispered.

'A few more months won't make much difference. I'll be relaxed at home and you'll have been off the Pill for two months. OK?' he studied her anxiously.

'Promise.' Her blue eyes glittered in the moonlight.

'I promise, Shauna,' he said earnestly, holding his arms open to her.

'Oh, Greg, thank you, thank you,' Shauna whispered, resting her head on his shoulder, reproaching herself for comparing her husband to her father. They were chalk and cheese. She really had lost it for a while earlier and overreacted. At last it was finally sorted between them and she felt as if a huge burden had lifted from her.

20

'MORNING, MR MAC. SORRY ABOUT CALLING IN SO EARLY. CAN I have a quick word?' Dan stood on Noel's doorstep, squinting in the early morning sun.

'Of course.' Noel's heart sank. He knew exactly why Dan was here. 'Come in,' he invited, tightening the belt of his dressing gown. He'd been in bed when the doorbell rang.

'I won't stay long,' Dan said calmly, stepping into the hall and closing over the door. 'You know, Carrie was very upset when she came home last night. I believe she told you we were going on holiday.'

'Well, she did mention it,' Noel blustered agitatedly. 'I don't know why she was upset. I just said it would be lonely with everyone gone for Easter.' He could feel his heart beginning to race. Dan looked very stern indeed.

'Now, Mr Mac, you know that Carrie is very good to you. She deserves to go off on this holiday without any worries or concerns. I don't want you moaning to her about being on your own. She's going to cook your dinners for you and put them in your freezer so you won't starve. Although I would suggest you try going out once in a while for lunch for a bit of variety while we're gone. Malone's does a very good lunch.' Dan stood arms folded, his gaze unwavering, and Noel felt like a naughty little boy. His temper began to rise.

'She doesn't have to do any cooking. I'll not be dependent on—'

'Now Mr Mac, don't take that tone with me, we're not going to fall out about this. I'm just telling you the way it is,' Dan said quietly. 'You're going to send Carrie off on her holiday with an easy mind. Sadie is going to call in on you every couple of days, so you won't be on your own. I don't like having to have words with you, Mr Mac, but Carrie is my wife and I have to look out for her and I don't like to see her upset. I'm sure you understand. We'll keep this little conversation just between the two of us. There's no need for her to know about it, OK?'

Noel nodded, unable to speak.

'Good, we understand each other.' Dan smiled. 'I'll be off so. And come back soon for your meals with us. The children miss you,' he added kindly as he opened the door and walked out.

Noel watched him go down the drive and felt myriad emotions. Fury at being spoken to like a child, and being very firmly put in his place, but also a grudging admiration for Dan's manliness. He hadn't been rude or abusive as Greg would have been. Dan had been respectful. Respectful but very, very firm.

Noel cleared his throat. He felt like crying. He, whose word had once been law in his household, had no power any more. People were telling him what to do and ordering him around. His son had turned his back on him, one daughter was thousands of miles away and the other was upset with him. How he missed his dear wife. Anna had been a soft-hearted woman who had looked up to him. If she were alive none of this would be happening. Tears slid down his cheeks. He'd go to the grave and bring some spring flowers and talk to her as he tidied the plot. That always eased his pain and helped him feel close to her.

He'd want to get dressed. It hadn't helped that he'd been in his dressing gown and unshaved. It had put him on a less dignified footing. What an uncivilized hour of the morning to visit anyone, he thought crossly, glancing at his watch and seeing that it was only seven forty-five. He shivered. There was a sharp nip out today. A cup of tea might warm him up.

Twiskers rubbed her little black and white nose against his leg and he lifted her up and buried his face in her fur. 'Oh, Twiskers, what's to become of me? Everyone's vexed with me except yourself. How could Carrie possibly expect me to contact that son of mine after the terrible things he said to me? Has she no understanding at all of how grievously he hurt me? Why doesn't she tell him to ring *me* and apologize? No-one understands how lonely a life it is.' Twiskers purred comfortingly. 'What would I do without you?' he murmured. He walked into the kitchen and opened a can of tuna for her, her favourite treat. She rubbed herself against his leg ecstatically and he managed a small smile. At least someone appreciated him, he thought forlornly as he bent down and patted her soft, furry head.

Dear Bobby
    How's life? Gay and glitzy I hope. Same old, same old, here. I'm so looking forward to visiting Shauna, or at least I was until Dad had a go at me yesterday about leaving him on his own, especially at Easter. He made me feel like such a heel, but I was feeling bad about it before he said anything anyway. I wish you and he would sort out your differences. It would make my life much easier. I know you probably think it's selfish of me to say that to you, but I'm in a selfish humour today and am very fed up with the two of you. You know it really hurts that you haven't even seen Hannah yet. Aren't you ever

201

going to come home for a visit? Dan and I did nothing to offend you. Why should we have to endure the fall-out of your run-in with Dad? Davey and Olivia are always asking about you. You're their favourite uncle for some reason!!!!! I know that you send great presents but it's not the same.

I suppose you'll get in a huff when you get this and not ring me for ages. But I'm sending it anyway. That's the sort of humour I'm in and it's not PMT either. It's me, fed up, and making my feelings plain for once.

Your browned-off sister,

C xx

Bobby read Carrie's email and felt a flash of guilt. He'd been waiting for Carrie to bring him to book yet again about not seeing his new niece. She was right. She and Dan had done nothing to offend him. They had been very decent to him. He was going to have to sort something out about seeing them. But how could he possibly go home and visit them and be in the same village as his father and not see him? The odds of bumping into him on the street were practically a certainty. That would be highly awkward. If he didn't visit it would be noted and that would be the subject of gossip and speculation. Noel would hate that. His standing in the community was very important to him, much more important to him than his son was. Bobby couldn't help the bitterness he felt; whoever said time healed didn't know what the hell they were talking about.

How did he deal with this? he wondered tiredly. He was bushed. It had been a busy shift. One of the chambermaids had fallen over her bucket and broken her arm. A guest had locked the keys of her car in the boot and got highly agitated when he'd suggested that she call her husband to come to the hotel with the spares. She was obviously having an affair, not that he cared if she was shagging the whole of London, but he and the porter had spent twenty-five minutes with a coat hanger trying to break into the car. He should have stayed a receptionist instead of working his way up to assistant manager, he thought glumly as he stretched out on the sofa and flicked through the channels to see whether there was anything to take his mind off his family problems.

An episode of *Frasier* had just started and he tried to immerse himself in it but failed. He knew he should ring Carrie but he just couldn't bring himself to. How did he answer that email? It was clear his sister was way down in the dumps. How typical of Noel to lay a guilt trip on her. Guilt trips were his father's speciality.

He got up and went to the fridge and pulled out a bottle of Bud and opened it. He took a long draught and stood staring out the window. It was spitting rain, the drops hitting the pavement relentlessly. A couple hurried by hand in hand, collars pulled up against the rain, laughing at each other, happy. He looked at them enviously. He'd like to be part of a couple. He had loads of friends and acquaintances and he'd had several flings, but so far he hadn't met someone to settle down with.

The lights in the windows of the highrise flats shone yellows and pinks and blues and greens. So many people living in such a small area. Families, singles, separated, divorced, hetero, gay, bi. That was what he loved about London. Here he was as normal as anyone else. In Whiteshells Bay he was very much the odd one out. And it was a horrible feeling. Maybe Carrie, Dan and the kids could come to London for a weekend. He'd get a good rate for them in the hotel; there wouldn't be enough room for them all in the flat. Suddenly he felt lonely for all of them. For Davey and his great infectious laugh, for Olivia and her sense of high drama, for Chloe. How could he ever forget Chloe singing 'BimBamBom' and lifting him out of himself when he'd been near to crying that Christmas morning at the grave? She was five now. Starting school in September. Carrie was right. He *was* being a fool. These beautiful darlings were his kith and kin. He'd want to make an effort or he'd end up a lonely old geezer . . . just like his dad.

21

SHAUNA PEELED AND DICED A CUCUMBER, ADDED A FINELY chopped clove of garlic, chopped dried mint to a bowl of natural yoghurt and flavoured it with salt before giving it a good stir. It would be a tasty accompaniment to the couscous and chicken dish she was bringing to the picnic on the island. She had a platter of smoked salmon and cream cheese wraps already prepared and Filomena was making potato salad. Greg was in the shower, whistling. He was in great form and it was rubbing off on the household.

She felt like whistling herself. She smiled. They had made love last night and it was as if all the tension that had simmered on and off between them for such a long time had faded away. For the first time in ages she felt comfortable in her marriage again. It was a great feeling. Like when she was first married and Greg had bent over backwards to make her happy. Before he'd become distracted and absorbed in work and climbing the career ladder. He'd become so competitive over the years it disturbed her. When she'd challenged him on it he'd told her that she didn't complain about the lifestyle his competitiveness gave her. He had a point, she'd admitted. She'd got used to a life of relative luxury. She'd got used very quickly to having her own credit card, an au pair, membership of an exclusive beach club and a very social, affluent lifestyle. But although she enjoyed it hugely it didn't fill the need and want deep inside her.

Last night had been different. Greg had made her feel happy again, especially when he'd apologized for not accepting that her biological clock was ticking fast. At last, he'd acknowledged her need. That was a big step for them as a couple. Now they were working as a partnership again and she'd even decided as a gesture of goodwill that if Jenna would take Chloe with Carly in their boat, she'd endure Pierre's speedboat nightmare.

'Chloe,' she called. Her daughter was watching a Barney video. Personally, Shauna couldn't stand the great purple dollop of saccharine and had an irrational wish to kick him hard in the goolies, but Chloe lapped it up.

'Mom, I'm busy,' her daughter called back.

'I want to ask you something. Quick, it's exciting.'

Chloe padded into the kitchen. She looked adorable in her pink frilly top and matching trousers, but she wouldn't get much more wear out of them, Shauna noted. She was getting big, and filling out. Shauna must warn Filomena about giving her too many treats.

'What do you want to ask me?' Her daughter gazed at her with her big blue eyes.

'Would you like to go with Carly in her boat?'

'*Yessss!* Can I, Mom? Carly is my very best friend.'

Shauna smiled at her. 'I know, that's why I asked. Would you like her to have a sleepover?'

'Oh, Mom, I love you. You're my best Mom.' Chloe launched herself at her. Shauna hugged her tightly.

'In a few minutes we'll be getting ready to go. I want you to get your sunscreen for Filomena, OK.'

'OK.' Her daughter made a face. She still hated having her sunscreen put on. Shauna made a face back.

'I know it's a nuisance but we don't want to get sunburnt, sure we don't.'

'No, Mom.'

'And don't forget your sunglasses and hat.'

Chloe gave an exasperated sigh. 'I won't, Mom. You don't have to keep telling me.'

'Sorry,' murmured Shauna, understanding completely her daughter's irritation. She was growing up fast and developing a most determined and stubborn little personality. It was fascinating to watch.

Three-quarters of an hour later they were driving past the clock tower along the Corniche road on their way to the marina in the Intercontinental Hotel. Shauna had phoned Jenna and asked if Chloe could travel with them.

'Great idea; they'll have each other for company. Are you sure you won't come with us?' her friend had asked.

'Believe me, I'd love to go with you. But Greg thought it would be rude, seeing as Pierre issued a personal invite.'

'He fancies you,' teased Jenna.

'Ugh! You wash your mouth out. That greasy little toad. Did you ever see anything like the comb-over? How does Chantal put up with him?'

'She's a real cold fish. That's probably why he's the way he is, because he doesn't get anything from her,' Jenna remarked sagely.

'Well let them get over themselves. I'll do as little "polite conversation" as I absolutely have to,' Shauna said dryly.

'Me too,' Jenna agreed. 'Thank God we have the children, we can use them as an excuse to withdraw and be on our own for a while. See you soon.'

The Williamses were already at Kareem's boat, loading up windbreaks and picnic table and chairs, when Greg, Shauna and

Chloe clattered along the wooden pontoon. Pierre waved expansively from his speedboat a few berths away. '*Bonjour, Shauna.* You are coming with us, yes?' he called. His wife, Chantal, sat stony-faced in the stern, giving the slightest wave of recognition.

'Yes, Pierre. Chloe is going with Jenna,' Shauna called back.

'Excellent. Jenna, come have some champagne before you set off,' he ordered.

'Oh *noooo*,' Jenna groaned quietly as she waved and nodded acquiescence.

Five minutes later, when they had packed away the picnic and beach gear, the two girls strolled over to the MD's boat, followed by Greg, leaving the children with Brett.

'My favourite ladies.' Pierre bowed with exaggerated Gallic charm, kissing each of their hands. '*Enchanté.*'

Another couple, Monique and Rashid al Hamade, were already sipping their champagne, seated beside Chantal.

'Hello, Chantal.' Shauna greeted the French woman politely with a kiss on each cheek.

'Shauna, very nice to see you. You look *très chic*.' She gave a small tight smile, her bright, beady eyes going over Shauna from head to toe. Shauna was wearing an elegant green sundress with a matching chiffon jacket to cover her arms. If she had just been going with Jenna and Brett she would have worn her shorts and a top, but once Pierre and Chantal were involved the dress code notched up a gear or two. Chantal herself was wearing white linen pants and a red silk blouse. A floppy white sun hat was draped with a red scarf that matched the colour of her sandals and bag *precisely*. She looked the height of French chic.

Pierre, on the other hand, looked like a little barrel in his brightly coloured Hawaiian shirt and white chinos. His lank, dyed black hair blew all over the place in the fresh breeze that blew in off the sea.

'Breezy day for a picnic,' Shauna murmured, taking the flute of champagne that he handed her.

'*Mais non*, it will be wonderful. Refreshing after the humidity of last week. Greg, *mon ami*, how goes it?' He shook hands with Greg and motioned him to the bow of the boat. 'You will drive this beauty when we leave the marina. *Oui?*'

Greg's eyes gleamed with anticipation. 'I'd love to, Pierre. Just say the word.' He turned to Chantal. 'I'll drive carefully,' he said smoothly, giving her a charming smile. She gave a little simper. She liked Greg, and he knew how to play up to her, Shauna thought in amusement as she sat down beside the fourth woman on the boat.

'Monique, how are you?' She smiled at the tall, elegant French-woman.

'Very well. And you?' The glamorous brunette smiled warmly. Her husband, Rashid, worked as a financial consultant within the company. Shauna liked him, a warm, friendly Lebanese man; he had shown wonderful Arabic hospitality to her and Greg since they'd come to live in the Emirate. A party in Monique and Rashid's villa was always something to look forward to.

'You didn't bring Nadia and Rafik?' Jenna joined them.

'Hala Mattar was taking her two boys to Al Ain zoo and staying overnight with her friends so my two were invited and couldn't wait to go. Rashid and I are having a day and night all to ourselves. Bliss.' She smiled at her tall, good-looking husband, who always reminded Shauna of Tom Selleck with his black bushy moustache.

'We should go,' decreed Chantal. 'Time is passing.'

It was about a fifty-minute trip to the islands and by the time everything was set up and lunch served it would be well after noon. That wouldn't leave them a lot of time to relax. It was always safer to be back at the marina before it got dark.

209

Ten minutes later they were on their way. As soon as Pierre had eased his way out of the marina, past the palaces and boat yards, and was into the deep sea channels, he pushed forward on the throttle, and for Shauna at least the pleasure went out of the trip as the powerful boat surged forward at high speed.

It was a windy day with whitecaps on the normally glassy sea. Spume and spray shot past them and the engine was so noisy she soon gave up trying to have a conversation with Chantal. The smell of petrol fumes made her feel queasy and she glanced back longingly at Jenna and Brett's boat, dawdling along far behind them.

The men were in the bow discussing the speed and manoeuvrability of the boat. They were in their element. Shauna was glad that Chloe wasn't with them as they bounced up and down. Pierre hadn't offered anyone one of the lifejackets that were stowed under the seat they were sitting on, and Shauna couldn't help feeling nervous as they rattled along. It was a relief fifteen minutes later when their host was forced to slow to a stop to show his papers to one of the police launches that patrolled the coast.

The sun was blazing high in a dazzling sapphire sky and the glitter on the water was intense. Shauna was glad of her Ray-Bans. Chantal had a lovely pair of Prada sunglasses that gave her a very Jackie O look. She wore her sunglasses as an accessory and had dozens of pairs. She had a knack for matching the perfect pair with every outfit.

Shauna watched as Pierre motioned Greg to take the wheel. Her husband, dressed in a pale green short-sleeved shirt and khaki shorts, looked tanned and impressive as he stood at the wheel of the powerful boat, his black hair raffishly tousled in the breeze. He had spoken of buying a boat for them. Shauna wasn't pushed either way. Going to the islands for picnics was nearly more trouble than it was worth by the time everything was packed into the car, unpacked into the boat, unpacked from the boat at the island and then the whole palaver repeated going home. Picnic tables, chairs, windbreaks, snorkels, ice coolers. The list was endless. Having a boat was nice for cruising slowly along the coastline, particularly when the sun was setting. She'd like that. But if Greg was going to do a Pierre on it, he was on his own, she thought grimly as they bounced hard over a choppy wave. She watched him chatting easily to Pierre and Rashid. He was completely at ease. The life and soul of the party. Didn't he ever weary of it? The constant 'performing'? She did, but Greg seemed to thrive on it.

It was a huge relief to her ten minutes later when Greg eased back on the throttle and they cruised into the emerald waters at the island's edge. She caught Monique's gaze; her friend raised her eyes to heaven. Chantal sat grim-faced. She'd had to hold on to her hat on one or two occasions to stop it from blowing away. Pierre threw out the anchor and the boat bobbed gently in the warm Gulf waters. Greg helped Chantal onto the inflatable dinghy. 'Anyone else want to be rowed in?' He squinted up at them.

'I'm fine, I'll paddle,' Shauna said.

'Me too.' Monique slipped off her sandals and stepped into the warm green waters from the diving board at the back of the boat. Shauna hoisted up her dress and followed her in. The water was bath-warm, and she wriggled her toes in the soft sand. She was looking forward to a swim before lunch.

The wind had not abated and a stiff breeze whipped the fine white sand around her legs as she padded ashore. It really wasn't the ideal day for a picnic; if she and Jenna had been left to their own devices they wouldn't have chosen a windy day for an island trip, but Pierre never liked to be thwarted.

211

Twenty minutes later Jenna, Brett and the children joined them. Pierre, Rashid and Greg were struggling to erect the sun canopy, which was proving to be rather difficult because of the breeze. Monique and Shauna had arranged the chairs and were trying to set up the windbreaks, which were flapping madly between their poles.

'*Zut.*' Pierre's exasperated imprecation carried on the breeze as the rope was torn out of his hand.

'This is ridiculous,' Monique murmured as she hammered a pole as hard as she could. 'There's sand everywhere. I suggested we all go and have lunch in the club but Pierre wouldn't have it. He was coming out on his precious boat and that was that. He and Chantal had a row about it and that's why she's in a bad humour.'

'Just what we need, Chantal in a bad humour.' Shauna grinned as she tried to get her rug to lie flat.

'Mom, can we go swimming?' Chloe danced across the beach to her.

'Sure, I'm going to come in a minute. Slip out of your trousers and T-shirt and don't go out too far.'

'OK, Mom,' her daughter agreed, pulling her trousers off as quickly as she could. Carly was doing the same and Shauna watched the two little girls run shrieking happily to the water's edge. It was wonderful for her daughter to have a good friend. If Greg got the Dubai posting she hoped desperately that Jenna and Brett were going too.

'Are you comfortable, Chantal? Is there anything I can get for you before I go in for a swim?' She walked over to where the older woman was sitting in a black canvas chair, waiting for the canopy to be sorted.

'*Non*, but thank you for asking. I'm going to read my magazine, if that's possible,' she said dryly as a gust of wind fluttered the pages of her *Paris Match*.

'It's a little windy all right.' Shauna smiled at her.

'Hrummp,' she snorted expressively. 'Monique suggested we go to the club; it was a very sensible suggestion. These men and their toys!' She arched an eyebrow and cast a dismissive glance towards her husband, who was tightening the ropes of the canopy. Shauna went back to her windbreak and slipped out of her sundress. She was wearing a turquoise one-piece swimsuit and it showed off her golden tan to perfection. She kept her figure in shape through gym work and walking on the Corniche early in the morning three days a week. This time next year she could have a big bump, she thought happily as she ran into the sea to join the girls. The water was utterly refreshing and she began a lazy crawl around Chloe and Carly, who were splashing and chatting and having fun. The island gleamed and shimmered. She had never seen such fine white sand as there was here. It was almost powdery; not at all like the harsh, coarse grains of home.

She closed her eyes and listened to the swish swish of the waves against the shore. She liked the peace of the islands. No noisy roar of traffic, none of the fumes that were part and parcel of life in a very cosmopolitan city like Abu Dhabi. Pity about the wind, she thought as she drifted indolently along. The sun was hot on her arms; in another few months it would be unbearable. This was a lovely time of the year in the Gulf and she was glad Carrie was coming out when the weather would still be tolerable.

The others, apart from Chantal, who sat like a sphinx under the flapping canopy, joined them a while later and they chatted and joked as they swam. Pierre made sure not to swim out of his depth or get his hair wet. Shauna could see that it had been well gelled down after the windblasting it had got on the trip out. He would look so much better if he got his hair cut short and just gave in to his baldness.

'That's a very pretty swimsuit,' he told her admiringly as he circled round her. *Almost like a shark*, she thought, annoyed. Pierre had a lascivious way of looking at her that made her feel uncomfortable. 'He's French. He flirts,' Greg had said dismissively when she'd complained about it. He hadn't even been the slightest bit jealous, she'd thought, miffed.

'Thank you, Pierre. Chantal not coming in?' She kept her tone light.

He shook his head. 'She hates the water.'

'Why did she come?' Shauna asked.

He gave a low chuckle. 'Do you think she would let me come alone with all you beautiful women?' He waved his hand expansively, his gold Rolex watch glittering in the sunlight.

As if you'd have a chance with any of us, you prat, Shauna thought derisively but she smiled sweetly and said 'Wise woman' before swimming out deeper where he wouldn't venture. She'd done enough brown-nosing.

'Was the lech trying it on with you?' Jenna joined her and they swam together parallel to the shore.

'Yeah. It's really irritating. He's pathetic, isn't he? And I hate myself for pandering to him. I feel like telling him to get lost. Could you imagine Greg's face if I said that?' She scowled.

'I know. It's so false out here sometimes, isn't it? With everybody trying to impress somebody. And the "position" or the "big contract" the most important thing. Brett and I are getting sick of it, to be honest. And there's the political stuff too. It's got a lot more tense out here. It's going to get worse. Americans aren't the most popular expats,' she said wryly.

'Don't say that,' Shauna protested.

'It's true, unfortunately, and facts have to be faced. If he doesn't get the Dubai job we think we might head home,' she confided.

Shauna's heart sank. 'Oh no!' She stopped swimming and began to tread water. 'Are you serious?'

'Yup. Carly's due to start school and we have to think of what we want for her. I'd like her to have more stability. If we get Dubai it's going to be our last move, then we're definitely going back home. If we don't get it, we're thinking of going back home later this year.'

'Oh, no. Don't do that. I'd really miss you, Jenna.' Shauna couldn't hide her dismay. 'I can be myself with you. We think the same. We can have a joke about some of those dreadful women we meet on the circuit. Don't go,' she urged. 'Don't leave me to Chantal and Pierre's tender mercies.'

'I didn't think you were going to stay out here this long,' Jenna remarked as they turned and began to swim back towards the shore.

'Greg loves it. I don't think he'll ever settle down at home. We're going to try for a baby in the summer. At least if I get pregnant and have another child, I'll feel we're more of a family,' Shauna told her.

'That's great, honey. I know you're longing for another baby. I hope it all works out,' Jenna said warmly.

'Thanks. Me too. Poor Chloe will be devastated if Carly leaves.' Shauna sighed.

'She'll make new friends at school,' Jenna said comfortingly. 'Anyway, we might all be going to Dubai so let's not worry about it until it happens. We'd better go in and get the lunch. I don't expect her ladyship will have got it all ready for us, or even set the table.'

They waded in to the shore and Shauna grimaced as the fine sand whipped around her wet legs. It was almost a mini-sandstorm, she thought crossly as she dried herself off and wrapped a sarong round her waist.

215

Although on the surface the lunch was a jolly affair and Shauna chatted and laughed with the others she was dismayed by her friend's news.

That was the problem with life out here, she thought glumly as she sipped a white wine spritzer and nibbled on a stuffed mushroom that Chantal had prepared. Friendships never lasted. People moved on. If they went to Dubai she was going to have to start all over again making a new circle of friends. So would poor Chloe. Was it worth it? she wondered, listening to the gay, superficial chat around the table.

They began to pack up two hours later, the wind having increased as the afternoon progressed. 'I'm going to go with Chloe in Brett and Jenna's boat,' she told Pierre. 'Carly's having a sleepover in our house.' She was damned if she was going to put up with another endurance test on the way home.

'Oh! But I so enjoy driving you in my boat.' Pierre made a face.

'I know, Pierre, but you know the way it is with children. Thank you for a lovely day.' She turned to Chantal and kissed her on the cheek.

'You're welcome. You enjoyed your swim, I noticed,' the other woman said tightly.

Oh, get a life; I wouldn't look at Pierre if he were the last man on earth, she groaned silently. *You're welcome to him.*

'Yes, I had fun with the children,' she said gaily. 'See you at the ballet next week. Say goodbye, Chloe,' she instructed her daughter, relieved that the day was almost over.

'I'm going to take everyone to dinner. Do you want to join us later?' Greg murmured. 'We should repay Pierre and Chantal's hospitality for taking us out on his boat.'

'No, Greg. I promised the girls a sleepover.' She was glad of the excuse.

'Filomena can babysit,' he retorted. 'Come on, Shauna.'

'Not tonight, Greg. I want to spend time with Chloe,' she said pointedly.

'It might be good for—'

'No, Greg. I spent the day with your colleagues. I'm spending the night with our daughter,' she hissed and didn't care if he was annoyed.

As she watched the two little girls asleep in Chloe's bedroom that night she knew that the time was going to come when her loyalties would be divided over what was right for Chloe and what was right for Greg. Jenna and Brett had already made their decisions in that regard for their daughter. They were united about putting Carly first. They had their priorities right.

Carrie never had divided loyalties with Dan and the kids; they all seemed to pull together. But then, according to Greg, they had a boring life. Certainly, compared to theirs, that was a pertinent comment. But as regards family unity and stability, Carrie and Dan had what it took. Would her husband's priority always be work? she wondered. It was something she didn't care to dwell on because she was afraid of what the answer might be.

It would be interesting to see what her sister thought of the lifestyle out here, she thought wryly as she closed the door gently on the sleeping children. She was looking forward immensely to Carrie's visit. It would be very different from having that lazy lump Della to stay. Della expected to be entertained and wined and dined. She'd attempted to treat Filomena like a servant. She'd even left her used bath towels lying on the floor for Filomena to pick up until Shauna had seen Filomena doing it and put a stop to it there and then.

'Right, that's it, Filomena. You are not to so much as make their bed or hoover that room until they're gone,' Shauna had instructed grimly on the fifth day of their first visit.

'The maid never cleaned our room today,' Della had complained later that evening, after a day at the club.

'I told her to leave it. That's not part of her duties; she has enough to be doing,' Shauna said coolly. 'This isn't a hotel,' she'd added caustically, not that it made any impact on Della, who was immune to such sarcasms.

She was dying to tell Carrie all about her trials and tribulations with her sister-in-law. They'd have a laugh together, she thought, cheering up. She'd send her an email to fill her in on the day's events and then she'd have a nice long soak in the bath with a glass of wine.

Greg wouldn't be home too late, as he had to get up for work in the morning. He was driving to Al Ain so it would be an early start. She'd like to be asleep before he got home. She didn't want an earbashing about not going out to dinner.

22

'SHAUNA, WE'VE LOADS OF FOOD. WE'LL BE TAKING THEM OUT TO eat, and we can shop every day. Will you stop panicking,' Greg said irritably as he pushed a laden trolley round the huge Co-op.

'Don't forget there's five of them coming. Now, do you think we've enough cereal? I wonder is there anything in particular that they like? I should have checked with Carrie.' Shauna stood in front of the cereals, pondering.

Greg had had enough. 'Shauna, we're going. I've to meet Amir Saeedi for coffee to discuss the revisions on the plans for the Buraimi Oasis project and I don't want to be late.' He pushed the trolley purposefully towards the checkout. He knew Shauna wasn't impressed that he'd arranged to meet Amir on his day off, but it was the only time that suited them both as his colleague was heading off to New York for a week of meetings. Life didn't stop just because the bloody Waltons were coming, he thought grumpily as he began unloading the shopping onto the belt, having had to queue behind a very slow, elderly lady.

'Right, see you later,' he said twenty minutes later, after he had packed the shopping into the boot of Shauna's car.

''Bye,' she said in a none-too-friendly tone and he scowled as he strode to his own car. She never went to such trouble when *his* family was coming, he thought sourly as he nosed out into the traffic. He liked Carrie and Dan and the kids, but Shauna was always rubbing his nose in it, saying how they were the perfect family, and how she would like to have a new baby to make their family more like the Morgans. He wasn't convinced that Chloe would like a new baby as much as Shauna seemed to think she would. He remembered well how neglected and put out he'd felt when Della had been born. He'd been the one everyone had made a fuss of. The one his parents had doted on. Then *she* had arrived. In the blink of an eye, as far as Greg had been concerned, his position had been usurped by the squawking intruder, never to be regained.

After Della was born life revolved round her and her whims and fancies. And so it had been into adulthood. Even to this day she was still 'the queen', expecting everyone to run around after her. As far as Greg was concerned he was doing Chloe a *favour* by not exposing her to the hurt, trauma and jealousy that a new baby in the family could cause, especially when a child has been the centre of attention for so long.

The traffic was heavy and slow-moving on Zayed Street due to an accident, and he inched along towards the Emirates Plaza where he was meeting Amir.

He was annoyed to see his colleague there before him, seated sipping coffee in the foyer. Greg liked arriving first at hotel meetings; it always gave him that feeling of being in control. He took a deep breath, strode forward and held out his hand, beaming. It could be worse, he could be at home unpacking the shopping, he thought with a flash of humour as he sat down opposite the other man and waved his hand to attract the attention of a waiter.

Hi Carrie

Well I've just unpacked the shopping and the fridge is bursting, so you won't starve!! Chloe is in a tizzy of excitement. When we put the extra fold-up bed into her room she informed me that she wanted to sleep on it and that Davey could have her bed. I didn't even go there. They can sort it out among themselves. Don't forget the King crisps. I'm dying for a packet. And the Club Milks. Yum! Oh what a feast I'm going to have! And bring some newspapers and magazines so I catch up with what's going on at home.

Weather is gorgeous. The high seventies, low eighties, but it hasn't been too humid. Don't forget to come to the glass partition so that I can throw your visa over to you before you go to the passport control. Switch on your mobile as soon as you get into Arrivals and ring me. I'm dying to see you. I can't think when I've been so excited. I'm just as bad as Chloe!!!!!

Lots and lots of love,
    S xxx

'I can't believe I drove down without the bag of bits and pieces I'd bought for Chloe and Shauna and Greg.' Della tutted with feigned disgust. Carrie wasn't fooled. She knew full well that Della hadn't bought anything and was just visiting to be fed and entertained. Well she'd picked the wrong day for it, Carrie thought, highly annoyed.

'That's a shame,' she said coolly. 'Listen, Della, I've cleared out the fridge, seeing as we're going for two weeks, so will you come down to Seashells for a bowl of soup? And then I'll have to love you and leave you because I've to do a supermarket shop for Dad and get a thousand and one other bits and pieces. You know

221

yourself what its like when you're going away en masse,' she added pointedly, ushering Della and Ashley out the door.

Hannah held her tightly by the hand. She didn't like Ashley. He was rough and aggressive, always demanding attention. Della's little son was thoroughly spoilt and she rarely chastised him.

'Oh, I thought we'd have time for a chat and catch-up.' Della made a moue of disappointment.

'We will, in the café,' Carrie said airily as she fastened the seat belt on Hannah's booster seat. 'Just follow me.'

It was so typical of Della to arrive unannounced, she thought crossly as she drove out onto the road. Carrie had phoned Shauna's sister-in-law three weeks before to say that they were going to Abu Dhabi, if she wanted to send anything out. Della had said that she'd get back to her. When Carrie hadn't heard from her, she hadn't made any attempts to contact the other woman, figuring that once was enough to tell her of their impending trip. She hadn't bargained on Della's arriving the day before they were leaving. And then arriving empty-handed, she thought in disgust. Imagine *pretending* to forget her gifts. With anyone else she would have accepted the excuse, but with Della she knew full well what lay behind it. Now she was going to have to waste a good hour of her precious time entertaining her, but at least she was out of the house. That was half the battle with Della, who could spend a full hour saying goodbye.

Thank God she'd brought Davey and Olivia to get their hair cut after school yesterday and hadn't left it to the last minute. She was only going to spend the shortest time she could get away with lunching with Della, she decided. It would take her an hour at least to do her father's shopping and unpack it. She'd just be home in time for the kids to get out of school.

Fortunately it was just before the lunchtime rush and they got a window table for four. Carrie sorted Hannah in her high chair.

Ashley insisted on sitting in a big chair at the table even though his head hardly came up over the top of it.

'I might have the seafood cocktail for starters. I wonder is the meat organic? I haven't had steak for ages,' Della said brightly. 'Too much red meat is bad for you.

'I won't have time for starters,' Carrie murmured. 'I'll just have the chicken and mushroom vol-au-vent, but you go ahead.' Typical of Della to go for the most expensive dishes on the menu. Well, if she thought Carrie was treating her to lunch today she had another think coming, for her cheek.

'Oh, dear, that's a shame. I'll have one anyway.' Della smiled at the waitress who'd come to take their order. 'The seafood cocktail and the steak well done with a side salad and baked potato,' she said, and raised an eyebrow at Carrie.

'Vol-au-vent and chips for me, and could I have a very small portion of chicken, mashed potatoes, broccoli and gravy for Hannah? And you can bring ours with Della's starter. I don't have a lot of time.' She smiled at Gina, the waitress, whom she knew well.

'Sure, Carrie. No problem. Are you up to your eyes getting ready to go?'

'You can say that again.' Carrie laughed.

'And for the little lad?' Gina turned to Della.

'Are your vegetables organic?' Della enquired.

'They are,' Gina assured her.

'Hmm. Could I have a small dish of vegetables and a slice of chicken breast? Is it corn fed?'

'Indeed.' Gina's smile never wavered but Carrie could detect a certain hardness in the eyes. Gina was a very no-nonsense type, and well used to dealing with pretentious, disagreeable customers. Della was so irritating. Who did she think she was impressing?

'Now you simply must go to the souk to buy the spices;

223

they're out of this world. Would you bring me back some cardamom, cumin and cinnamon? I'll fix you up when you get home.' Della sat back in her chair and fixed Carrie with her sly brown eyes once their order had been taken. 'And would you ask Shauna to get me a couple of yards of that gorgeous raw silk I got at Christmas? I'm going to get another jacket with long sleeves made up. I bought the red at Christmas; tell her I'd like it in the green and I'll fix her up when she comes home for the summer.'

'Sure.' Carrie made a mental note to say no such thing to Shauna. She too could conveniently forget things when she had to.

Ashley wriggled off his chair and began to wander around. The café had begun to fill up with the lunchtime trade. Della ignored him as he weaved in and out between the tables pretending to be an aeroplane.

'Maybe he should sit down,' Carrie suggested grimly.

'Oh, he's got oodles of energy. I never know what to do with him. I should have left him in the crèche but it's just got so expensive lately,' Della complained.

Ashley careered into Gina, who was carrying a bowl of soup to a table.

'Della, you'd want to get him. Gina could have spilt the hot soup on him,' Carrie exclaimed exasperatedly.

'Ah he's grand,' Della said dismissively. 'Now you have to go and spend a night camping in the desert. We did it and the stars were stunning. And you simply must go snorkelling. And you've got to try the Chinese restaurant in the Sheraton. We go there every time. It's magnificent,' she gushed, clearly relishing rubbing Carrie's nose in it that she had been out to the Gulf so many times.

'Excuse me.' Gina arrived at their table with a firm hand round Ashley's wrist. 'This young man needs to sit down or he's going to get hurt. I'll get you a high chair for him.' Her tone brooked no argument.

'Be a good boy,' Della said, annoyed. A minute later, Gina arrived with a high chair.

'There you go,' she said firmly. 'Your meal will be ready in a few minutes.'

'No, *no*. NO!' screamed Ashley, kicking wildly as his mother dumped him in the high chair. He banged his fists on the plastic top and squealed and howled until everyone in the little café was looking in their direction. Carrie could feel a hot sweat rising as Della sat there ignoring the carry-on.

'Stop that, Ashley,' she said crossly, mortified.

'Noooooo,' the toddler yelled, and spat at her.

Carrie's hand itched. If one of hers had done that they would have been mighty sorry. Della simply threw her eyes up to heaven. *She's something else. No wonder the child is the way he is*, Carrie thought furiously.

Hannah studied him intently. 'Bold, Mameee,' she announced loudly. Ashley leaned across and pulled her hair. Hannah howled in pained dismay.

'Della, sort him out,' Carrie snapped, civility out the window. She lifted Hannah onto her lap as Gina arrived with their food.

'Say sorry, Ashley,' Della said irritably as Gina placed her seafood cocktail in front of her and a small dish of food in front of Ashley, who promptly threw a carrot at her.

Another waitress had placed Carrie's and Hannah's meals in front of them and Carrie began to feed Hannah on her lap, determined to scarper as soon as she possibly could.

'This is delicious,' Della exclaimed as Ashley hurled bits of his food all over their table.

'They do nice food here,' Carrie remarked, wishing heartily that she was on her own with Hannah.

225

'You know you really should go for the salad option, Carrie. Chips are laden with fats. Terribly bad for your cholesterol,' Della lectured, forking some healthy lettuce into her big gob.

Oh, shut up, Carrie longed to say but she didn't have the energy to argue, so she merely nodded and pronged a chip with her fork. Once her daughter had finished her dinner, she shoved a few forkfuls of vol-au-vent into her mouth, her appetite non-existent thanks to her lunch companions.

Della had been served her steak and was thoroughly enjoying it. Ashley was still whinging and misbehaving and all Carrie wanted was to get out as quickly as she could. She rooted in her bag for a tissue and wiped Hannah's mouth. Then she pulled a ten and a five euro note out of her purse, which covered her and Hannah's meals, with enough left over for a tip, and placed it in front of an astonished Della.

'Here you go, Della, that takes care of our lunch. Sorry I can't stay for coffee, but I'm on a very tight timescale. I'll tell them all you were asking for them. Safe journey home,' she said briskly, wrapping Hannah up warmly in her coat and hat.

'Well, I'd have thought that you at least have time to finish your meal and have a cup of coffee.' Della was clearly put out.

'You should have let me know earlier that you intended to come down and I could have arranged something. But you know yourself what it's like when you're going away on holiday. Enjoy the rest of your meal. See you.'

She took Hannah by the hand and hurried out of the restaurant, half afraid that Della and the brat would want to come shopping with her. She had rampant indigestion from eating too fast but at least she hadn't been stung for the whole meal. Della was such a cool customer. Carrie knew that she'd expected her to pay for their lunch. Well, that would give her something to think about. She smiled as she lifted Hannah into

226

her car seat. Shauna would have a good laugh when she heard that Carrie had succeeded in pulling a fast one on her sister-in-law.

Della paid for her lunch with bad grace and bundled Ashley out the door of the café despite his protests. Her day had not gone as planned. Carrie had been brusque, rude almost, which was unusual for her. Lunch had not been relaxed. She'd been looking forward to her trip to Whiteshells Bay and being entertained by Carrie. But it hadn't turned out like that.

She could go for a walk on the beach with Ashley, she supposed, seeing as Kathryn was going to a friend's house after school, but it wasn't much fun going on her own. She did a lot of things on her own, she thought forlornly as she looked out at the glistening sea that whooshed gently backwards and forwards along the shore. It struck her that she hadn't what she would call 'real friends'. She mostly had acquaintances whom she met through her work in the shop, or in her yoga class, or at the alternative medicine workshops that she attended. She wished she had a sister to share her life with. Carrie and Shauna were so lucky to have each other. It wasn't the same with a brother. Greg wasn't really interested, and if she was absolutely honest, neither was her husband. At heart Eddie Keegan was a lazy slob who was happy enough having his few pints and getting a ride every weekend. She'd married him so that she wouldn't be left on the shelf and because there was no-one else on her horizon.

Not that she'd admit that to a sinner, Della thought disconsolately as she took her son by the hand and walked down the stone steps that led to the beach. Pride and appearances were everything. She'd never let on to anyone that her life was less than perfect. That was one little secret that Madams Shauna and Carrie would never know. Snooty cows, always making her feel excluded, she thought angrily, trying to swallow the lump in her throat and banish the sudden loneliness that unexpectedly threatened to overwhelm her.

Noel sat with Davey on one side and Olivia on the other and cut up a slice of roast beef. Carrie had cooked his favourite dinner for him: roast beef, roast potatoes, Yorkshire pudding and mushy peas. It always reminded him of Sunday lunch when Anna was alive. He'd been about to say that he would miss them but had stopped in time. After Dan's little lecture he was being very careful about what he said to Carrie.

'Guess what, Grandpa?' Olivia whispered, 'Mam made your favourite sweet. Rhubarb crumble and ice cream and cream.'

Noel smiled at her and felt a wave of affection for his eldest granddaughter. She could never keep a secret from when she was a toddler. 'That was very kind of her. And this is a lovely dinner.' He smiled at his granddaughter. Olivia had a soft heart just like her mother, he realized, wondering why he was noticing these things for the first time. Was it because they were all going away and leaving him on his own that he was beginning to appreciate them a little more? he thought with a dart of guilt.

It was a delicious meal but he wasn't very hungry. He was dreading their going, but of course he couldn't say so. He sighed deeply. When Carrie had come to the house with his dinner the day Dan had chastised him he'd apologized for upsetting her.

'That's OK, Dad. It's only for two weeks. It will fly by,' she'd said quietly.

'I know it will and of course I really want you to enjoy yourself. You deserve it,' he'd assured her.

'Well, I'll enjoy it better if I know that you're not sitting here moping, waiting for us to come home,' Carrie said, but her tone was kind and he knew that she didn't mean it as a rebuke.

'Actually, I'm going bowling with Mrs O'Neill. She's roped me in to their bowling group. She said they needed more men,' he told her sheepishly.

'Dad, that's great news.' She'd been delighted for him. Noel hadn't been as enthusiastic. He wasn't sure if bowling would be his 'thing', as young people said. Mrs O'Neill had been at him for ages to join the club. It would give him some exercise instead of wearing his knees out praying, she'd said with a glint in her eye, and he'd had to laugh.

To his surprise he'd enjoyed himself once he'd got used to making a fool of himself as he learned how to roll the ball properly. 'It's all in the flick of the wrist,' his neighbour informed him as she knocked the skittles for six.

He now went bowling two afternoons a week. It was enjoyable to be in the company of his peers. The conversations were interesting. Some of the men were widowers like him and he'd begun to realize from listening to their chat that he was extremely lucky the way Carrie and Dan took care of him and supported him. One rotund chap a little older than himself confided that he lived on tinned steak and kidney pie and Smash. His children rarely came to visit; and he'd spent Christmas alone. Noel felt so sorry for him that he'd invited him to accompany him to Malone's for lunch one day when Carrie was away. The fellow ought to eat properly a couple of times a week at least, and Dan had said the food in Malone's was good.

At least he'd have his bowling and his lunch appointment to keep him occupied while he was on his own, he comforted himself, lost in thought.

'Eat up there, Dad,' Carrie urged, noticing that he hadn't cleared his plate.

'You gave me a lot,' he protested.

'That's to keep you going until we get back, Grandpa,' Davey teased. 'You'll be sure to feed my fish, won't you?'

'Indeed I will, Davey. Don't worry your head about them. They'll get the best of attention,' his grandfather assured him. 'Now take plenty of photos for me. I'll be very interested to hear all about your holiday.'

'I'm going to take *loads*, Grandpa. I've got three films. And we're bringing the video as well so we'll have a video and photo night when we come home,' Davey said earnestly. 'How is your bowling league going?'

'Well, would you believe, we were playing St Mel's on Tuesday and I managed to win a few points for the team and we won,' Noel said proudly.

'Deadly, Grandpa,' Davey enthused, much to his grandfather's delight. His grandson was a great little chap, he thought with uncharacteristic pride.

Dan arrived home just as Carrie was clearing away the dinner plates, and took his place at the table. 'Sorry I'm late. Did you enjoy your special dinner, Mr Mac?' he asked cheerfully.

One thing about his son-in-law, he didn't hold things against you, Noel reflected. Dan had treated him just as he normally did since their recent early-morning conversation. 'It was very tasty and much appreciated. And now I'd like to show my appreciation,' he said, clearing his throat awkwardly. He reached into his jacket pocket and took out four envelopes, one marked 'Carrie and Dan' and the other three each with one of the children's names on it. He handed them round. 'Open them,' he urged.

'Oh my *God*, Grandpa!' Olivia exclaimed dramatically, as five notes fluttered out of her envelope. 'That's five tens in paper money. I'm *really* rich.' She had recently made the discovery that paper money was much better than coins.

'Oh, Dad!' Carrie exclaimed as she opened theirs and saw four fifty euro notes. 'That's far too much.'

'Mam, look. I got the same as Olivia.' Davey waved his around exuberantly. Such riches. He couldn't wait for his holidays. His other grandparents had given him cash as well and he'd been saving hard. He was the richest boy in his class at the moment. Even Willie O'Shea whose dad was a doctor, and who was usually loaded with money, hadn't as much as Davey had right now.

'Dad, really,' Carrie protested. 'There's no need to—'

Noel held up his hand. 'Stop. Carrie, this is going to be the holiday of a lifetime for you, Dan and the children and I'd like to make my contribution towards it.' He cleared his throat again. 'I'd like to take this opportunity to say how much I appreciate . . . umm . . . how much I appreciate all your . . . er . . . love and kindness.' He flushed a deep beetroot red, unused to such speeches.

'Oh, Dad.' Carrie had tears in her eyes. 'We're glad to have you with us.'

'You're part of our family, Mr Mac.' Dan patted him kindly on the shoulder.

'You're our Grandpa,' Davey said stoutly, hugging his grand-father. Noel hugged him back awkwardly. He had a strange feeling in his heart. An emotion he wasn't used to. He felt he could almost cry, he thought in panic. Hannah toddled over to him and gave him one of her dollies.

'Thank you, pet,' he managed, glad when they all laughed and the tension was broken.

'We've another surprise for you,' Olivia said smugly. 'Haven't we, Mam?'

'We sure have,' Carrie agreed. She went over to one of her cupboards and took out a plate on which reposed a large iced chocolate cake, decorated with Smarties and a small almond paste nest with little sweet eggs in it. 'It's your Easter cake,' she said brightly and he instantly realized that she still felt guilty about going away on holiday. And the only reason she felt guilty was because he'd made her feel it with his martyr act, he acknowledged, in a rare moment of self-awareness. Carrie didn't deserve that, he admitted, feeling a sudden surge of shame.

'Oh my goodness, I can't possibly wait until Easter Sunday to eat this, and I'll certainly need some help,' he exclaimed, hastily brushing away his very uncomfortable feelings. His grand-children reacted with delight.

'Yippee!' yelled Davey who *adored* chocolate cake.

'I just knew you'd say that, Grandpa,' Olivia assured him. 'Can I have a piece of the nest?'

'Well, just a small bit, now,' warned Carrie. 'Don't forget we're going very early in the morning and we don't want any sore tummies.'

'Just a small slice each then, Carrie,' Noel urged, winking at Davey and wishing that he didn't feel so ashamed. It was a feeling he wasn't used to. It was *most* uncomfortable.

'I think we should put a candle on it and sing "For He's a Jolly Good Fellow" to Grandpa,' Olivia suggested, always ready for a bit of theatre.

'Terrific idea,' Dan agreed. 'Candle please, wife.'

'Certainly, husband.' She smiled, loving him for the way he always did his best to make Noel feel cherished and welcome. She placed the candle in the centre of the cake and lit it and they all sang loudly and lustily, much to Noel's embarrassment.

After they'd had a cup of tea and a slice of the scrumptious cake, Noel reluctantly stood up and put his coat on. 'I should be off. You've things to do and you need to get to bed early. Will you give this envelope to Chloe for me and wish her a happy

Easter? And I got a little bottle of perfume for Shauna. I hope she likes it. I asked Mrs O'Neill's advice.' He handed Carrie another envelope and a small package.

'I will of course, Dad. Say goodnight to Grandpa, everyone, and wish him a happy Easter and thank him for all that money,' Carrie said to the children. They crowded round him, hugging him and kissing him.

'Gank you.' Hannah hugged his leg and he bent down and picked her up.

'Will you give your old grandpa a curl?' he asked, smiling at her upturned little face, which was just now eager for fun.

She loved that game and tugged at one of her copper curls and patted his head with her palm. 'There, Gankgank,' she said kindly, chuckling as he gave her one back.

'She's a grand little girl,' he said to Carrie, his eyes bright with emotion.

'See you soon and take care of yourself.' Dan held out his hand and gripped Noel's in a firm handshake.

'Have a good holiday, Dan,' Noel said sincerely, handing Hannah over to him.

'I will.' His son-in-law smiled back at him and Noel realized yet again what a solid, kind man his daughter had married. Dan was not the sort of man who would make someone feel guilty, he thought, another wave of shame washing over him.

'I'll walk you to the car, Dad,' Carrie murmured, leading the way to the hall and opening the front door.

It was a balmy spring evening. Wisps of cloud were tinted pink and gold and the trees sported their new spring coats as buds of white and pink blossoms burst out effervescently. The breeze off the sea was only slightly chilly and there was definitely the merest hint of the summer to come in the air.

'I'll phone you tomorrow when we land in Schiphol and I'll

ring you from Shauna's when we arrive. And we'll keep in touch,' she assured him.

'I appreciate that, Carrie, but don't be worrying about me, I'll be grand. Enjoy your holiday and we'll have a good night when you get back and you can tell me all about it,' he said heartily, hating having to say goodbye to her.

'Just be sure to defrost your dinners the night before and make certain they're thoroughly heated,' she instructed.

'I will and . . . er . . . thank you.' His grey eyes met hers and a flash of affection passed between them. For the first time in his life he held out his arms and drew her to him in a hug.

They held each other tightly for a brief moment and he patted her back awkwardly as he felt her tears against his cheeks. 'We'll be home before you know it,' she gulped, trying not to cry.

'I know that. Have a good time now,' he murmured, before drawing away from her and getting into the car. She stood waving forlornly and he rolled down his window and waved back at her, his eyes blurry.

It was a miracle that he got home without having an accident, he thought as he drove into his drive, stricken with such un-expected emotions. The last time he'd felt this lonely was when Anna had died.

He locked the car and was about to go into his house when Mrs O'Neill called to him.

Not now, he thought in desperation, but he couldn't ignore the woman. He walked slowly over to the small wall that divided their properties.

'Are you all right, Noel?' She looked at him in concern, noting his watery eyes.

He swallowed hard. 'Just saying goodbye to Carrie,' he mumbled.

Comprehension dawned. 'Ah yes, but sure it's only two weeks

and I'll keep an eye on you,' she said reassuringly, her bright blue eyes kind and concerned. It was the last straw. Tears welled up in Noel's eyes and he gave a strangled little sob.

'Sorry, sorry,' he muttered, mortified, and turned away.

'Ah you poor old craythur,' Mrs O'Neill exclaimed. 'Come in to me this minute and we'll have a cup of tea. I know *exactly* what you're going through. I go through it every time mine come home from abroad and have to go away again.'

'I don't want to put you to trouble,' Noel sniffled.

'What are you talking about, trouble? Aren't you me next-door neighbour and haven't we been through a lot down the years? Come in now and get it off your chest and you'll feel the better of it,' she urged.

And somehow, knowing that Mrs O'Neill understood what it was like to be lonely helped him enormously and it ceased to bother him that he'd made a show of himself crying in front of her. He followed her into her neat little kitchen and sat at her kitchen table and didn't feel as alone as he'd feared he'd be.

As for the feelings of guilt and shame, he wouldn't think about them any more. It was too uncomfortable. He could deal with feelings of loneliness better and besides, it felt good to have Mrs O'Neill feeling sorry for him. No-one else did. He couldn't help the feelings of self-pity that washed over him. His life was difficult enough. There was no point in being too hard on himself, he decided as he took the cup of hot, sweet tea from his neighbour and bit into one of her delicious cherry buns.

23

'I CAN'T BELIEVE YOU'RE FINALLY HERE. I'M *SO* EXCITED.' SHAUNA hugged the daylights out of Carrie, who had tears in her eyes as she hugged her sister back tightly. 'Oh my God, look at the size of Hannah. Oh, darling, aren't you beautiful?' She knelt down to the toddler who was yawning her head off in her buggy. 'And Davey and Olivia. Quick! Give me a hug.'

'Come on, Shauna, let's get these poor travellers home,' Greg suggested as his wife was enveloped in a flurry of hugs.

'We brought you the King crisps and Club Milks and lots of other treats,' Olivia informed her aunt breathlessly, surfacing from her bear hug.

'And some Barry's tea bags,' Davey added.

'*Barry's tea bags!* Did you hear that, Greg? Let's go home and put on the kettle.' Shauna laughed, thrilled to be surrounded by her beloved family.

'That sounds like a great idea to me.' Dan angled the laden trolley towards the exit.

'It's very warm, isn't it?' Carrie exclaimed as they emerged into the humid, starry darkness and the warm night air enveloped them.

'I thought it was a little cool, actually,' Shauna remarked. She was wearing a light cardigan over her sundress.

Carrie looked at her, amazed. 'You really have acclimatized, haven't you? It's *warm*, Shauna.'

'We've got AC in the car,' Greg said, leading them over to a large SUV.

Dan whistled. 'Nice going, Greg. A Merc jeep. Bet it's a dream to drive.'

'Does the biz all right. Great road holding,' Greg agreed.

'Deadly.' Davey gazed at the huge car with undisguised admiration.

'You like it, Davey?' Greg was delighted with their reactions.

'Dad, can we get one?' Davey asked eagerly.

'Sure.' Dan laughed, winking at Carrie.

They settled themselves in for the trip through the desert out to the island city. 'Fabulous road, isn't it,' Carrie enthused as they drove under the inky, starry skies along the straight highway that led to Abu Dhabi.

'Tell us all the news. How's Dad?' Shauna asked eagerly. 'He got used to the idea of you coming?'

'Yeah.' Carrie nodded as she snuggled Hannah in close to her. 'He actually came round very well, believe it or not. I've got an Easter present for you.'

Shauna's eyes widened. 'Really!' she exclaimed. 'I certainly wasn't expecting that.'

'I was slightly gobsmacked myself. He gave us all a load of cash and I've got an envelope for Chloe as well. There's fifty euros in it for her.'

Shauna gave a low whistle. 'Are you serious? What's going on? Is he OK?' she asked, a note of concern in her voice.

'I think he's fine. Maybe he's starting to mellow a bit. He's taken up bowling,' Carrie informed her.

'So you were saying in your emails. Well done Mrs O'Neill.'

'You can say that again,' Carrie agreed. 'She's a great neighbour.

I'll give him a ring when we get in if that's OK. I told him I would.'

'Fine. I'd like to thank him for the gifts.' Shauna smiled at her sister as they raced along the desert highway and the lights of the city began to sparkle more brightly against the dark velvet sky, the outlines of the highrises silhouetted against the horizon.

'It's a big city, isn't it?' Dan observed as they reached the suburbs that lined the airport road, passing beautiful mosaic-decorated mosques along the route.

'I love their roundabouts. They're works of art, aren't they?' Carrie enthused as they drove past the huge roundabout at Zayed the Second Street.

'That's the Cultural Foundation over there.' Shauna pointed out an impressive building to the left of them. 'We'll be going there one evening. We're right in the centre now. This is Sheikh Hamdan Bin Mohammed Street that we're crossing and we're coming to Sheikh Khalifa Bin Zayed Street,' she explained to Davey, who was fascinated.

'Quite a mouthful,' Carrie observed as they emerged onto the Corniche road.

'You'd just say Khalifa Street or Hamdan Street. You wouldn't have to say the whole palaver.' Shauna laughed as she pointed out a magnificent illuminated fountain. 'This is called the Volcano Fountain. Isn't it something else? It's the most spectacular fountain in the city. See the way it gushes out.'

Olivia and Davey, eyes on stalks, were oohing and aahing at the splendid illuminated showpiece that was a great focal point in the city.

'This is stunning. Aren't the gardens magnificent? I can't believe how green the city is.' Carrie's head was on a swivel.

'Sheikh Zayed, the ruler of Abu Dhabi at the time, wanted to

238

have beautiful gardens all over the city. It was very important to him and you'll see in the morning just how terrifically he succeeded. The city is so built up; the gardens really enhance it and take the harshness out of it. And don't forget it's built out of the desert,' Shauna clarified, feeling very proprietorial and proud of her adopted city.

'Oh, Dad, look. Look at the boat,' Davey exclaimed, pointing out to sea at a boat lit up as brightly as a Christmas tree.

'That's a dhow,' Greg explained. 'We're going to take you on a trip in one.'

'Did you hear that, Dad?' Davey was jiggling with excitement.

'And we're going to go out to the islands for a picnic on one of my friends' speedboats,' Greg assured him as he swung down to the underground car park below the apartment block.

'Isn't it great that you've got a view of the sea?' Carrie exclaimed.

'Yeah, we were very lucky. Only two of the company apartments have sea views and we got one of them. The balcony from the lounge is a wraparound and the end bit of it overlooks the sea. They used to have an apartment block out on the airport road but they relocated to this more modern block a year before we came out, so we were dead lucky. Lots of my friends have apartments that don't have great views. Friends of ours that you'll like have invited us to a party next week and they have a villa with a garden. It's gorgeous. Private houses with gardens are like gold dust out here.'

'I'd say so,' Carrie said, trying to imagine herself with three children and no garden to play in. She took her gardens so much for granted. Her back garden was like an extra room in their house.

Carrie, Shauna and the children travelled up first in the silent lift, and Carrie raised an eyebrow when it opened on to a small, marble-floored, mirrored landing, off which there were only two front doors.

'Nice and private, isn't it?' she remarked.

'Yep. We share the landing with a very quiet couple, the Mansours. She's a nurse and he's an IT specialist,' Shauna told her as Filomena opened the door of the apartment to welcome the visitors.

'You know Filomena. I'd be lost without her,' Shauna said, smiling at her au pair.

'Thank you, ma'am,' Filomena said shyly, but Shauna knew she was pleased.

'Hi, Filomena,' Carrie said warmly. 'Nice to see you again.'

'Is this your house?' Olivia asked, peering into the hall.

'It's called an apartment. Come in, everyone,' Shauna invited and stood back to enjoy Carrie's reaction to her home.

'It's gorgeous,' breathed Carrie as she wandered along the hall and into the lounge. 'Where did you get the furniture, or did it come furnished?'

'The leather suite was here but the coffee table and the sideboards are antiques I've picked up. The Gulf's a great place for well crafted, unusual pieces. If you see anything you like we could get it and when someone's going home with a shipment I'll ask them to bring your piece with them. We do that all the time out here,' Shauna explained as she led them to the guest bedroom.

Carrie gazed round at the pale mint green and white room with the big bed dressed in green and gold. White wicker furniture and white muslin curtains lent an airy, tropical feel to the room. Shauna had turned on the air conditioning so it felt nice and cool. A cot stood beside the bed for Hannah, who gazed at her mother and said longingly, 'Bottle, Mamee.'

'Let's get this baba to bed,' Carrie suggested. 'What time is it here?'

'About one fifteen,' Shauna said ruefully. 'And Greg's got work in the morning. Our weekend is Thursday afternoon and Friday, generally. So even though tomorrow's Saturday, it's like Monday morning here.'

'Oh! Hadn't thought of that. That's a shame.' Carrie rummaged in her travel bag and found a bottle. 'I'll just pour some milk into it and stick it in the microwave.'

'No, you get her into her jimjams, I'll do that. Davey and Olivia are sleeping in Chloe's room. Do you want to have a peep in?' she asked her niece and nephew. 'One of you can sleep in the fold-up bed and the other can sleep in the top bunk.'

'Fold-up, fold-up.' Davey raised his arm.

'That's not fair,' Olivia sulked. 'Why does he always get what he wants?'

'Now don't start, it's been a very long day,' Carrie warned as Dan lugged their cases into the bedroom.

'Look, you can swap between you and all have a go of the fold-up bed. OK?' Shauna said soothingly as she opened the door to Chloe's bedroom a little wider.

'Look at the size of her. She's growing up fast, isn't she?' Carrie said regretfully as she saw her niece's tousled blond head on the pillow.

'I know.' Shauna sighed as she closed the door. 'Where are the years going? Come on now; I've a light meal of chicken, salads and dips for you. I bet you're hungry after the flight and I'm dying for a cup of Barry's tea.' Shauna led them down the hall to the kitchen. The dining room led off it and the big mahogany table was laden with a selection of platters and dishes of food. 'I'll make the tea while you're putting Hannah to bed.'

'Good thinking,' yawned Carrie as she filled the toddler's

bottle with milk and gave it to Filomena to put in the microwave. Ten minutes later Hannah was in her cotton pyjamas and almost asleep as she drank her bottle in the cot.

Supper was a jolly meal as they caught up with the news and gossip. Davey and Olivia laughed as Shauna and Greg licked their fingers after devouring a packet of crisps each.

'That was to die for. I was longing for a packet of proper crisps. The ones out here are very greasy. I'm nearly tempted to have another packet.' Shauna ran her finger around the inside of the packet to get the last precious crumbs.

'Go ahead,' Dan urged. 'We brought plenty.'

'No, I think I'll have a Club Milk with my cup of tea and let the hot tea melt the chocolate when I take my first bite,' Shauna decided, feeling like a miser with her treasure.

Greg yawned.

'You should go to bed. We should all go,' Carrie suggested, aware that her brother-in-law had an early start in the morning. She hadn't thought that he would be working on a Saturday when she'd booked the flights.

'I will if you don't mind. I have to be at the office for seven. Listen, Dan, I have to go to Dubai early next week. How would you and Davey like to come with me for an overnighter and we could go to the camel races? It's a great experience, and the girls could do their girly thing or else come with us and go shopping?' he suggested.

'Sounds good,' Dan agreed. 'We'll think about it – it might be too long a drive for Hannah.'

'Fine. We'll play it by ear. 'Night all.' He waved a hand in salute and headed for bed.

'Camel racing. Wait until I tell the gang at school.' Davey was in ecstasy.

'We'll have a girls' day.' Shauna noted Olivia's crestfallen face.

'It's about a two-hour drive to Dubai, and you wouldn't have much peace shopping, unless you'd like to leave Hannah with Filomena?' Shauna eyed her sister across the table.

'I don't think so. It wouldn't be very fair on either of them. They don't know one another. We'll see,' Carrie demurred. 'Right now I think we should all hit the sack. Even though we all snoozed on the plane we've been up since five this morning.'

'Well look, there's no rush at all getting up in the morning. We'll have a lazy day tomorrow and get you settled in and then I'll start showing you the sights.' Shauna licked her lips for every sliver of melted chocolate.

Dan laughed. 'Have another one. Go on. You deserve it.'

'I do, don't I?' she agreed and unwrapped another precious Club Milk and dunked it in her tea.

Half an hour later she lay in bed beside her snoring husband and stretched like a cat. It had been a great day. And what a surprise to get a bottle of perfume from her father. It was Shalimar and she guessed that he must have asked Mrs O'Neill's advice. He'd sounded pleased when she'd spoken to him on the phone and told him how much she liked it. It was good to have a peace of sorts between them. She wondered whether he and Bobby could ever come to an understanding. That might need a miracle, she thought wryly. She yawned. It had been a long day.

She had a full itinerary for Carrie, Dan and the kids. She wanted them to have the holiday of their lives. And she had a big treat planned for them. Shauna lay in bed, eyes sparkling with anticipation before she eventually drifted off to sleep.

It seemed like no time before she heard Chloe's voice yelling, 'Mom, Mom, my cousins are here.' She roused herself from a deep sleep and glanced at the small clock on her bedside locker. It showed six forty-five. She hadn't even heard Greg showering or leaving.

Chloe appeared at her bedroom door, tousled and excited. 'Mom, they're here. Davey and Olivia are here and I never heard them coming and you *promised* to wake me up!' she scolded.

'I tried to but you were fast asleep,' fibbed Shauna, hauling herself up onto her elbow.

'Come along, Chloe.' Filomena appeared at the door. 'Let me get your breakfast.'

'I want to have breakfast with my cousins,' Chloe demanded.

'Don't wake them up,' Shauna warned. 'Filomena, I'm going back to sleep for a little while. Wake me as soon as Carrie and Dan are up.'

'Yes, ma'am,' the au pair said, taking Chloe by the hand and closing the bedroom door.

Shauna was back asleep in minutes. Having Filomena was a great bonus, she told Carrie an hour and a half later as they sat in the middle of a rowdy group of children, having a lazy breakfast.

'I wouldn't mind having a Filomena myself.' Carrie grinned as she watched the young girl feeding mashed banana to Hannah.

'It's as good as Christmas. I feel just the way I do when Santa comes.' Chloe danced over and threw her arms round Carrie. 'I wish you could stay for ever.' Carrie hugged her back.

'Just think of our lovely long holiday in the summer,' she reminded her niece. 'We'll all be together again.'

'I like being together.' Chloe ran back to Olivia who was playing with one of her cousin's Barbies, and kissed her excitedly.

'Me too,' Shauna said ruefully to Carrie, 'but Greg's talking about a new job that's coming up in Dubai and I'm beginning to wonder if we'll ever get home for good.'

'Don't say that,' Carrie said quickly.

'I know, but it's something I'm going to have to deal with and possibly sooner rather than later.'

'Oh.' Carrie couldn't hide her surprise at the news.

'Let's not even think about it now, we'll talk about it in the summer,' Shauna said briskly, realizing that Carrie was a little dismayed. 'Right, I think we should all get our togs on. I'm going to bring you to our beach club and we can have a bite of lunch there. What do you think?'

'Deadly. Can we snorkel?'

'Can I wear my new pink togs?'

'Our beach club is the best one in Abu Dhabi. My dad's friend has a boat there.'

'Want gocklat.'

A cacophony of voices assaulted the two sisters.

'Just like old times.' Shauna laughed as she picked up Hannah and cuddled her tightly. She was going to enjoy every precious moment of the Morgans' visit. She wanted Chloe to know that family was more important than anything.

24

'IT'S SO DIFFERENT.' SHAUNA SMILED AS SHE POKED HER HEAD round the door of Carrie's en suite to see her sister wiping the bath.

'What's so different?' Carrie looked at her in surprise as Shauna flipped down the lid of the loo and sat on it.

'Having you to stay. Filomena can't believe the difference between you and Della, and your kids and hers. Honest to God, Carrie, she was such a bitch. She would have treated Filomena like a skivvy if I'd let her. She wouldn't even pick her towels up off the floor. You have no idea. I was furious with her. You know the way you arrived with bags of goodies and magazines and gifts? They arrived with a couple of packets of sweets that they'd bought at the airport.'

'You're joking!' Carrie exclaimed.

'I'm not, and they bought a boxed set of candles and a story book out of Tesco's for the Christmas presents. They're so mean they piss me off. They just take, take, take, as if it's their due. Greg's worked hard for what we've got and I did too when we were in Saudi. We didn't just pluck it off a tree, but Della thinks it got handed to us on a plate and she's always making sly little digs about how rich we are,' Shauna complained.

'Well, you are rich,' Carrie said, straight-faced.

'Smarty.' Shauna laughed, caught off guard for a second. 'Sorry for the rant,' she added sheepishly.

'Rant away,' Carrie invited as she folded the fluffy peach bath towel neatly and hung it on the rail. 'I just wouldn't be able to walk out of any bathroom and leave a towel on the floor. Am I sad or what?'

'No, we were just brought up properly,' Shauna retorted. 'We've got respect for others. Some of the maids have terrible lives here. People treat them like dirt.'

'There's lots of poor unfortunate immigrants at home have terrible lives too, being underpaid and housed in dreadful conditions. Dan employs migrant workers but he pays them the going rate, the same as everyone else. It wouldn't cross his mind to do otherwise. That's one of the things I love about him. He has real respect for people.'

'Dan's a very decent guy,' Shauna said quietly. 'You're lucky.'

'I know.' Carrie smiled. 'I'm so glad he's with us. He's really enjoying himself. He works very hard for us. It's great to see him having fun. How are things with you and Greg? You seem to enjoy the life here.' Carrie perched on the side of the bath and started to fold up Hannah's pyjamas.

'It's different. It's varied; you meet so many different people and are exposed to a multitude of cultures. But it's unsettling on kids, I think. They make friends and then they move, or you move, and you have to start off all over again. Greg might have a chance of working on a big project in Dubai and he desperately wants to give it a go. I'd have preferred to come home and get Chloe settled in a school at home. And there's a worry at the back of your mind about the political situation; the war in Iraq is unsettling and you can't help wondering if some misguided fanatic will set off a bomb in the souk or some other public place.' She gave a deep sigh. 'It just adds to my list of pros for

247

going home, but of course Greg doesn't want to know.' She made a face. 'At least he's finally agreed to try for a baby when we do go home this summer, not that it will be much company for Chloe. There's too much of an age difference now, but I'd really like her to have a brother or sister so that she won't be on her own when she's older . . . our age even.' She smiled wryly at her sister.

'Forty's the pits. At least you're still in your thirties,' Carrie said ruefully.

'Just about.' Shauna grimaced. 'It's hard to believe, isn't it? Where does the time go? Just look at the kids. I remember when you were pregnant with Davey; it only seems like yesterday. Carrie, do you think Chloe's happy?' she blurted out. 'I think she's a bit insecure and clingy. Olivia and Davey are much more confident.'

'Don't compare, Shauna,' Carrie said gently. 'Our circumstances and lifestyles are very different and they are that bit older.'

'I don't know if it's that, even. Greg's hardly at home to see her. He works all hours and then the social scene here is very tied up with work. He likes me to be out and about with him and Chloe's left with Filomena a lot. And I know we're really lucky with her, she's a great girl, but when I see you all together there's such a sense of family about you and I always wanted that for Chloe. I think we've failed her in some ways.' She bit her lip, her eyes dark with anxiety.

'Don't be so hard on yourself, Shauna,' Carrie comforted, at a loss what to say. Her sister's fears and worries were not entirely baseless. Carrie could see how clingy and attention-seeking Chloe was. It was true; Greg was gone from early morning until late at night. Spending time with his daughter did not seem to be a priority, she thought ruefully, but she certainly

248

wasn't going to say anything to Shauna about it. Her sister was well aware of the negatives in their lives because of their life choices. 'Don't forget the summer's coming and we'll be spending a lot of time together and Chloe *will* have a sense of family, so stop fretting.'

'You got the kind genes in our family, Carrie.' Shauna stood up and hugged her sister.

'You must be joking. I wasn't very kind to Della last week, although after what you've just told me, I'm not sorry. The cheek of her treating Filomena like that. Thinking about it, though, why would I be surprised? It's typical of her. Wait until I tell you what happened the day she arrived at my door, pretending to have "forgotten" your presents.' Carrie launched into the story of the trip to the café and how Della had assumed Carrie would be footing the bill for the meal.

Shauna's peals of laughter carried out into the hall and Dan stuck his head round the door. 'What's so funny?' he asked.

'Della,' the two of them chorused and he grinned.

'Tsk tsk! Having a good backbite, are we? What's on the agenda today, women?' It was the fourth day of their holiday and they'd already been to the souk, the Cultural Foundation, the beach club and a party at the Hilton.

'I was thinking I might bring you to some of the antique and rug shops on al Nasr Street, behind the big gold building we can see from the balcony. We could go there for an hour or so and Filomena could bring the kids to the women's and children's park and we could meet them in the Pizza Hut for a treat.'

'It's not really fair on Filomena, though, is it?' Carrie murmured. 'Four kids are a lot to take care of.'

'Listen, your children are angels compared to Della's pair. Filomena doesn't mind and it's only for an hour. We can go to the beach club later, and then tonight we've been invited to a party at the al Hamades' villa. Tomorrow I'm going to bring you to Al Ain, the university city. There's a great zoo there. And we're going camping in the desert and for a picnic on the island at the weekend. Then next week the lads are off to Dubai and you and I are going to a ladies' night and we're going to—'

'Stop! I'm exhausted.' Carrie held up her hand, laughing. 'You don't have to plan for every day. Let's just chill out and spend time with each other,' she added gently. They'd been out every night partaking in the gay social whirl of expat society and while it was enjoyable, Carrie was feeling a little over-whelmed.

'Oh, OK,' Shauna agreed. 'I just want to make sure that you're having a good time.'

'We're having a *great* time,' Dan assured her. 'We'll need a holiday to get over this one.'

'But I want to come to the shops too,' Chloe whined when Shauna explained what was happening, ten minutes later. 'I don't want you to leave me, Mom.'

'Now, Chloe, be a good girl and don't be silly. You'd be bored in a furniture shop, you know you would. Wouldn't you much rather go and play in the park with your cousins and then meet us in the Pizza Hut or Kentucky Fried Chicken? You can pick,' Shauna wheedled.

'Don't want to go to those places. Want to go with you,' Chloe sulked.

'Sure they can come with us,' Carrie said easily.

'They'll be bored,' Shauna protested.

'Come on, Chloe, we could play games in the park. You can push Hannah in her buggy,' Olivia offered kindly and Carrie felt like hugging her daughter when Chloe's face split into a wide beam.

'Can I? I like pushing the buggy. I wish I had a baby sister,' she said wistfully and Shauna felt a dart of sadness. Chloe was having a ball with her cousins. She'd really come out of herself, showing off her favourite places, proudly introducing her friends to them, even boasting about how rich her daddy was. Shauna had nipped that smartly in the bud, noting Olivia's frown at Chloe's implication that Greg was superior to Dan.

'My dad's got millions of glasshouses,' she'd countered stoutly, much to Shauna's amusement.

"Oee, 'Oee, push,' Hannah demanded, clambering into her buggy, and Chloe forgot her sulks and became engrossed in manoeuvring her cousin out into the lift, much to her mother's relief. It was stressful when Chloe was acting up in front of Carrie and the kids.

Two hours later, Carrie had bought two oriental rugs, a kilim, a hand-carved figurine of an Arab girl holding a baby, and a set of wooden napkin holders. Dan had treated himself, urged on by Carrie, to a hand-carved marble and wood chess set. It had been a very satisfying spree and it was made all the better by the reaction of the children when they saw the purchases unwrapped as they waited for their pizza to be served.

'Cool, Dad. We'll have a great game of chess with that,' Davey enthused as he fingered an exquisitely carved pawn.

'Oh, Mam, isn't she gorgeous? That's a brill thing to buy.' Olivia was enthralled with the Arab girl.

'You guys are going to have to buy another suitcase before you go home,' Shauna remarked as a waiter arrived with a steaming pepperoni and pineapple pizza in one hand and a chicken, mushroom and cheese one in the other.

'Oh, goody, I'm starving,' Chloe declared. Shauna threw her eyes up to heaven. 'You'd think she never got a bite,' she said defensively.

'Don't say that, Mom!' Chloe flashed a glare at her mother,

stung at being made a show of. 'Auntie Della says you don't feed me properly, anyway,' she added petulantly.

'What!' demanded Shauna, eyes flashing.

'Auntie Della said you don't feed me properly. She said I eat too much rubbish and that you don't know how to cook properly like she does,' Chloe riposted defiantly.

'Is that so?' Shauna said grimly. 'When did she say this?'

'At Christmas when you and Dad had to go to the office party and Filomena got us some chawirma.'

'Oh, I loved the chicken chawirma we had last night,' Olivia announced matter-of-factly. 'It's my favourite thing since I came here.' They'd all gone walking in the gardens along the Corniche, as was the custom in the cooler evening, and Shauna had introduced them to the spicy treat.

'I liked the lamb one,' Davey remarked, his mouth bulging with pizza. 'What did you prefer, Dad?'

'I liked the lamb too,' Dan said easily.

'And I liked the chicken,' Carrie said brightly, glad of Olivia's timely intervention. She could see that Shauna was raging at Della's remarks. And why wouldn't she be? It was highly inappropriate of Della to undermine Shauna to Chloe and just the type of thing she'd do. Even if she *had* a point, Carrie thought ruefully. Chloe and Filomena seemed to eat an awful lot of fast food.

'Isn't that Della a real bitch?' Shauna murmured to Carrie that evening as Greg drove them through the city to the al Hamades' villa near the embassy belt. She and Carrie were sitting in the back and the two men in the front were engrossed in a discussion of property versus shares in terms of investment.

'Take no notice of her,' Carrie advised.

'Imagine saying that about me to my daughter. How underhand is that? And how ungracious after all the hospitality she's had at my hands. I detest that woman. She's one to talk about nutrition. Did you ever see the crap she feeds her family? Beans and lentils and lettuce leaves because she's too lazy to cook a proper dinner.'

'Forget her,' Carrie urged as Greg drove up to a pair of high wooden gates set into the big walls that surrounded the villa. He parked between a Mercedes and a Range Rover.

The noise of laughter and chat carried on the breeze. Monique greeted her guests warmly, leading them into a large garden full of luscious flowering shrubs and frangipani trees. Fairy lights strung between the trees lent a magical air and Carrie recognized several people she'd already been introduced to at the functions she'd been to with Shauna.

A plump American woman swooped down on Shauna and planted a kiss on each cheek. 'My, honey, don't you look swell? I like the dress. Is that a new piece you're wearing? Where did you get it?' She stood back to admire the gold and ruby necklace and earrings that Shauna wore.

'Hello, Darlene. You don't miss a thing. Greg bought it for me at Al Manara's. They have a new collection in,' Shauna informed her dryly.

'Oh, I must check it out,' the other woman said enviously, her eyes flicking up and down over Shauna, who looked stylish and elegant in a crimson silk sheath dress and a pair of impossibly high Manolo Blahniks.

Monique smiled at Carrie and Dan. 'Why don't I get you both a nice cool drink? We're having a buffet supper so feel free to help yourselves. I must get Rashid to come over and say hello.' She waved at a waiter who was carrying a tray of drinks. 'It's great that you're here. Shauna has been so looking forward to your visit. Are you enjoying your trip?'

'We're having a fantastic time,' Carrie assured her. 'And it's so nice to be able to put faces to names. We hear all about you. I feel as if I know you.'

'Nice to meet you folks. Shauna should throw a party to introduce you properly to Abu Dhabi society. It's been a while since you had a bash, Shauna.' Darlene beamed and then saw some new arrivals and made a beeline for them.

'That's Darlene Whitman and she's the nosiest busybody in the Emirates. And I won't be inviting her to any bash in the near future,' Shauna informed them as she waved at Jenna and Brett, whom Carrie and Dan had already met.

'Darlene's husband works with Rashid and he's as quiet as a mouse and so nice. I feel very sorry for him with a wife like her. And she goes to every single party they're invited to and never hosts one in return,' Monique explained, laughing at Carrie's bemused expression.

'This place is mad,' Dan murmured a couple of hours later as he and Carrie sat on a swing seat in a corner of the garden and watched the guests chatting animatedly as though it had been months since they'd seen each other rather than days or, in some cases, hours.

'It's all a bit frantic, isn't it?' Carrie remarked as she watched Shauna, Jenna and a slender Asian woman gesticulating vivaciously as they discussed the latest gossip.

'Would you like to live here?' her husband asked as he took a long draught of beer.

'For a couple of months maybe, but not for as long as Shauna has. It's a kind of superficial lifestyle, isn't it? All these parties and coffee mornings and social gatherings. Shauna told me she often changes her outfits three and four times a day if she's got a lot on.' Carrie wrinkled her nose, brushing away some irritating insect that was taking a big interest in her upper arms.

Dan laughed. 'You might have to expand your wardrobe. You've about five outfits in *total*.'

'*Exactly!*' She grinned, kissing him on the cheek. 'I couldn't bear the hassle of having to worry about what clothes and what accessories to wear. They even try to outdo each other in the jewellery stakes. Darlene isn't the only one who commented on Shauna's new "piece".'

'Shauna has a lot of jewellery all right,' Dan said wryly. 'I should buy you a couple of "pieces" while we're here.' He smiled down at her, his eyes crinkling good-humouredly in his tanned face.

'Don't be daft! We don't have to keep up with the Joneses like Greg and Shauna do. I'd prefer you to buy me a piece as a love token rather than a trophy to flash in front of the neighbours.' Carrie nestled in to the crook of his arm and yawned. The humidity was getting to her and she was tired. Although the holiday was fun and exhilarating, the pace was unrelenting. They were going to Al Ain the following day and Shauna and Greg had a full itinerary of things to do and see planned for the weekend.

'Greg's very driven, isn't he?' Carrie glanced over at her brother-in-law, who was deep in conversation with a stocky, balding man with a bad comb-over.

'It's paying off. He's loaded. They've ten properties at home and land in Cavan. And he's buying a place in Dubai,' Dan observed laconically.

'We've land in North County Dublin,' Carrie retorted.

Dan laughed. 'I suppose we have.'

'And, more to the point, we're a happy family. That counts for a lot, doesn't it?' She arched an eyebrow at him.

'A hell of a lot. We're lucky, aren't we, Carrie?' Dan's blue eyes studied her intently.

'You bet we are, Dan. I wouldn't swap our life for all the jewels in the Orient.'

'I guess we're just two boring old codgers. Sad but true.' He grinned at her, his teeth pearly white in the dark. His tan had deepened and he looked ruggedly handsome in his maroon Lacoste shirt and beige chinos.

'Well, you're a dead *sexy* boring old codger and I wish we were at home so I could ride you ragged,' Carrie murmured longingly, running her finger along the dark hairs on his forearm.

'Stop!' he warned. 'Don't talk dirty to me, or I might jump on you and that would give good ole Darlene and her folks something to talk about.'

Carrie guffawed and didn't notice that Shauna looked at her with a wistful envy in her eyes.

'You're very quiet. What's wrong with you?' Greg asked as he and Shauna undressed for bed.

'I'm tired. It was a long day and a long night,' she murmured, sliding her nightdress over her head.

'I think Carrie and Dan are enjoying themselves. Sorry I can't go to Al Ain with you tomorrow. Pierre rescheduled a meeting that I just can't get out of.' Greg yawned as he stepped out of his trousers.

'What's new?' Shauna said sourly.

'Hey, don't be like that, Shauna,' he said irritably as he emptied his change onto the bedside locker and flung his trousers onto the chaise longue by the French windows.

'There's more to life than work, Greg,' she snapped. 'Look at us. You're gone in the morning before I get up. You come home; we go out to a function or for dinner with other people and spend the night talking to the world and his mother. We have five minutes' chat, maybe, at bedtime and that's it. We're like ships that pass in the night. I was just looking at Carrie and Dan tonight. They sat together for nearly an hour chatting and laughing, completely happy in each other's company, and I envied them. I really envied them, Greg,' she said reproachfully. 'We don't have that any more, and I miss it.'

'Oh, for fuck's sake, Shauna, the hour of the night you pick to have a conversation like this. Your timing is *lousy*!' He glared at her as he flung himself down on the bed.

'Don't take the nose off me,' she snapped back. 'You asked me what was wrong with me and I'm telling you.'

'Look,' he said exasperatedly, 'we're not Carrie and Dan, we're us, and I wish you'd stop ramming them down my neck as the perfect family and the perfect couple. There were a lot of very interesting people at that party tonight; they should have mixed and mingled more when they had the opportunity. When are they going to attend a party like that again? They can sit talking to each other at home any time.'

'They did mix but they sat talking to each other as well, because to each other they *are* the most interesting people. That's my point. They don't need to go outside their marriage to be entertained. They entertain each other.' She didn't try to disguise her frustration. Greg had hardly spoken to her, Dan or Carrie at the party, he'd been so busy networking.

'How boring for them,' he said derisively.

'Don't be so superior.' She couldn't hide her disgust.

'Shauna, *why* did you marry me?' He sat up and eyeballed her.

'I . . . I . . .' she stuttered, surprised by his question.

'Why did you marry me? What attracted you to me?' he persisted.

'I liked it that you were outgoing and fun-loving . . . different from what I'd grown up with,' she admitted sulkily.

'Well, I haven't changed,' he said coldly.

'Yes you have, Greg, you don't have time for *me* any more,

you don't have time for Chloe, all you care about is impressing the so-called big guys and making money—'

'Money so that you and Chloe can have a very comfortable lifestyle,' he interrupted angrily. 'What's wrong with that, for crying out loud? I haven't heard you complaining before.'

'There's more to life, Greg,' she argued.

'You didn't think so when we met first. You were into making money as much as I was.' His eyes were like flints, hard and cold.

'Things change. We've a child to consider. I've changed. My needs have changed,' she retorted, trying not to let her voice shake. She hated having rows with Greg. It made her feel sick. It reminded her of the bad old days when she had to stand up for herself to Noel. Even though she hadn't flinched from it, it had always left her shaking afterwards. She could feel that old familiar quiver in her tummy that brought her right back to childhood, and was half sorry she'd started the argument.

'Yes, you have changed.' Greg was snarling at her. 'You're never satisfied. You've turned into a moany, needy *nag* and I'm getting tired of it.' He lay down and turned his back on her.

'You're a bastard, Greg. That was totally uncalled for.' Shauna felt tears smarting in her eyes. She was shocked at his vehemence and his uncharacteristic viciousness.

He remained stubbornly silent.

Unwilling to let him see her cry she stalked into the en suite and closed the door behind her. They'd had their rows before but this was a new low. She rested her forehead against the cool oyster-coloured tiles. He was right about one thing: her timing *was* lousy. There was nothing worse than having to pretend that everything was all right in front of visitors, when everything was very, very wrong.

* * *

Greg lay in bed fuming. Was there no pleasing the bloody woman? He worked his ass off to buy her jewellery and clothes that cost an arm and a leg, and to provide her with luxury homes and a great lifestyle, and what thanks did he get for it? Damn all. Instead he got plodding, boring Dan and Carrie shoved down his neck as role models for a marriage. If he had to descend to their level of dull he'd hang himself, he thought angrily as he pummelled his pillow into a more comfortable shape.

He supposed he was lucky she hadn't started on him about having a baby again. He'd bought himself some breathing space there. Nice and all as Hannah was, having her around 24/7 just brought back bad memories of high chairs in restaurants, and a social life arranged around nap times and feeding times, and cranky crying when tiredness got the better of her. If there was one thing this visit of Shauna's family had confirmed for him it was that he emphatically did not want another child. He hadn't the patience for children. He had no empathy with them and that was the honest truth.

Chloe got up his nose with her whining, which seemed to be getting worse. When she was good she was gorgeous, but he didn't *want* any more kids. Why should he have to apologize for that? He wasn't Saint Dan and the sooner Shauna realized that and stopped trying to make him feel like a heel the better.

It wasn't that he didn't like his brother-in-law, he mused. Dan was an OK guy and intelligent with it, but he was happy to work away on his market gardening business and spend time with his family and as far as Greg could see that was the height of his ambition. He'd find that stultifyingly boring. He needed to push himself, to challenge himself to even greater success. If he lost that hunger and drive he might as well give up. If Shauna loved him she'd accept that as part and parcel of who he was.

What a bummer of a way to end the evening. He'd been so

proud watching his wife show off her new jewellery. She'd looked stunning with her blond hair swept up in a classy chignon and that gorgeous crimson dress showing off her great chassis. He'd enjoyed seeing the flashes of admiration in other men's eyes and the spark of envy in the women's. This lifestyle was his forte, this was where he shone, and it had given him pleasure to show Carrie and Dan how far he and Shauna had come. He'd thought his wife felt the same. She'd seemed to really enjoy showing them all the sights and delights of this multi-faceted country.

And then she hits him with this! Out of the blue. How could he be so off beam? Couldn't Shauna see that he only wanted the best for them? What was so awful about that? It was just as well that he wasn't going to Al Ain with them tomorrow. He wouldn't be able to keep a civil tongue in his head with her, he was so pissed off with her ingratitude.

He heard the bathroom door open and Shauna padding over to the bed. He turned away and pulled over to the far edge of the mattress. Right now he wanted nothing to do with his wife. If she'd kicked him in the balls it wouldn't have hurt as much as this did. He attempted to focus his thoughts on the strategy meeting he had to attend in the morning. It was important that he make a good impression. At least it would take his mind off his domestic problems, he thought grimly, wishing that he could go asleep. But sleep was hard to come by and he tossed and turned restlessly, wondering how his and Shauna's paths could have diverged so drastically without his even realizing it.

25

'HAPPY EASTER, NOEL.'

'And the same to you, Mrs O'Neill.' Noel tried his best to appear cheerful but he was feeling very lonely indeed. The last week seemed to have crawled by. He'd developed a heavy cold on his chest and hadn't been able to go bowling or, even worse, take part in the Easter church ceremonies.

'This is for you.' His neighbour handed him a big Malteser Easter egg.

'Good heavens! Er . . . thanks very much, but I'm afraid I don't have one for you.' He was completely flustered.

Mrs O'Neill gave a hearty chuckle. 'It's all right, Noel, I didn't buy you one either. This is from Carrie and the children. She asked me to keep it for you until Easter Sunday. She told me you had a great fondness for Maltesers.'

'Indeed I do. Wasn't that good of them, all the same?' he exclaimed, touched at his daughter's kindness.

'She's a great girl,' Mrs O'Neill agreed.

'She'll be ringing me shortly. She thinks I was at half ten Mass—'

'And you let her go on thinking it,' his neighbour warned. 'We don't want her holiday spoilt worrying about a little cold.'

'Oh now, it's more than a cold, I'm afraid. It's gone into my chest. And the antibiotics aren't clearing it up. It could turn to pneumonia or pleurisy if it's not something more sinister,' he said gravely.

'Now stop that nonsense, Noel. You've got a cold,' Mrs O'Neill said briskly. 'Go inside and I'll make you a cup of tea. Are you all right for your dinner today? Did you defrost one of Carrie's frozen ones?'

'No, her sister-in-law Sadie is bringing me over a turkey dinner. That's if I can eat it.' He led the way into the kitchen.

'You'll be well hungry for it if you don't eat too many Maltesers,' Mrs O'Neill assured him as she bustled into the kitchen and put on the kettle. 'Would you like a slice of toast or a biscuit with your tea?'

'Sure I'll try a piece of toast. I've lost my appetite over the past few days, but I suppose I need to keep my strength up.'

'Indeed you do,' Mrs O'Neill told him. 'I always knew when my Ted was really sick. He'd lose his appetite completely. That's when I'd start to worry. And to think he died, hit by a drunken driver and him a teetotaller all his life. Life's very strange, isn't it?'

'It is, Mrs O'Neill,' he agreed, sitting down at the kitchen table. Twiskers hopped up onto his lap.

'That cat is terrible fond of you.' She studied the pair of them.

'Just as well someone is.' Noel stroked Twiskers's velvety head.

'Ah don't be saying things like that. Haven't you three lovely children and four precious grandchildren?'

'I suppose you're right.' He sighed.

'Of course I'm right,' she retorted crisply. Noel was really feeling sorry for himself, she thought with wry amusement as she popped a piece of bread under the grill. Typical man. 'How's

262

Bobby getting on? He hasn't been home in a long time. Is he doing well for himself over yonder?' she asked chattily.

'All right, I suppose,' Noel said gruffly, his lips thinning.

'You suppose?' She looked at him in surprise. 'Do you not keep in touch?'

'Don't be asking me questions like that,' he grumbled.

'Well I didn't mean to pry, Noel. I'm sorry if you felt I was.' Mrs O'Neill wasn't at all abashed at his rebuke. She was used to his pernickety ways.

'We don't get on too well,' Noel explained, regretting his crankiness.

'I'm sorry to hear that, Noel. I always thought he was a lovely lad.' She poured the boiling water into the teapot and gave it a swirl.

'Oh, you might think that. But I've had terrible trouble with him,' Noel confided, rubbing his hands agitatedly. He was starting to show his age, Mrs O'Neill observed as she watched him slumped in his chair. His hair was thinning, and the liver spots on his knobbly hands had darkened. There was an egg stain on his bottle green pullover and a snag in his grey trousers. Men weren't able to cope with being widowed like women were, she thought stoically as she let him unburden himself.

'No-one knows the worry and upset I've endured because of him. It put a terrible strain on his mother, God rest her. I think she'd still be alive, only for him.' It all came tumbling out in a torrent of confession.

'Why? What did he do?' she asked, shocked at this revelation.

'Ach, he caused us nothing but worry. You know the way he carries on.'

'Well I've never noticed anything out of the ordinary.' She frowned, buttering the crispy brown toast, wondering what on earth Noel could be referring to. She always remembered Bobby as a mischievous, irrepressible little chap who'd grown up to be a very nice young man. He had been Anna's pride and joy. She'd doted on him.

'He's . . . he's . . . he's not like other fellows,' Noel mumbled, avoiding her gaze.

'Noel, are you trying to tell me that he's *gay*?' Mrs O'Neill said incredulously as comprehension dawned.

'Yes, if you want to put it like that.' Noel fidgeted in his chair, wishing he were a million miles away.

'Ah for goodness' sake, is that all?' His neighbour placed the hot buttered toast in front of him. 'I knew that from when he was a little lad. You'd know by the prancing around of him, for goodness' sake.'

Noel couldn't believe his ears. He'd expected her to be shocked and sympathetic, not . . . not matter-of-fact and un-affected. 'You're very blasé about it,' he accused, annoyed at her reaction. How dare she make such light of so distressing a revelation? 'How would you like it if it was one of your lads?' he demanded truculently as he fed Twiskers a piece of toast.

'It wouldn't make a blind bit of difference to me, Noel. If that's the way they're made, there's nothing you and I can do about it.' She poured the tea and sat down at the table opposite him. 'Don't tell me you're holding that against the poor lad?'

'Well it's . . . unnatural . . . it's a very unchristian way of life,' he blustered.

'Who says so?' she challenged.

'Good heavens, Mrs O'Neill! The Church says so.' Noel brushed back a stray strand of grey hair that had flopped over his eye and stared at her in dismay.

'That lot, that shower in the Vatican,' she snorted. 'They're fine ones to talk. Half of them don't have a bit of Christianity in them. Going on with the nonsense they go on with. All them old lads wearing their funny hats and flowing robes and living in palaces, issuing rules and regulations. You can't take communion here; you can't take communion there. We're the real Church. The rest of you are only impostors. What did that "Prince of the Church" down in Dublin say about sharing communion?' She wrinkled her brow. '"A sham", that's it. Sharing communion was a sham! There's Christianity for you. Do you think that Jesus would say that, Noel?' She eyed him sternly.

'Ah well now, the Cardinal's a very learned man. He knows these things,' Noel explained patiently.

'Tosh, Noel,' she scoffed, unimpressed. 'If you call that learning, you can keep it as far as I'm concerned. Did you ever hear such childish nonsense? And look at the way women were treated, and still are. There's no equality in the Church for women, Noel, and us all supposed to be made equal in God's image and likeness—'

'You can't be saying things like that, Mrs O'Neill,' Noel spluttered in consternation. 'Women have their place too.' He had thought his neighbour was a God-fearing righteous woman. She was sitting opposite him talking . . . heresy.

'I can say what I want, Noel McCarthy. I had to find my God the hard way,' she said firmly. 'When my Ted was taken from me in such a cruel and horrible way I was in a dark and lonely place and I questioned God. My faith was gone. How could He allow this to happen to a good hard-working man who never did any harm to anyone? I had my dark night of the soul when I was on my knees, I can tell you, and then I read a book called *Embraced by the Light* by a woman called Betty J. Eadie, about what happens when you die. And it made me think and question *everything* I was taught. And I was taught like yourself, Noel.' She wagged a finger at him. 'But the difference between us now is that I found a God of compassion. Not the harsh, judgemental, wrathful God we were reared on. And what a joy it is to me.' Her eyes brimmed with tears and she wiped them away with the corner of her floral apron.

'I started reading other books, spiritual books that were very different in outlook from what I was used to and it made me reassess every single thing I'd ever been taught about religion. And that was the best thing that ever happened to me, Noel. Because now I think for *myself*. And I don't have so-called pious men as buffers between my God and me. I know there are some lovely priests out there. We have one in the parish, but I don't need him any more to tell me about God. I'm learning all about Him myself. And I don't let any of them tell me what to do,' she said stoutly.

Noel couldn't believe the apostasy that was issuing from his neighbour's lips. 'But you still go to church,' he said weakly.

'I do, and I enjoy it. But I do it my own way now.' Mrs O'Neill took a sip of tea and gazed at him calmly. For a moment she even found it in herself to feel sorry for her neighbour. His red, watery eyes were staring at her with undisguised consternation. It was obvious she had totally shocked him. She took another sip of tea and put down her cup and said kindly, 'Noel, would you agree that we are all created by God?'

'Indeed. Of course.' He nodded earnestly.

'So all of us are sons and daughters of God?'

'Oh yes.' He pursed his lips, wondering where she was heading.

'Well, my take on it now is that we're all part of the Divine Creator. He created us. Am I right?'

'Yes,' Noel agreed, wondering what she was going to come out with next.

'We're in agreement, then. So now, before Holy Communion, instead of saying "Lord I am *not* worthy to receive you", as we were taught, I say "Lord I *am* worthy to receive you". And in that way I acknowledge my Divinity. It's very simple really and much more positive,' she explained cheerfully, pouring herself another cup of tea.

'Good heavens!' He was astonished at her misguided irreverence.

'We've all been kept down, you see, and made to feel guilty. Religions are great for that sort of thing. And that's why the likes of poor Bobby have such a hard life. Let me ask you a question.' She fixed him with a laser-eyed stare. 'You're very fond of young Davey, aren't you?'

'Of course I am.' Noel drank a reviving sup of tea. He wasn't the better for this conversation. 'He's a great little lad,' he added, thinking how much he was looking forward to seeing them all again.

'Well what would you say if he came to you and said he was gay?'

'I . . . I . . . Don't be ridiculous,' he stuttered, affronted.

'I'm not being in the slightest bit ridiculous,' she insisted. 'Who's to know what life throws at us? So don't be so harsh on Bobby. He needs even more love than the rest of them. And you know, Anna *knew* he was different, Noel.' She kept her gaze steady. 'She said it to me a long time ago and it didn't bother her, so don't be blaming her death on Bobby. Her big worry was the way you'd take it.' She had no intention of letting him off the hook. 'If she knew that you were estranged because of it she'd be very troubled and disappointed.'

'Don't be saying things like that,' Noel muttered wretchedly.

'You know, Noel, we're in our second half of life and we have to stop acting like sheep and swallowing everything we're told. We have to think for ourselves and work it out as best we can. And that's my advice to you. Think for yourself and stop making life hard for the pair of you. God's compassion is there for us all if we want it. Bobby's a lovely lad. What harm if he finds love with a chap like him? Love is love no matter who's giving and receiving it. And isn't that what we all want? A little bit of love?'

The phone rang. She smiled at him benevolently, aware that she had shocked him to his core. 'There's Carrie now, I'd say. Go and answer it and don't let on there's a thing wrong with you, while I wash up these cups,' she ordered.

'Right,' he said meekly, wondering whether she had turned into some sort of she-devil. He went out to the hall and picked up the phone and heard a chorus of 'Happy Easter, Grandpa' in his ear. His heart lifted at the sound of his grandchildren's childish glee. Tempted as he was to play the martyr and get some sympathy, he knew that Mrs O'Neill had her ear cocked in the kitchen and would give him a sharp telling off if he played the old soldier. Anyway, there was less than a week to go now until they got back; he'd struggle on until they got home. It would be mean to ruin Carrie's holiday by having her worry about him.

'Hello, Dad? How are you?' He felt a surge of emotion and affection as he heard Carrie's voice on the line.

'I'm fine, Carrie. Are you having a good time? How are the children? Is it too hot for them?'

'Not at all, Dad. We go swimming in the Gulf every day, and they're having a great time. We went camping in the desert on Friday. It was fantastic. The time is flying. Sure we'll be home before we know it. You sound as if you've a cold.'

'Ah it's only a sniffle,' he said heartily, triumphantly resisting the urge to enact the role of the abandoned invalid.

'Well, mind yourself, Dad. What are you doing for your dinner today?'

'Sadie's bringing me a turkey dinner, so I'll be grand. Mrs

O'Neill is with me at the minute. We were having a cup of tea. She brought me in your Easter egg. It was very kind of you, Carrie. Thanks a lot.'

'You're welcome, Dad. Here's Shauna, she wants to say hello.' Carrie passed the phone over to her sister, and Shauna came on the line. 'Hi, Dad. Happy Easter.'

'Hello, love. Are you having a good time with the gang?'

'It's great to have them here. I'll miss them when they're gone.'

'Why don't you come home yourself for good? That place is a bit of a powder keg with the war in Iraq and all of that,' he urged.

'We'll see,' she said non-committally. 'Chloe wants to say hello to you.'

He spoke to all of the children, even Hannah, who was all talk of her Easter eggs. He felt lonely hanging up. It was amazing how much he missed them. He supposed he'd taken them for granted over the years, he acknowledged uncomfortably.

'They'll be home soon, Noel, don't be fretting now,' Mrs O'Neill said when she saw his crestfallen face as he came back into the kitchen. 'Phone calls are all I have. At least Carrie will be home soon and Shauna will be home for the summer.'

'What are you going to do for the rest of the day?' he asked, beginning to realize how lonely a life his neighbour must have in spite of all her social activities.

'I'm going to lunch with another widowed friend of mine. But I'll call in on my way home and see how you're getting on. Is there anything I can get you when I'm out?'

'I have everything I need, thanks. And . . . er . . . thank you for all your kindness,' he said awkwardly.

'Even if I'm a bit of a heretic?' Her bright blue eyes twinkled at him mischievously.

Noel laughed. Mrs O'Neill was a good-humoured woman and always had been. 'We're different,' he conceded.

'Anyone can change. Make your peace with Bobby; it's what Anna would want. Life's too short to be fighting. We don't know what's round the corner. We could be gone tomorrow. And besides, it would be the *Christian* thing to do,' Mrs O'Neill advised as she folded the tea towel and hung it up.

He watched her go, chewing the side of his jaw. From anyone else he would have taken it as nosy interference, but he had a high regard for his neighbour. She'd been a great friend of his wife's and she'd coped with her husband's sudden death and her children's departures to foreign climes with stoic determination and bravery. He was still pondering on her words even as he ate the tasty roast turkey dinner Dan's sister brought him a couple of hours later.

Had he been too harsh and judgemental on Bobby? What would he do if Davey came to him when he was older and said that he was gay? Kind, loving Davey who always made a fuss of him. Bobby had been a kind and loving child, he thought with a little dart of shock. He and his nephew were very alike in some respects, but Noel had spent so much time chastising him, wanting him to do manly things, that they'd ended up at loggerheads.

'But I was only trying to do my best for him,' he said aloud as he washed his dishes, angry with himself and Mrs O'Neill that he was having to justify the upbringing he had given his child. He'd tried to set his son on the right path, as any good father would. Why should he be judged harshly for that?

Because you *judged harshly*. The thought hit him like a thunderbolt. He stared out at the garden. The damson trees, Anna's pride and joy, were a riot of snowy blossoms bursting gloriously from their branches. A bright yellow gorse raised its flowers to the deep blue sky. A pink camellia was poised to bloom, its tight buds straining to be free. Such a place of beauty, the garden he and his late wife had created, he mused. Bobby had often helped his mother in it when he was young. He and she would talk away and he'd see her laughing at something her son had said and be jealous. His heart contracted. He had been jealous of the bond Anna and Bobby had. She'd always been so protective of her son, and he had accused her of mollycoddling him.

Was it jealousy that had made him say those things?

He shook his head at the notion. That was ridiculous. It was abhorrence at the thought of his son physically loving another man. The thought repulsed him. It was unnatural. And how shocking that one of *his* offspring would have such a perverted inclination. It must have come from Anna's side of the family. There was *nothing* like that in *his* family, he thought angrily.

A flicker of remorse shot through him. What a thing to blame on his poor dead wife.

'I'm sorry, my dear,' he murmured, ashamed.

Was he a harsh and judgemental person? He had always thought that he was a good, decent, upright man who took his duties as a husband and father seriously. But listening to Mrs O'Neill today when she'd talked about God and compassion had made him feel uncomfortable. Maybe he could have been more compassionate in his life, he thought guiltily.

Why had she brought up all those subjects? Why couldn't she just leave him be? Why did he have to think about these dreadful things now when he just wanted a bit of peace? He made himself a cup of tea and went into the sitting room and sat down by the fire. There was still a little nip in the wind and he'd lit the fire to take the chill off the room. The flames flickered comfortingly and Twiskers jumped up onto his lap. He stroked her head and felt a measure of comfort when he heard the deep purr roll from the back of her throat. At least he made someone happy even if it was only the cat, he thought sorrowfully as memories of the harsh words that both Shauna and Bobby had flung at him over the years came back to haunt him. After a while, weary of his turmoil, he closed his eyes. His chin drooped onto his chest and he slept.

'Dad sounded as though he has a cold on him,' Carrie turned her head and squinted at her sister as the afternoon sun sparkled on the jade waters of the Gulf. Dan was swimming with the children and Carrie and Shauna lay on emerald green loungers under coconut straw umbrellas, sipping ice-cold Pimms.

'He didn't go on about it the way he usually would. You know if Dad gets a sniffle he's usually convinced he's getting pneumonia,' Shauna remarked lazily, smoothing more suncream onto her golden limbs.

'I think he was making the effort to let on that he was all right. He's mellowed a little. He's not as bad as he used to be at all. I think the kids have a lot to do with it. He's mad about them.' Carrie stretched luxuriously.

'Pity he wasn't like that when we were young,' Shauna retorted.

'What's wrong with you? You're not in great form.' Carrie eyed her knowingly. 'You and Greg are having a row, aren't you?'

'No we're not,' Shauna retorted hotly.

'Look, the two of you are being so extra polite to each other in front of us, it's excruciating. I know something's up. What's wrong? You might as well tell me while we have a few minutes to ourselves.' Carrie leaned on her elbow and looked over at her.

'I had a go at him about not spending more time with Chloe and me, the way Dan spends time with you and the kids. Of course he went ballistic and flew off the handle and said some very hurtful things. He's a bollox,' Shauna said sulkily.

'He works hard for you, Shauna,' Carrie said gently.

'Dan works hard for you, too, and he spends time with you. Look at him out there with the kids.'

They raised themselves up on their elbows and saw Dan surrounded by a horde of squealing children splashing and jumping around. Behind him, bright orange buoys undulated on top of the water where the shark nets lay strung across the bay.

'Don't forget, Dan's on holiday,' Carrie pointed out.

'Greg comes home to us for three weeks in the summer and he still doesn't have time for us, he's so busy sorting out his property portfolio.' Shauna dismissed that argument out of hand. 'You're a family, Carrie, a tightly knit unit. Sometimes I just feel I'm a trophy that Greg can deck out in jewels and designer clothes to show off to his colleagues. And as for Chloe, he couldn't be happier that we have Filomena to look after her. It means he can abdicate all his parental responsibilities. He thinks he's the perfect father and husband by simply providing for us financially. He can't understand why I get pissed off. It's not what I imagined our life would be,' she ended glumly.

'Come on now, Shauna, don't tell me you'd be happy in a three-bedroom semi-detached with a nine to five husband like most ordinary mortals,' Carrie mocked. 'That was never you and never will be.'

'OK, well, not quite that, but I can't help envying you and Dan. You're so close and you have such fun together.'

'We have our ups and downs too. Don't forget I'm competing with bloody glasshouses.' Carrie lay back against her cushions enjoying the feeling of lethargy that was spreading through her.

'But you still *like* each other,' Shauna muttered. 'I don't think I like Greg any more.'

'Don't say that,' Carrie protested. 'You only feel that now because you had a row. It will blow over.'

'Do you think I should try for another baby?'

'Do you want the truth?' Carrie sat up and swung her legs onto the sand so that she was facing her sister.

'Oh, OK, then.' Shauna eyed her warily, knowing that her sister wasn't going to pull her punches.

'If you think having another baby will change Greg, it won't,' Carrie said bluntly, 'especially as he's been putting it off for so long. If he was any different with a new baby from how he is with Chloe it would be a big surprise. I think if you're going to have another baby you're on your own, more or less, and that's being honest, Shauna. I don't think his heart's in it and you have to be realistic.'

'I know, but I really do want a brother or sister for Chloe.'

'Have one, but just be sure you're not going into it with false expectations. Oh, I don't know. Maybe I'm wronging the chap.' Carrie shrugged and took a long sip of her drink.

'Do you think I'm a bitch? Do you think I'm being disloyal saying these things to you?' Shauna pushed her sunglasses up on top of her head and stared at her sister.

'Don't be silly, it's *me* you're talking to. That's what sisters are for.'

'I know, and I really appreciate having you to talk to. That's why I want someone for Chloe. I'd hate her to be on her own.'

'She does have my gang, don't forget,' Carrie assured her. 'And Greg *has* been a kind and generous husband.'

'I know. Maybe it's just me. Maybe I'm starting my midlife crisis.'

'Give over. I haven't had mine yet and I'm older than you are,' Carrie teased. 'Now order me another drink, I'm on my holliers!'

* * *

'Greg, can we make up before you go to Dubai with Dan and Davey tomorrow? It's really stressful having a row when visitors are here and Carrie has copped it.' Shauna turned to her husband, who had just got into bed.

'Well you started it, Shauna,' he retorted. 'And you made me feel really bad. I felt totally unappreciated. I felt nothing I do for you matters. I'm not working my ass off just for me, you know,' he added plaintively.

'I know,' she muttered. 'I'm sorry. I didn't mean to make you feel like that. I do appreciate how hard you work for us. I'd just like us to spend a little more time together.'

'We will, I promise,' Greg said placatingly, relieved the coolness was over and that his wife had made the first move. 'This summer will be our best ever,' he assured her. 'We could spend a few days in Paris on the way back after the holidays, if you like.'

'Don't forget Chloe will be starting school,' she reminded him.

'Damn, forgot that. Nix Paris,' he said grumpily.

'I know what we could do!' she exclaimed eagerly. 'I'm sure Carrie would mind Chloe for a few days and I could fly to meet you there on your way home in August. We could have a romantic few days.' Her eyes sparkled at the idea. She'd be off the Pill and wouldn't it be wonderful to conceive a baby in Paris? Not that she'd mention it to her husband right now. She didn't want him getting into a bad humour again.

'*Brilliant* idea,' Greg approved, bending down to kiss her soundly. 'A romantic holiday in Paris is just what we need.'

26

Everything organized! Leaving now. Here's to reunions!!!

Shauna read the email and smiled. It had been sent hours earlier. Excellent. Things were going as planned and she liked being on top of things.

'Carrie,' she called to her sister who was ironing on the balcony.

'Yep?'

'Filomena will do that when she gets back from the park.'

'She has enough to be doing, and anyway I'm finished now.' Carrie unplugged the iron and stepped into the lounge. It was uncomfortably warm and she was perspiring. She couldn't understand how her sister remained so unaffected by the heat. They had three days left of their holidays and although she'd had a ball she was looking forward to a walk along the beach at home in a bracing breeze. 'I'm going into my bedroom to read my book until the kids get back,' she announced.

'It's like the Arctic in there,' grumbled Shauna. Dan had taken Hannah for a walk in her buggy along the breakwater. Jenna had invited Chloe, Olivia and Davey over to her apartment and the sisters were enjoying a few hours together. 'So will you come to the airport with me while I pick up our guest? It's a pain in the ass that Gabrielle Reed can't pick her up. Honestly, if you invite a guest to give a talk to your Emirates Historical Society you pick them up yourself.' Shauna threw her eyes up to heaven. 'Her and her bloody migraines.'

'Don't be so unsympathetic,' Carrie rebuked. 'Would she do it for you if the positions were reversed?'

'That old warthog? You must be joking,' Shauna scoffed.

'Well then, why are you doing it?'

'Because Linda Faradi is the vice president of the society and she was supposed to do it but one of her kids has a bug and she doesn't want to spread it around. So she asked me.'

'Well at least your car is air-conditioned. What time have you to go at?' Carrie poured herself a glass of fresh orange juice.

'About six. We'll be home by half seven and Greg has booked a table in a Mexican restaurant which is fairly laid back and the kids will like it as well. Is that OK?'

'Fine,' Carrie assured her. 'I've put on a half a stone since I came out here. I've never been to so many restaurants. My waistbands are getting tight.'

'A week at home and it will be gone,' Shauna assured her. 'What are you reading?'

'The new Michael Palin, I love him.'

'Go and make the most of it. I've to make a few calls about the art group's annual dinner.'

'Don't you ever get fed up of all the socializing?' Carrie perched on a stool at the breakfast counter, enjoying the couple of hours alone with Shauna.

'If you didn't socialize here you'd go mad,' Shauna said dryly. 'It takes your mind off how far away from home you are and how much of an outsider you are in such a different culture. It gives you a false sense of security, if you like. Every expat is in the same boat. It's our common denominator.'

'I suppose so. I just wouldn't have the energy for it. Or the wardrobe,' Carrie joked.

'Della loved it.' Shauna made a face. 'I wonder does that mean we're alike?'

'Wash your mouth out with soap.' Carrie grinned. 'She's unique and I don't mean that as a compliment. I don't know how she and Greg can be so different. He's very hospitable and not at all mean. And she's such a tightwad.'

'She takes after their mother. You've met Joanna; you've seen how odd she is. She rarely sees him or Della. Greg is more like his father, I think. It was such a pity he died when Greg was in his teens. Joanna's a very self-centred woman. She does her own thing and to hell with anyone else. No wonder Della turned out the way she did.'

'Thank God my in-laws are not only normal, but nice too.' Carrie yawned. 'Right, see you in an hour or so.'

'Enjoy it.' Shauna followed her to the bedroom. Carrie flung herself down on the big bed.

'This is such a luxury,' she purred. 'The only time I get the chance to read at home is when I get into bed at night, and I usually fall asleep after a few pages.'

'Well make the most of it then. Would you like a mango smoothie?'

'Oooh, I'd love one. The mangoes here are *gorgeous*!'

'Coming up.' Shauna smiled, enjoying the fact that Carrie was totally relaxing on her holiday. Her sister was always very good to her when she went home to Ireland in the summer. It was nice to be able to reciprocate the kindness.

Noel slid on his glasses and peered at the telephone number in front of him. Should he dial? He dithered. What would he say? It had been a long time. He sat down on the small phone seat and picked up the receiver and slowly dialled the number written on the pad. His heart began to thump as he heard the ringing tone. His palms moistened. Hastily he replaced the receiver and went back out to the kitchen. The fire was low in the grate so he threw on a log and a couple of briquettes. It began to spark and flames licked around the ends of the log.

Hanging up like that had been the coward's way out, he thought, staring into the flickering fire. If it was Mrs O'Neill, she would have just plunged in and got on with it. His neighbour was a stalwart woman, he acknowledged. Carrie had only been away less than two weeks and he was just about coping. Mrs O'Neill had fended for herself for the past few years, apart from a couple of visits from children who lived on the other side of the world. She was someone to look up to, he admitted as he took a deep breath and went back out to the phone.

He redialled nervously and waited for an answer but the phone rang and rang and eventually he hung up. He didn't know whether he was relieved or sorry that Bobby hadn't been there. With a deep sigh he pulled on his coat. He'd promised Davey that he would feed his fish. Mrs O'Neill had kindly performed the deed while he'd been incapacitated, but he was feeling better and he needed to get out and about again. He'd been racking his brains as to how he could thank his neighbour for her kindness and he'd decided to plant up two hanging baskets for her to hang on either side of her front door. She'd be delighted with that, he knew. She wasn't much of a gardener but she loved flowers. He'd go to the garden centre and get some bedding plants. Noel felt quite cheerful as he locked his front door after him. If he'd lifted the phone once to try to contact his son he could do it again. If his wife was looking down on him she'd be pleased. The thought gave him comfort and he decided he'd stop at the grave on his way home and have a chat with his dear Anna.

279

*   *   *

'What does this woman look like?' Carrie asked as passengers began to emerge into the arrivals hall and crowd along the glass barrier to get their visas.

'Blondish, from what I remember. Tall and skinny. She'll know me when she sees me.' Shauna strained to see if she could recognize a face in the throng.

'You should have made a sign.' Carrie could see other greeters holding up signs with names written on them.

'No need for that; there's the person I'm looking for.' Shauna pointed towards another wave of arrivals.

'I don't see any tall, skinny blond wom—' Carrie's jaw dropped in recognition. 'Oh my God! Bobby! It's Bobby!' she exclaimed, turning to Shauna, who was grinning from ear to ear.

'Surprise surprise!'

Bobby was waving dramatically, his face wreathed in smiles as Shauna stood on her tippy toes and handed over his visa.

'How are my darlings?' he called through the glass.

'Hurry on and get your skinny ass out here,' Shauna ordered, trying not to cry as she saw tears slide down her sister's cheeks. 'Stop it,' she gulped, 'or you'll have me at it.'

'When did you plan this?' Carrie rooted in her bag for a tissue. She was overwhelmed.

'Ages ago. I thought it would be nice to be together and I know that he won't go home for a visit. It's such a shame. He hasn't seen Chloe since she was a toddler.'

'He hasn't seen Hannah at all.' Carrie sniffled. 'He's an awful brat.'

'It's a terrible way to be, estranged from your father. I never thought he'd stay away from home so long,' Shauna murmured as she watched her brother join the queue for passport and immigration control.

280

'Both of them are as stubborn as each other.' Carrie sighed.

'Here he is, come on.' Shauna grabbed her by the arm and they moved towards the exit. Moments later Bobby's long, thin arms were wrapped round them as he hugged the daylights out of them.

'The two of you look fantastic. Aw, girls, it's *great* to see you. Where are the kids?'

'We're meeting them for dinner in a Mexican restaurant.' Shauna squeezed him tight, thrilled at how well her surprise had worked.

'I can't believe it.' Carrie shook her head as they walked out of the airport. 'How did you keep it to yourself?'

'With great difficulty.' Shauna laughed as she led the way to the car. 'I'd say something and have to stop in the middle of it. My nerves were shot.'

There were squeals of delight when they walked into the restaurant three-quarters of an hour later. 'Bobby, Bobby!' Davey and Olivia shot out of their seats and Dan did a double take as he saw the laughing trio walk towards their table.

'Hello, stranger.' He stood up and held out his hand to his brother-in-law.

'How are you, Bobby?' Greg stood up and shook hands before calling to the waiter. 'A beer?'

'You bet,' Bobby said gratefully, untangling himself from his niece and nephew.

'A pitcher of margaritas for you ladies?' Greg, ever the urbane host, asked.

'Lovely.' Carrie took Hannah out of her high chair. 'Meet your Uncle Bobby, Hannah.' She smiled at her daughter.

'Well hellooo, beautiful!' Bobby stared at his little redheaded niece. Hannah hid her face in her mother's neck. 'Don't be shy with me,' he urged.

'What can you expect?' Carrie said a little tartly.

'You can give out to me later, Carrie, I'm thirsty and I'm starving and I know I've a lecture coming.' Bobby grimaced.

'Sorry.' She had the grace to apologize.

'Yeah, stop doing the older sister bit,' Shauna teased, lightening the atmosphere.

'OK OK.' Carrie held up her hands.

'And how is my Chloe?' Bobby kissed the top of his niece's curls.

'Hello.' She dimpled shyly.

'Hello yourself,' he said easily, sitting beside her.

'Sit by me,' Olivia pouted.

'No, me,' Chloe insisted.

'Me.' Hannah joined in.

'He's here five minutes and he's causing a row.' Shauna smiled at her younger brother as she handed him the menu. 'Choose and let's tuck in.'

It was an uproarious and joyful meal. The children, sensing their parents' infectious good humour, were giddy and excited and Shauna was delighted, and hugely relieved that her row with Greg was over. She was in terrific form. Greg had told her to leave the car in the restaurant car park. They'd get a taxi home. By her third margarita she was flying.

'Exotic city,' Bobby said admiringly a couple of hours later as they drove past Davey's favourite roundabout, the one with the massive coffee pot with the three cups illuminated against the inky black sky.

'We've loads to show you,' Davey assured him. 'Wait until you see the dhows.'

'No, wait until you see the souk. They have *everything*. Gold as well,' Olivia informed him.

'Gold! Wow!'

'I have a gold charm bracelet,' Chloe piped up.

'Stop boasting, Chloe. You're always boasting,' Olivia said irritably.

'I'm not boasting,' Chloe retorted. 'I *have* got a charm bracelet and a gold bangle *and* a gold chain. 'Cos my dad's rich.'

'So is mine,' snapped her cousin.

'Stop fighting, you girls,' Davey ordered. 'It's great that you're here, Bobby, you just get fed up of girls sometimes.'

'Indeed,' Bobby drawled. 'Tell me about it.'

Shauna giggled. She was well on.

Two hours later, when the children were in bed and Filomena had gone to her room, Bobby rummaged in his rucksack and produced a bottle of Baileys and one of Tia Maria.

'Oooh, Baileys! Lovely,' sighed Carrie, sprawled barefoot on the sofa.

'I was petrified those police that got on the plane at Dhahran were going to discover it,' Bobby remarked, referring to the religious police who boarded the flight when it touched down in the Saudi airport. 'It's a bit nerve-racking, isn't it? Don't think Saudi would be my scene.'

'*This* is my scene,' grinned Shauna as she waved some liqueur glasses around. 'Get some ice, Greg, and let's party.'

'Oh, I bought some crisps as well,' Bobby remembered.

'Proper crisps! Oh, I've died and gone to heaven.' Shauna sighed, as happy as a lark, thrilled to have her siblings together so far from home. It was the best night of Carrie's stay, they agreed as they wended their woozy ways to bed several hours later.

'I'm dying,' Shauna muttered when she woke to see Greg emerging from the en suite, showered and shaved for work.

'I did try to tell you not to mix your drinks,' he said

unsympathetically as he tightened the knot in his tie. 'I'll be home late, I've got that business dinner in the Hilton.'

'Don't talk about dinner.' Shauna groaned as a devil danced a hornpipe in her head. She closed her eyes and never heard him leave for work.

Carrie looked the worse for wear as she staggered along to the kitchen a couple of hours later. Dan had taken the children for a walk by the sea and Bobby was snoring his head off on the sofa. It was Filomena's day off.

'Wake up, you.' Shauna poked her brother in the rump and stood over him with a cup of steaming coffee.

'Aaaagh! Oh, my head.' He struggled to sit up, his hair a straw yellow mop on his head.

'You look a sight.' Carrie grinned.

'Did you look in the mirror yourself this morning?' he retorted grumpily. 'Hell! I'm renouncing drink,' he moaned as he sipped his coffee. 'Where's everyone?'

'Dan, who can hold his liquor, thank God, has taken the kids for a walk to allow us time to sober up and make ourselves presentable.' Carrie yawned and winced as the movement caused her needles of pain.

'Do something about that sun, turn it down or something.' Bobby squinted at Shauna.

'Deal with it,' she muttered, handing him her sunglasses.

An hour later, feeling slightly revived after showering and dressing, they sat on the balcony eating croissants dripping with butter and jam.

'Have some fruit and yoghurt,' Shauna urged, proffering a dish of fresh fruit that she'd sliced and diced.

'Fresh strawberries and mangoes for brekkie. I could learn to adapt to this lifestyle.' Bobby helped himself to a generous portion and spooned some yoghurt over it.

'Do you think I should get those spices for Della?' Carrie buttered another croissant and tried not to think of the calorie content.

'Don't even think about it,' Shauna advised.

'OK,' Carrie agreed, not needing much persuasion.

'Did you ever think we'd end up all together eating brekkie in a posh apartment in the Persian Gulf?' Bobby sat back in his chair contentedly. 'You've done well for yourself, Shauna.'

'I suppose I have,' she agreed. 'Even though it's taken you long enough to come out here.'

'Ah don't give out to me,' he wheedled.

'Why not? You deserve giving out to.' She eyed him caustically.

'OK! Get it over with. So I'm a black sheep for not visiting, or coming home.' He looked at Carrie, waiting for her to chip in.

She shrugged. 'If you don't want to come home that's up to you, but just because you're not speaking to Dad doesn't mean you can't come and visit us.'

'Aw, come on now, Carrie, be reasonable. How could I do that? Come home to Whiteshells Bay and not visit the old buzzard? Even *I'm* not that callous,' he retorted.

'So we all have to suffer,' Carrie said dryly.

'Look, Carrie, you're his favourite and always have been, you don't *quite* know what it's like,' Bobby said tightly.

'True,' murmured Shauna.

'Don't give me that,' Carrie snorted. 'I've had my ups and downs with him too.'

'Not as bad as we have, in all fairness.' Shauna was firmly on Bobby's side.

'Well, all I'm saying is that he's getting old and he's not as bad as he was, and maybe you should try and make some sort of peace with him so that you won't have regrets when he does . . . die,' Carrie said exasperatedly.

'I won't have any regrets,' Bobby said sulkily.

'You know, in your own way you're as stubborn and intransigent as he is. You were pretty hard on him too,' she pointed out.

'Oh, let's not fight,' Shauna said wearily. 'We haven't all been together for three years. Let's enjoy ourselves.'

'Let's, by all means,' Carrie agreed. 'But there's no point in brushing things under the carpet, they've got to be faced sometime or another, and, Bobby, I don't care what you say now, but I do think you'll have regrets if you don't make some sort of effort at reconciliation.'

'And I suppose if I do kiss and make up he's going to have me and my partner over to stay,' Bobby said sarcastically.

'You've got a partner!' they exclaimed in unison.

Bobby grinned. 'Yes, you smug marrieds! I'm spoken for.'

'What's he like?'

'What's his name?'

'He's divine,' Bobby raved. 'His name is Anton, he's tall, dark and handsome, and slightly Colin Firth-ish. He's a web designer, and I just adore him.' He pulled his wallet from his shorts pocket and drew out a photo of his beloved.

'Hmmm, dishy,' Shauna approved as she studied the dark-haired young man with the smiling eyes.

'He's nice. I'm glad for you, Bobby.' Carrie leaned over and kissed him. 'How long have you been together?'

'Actually only very recently as a couple,' Bobby confessed, 'although we've known each other for yonks. We didn't actually click until just before I came out here. It's very, very early days but I'm really happy,' he confided.

'Are you living together?'

'Not yet. He's subletting in Notting Hill from a guy who's in New York for a year, but he's only got four months to go and then we're going to set up home together. I'm dying for you to meet him.'

'Why don't you both come and stay with me in Malahide for a few days in July when I'm home?' Shauna suggested.

'Wouldn't Greg mind?' her brother queried.

'Not at all, but he won't be home until August anyway.'

'You're on,' Bobby agreed eagerly.

'Will you visit Dad?' Carrie licked a smear of jam off her finger.

'Well, if I do, I won't bring Anton. That might be just *toooo* fraught.'

'You can say that again,' chortled Shauna. 'Could you imagine poor old Dad if you pranced in with Anton and introduced him as your partner?'

'I know. Some things are never going to happen and that's one of them, no matter how much I'd like it. You two don't know what it's like,' he accused.

'No, we don't,' Carrie agreed. 'And you're dead right, some things will never change, but at least you can introduce him to us, so be thankful for small mercies and stop feeling sorry for yourself and try to let go of the past.'

'You always *were* the bossy big sister,' Bobby said affectionately as yells and laughter signalled the return of Dan and the children.

'Let's have a lazy day and go to the beach club for lunch and a swim,' Shauna suggested.

'Sounds perfect to me,' Carrie agreed. 'I've just finished Michael Palin and I'm going to start—'

'You're *not* reading. I haven't seen you for three years,' Bobby protested.

'Tough! I'm on my holliers!' Carrie retorted.

'That's all I've got from her since she arrived,' Shauna said fondly, smiling happily at her dearly loved siblings.

Dear Son

I tried to phone you last night and tonight and have got no answer. I hope that you're all right. As this is Easter and a time of reconciliation I'd like to hold out the olive branch to you after all this time in the hope that we could put the past behind us and start afresh.

I realize that I may have been somewhat harsh with you in the past but my desire was always to be a good and loving father. Perhaps I've failed. I think your dear mother would be very unhappy with the estrangement there is between us; I know it troubles me. So if you can find it in your heart to accept my apologies for any hurt I've caused you I would be very grateful.

I hope all is well with you. Your sister Carrie is on holiday with Shauna in the Gulf. I miss them all sorely and will be glad to see them all home safe and sound.

I trust this letter finds you well and happy. I'm afflicted with bronchitis and am on antibiotics. I was lucky not to get pneumonia. God willing, I'll recover.

Your affectionate Father

Noel studied the letter he had written to Bobby for the umpteenth time. It had taken a long time to draft but he felt he'd got it right. He'd crossed out and rewritten every second word until he was happy, and then he'd come to the end when he'd had to put in the closing line. He couldn't quite bring himself to write your 'loving' father. A little too hypocritical and not quite accurate, he'd thought uncomfortably. Love wasn't a word he associated with his feelings for his son, but 'affectionate' was a good word, he thought with satisfaction.

He would post the letter first thing. He had Bobby's address. He'd had to forward him post when he'd first moved to London and as far as he knew he hadn't changed flats. Carrie would have told him if he had.

Anna would be well pleased, he thought with satisfaction as he tidied away his writing materials and made his hot chocolate before going to bed. He had made a move towards reconciliation, the Christian thing to do, as Mrs O'Neill had advised. The next step was up to Bobby.

It was their last night in Abu Dhabi and they all strolled through the souk absorbing the smells and sounds and colours that were a feast for the senses. Bobby was stocking up on spices, having already treated himself to a richly woven rug in crimson and gold. Davey had bought an Action Man that crawled on his belly and Chloe and Olivia were torn between various items of bling and Barbies. Hannah was happy with her Winnie-the-Pooh and Carrie had treated herself to another couple of lengths of beautiful silks. Shauna was subdued, feeling lonely already at the thought of their leaving.

An hour later they sat on the balcony eating chawirma and salads, watching the dhows sailing up and down the silver Gulf as the moon hung low in the pitch black sky and stars glimmered enchantingly. Jenna and Brett had called in to say goodbye and there was laughter and relaxed chat between the adults as the children began to get drowsy and Filomena discreetly and efficiently undertook the bedtime duties.

Carrie slipped Hannah's pyjama top over her head and smiled as the toddler's curly head lolled against her shoulder. Poor

Hannah was out for the count. She'd be back in her routine next week and late night bedtimes would be but a dream.

It was a relaxing evening. Shauna had turned down invites to a barbecue in the beach club in favour of a family night and Carrie was glad. She'd enjoyed her last browse through the souk with the children and Bobby but she knew that Shauna was feeling down despite her bright facade in front of Jenna and Brett. She was torn herself, hating to leave her brother and sister but looking forward to seeing her father and getting home.

'You'll be home too for the summer,' she comforted Shauna as they filled the dishwasher before going to bed.

'I know. It was just so lovely having you and Bobby here. You're a great sister, Carrie, and I love the kids and Dan. I really miss home sometimes. It's getting harder to come back after each summer.'

'Would you not be bored if you came home? This is a very exotic, jazzy life.'

'When I go home I'm perfectly happy having elbows-on-the-table lunches with you and Sadie, and Chloe is always very settled with her cousins.' Shauna turned the dial to the cycle and switched on the dishwasher. 'Greg would hate it,' she added wryly.

'Tough choice,' Carrie murmured, not envying her sister one bit.

'And Della thinks my life is a bed of roses.' Shauna shook her head.

'Let's not even waste our breath talking about her. Let's have a nightcap with the lads.'

'OK. And thanks for listening.'

'A regular agony aunt, that's me. Stop getting maudlin, for heaven's sake,' Carrie urged, waving a bottle of gin. 'Bring the lemon and the Pringles. Might as well add another couple of pounds and go up a full stone while I'm at it.'

Shauna laughed and did as she was told.

'Dad, we're just leaving Shauna's now. The flight's at midnight and we'll be flying from Schiphol at eight in the morning. We'll be home around half ten, all going well.' Carrie's voice sounded as though it was coming from next door.

'I'll have the kettle on and the place aired,' Noel promised, longing to see them all.

'The time went fast, didn't it? I can't believe we're coming home.' Carrie smiled at the excitement in his voice.

'I'm looking forward to seeing you. And you know what, Carrie? You might be pleased to know that I wrote a letter to your brother, hoping that he might let bygones be bygones. I tried to phone a couple of times earlier in the week but there was no answer.' Noel couldn't disguise the note of self-satisfaction in his voice.

'You wrote a letter to *Bobby*?' Carrie couldn't hide her surprise.

'It's been too long.' Noel sighed. 'Your mother wouldn't be happy the way things are.'

'No, Dad, Mam wouldn't be at all happy. She'd be delighted you wrote asking him to let bygones be bygones.' Carrie stared questioningly at Bobby, who was sitting at the kitchen counter drinking coffee. He looked shocked and made a face. She beckoned him over sternly.

'Dad, the reason you didn't catch Bobby in London is because he flew out here to give us a surprise. I'll put him on to you.' She handed the phone to a reluctant Bobby. 'Go *on*. He's written a letter of reconciliation to you,' she hissed. 'That was hard for him. Do your bit.'

Bobby cleared his throat. 'Hello, Dad.'

There was silence at the other end of the phone and then he heard Noel's well-remembered voice.

'Hello, son,' his father said gruffly. 'Are you having a good holiday?'

'Er . . . great. It was terrific to see the girls and the kids . . . um . . . it's been a while,' he managed.

'Too long. Maybe you might get home in the summer. It would be . . . it would be good to see you.'

'That would be nice, Dad,' Bobby said quietly.

'Yes, well, there's a letter in the post for you. Maybe we can put the past behind us and start afresh,' his father said hesitantly.

'Of course we can.' Bobby's heart softened. Holding a grudge was not in his nature. 'I'll see you in the summer. And Dad . . .'

'Yes, son?'

'Thanks for the letter. I'll be looking forward to reading it when I get home.'

'Well I'm not the best at writing letters,' Noel admitted with a dry chuckle. 'I just muddled along with it. Enjoy the rest of your holiday now. I'll just say a quick hello to Shauna.'

''Bye, Dad.' Bobby swallowed hard as he handed the phone over to his sister. Who would have believed that his father would make the first move towards forgiveness? A pang of shame made his heart constrict. If it had been left to him, it might never have happened. Maybe Carrie *was* right; maybe he was more like his father than he cared to admit. It wasn't something he wanted to dwell on too long.

'What a wonderful way to end the best holiday I've ever had,' Carrie whispered as she hugged him tight.

'Stop. I don't want to bawl,' he grimaced.

'OK, but I'm glad,' she murmured.

'Me too. I'm looking forward to visiting in the summer now.'

'It's going to be the best summer ever,' Shauna declared. She was glad that Bobby was here for another few days. Saying goodbye to Carrie was the pits.

'At least the kids will sleep on the plane,' she said to Carrie an hour later as they tumbled out of the SUV, excited at the thought of going home and wondering what film would be shown on the flight. Hannah was falling asleep in Dan's arms.

'Thanks for a great holiday. Don't come in,' Carrie urged. 'It's much better not to prolong the goodbyes. We'll see you in the summer and it won't be long coming.'

'OK.' Shauna couldn't hide her tears.

'Stop, please, Shauna.' Carrie tried to swallow the lump in her throat.

'Shauna, get your ass out of here.' Dan laid Hannah in her buggy and turned to his sister-in-law and enveloped her in a bear hug before giving her a whoosh up into the front seat. 'And a nice ass it is too.' He winked and she laughed. Greg waved and started the engine and before Dan had pushed their trolley through Departures they were roaring off in the darkness along the highway that crossed the desert.

Noel flipped the last of the rashers into the dish holding the sausages, covered it and slid it into the oven. He filled the sizzling pan with sliced mushrooms and seasoned them with pepper and salt and threw in an extra knob of butter. While he was waiting for them to cook, he buttered slices of brown and white bread and laid them in two bread baskets.

A warm breeze blew in the kitchen window and Davey's fish swam happily in their tank. Noel had cut the grass front and back and on the island in the kitchen stood a big steak and vegetable casserole that Mrs O'Neill had thoughtfully cooked for Carrie.

'The last thing that poor girl will want to do is cook dinner later on so she can pop this in the microwave,' his friend assured him as she handed him the dish of aromatic food. 'And make sure to have milk and bread for them until she has time to do a shop,' she advised. It was good advice. He wouldn't have thought of it, he reflected, giving the mushrooms a stir.

He opened a can of beans and tipped them into a saucepan. Davey and Dan loved beans with a fry so they'd go down a treat. He was peckish too, he realized, as the smell of frying mushrooms made his mouth water.

He heard the crunch of tyres on gravel and his heart leapt as he hurried out to the hall and peered out the window beside the front door. A big maroon people carrier taxi had pulled up outside and he could see Davey jumping out. Noel flung open the front door, a beam creasing his lined face.

'Grandpa!' Davey raced over to him and embraced him tightly. Noel ruffled his tawny head, unable to speak, as Olivia and Hannah galloped over to him squealing with delight.

'Hello, hello,' he said gruffly and then Carrie was beside him hugging him, tears in her eyes, and Noel felt more loved than he'd ever felt in his life.

'Hello, Mr Mac.' Dan gripped him by the hand and inhaled appreciatively. 'Is that rashers and sausages I smell?'

'It certainly is,' Noel said proudly. 'I've cooked us all a big fry-up. I thought you'd be hungry.'

'Deadly, Grandpa, we're *starving*!' Davey exclaimed. 'How are my fish?'

'Alive and kicking – or should I say swimming,' he joked, delighted that they were home at last.

'That smells great, Dad. I'm dying for a cup of tea,' Carrie exclaimed, as Hannah made straight for her toys.

'Well, sit down there now and I'll dish up and you can tell me all the news.' Noel opened the oven and lifted out a big dish of sausages, rashers and fried tomatoes. 'You might put them on the plates, Carrie, and I'll serve the beans and make the tea.'

'Right,' she agreed, thinking that he looked a bit pale, and watery around the eyes.

'Grandpa, this is the best breakfast ever,' Olivia declared ten minutes later as they settled down round the big pine table and Dan poured tea into their mugs.

'That's good.' Noel smiled at her. 'It's the best breakfast ever for the best family in the world. Now tell me *all* the news.'

As Carrie sat listening to her children regaling their grand-father with every detail of their holiday she gave a little prayer of thanks. For the first time in years their family was on an even keel again and it was a huge relief. Her father and brother's estrangement had been an underlying worry to her and even the fact that Noel had cooked them a welcome-home breakfast was a surprising change in behaviour. Maybe their short absence had made him appreciate them. It certainly seemed that way.

Shauna had said that it was going to be the best summer ever and perhaps she was right. Old wounds would be healed and fresh starts would be made. What more could they all ask for?

SUMMER

(the same year)

27

'LOOK, CHLOE, IT'S OUR PLANE. THE GREEN ONE WITH THE BIG shamrock on the tail. We'll be home soon. Isn't it exciting?' With mounting excitement Shauna pointed out the big Aer Lingus jet taxiing to a halt at the jetway on the tarmac in front of them.

There was nothing like seeing an Aer Lingus plane in a foreign airport to lift a weary traveller's heart, she thought happily. Stepping on board was the first real feeling of being home. No matter how many times she flew, alone or with Greg, she always felt that same frisson of excitement when she saw the familiar green logo on her journey back to Ireland.

'I'm tired, Mom,' Chloe whined.

'I know, darling, but it won't be long now and then you can go straight to bed and when we wake up we'll unpack and settle in and then maybe tomorrow we'll drive out to see your cousins.' Shauna tried to jolly her weary daughter along. It had been a tiring midnight flight from the Gulf on the KLM Airbus and they'd had to wait several hours for their connecting flight to Dublin. Filomena was nodding off in her seat, surrounded by various duty free bags and two of Chloe's dollies.

Shauna was longing for a cup of tea and a slice of brown soda bread smeared with butter and marmalade and then a shower and a long sleep in a freshly changed bed, at home, without being disturbed by the rattle and whine of air-conditioning.

The humidity in the Emirates in the last few weeks had been unbearable. Ten minutes in the open had the perspiration running in rivulets down her back and if it weren't for the air-conditioning she would have melted. The breeze that had whispered between the jetway and the cabin door when she'd disembarked at Schiphol had given her a taste of fresh, refreshing breezes to come. The smell of the air was different, too: no heady scents of the desert, no oven blast of heat. It was great. She didn't know how Greg stuck it in the Gulf in high summer. She'd been utterly wilted the last few weeks as the temperatures had soared to over a hundred and the humidity had been intense.

'Mom, when are we getting on the plane?'

'Soon,' Shauna fibbed, watching the disembarking passengers. It would be at least another half an hour before the turnaround. 'Let's have one last cup of hot chocolate,' she suggested. The hot chocolate in Schiphol was particularly tasty and a firm favourite of her daughter's.

'OK.' Chloe perked up. 'And some biscuits?'

'Just this last time now, Chloe,' she warned. 'We're definitely cutting down on the junk this summer.'

'OK, Mom.' Chloe rolled her eyes heavenward. She'd heard all this before.

Two hours later Shauna peered eagerly out the cabin window and saw the unmistakable red and white ESB towers, Dublin port, and Dun Laoghaire to the left of her as they flew low over the glittering blue-green waters of the Irish Sea. The plane banked and straightened for its final approach, minutes away from landing. She could see the Seacat skimming across the white-capped sea below and two trawlers chugging along towards

Howth with their catch of the day. To the right, North County Dublin was flashes of emerald green and gold.

Her heart began to race as the sea disappeared and fields, roads and houses came into clear focus. She could see lanes of traffic streaming in towards the city in the morning rush hour. To the drivers, hers was just another plane coming in to land, but she was coming home and her heart was singing.

Chloe was asleep and she wanted badly to wake her and have her share her sense of excitement. But Ireland wasn't home to Chloe, Shauna thought with a sudden jolt. Home to Chloe was a hot, humid country carved out of desert and Ireland was a place to go for a couple of months for the summer holidays. How awful! she thought in dismay and tried not to let the realization burst her bubble of excitement.

Filomena was flicking through *Hello!* unaware of her employer's mixed emotions. Poor Filomena, she was far from home too. Why would she be excited landing in a foreign country? She was going home to the Philippines for a month in August, and Shauna was going to make sure to give her an extra generous bonus, she decided, as the wings seemed to dip and waver and the ground got closer and closer. They landed in a blur of green, the wheels hitting the runway with a slight thud.

I'm home, I'm home, she thought, exhilarated, and closed her eyes, savouring the moment as the brakes eventually slowed the airliner to a gradual crawl. The trees looked impossibly green, the fields and surrounding grassland lush and rich after the parched thin grass back in the Emirates.

How ordinary everyone looked compared to the richly robed Arabs and veiled Muslim women who had thronged Abu Dhabi airport, she noted, as she emerged from the jetway and began the long walk to Passport Control followed by a yawning Filomena and a cross, tired Chloe.

'It's very cold here, Mom, I'm freezing,' her daughter complained.

'Put your cardigan on. Filomena, can you give her a hand, please?' Shauna instructed as she keyed in her pin number and waited for her phone to connect to the network. A text message came up and she smiled, seeing that it was from Carrie. Welcome home c u in a few minutes, it said, and she knew that Carrie was outside in Arrivals.

It was another twenty-five minutes before they cleared immigration and collected their luggage and she was in a fever of impatience as she manoeuvred her loaded trolley through the big glass doors out to the meeting area.

'Shauna!' She heard Carrie's call and turned to see her sister at the barrier, waving madly and smiling broadly. Leaving the trolley where it was she ran to her and they hugged tightly.

'Told you the time would fly.' Carrie drew away from her and turned to cuddle Chloe.

'Where are my cousins?' she asked excitedly.

'I came by myself,' Carrie said lightly as she turned to hug Filomena.

'Aw, I wanted to see them,' pouted Chloe.

'You will. You've the whole summer ahead of you.' Shauna tried not to give in to irritability.

'Right, let's go. Follow me,' Carrie instructed crisply as they emerged into a fresh, easterly breeze. Shauna stood inhaling the heavy, salty air. 'Gorgeous,' she breathed. 'Gorgeous! It smells like home.'

Filomena shivered and zipped up her fleece.

'I slept for a week after I got home.' Carrie laughed. 'The air's just so rich on the coast.'

'I'll probably sleep for a month. I'm knackered. I couldn't sleep on the flight. I was sitting beside this fat lump who smelt of garlic and farted and snored his way through the flight. It was a nightmare.' Shauna grimaced as they crossed to the pay machines and car park.

'Yeah, it was gross.' Chloe wrinkled her nose at the memory.

'You're here now and you're going to have a good breakfast, have a shower and tumble into bed. The house is aired, the heating is on like you asked, the fridge and freezer are stocked, and you've nothing to do except fall into bed,' Carrie said.

'Thanks a million, Carrie.' Shauna yawned so hard she nearly dislocated her jaw.

'I brought the station wagon, I figured you'd have a load of luggage.' Carrie grinned.

'You know me, I can never travel light,' Shauna reminded her. 'And Miss Chloe's as bad. We have five dolls in the case *and* their wardrobes.'

'The bad news is that we're in outer Siberia. I could only get parking in Block C. It's crazy. So we've a bit of a trek, sorry about that.'

'No problem, the walk will do us good. How's everyone? How's Dad?'

'Good form; looking forward to seeing you,' Carrie said as she led them to the lift. Ten minutes later they were through the exit barrier.

'At least we're going against the traffic,' Carrie remarked as they slid into the lane heading for Malahide.

'Look at the traffic jam on the other side. I wouldn't like to be commuting into the city to work,' Shauna observed, settling back for the journey home, glad that she didn't have to negotiate the traffic and the roundabouts. It was great being picked up at the airport. Carrie was always really good about making sure to be there to welcome her home.

'That's Dad's car,' she exclaimed twenty minutes later as Carrie pulled into the drive.

'He wanted to see you. But there wouldn't have been enough room for all of us *and* the luggage so he's got the kettle on,' Carrie explained as she pulled up the handbrake. The front door opened and Olivia, Davey and Hannah shot out, followed by Noel, who stood squinting in the sunlight, a tea towel over his shoulder.

'He's got stooped,' Shauna observed, taken aback by the first sight of her father. 'When I was young he always seemed so . . . so imposing. Strange, isn't it?' she murmured, unable to quell the myriad emotions she felt at the sight of him. There were still resentments and hurts but she was conscious of a feeling akin to affection that certainly wouldn't have been there before. The fact that he'd written a letter of reconciliation to Bobby had softened her feelings towards him and she was able to hold out her arms to him with a warmth that had been sadly lacking in their relationship over the years.

'Hello, Dad. Thanks for coming out to the house,' she said, kissing his wrinkled, liver-spotted cheek. He really was starting to show his age, she thought with a sense of dismay.

'Welcome home, Shauna. I've a breakfast cooked for us all,' Noel said proudly, patting her awkwardly on the arm.

'A fry-up?' she asked hopefully, smiling into his faded grey eyes.

'What else for someone who hasn't had a decent rasher and sausage in months?' he chuckled. 'Where's my girl?' He turned to Chloe, who was surrounded by her excited cousins.

'Hello, Grandpa. We've got presents for you.' She wrapped her arms round him.

'Well, look at you. Haven't you got big?' Noel hugged her back, beaming down at her. 'Thanks very much for the lovely shirt you sent home with Carrie. I was delighted with it. Come on in now, I've made your favourite thing.'

'Fried brown bread?' Her eyes lit up; she was starving.

'Fried brown bread,' her grandfather assured her. 'Especially for you.'

'Did you hear that, Mom? Grandpa made fried brown bread 'specially for *me*!' Chloe was chuffed. She loved being centre stage.

'We're getting some too.' Olivia was a tad miffed at the fuss Noel was making of Chloe.

'There's fried brown bread for everyone,' Carrie said firmly, ushering her brood in before her.

'Dad's great at cooking breakfast but he certainly leaves a fine mess,' Carrie murmured to Shauna an hour later as she filled the dishwasher.

'I know, but it was so tasty. I really enjoyed it.' Shauna handed her the greasy grill pan. 'Those rashers and sausages were to die for.'

'Well, I've left a lasagne in the fridge for you. You can have it with a side salad tonight, it will save you cooking.' Carrie slotted in the last mug, closed the door and set the cycle.

'You're so good to me, Carrie,' Shauna said gratefully.

'It works both ways.' Carrie shrugged. 'I really enjoyed our holiday at Easter. It was good for me. I was in a bit of a rut before I went out, to be honest. It made me get off my ass and do something different. You'll find out what I'm up to tomorrow. I've a surprise for you.' Her eyes danced in her tanned face.

'Tell me. Come on, don't be mean. What are you up to?' Shauna demanded.

'You'll see when you come up to us. Patience,' Carrie said tantalizingly.

'Aw, Carrie,' Shauna protested. 'That's not fair.'

'Go to bed. Have a good sleep, drive over to us tomorrow and all will be revealed,' her sister teased.

'Meanie,' Shauna retorted, intrigued. She yawned. 'God, I'm bushed. I'm going to hit the sack.'

'You do that. We'll go now. Ring me when you wake up. Come on, you lot,' she called to her gang, who were upstairs in the Aladdin's cave of toys that was Chloe's bedroom.

'Dad, thanks for a great breakfast. I'm going to go to bed now. I'll drive over to Whiteshells Bay tomorrow.' Shauna went into the lounge where Noel was reading the paper and gave her father a peck on the cheek.

'You have a good sleep for yourself. You look very tired,' her father advised as he slipped into his jacket.

Olivia, Chloe, Hannah and Davey clattered down the stairs, all talking at the same time. Noisy chaos ensued as goodbyes were said and then her family was gone and a sudden peace descended on the house.

'Let's have our showers and go to bed,' Shauna said tiredly, her energy dipping all of a sudden.

'Come on, Chloe,' Filomena said firmly.

'Do I have to get my hair washed?' Chloe scowled.

'No. Just have a little bath if you prefer, to freshen you up after travelling,' Shauna urged.

'OK, Mom.' Her daughter was too tired to argue and she followed the au pair up the stairs. Twenty minutes later, clean and sweet-smelling, she was fast asleep. Shauna closed her bedroom door slightly to try to shut out the sunlight that was spilling in from the landing.

It was a relief to stretch out in the big king-sized bed and feel the Egyptian cotton sheets cool against her skin. The ordeal of travelling home was over. She had three months to relax and wind down. Three months to share with Carrie and the family, a trip to Paris with Greg, and hopefully, with luck and the grace of God, she might even be pregnant by the time she was going back to Abu Dhabi.

She sighed. This was the last time she'd get to spend three months of the summer at home. Chloe would be starting school in September; all holidays would revolve around her schooling in the future.

Still, that was for another day. She was home, she was happy and she was very tired. Shauna turned onto her tummy and buried her head under her pillow. Filomena padded across the landing and closed the door to her room. Chloe was asleep. She'd sent Greg a text to let him know they were home, and that she'd call him later. She'd done all she had to do. Her eyelids drooped and she snuggled into her bed contentedly.

The doorbell shrilled.

Shauna jerked awake. 'Bloody hell,' she muttered, shooting up in the bed.

'I'll get it, ma'am.' Filomena appeared at her door moments later, black hair tousled, tying a dressing gown round her.

'Just tell whoever it is that I'm in bed. If they wake Chloe I'll burst them,' Shauna said crossly.

She heard Filomena hurry down the stairs and open the front door. There was a low murmur of voices and then she heard the door close.

'Who was it?' She ran her fingers through her hair, annoyed at having been jerked out of her dozy lethargy.

'Mrs next door, ma'am. I said you were asleep and she said that she would see you later.'

'Oh, for God's sake! They wouldn't give you a minute,' Shauna snapped irritably. 'She knows we've come in on the midnight flight. They'll all be knocking at the door today and tomorrow. Well, I don't care who else knocks, Filomena, don't answer it. Let's try and get some sleep. Thanks for all your help.'

'You're welcome, ma'am,' Filomena said with her usual good humour and closed the bedroom door gently.

Shauna lay back down. She liked her neighbours but sometimes they could be a little demanding. They'd all be wanting to talk to her and tell her the news and gossip and she'd spend the next two weeks making coffee for a stream of visitors. Sometimes she felt that she was their 'summer entertainment'. When Greg was home there'd be barbecues every weekend, and dinners and lunches in between. It could all be slightly wearing, and of course Della and co. would be visiting constantly. Her heart sank. Della!

She'd phoned, very put out when Carrie had arrived home without the silks and spices she'd ordered, and instructed Shauna to make sure to bring them home in the summer. Shauna had been raging at her cheek, and had determined that she wasn't in any circumstances going to go out of her way to buy the required items for her sister-in-law.

The week before she came home she'd chickened out and bought some material. She couldn't find the shade Della was looking for so she'd bought some royal blue. If her detested sister-in-law didn't like it she could lump it!

Shauna'd forgotten all about these aspects of coming home in the excitement of actually arriving and seeing Carrie and the gang. Her feel-good bubble began to evaporate. She felt a surge of annoyance with her next-door neighbour for reminding her of the 'arrival home negatives' as she called them. Anyone with a bit of cop-on would know that she'd be exhausted after the long journey. And she certainly wasn't going to entertain *any* visitors this evening, she decided drowsily as fatique overtook her and she finally fell asleep.

28

CARRIE HUMMED TO HERSELF AS SHE DROVE ALONG THE M1, trying to block out the sounds of Britney, who was playing on the CD player. There'd been a row between Olivia and Davey about what to listen to, with Davey insisting on Green Day. She'd solved that one by letting Davey listen to his CD on the way out. It was now Olivia's turn to listen to *her* absolute favourite. Britney was cool, according to her daughter. When the squabble had got particularly fraught she'd threatened them both with Hannah's nursery rhyme CD.

It was great having Shauna home. She was looking forward to a few girls' nights out with her and Sadie. And she was really looking forward to seeing Shauna's face when she showed off her new enterprise.

Carrie's face split in a broad grin. So much had happened since her holiday in the spring. She was now the proud owner of a small caravan park. It had been extremely hard not telling Shauna about it but she'd wanted to surprise her. It had all happened so quick she was finding it hard to believe herself.

This would be her first season; she was two-thirds booked out and had high hopes of having one hundred per cent occupancy for the high season. Was she mad, she wondered, going into a demanding business that would take over her whole summer? And saddling herself with a fairly hefty bank loan to boot?

She'd give it a whirl for a year, she'd told Dan when he'd pointed out that her work load was going to be trebled and he'd be too tied up with his own business to give much help. She was used to hard work, she'd said dryly. The difference was, this time she'd be working for herself.

She sighed, remembering how uncharacteristically depressed she'd become after the high of her holiday in the Gulf had dissipated. She'd found herself comparing her humdrum life to that of her sister. Shauna had done so much and seen so much, met so many people and travelled extensively with Greg. In comparison, Carrie felt her life seemed tame and uninspired.

She had worked briefly in Dublin for two years as a legal secretary before she'd married. She'd shared a house in Fairview with two other girls. She'd enjoyed a good social life and living in the capital but had been happy enough to settle in Whiteshells Bay when she'd married Dan. Seeing Shauna's fast-paced, social style of life, and comparing it to her own rather routine, day-in day-out stuff, had made her feel that middle age was creeping up fast and what had she to show for it? She wanted to get out of her comfortable rut. Because she *was* in a rut, even if it was a nice rut, she'd told Dan moodily.

'Look, you're both different people, with different personalities and different ways of life. You can't compare yourself with her,' Dan pointed out, half sorry they'd gone out to Abu Dhabi. It was very unusual for his beloved to get down in the dumps for more than a couple of hours. Now all this questioning and angst and talk of middle age was extremely unsettling.

'I'm boring,' Carrie wailed. 'All I do is cook and wash and shop and do homework and then I do the same thing the next day and the next.'

'Carrie, you make a home. You're the linchpin. Our children are happy, I'm happy—'

'And I'm *boring*,' she interrupted crossly.

'You're not, you're gorgeous and sexy and interesting,' Dan assured her. Then wondered whether he should have put in-teresting before gorgeous and sexy so that she wouldn't feel like an airhead. He wasn't used to walking on eggshells with Carrie. It was unnerving him.

'What else would you say?' She brushed his compliments aside irritably. 'You're hardly going to say that I'm fat and frumpy and dull. And that's the way I feel right now. I'm serious, Dan. Life's passing me by,' she said frustratedly.

'You only feel like that because you've a few extra pounds on you after the holiday,' he said soothingly. 'Once you get back into your routine it will fall off you.'

'So now you're telling me I *am* fat!' She stared at him in horror.

'No I'm *not*, Carrie. You said that you'd put on a few pounds. I think you're fine,' he exclaimed in exasperation. What had got into her? She wasn't usually this illogical.

'Make up your mind, Dan,' she snapped.

'Now stop it. Or we'll end up having a full-scale row over nothing,' he ordered, looking uncharacteristically stern.

'Sorry.' At least she had the grace to apologize, he thought, relieved. 'I just feel frustrated and unsettled since I came home.' She paced up and down the kitchen.

'Well what do you want to do?' he asked, perplexed at this unwelcome personality change.

'I don't know. I can't really get a job because I don't want to change the kids' routines. They've never been used to crèches and childminders and I wouldn't like that anyway.'

'Not even having someone like Filomena?' Dan asked, trying his best to be of help.

311

'I don't know,' Carrie said doubtfully. 'Chloe's been with her since she was two almost. She knows her as well as she knows Shauna.'

'Well, tell me what you want to do and I'll try and support you as much as I can.' Dan gave her a hug, optimistic that she'd be back to normal in the morning.

Carrie knew her husband well enough to know that he was desperately hoping that this was a passing phase and she'd get back to her old self sooner rather than later. What was it about men that they were so ill equipped to handle emotional stuff? All she wanted to do was talk about it. All he wanted to do was find a solution instantly and get on with things.

Dan was a very supportive husband. He didn't like it when she was upset or agitated. Just as she didn't like it when he was troubled, she reflected. She hadn't been very fair to him, exploding at him out of the blue like that. She'd better get over herself and get on with things, she'd thought glumly, remembering that she had to take her father to the dentist the following morning.

A week later they'd been walking on the beach with the children. It was a warm, pleasant evening without a hint of a breeze and the strand rang with the sound of children's laughter and barking dogs, and seagulls screeching and squawking as they wheeled and circled and soared and dipped over the waves. The sun was beginning to sink in the west and great slashes of peach, purple and gold had tinted the sky as they'd headed back home.

They strolled past Seafield, a large twelve-acre field, owned by Dan, which had been rented out since his father's time to a couple who ran a small, serviced caravan park on it.

'Billy Moran told me yesterday that himself and Rita are retiring. They've bought a place in Spain and they were wondering did I want to keep the field as a caravan park or should they sell off the vans. What do you think?' Dan remarked, as they glanced up at the five big mobiles that had the best view of the sea, high up on their green perch.

'Do you want to put more tunnels or glasshouses on it?' Carrie looked at him, thinking that if he did expand his market business it would be more work for him and she'd see less of him.

'It's an option. But the rent from the park is good as it is, and I like having it as another egg in my basket so that we're not completely dependent on the market gardening.' Dan skimmed a flat stone across the water and they watched it hop half a dozen times before it sank.

'That's true.' She knew how her husband valued having some regular financial security for his family.

'If Billy and Rita can get someone in to take it on as a going concern, I'm happy enough to keep it as it is, I think. I'll see how they get on.'

'There must be good money in it if they can retire to Spain.' Carrie tucked her arm in his. 'I wonder where will we retire to?'

'The back of the garden in a caravan.' Her husband grinned at her.

'Daddy, Mammy, look! We found two starfish,' Olivia yelled excitedly, as Hannah ran to them, dainty as a little ballerina, and started tugging at her father's hand.

'Daddy 'ish, 'ish,' she cried, her eyes wide with excitement.

'A fish, let's see.' Dan scooped her up and held her high over his head until she yelled with delight. Carrie watched them with pleasure and thought of her outburst a week earlier. She was lucky, very lucky, even if she was in a rut, she acknowledged.

She hadn't given the Morans' departure too much thought until she met Rita in the supermarket and congratulated her on her retirement. 'I'll miss my little park, we were happy running it,' the older woman confessed. 'It was a great life in the summer

313

and we closed it in the winter and went off to Spain for weeks at a time. It was ideal, really. That's why we decided to retire out there. We like it and we've been going for years.' Her permanent tan was the envy of her peers in the village who had to make do with a two-week charter holiday once a year, or else resort to sunbeds or tan wipes.

'Have you got anyone in mind to take it over?' Carrie asked casually.

'Colin Delaney and that young one he lives with seem to want to give it a try. He told Billy that he'd like to have a chat with him about it.' Rita made a face. 'I wouldn't be mad about him taking it over. He's a bit of a chancer, if you know what I mean.'

'I know, and he's a hard drinker too. I don't think Dan would be anxious to do business with him.' Carrie frowned.

'Would the two of you not do it yourselves? It's so near to your house and of course it's Dan's land. Sure you'd be free to look after it in the summer when the kids are off school, and to be honest our clients are mostly older couples and they're no trouble. We've a few young families but the children are well behaved and we close it in October.' Rita looked at her questioningly.

'I never thought of that. Neither did Dan,' Carrie said. 'Can I have a think about it, Rita?'

'Do that, Carrie. I think it would be a grand little sideline for the pair of you and I'd be delighted knowing that my clients would be well looked after.' Rita beamed at her.

'I don't know now, Rita. I need to talk to Dan. Don't say anything to anyone,' Carrie warned.

'Mum's the word.' Rita twinkled, pleased with her machinations.

'What would you think of me taking over the running of Seafield as a business?' Carrie asked Dan that evening as he handed her a glass of wine after the children had gone to bed.

314

'*You!*' he exclaimed.

'Yeah, *me*,' she said defensively. 'I feel I'd be well able for it. Rita suggested it when I met her down the village today.'

'Have you thought it out? We'd have to buy the vans. We'd have to insure the place, clean them before letting them, and maintain the grounds. And then what would we do, pay ourselves rent for the field?'

'The clients pay maintenance fees, and that covers all those costs, including the rent we have been getting,' Carrie explained.

'Yes, but Rita and Billy work together and live in one of the mobiles on the site during the season. How would you manage?'

'Well, I'd be able to free up the mobile they live in and rent that out and use the money from that rent to pay one of the lads from the village to look after the grounds and be a handyman. I'd get one of the women to help out with the cleaning every so often.'

'We'd have to get a loan to buy the vans.' Dan started scribbling figures on a piece of paper.

'Yeah. Maybe it wasn't such a good idea.' Carrie sighed. She'd felt it was feasible, ideal for her as a mother of three young children. It wouldn't be too much of an upheaval for them.

'No harm in seeing what the bank manager has to say.' Dan smiled down at her.

'Are you serious?' She felt a surge of excitement.

'It's on our doorstep. It's an opportunity. We'd be foolish not to investigate the pros and cons at least. And even more important, if it's what you want and it makes you happy, then let's go for it.' He bent his head and kissed her slow and deep and she groaned as flutters of desire spread out through her body. Even after all this time her husband could still turn her on with just a kiss.

Carrie smiled at the memory as she took the slip road off the

M1 and drove towards the village. One great thing about taking on the caravan park was the fact that she'd lost three-quarters of a stone from all the racing around and the cleaning of the six mobiles that were available to rent out. There were thirty mobiles on the site altogether. Twenty-four were privately owned and six were for renting.

It was a nicely laid out site, set out in tree- and shrub-lined enclaves. Each separate area had five mobiles in it, giving a sense of intimacy and privacy. It was much nicer than having rows of mobile homes facing each other. The trees and shrubs were mature and the owners kept their patches neat and tidy, with flowers and shrubs and hanging baskets bringing colour and variety. A small wooden chalet housed the office at the entrance to the site and there was a small pool and playground area on a grassy flat piece of ground directly opposite the entrance, which was electronically gated.

Needless to say, the children were ecstatic at their mother's business venture. To have access to a swimming pool and playground was beyond imagining, despite the fact that they had miles of fine white sandy beach and the sea on their door-step.

She'd got into a routine once she'd taken over from Rita and Billy. After she'd dropped the children to school, she went straight to the site and opened up the office. There she dealt with whatever queries or requirements her clients might have, mostly giving out tokens for the laundry room or putting petrol in the lawnmowers that the owners borrowed to cut the grass on their patches. She took bookings from people wishing to rent out the mobiles during the summer months. Most, as far as she could see, were customers who came year after year. Compared to the larger sites along the coast that offered restaurant, shop and child entertainment facilities, her site was very small and quiet, but many people liked that aspect of it and she had no intention of expanding it.

Saturday was her busiest day, when one set of customers departed the rented mobiles at eleven and they had to be spotless and ready for occupation by two in the afternoon. Until the past couple of weeks she'd managed by herself, as usually only two or three of the vans were rented. But now, at the beginning of June, when they were getting very busy, she'd taken on two women recommended by Rita to clean out the mobiles. It was a relief to have them on board. It freed her up to spend a little more time with the children, not that they felt neglected. They'd been having too much fun. If one of her mobiles was unoccupied, Carrie cooked their dinners there and used it as a base, much to their delight. Otherwise they stayed in the chalet.

Noel too had been roped in. He'd spent the month of May painting the verandas that surrounded the rented mobile homes. Neat and particular, he'd made a great job of it and Carrie had insisted on his taking some payment for his work. He'd also planted up the pots and beds at the entrance to the site and they were now a riot of colour and scent. He'd enjoyed that. Carrie had seen several of the private clients stop and talk to him, gardening obviously being a common interest, and she stopped feeling guilty about using him, realizing that he was enjoying meeting new people as well as spending time with her and the children. It was fun sitting together eating round the small table in the dining part of a mobile, and all the better when Dan was there. There was an air of gaiety and holiday that caravans always engendered. Hannah always got excited when Carrie said, 'Come on, let's go to the park.'

The children had been sworn to secrecy about telling Shauna and Chloe but she knew Olivia and Davey were bursting with pride about their new business. Chloe had enjoyed showing off in

317

Abu Dhabi; the shoe would be on the other foot for the summer. Carrie grinned, amused as always by their small displays of one-upmanship.

Even though it was tiring, she was exhilarated and determined to make a go of it. Their income from the site would be a little more than what it had been when they were just taking rent, even after her loan repayments and workers' wages. *That* was extremely satisfying. She could bring the family on a holiday or buy the new bunks with the desks underneath them that Olivia and Davey were longing for without having to dip into the household budget, and once the loan was paid off on the six mobiles it would mean a much bigger profit. It was certainly better than drifting aimlessly towards middle age, she thought with a rueful smile as she pressed the small pad on her keyring and the wrought iron gates that guarded the entrance to Seafield glided slowly open.

'Can we go for a swim, Mom?' Olivia and Davey chorused.

'As soon as Hannah's gone for her nap. How many times do I have to tell you not to say it in front of her?' she chided, pulling up outside the office.

'Swim. Swim,' Hannah said eagerly.

'I'll murder the pair of you,' she said crossly. 'Later, Hannah. It's time for your nap.'

'No nap, Mammy.'

'Yes nap,' Carrie reiterated as they piled out of the car. Olivia and Davey made for the group of children already playing in the playground and Hannah started howling.

'You're tired, pet. Come on in with Mammy and have a bottle and when you get up I'll bring you for a swim. OK?' She scooped her wailing daughter up in her arms and walked into the office.

'Hi, Carrie. Mrs Dempsey's van has a leak so I've called the plumber and there's a load of messages on the answering machine about bookings,' Kenny Walsh, the young man she'd hired to work part time with her, informed her briskly. 'Both lawnmowers are out, and I've done the litter and clean-up round and bagged up the rubbish. I'm going to mop out the laundry room now before I go on my lunch. Frances and Orla are cleaning out numbers two and six.'

'Thanks, Kenny. You're doing a great job.' Carrie smiled at him, standing lanky and tall in his royal blue overalls.

'That's me, Kenny the Great,' he grinned, tugging gently at one of Hannah's russet curls. 'Don't cry, Hannah. I'll give you a push on the swing after your nap,' he promised.

'Swing, swing.' Hannah struggled to get out of her mother's arms.

'After your nap.' Carrie said firmly.

The phone rang. 'Let the machine take it. I'll deal with it when I've got her down,' Carrie said, knowing she had a window of about an hour to deal with her phone enquiries once Hannah went asleep. Getting her to go asleep was the challenge.

She led her into the small back room that housed a large squashy sofa, a TV, a table and chairs and a small kitchen unit containing a sink, a microwave and a kettle. This was where they based themselves if one of the mobiles wasn't available. Carrie heated a bottle for Hannah in the microwave and led her over to the sofa. 'Lie down now, darling.' She whooshed the toddler onto the cushions, tucked a pillow under her head and covered her with her favourite blanket. Hannah was whacked, tired out after her early start, and only managed to finish half her bottle before her eyelids drooped and she was asleep.

'Great!' Carrie breathed a sigh of relief. It wouldn't be so bad when her daughter was older. Now she had to try to organize herself around her needs. She left the door open and went to the small office at the front and began the task of sorting her mail and phone calls. Outside, through the open window, she could hear Davey's loud guffaws. Carrie smiled and bent her head to her work. Dan was bringing them lunch in an hour or so. She wanted to be on top of things by then so that she was calm and in control and he could see that the business was running smoothly.

'Carrie, quick. Mr Feeney fell off his veranda and he's unconscious. Ring the ambulance.' Kenny raced into the office.

'Oh, Lord! OK.' Carrie picked up the phone and dialled 999 and gave out the information. 'Davey, come in and keep an eye on Hannah for me,' she yelled to her son who was shooting hoops.

'Aw, Mom!' he protested.

'Don't argue. It's an emergency. Quick!'

'What's wrong?' he demanded truculently when he got to the office.

'I've to go to Mr Feeney's mobile. He fell. Stay here.'

Carrie ran after Kenny, heart thumping. Maybe the poor man had had a heart attack. She hoped he wasn't dead. His wife was cradling his head in her lap and other neighbours were helping to keep her calm. 'Are you all right, Mr Feeney?' Carrie knelt beside him. He looked pasty and grey but at least he was conscious again.

'Did a damn fool thing, tripped over my watering can and fell down the steps. I think I've broken my arm.'

'I've phoned for the ambulance; it's on its way. Oh, Kenny, would you go up and open the gates so they won't be delayed getting in?'

'Sure.' Kenny took to his heels and Mrs Feeney had to laugh.

'I don't think it will be here that quick even though it's not that far up the road.'

It took the ambulance fifteen minutes, and another ten before Mr Feeney was assessed and given first aid before being lifted into the back of it. Much to the gathered children's disappointment it did not speed off with lights flashing and alarms wailing, but Carrie was relieved that her client hadn't had a heart attack, and that his condition wasn't too serious as far as they knew.

'I missed it all,' sulked Davey when she finally got back to the office.

'Don't be like that, Davey, it wasn't a nice thing to happen to poor Mr Feeney, and I needed your help. Don't make me feel bad for asking for it,' Carrie told him sternly.

'Sorry, Mam,' he apologized immediately. She loved her son's good nature and her hug was tight as they made up. She'd lost half an hour of her precious window, but Hannah was still sleeping so she settled down at her desk.

'Carrie, I was wondering about changing our mobile. We've bought a new one with central heating. Maher's in Dunboyne sold it to us. A lovely model called the Leven. It's got a bedroom with a bay window and en suite and integrated fridge freezer. It's the business.' Frank Coyle, a tall, broad man in his fifties, strolled into the office and sat down. 'Could you sort out a day with them when we could take delivery? Here's the number and here's the brochure. Isn't she a beauty?'

'Sure, Frank,' she said cheerfully, taking the brochure from him and studying it. His new mobile was a fine model; she just wished he hadn't come in right at this minute to tell her about it.

'I'll be needing a new veranda to go round it. Will you organize the carpenter?' Frank continued.

'Sure. I'll look after it, Frank.'

'Poor Des Feeney. That was a stroke of bad luck. If he's in plaster he's really stuck,' Frank continued chattily. The phone rang.

'Excuse me, Frank.' She smiled politely.

'I'll let you get on with it.' He uncoiled himself from the chair.

'Seafield Park, can I help you?' She waved at Frank and turned her attention to her caller.

'Hello, my name's Lorna Rooney. I was staying in one of your mobiles until this morning.' An elderly voice came down the line.

'Yes, Mrs Rooney, I remember. How are you? What's the problem?' Carrie continued opening her post, mostly bills unfortunately.

'I think I left my reading glasses in the main bedroom. Could you check for me? I'm terrible for putting them down and forgetting them,' the old lady quavered.

'Certainly, I'll do that. It will take a few minutes but I'll get back to you,' Carrie assured her and put the phone down. She looked out the window to see if she could catch sight of Olivia. Her daughter was coming out of the changing room, ready to go for her swim. Davey was already swimming up and down. He was a good swimmer. Carrie's rule with Olivia and Davey was that they could only swim if there were other parents at the pool.

'Olivia?' she called through the window. Olivia trotted over.

'Yes, Mam?' She jigged up and down impatiently.

'I need you to do something for me, pet. Run down to Frances in number two and ask her if there was a pair of glasses left in the bedroom.'

'Aw, Mammy, I'm going swimming.' Olivia scowled.

'For goodness' sake, Olivia, it's only a small thing I'm asking you to do. Now would you hurry on,' she exclaimed exasperatedly. Olivia stomped off in high dudgeon.

That pair were going to get a severe talking to, she decided crossly as the door opened again and a child came in looking for a washing machine token for his mother. Maybe Dan was right, she reflected ruefully. Had she taken on more than she could chew? She didn't feel half as good about her new business as she had earlier. Tension enveloped her as the flashing light on the so far unattended answering machine reminded her of something else not dealt with.

She pressed the button and the first call resounded tinnily around the office. Someone was looking to book a mobile for the middle of July. She took down the dates and flicked through the diary. One available. Excellent. She'd ring back and confirm.

The next caller was a wrong number.

The next, another caller wanting to book for two weeks in August. She knew straight away that they were out of luck. August was fully booked. So far so good. She felt her tension lift a little. She was getting through her work at last. Another twenty minutes of peace and quiet and she'd have the guts of it sorted.

'Mammy, I's awake.' Hannah trotted out from the back room all red-cheeked and tousled-haired. 'I's hungry.'

'Perfect timing then.' Dan strode into the office carrying two baskets and overheard his younger daughter's last remark. 'Lunch as instructed,' he declared breezily. 'How's it going?'

'Great,' she fibbed, cursing his punctuality.

Olivia barged in with the missing glasses and dumped them on Carrie's desk. 'Now I'm going swimming,' she announced defiantly. 'And I don't want to be disturbed.' She marched out without a backward glance.

'What was all that about?' Dan asked, highly entertained.

'An attitude problem that's going to be sorted.' Carrie frowned.

'Tell me about it over lunch. I'm off for the afternoon.' Her husband's eyes glinted with amusement.

'Well, I'm not,' she retorted and burst out laughing.

'Is there anything I can do for you before I go fishing, or reading, or golfing?' he teased, still grinning.

'Ah let's sit down and have our lunch while the other two are swimming and I'll tell you all the goings on,' she suggested.

'I'll set it out and call you when it's ready. You look a bit fraught,' Dan offered. Carrie reached up and gave him a kiss. She might be busy, and harassed, and wondering if she'd made a big mistake, but one thing was for sure. She had the best husband in the world.

29

GREG SWALLOWED WITH DIFFICULTY. HIS HEART WAS THUMPING.

'You OK there, buddy?' The surgeon gazed down over his surgical mask and patted him on the arm. 'Fifteen minutes max once the nurse has finished prepping you. You won't feel a thing down there when I give you the injection.'

'Fine. Fine,' Greg lied, wishing he were a million miles away. Vasectomy had seemed like the answer to all his problems. No more worries about Shauna getting pregnant. She could come off the Pill, and he wouldn't be up to ninety every time they made love, wondering if she'd conceived. She'd never know. The timing was perfect. She was in Ireland and he would have nearly two months to get over the procedure before he saw her again.

That was more than sufficient. He'd been assured he'd be over the op in less than a week. He could even have sex after a week, although he'd still have to use contraception until he had the two negative semen tests recommended. He wouldn't be having sex with Shauna until August. She'd never have a clue about his procedure. She'd never realize that it was his fault that she couldn't conceive. Guilt swept through him but he closed his mind to it. This wasn't the time or the place for thoughts of guilt. Time enough to fret over it later. He had enough to deal with at the moment, now that he was here in the clinic in Dubai.

He'd read all the literature that he'd been given, and been very relieved to find out that vasectomy did not affect the production or release of testosterone. His sex drive would not be affected, nor would any other masculine traits. His erections, climaxes and amount of ejaculate would all remain the same. He tried to tell himself these things as he lay on the operating table, but the negative things that he'd glossed over, and about which the urologist had reassured him, suddenly loomed large.

The very small chance of persistent chronic scrotal pain. Risks of prostate cancer, although recent studies suggested that there were no such risks. Complications such as swelling, bruising, inflammation and infection. The words reverberated through his brain. His heart started to race. Just say he was the one in a million who was affected by post-op complications. It had been bad enough suffering the utter mortification of being tended to by a nurse just out of her teens; now he was undergoing severe mental torment and the procedure hadn't started yet.

'Ready to go, mate?' Bob Kelly, the Aussie urologist, gave him the thumbs up. Greg felt a wave of nausea and terror wash over him. Spots danced before his eyes and then he knew nothing. 'I guess I'd faint myself if I was having one.' Bob grinned at the nurse. 'I might as well inject him while he's out.'

'You men are such wussies.' The nurse handed him the needle. Greg Cassidy wasn't the first patient to faint before his vasectomy and certainly wouldn't be the last. The chances were that he might even faint again. Once the surgeon had injected him with the local anaesthetic, she waved ammonia under his nose. 'Come on, Greg. Wake up. You've had your injection,' she said briskly, thinking that he was quite good-looking and very well hung. One of the finer specimens to come under her ministrations. Sometimes she wondered how she wasn't put off sex for life with what she saw.

Greg's long black eyelashes fluttered. He was as white as a sheet. 'Is it over?' he croaked.

'Just started,' she said cheerily. 'You won't feel a thing.'

'I don't believe it, Carrie, this is *fantastic*! When I was a kid I used to feel so envious of the people who lived in the caravans for the summer. I *longed* to be one of them,' Shauna exclaimed, gazing around the caravan park with amazement. 'I never realized how attractive it was inside the gates and what a little community it is.' She glanced over at one of the mobiles whose occupants were sitting under a sun umbrella having coffee on the veranda while chatting to their neighbour who was busy washing the outside of his mobile with a hose and mop. Another man was sitting on a deckchair on his small lawn reading the paper. There were no children around, much to Chloe's dismay, because it was Monday, and they were all at school. Hannah was just too small to have good games with, according to Chloe.

'One of the rented mobiles is vacant. Do you want to have a look at it?' Carrie asked, delighted with her sister's response.

'Yeah, I love caravans,' Shauna said, following her sister down a small hill and turning right into a small grassy area that contained five mobile homes, set well apart in a semicircle. Spruce trees and hedges separated them from the next section and all the small gardens were neatly tended and surrounded by masses of colourful shrubs and plants. 'You could live here,' Shauna remarked, gazing around in admiration.

'Lots of people do, in the sites that are open all year round in Bettystown,' Carrie said, stepping onto the veranda of the vacant mobile. She opened the door and stood back to let Shauna in.

'Wow!' Shauna exclaimed as Chloe and Hannah burst in behind them. 'It's so modern!'

The mobile was tastefully laid out with wraparound sofas and

327

light cream coffee table and TV unit. Over the fireplace hung a big mirror, which reflected the view from the wide window that dominated the lounge area. A small dining area led into a well fitted kitchen with all mod cons and then a narrow hallway led down to the three bedrooms and bathroom.

'Mommy, can we stay here, pleeessse, Mommy?' Chloe begged, entranced.

'Come and stay a night if you want. This one's vacant until Saturday,' Carrie invited. 'We could do a barbie on the veranda. That's what everyone does here. The smell would make your mouth water sometimes.'

'Pleesse, Mommy? Pleesse, Mommy, please, please, please?' Chloe got down on her knees and clasped her hands together.

'Just like Olivia. Actress!' Carrie murmured.

'We'll see,' Shauna declared. 'Don't forget Uncle Bobby's coming to stay.' She turned to Carrie. 'Isn't it an awful pity that Anton couldn't make it? His mother's having a knee replaced and he wants to be around to keep an eye on his dad while she's in hospital. I spoke to him on the phone. He's lovely. I'm looking forward to meeting him.'

'Me too. Bobby's really happy. It's great.' Carrie smiled.

'I want to stay here.' Chloe stuck out her lower lip and pouted.

'Be a good girl, Chloe,' Shauna warned, annoyed. 'Oh, Carrie, I've just thought. You won't be able to come into town and pop over to me the way you used to, now that you're tied up.' She made a face as realization hit.

'Well, not as much as before. I *am* a bit constrained now,' Carrie admitted. 'But I can take the odd morning or afternoon off and get Kenny to keep an eye on things. Will we have a cup of coffee on the veranda?' she suggested.

'Yeah. Let's pretend we really *are* on holiday,' Shauna agreed.

'You put the kettle on and I'll go up to the office and get some coffee and a few biscuits. I'll stick a note on the door to say that I'm in number six. You can stay here for the afternoon if you want. The kids will be coming here from school. They can all go swimming and I've made a big pot of saffron chicken for dinner. I could cook the rice here and we could eat outside, it's such a lovely day.'

'Perfect! Have you a few magazines or a book I could read?' Shauna felt herself starting to relax already.

'Sure, go up to the house and help yourself when we've had our coffee,' Carrie suggested as she stepped outside to go and get the provisions.

How very peaceful, Shauna thought as she filled the kettle and gazed out the small kitchen window, through which she could see a field full of green corn, rippling and swaying in the breeze, over the top of the hedge. Wouldn't it be lovely to stay here for a while and do nothing except read and sunbathe and spend time with Carrie. She sighed as she strolled out onto the veranda. She had Bobby coming to stay for a few days and Alice, one of her neighbours, had cornered her yesterday when she was going to get the Sunday papers to ask her when was she having her annual ladies' lunch.

'I'll let you know, Alice. I'm just home. I'm still jetlagged,' she'd said a trifle irritably.

'Oh, it's just that I'm going to the Caribbean for a fortnight, actually we're going cruising, and I'd really hate to miss your lunch. It's always such fun,' Alice twittered.

Shauna smiled at her upon hearing this little titbit. Now she knew why Alice had been so anxious to nab her. Her neighbour was absolutely *dying* to let her know that she was going on a Caribbean cruise. Alice was the queen of boasters. When Valerie, the neighbour directly opposite her, had got a new Saab convertible for her birthday, Alice had nagged her husband until he'd bought her the BMW model.

'Have you planned anything exciting for your holiday?' Alice smiled sweetly.

'I guess when life seems like a permanent holiday out in the Gulf it's actually nice to come home and just chill.' Shauna's smile was equally sweet. 'I'm meeting Greg in Paris for a few days. I need to update my wardrobe from last season, so that will be nice, but the great thing about being home for three months is that I can do things at the drop of a hat.'

Alice's eyes had narrowed at the 'updating the wardrobe' bit. 'I see,' she said tightly. 'Well, I must be off, Peter's playing a round in the K Club and then we're having lunch there. Great to have you home.' She air-kissed her and hurried across the road to her large double-fronted house, leaving Shauna half amused, half irritated. 'I should tell her I'm renting a caravan for two weeks,' she muttered as she watched Carrie striding along swinging a basket. Her sister looked great. She was wearing denim shorts and a pink halter-neck top and her legs were a lovely golden colour. Her auburn hair, lightened by the sun, had golden highlights that many women would pay a fortune for. Carrie always looked so healthy and natural. She rarely wore heavy make-up.

'Will you be able to come to my ladies' lunch this year? I've already been nabbed about it by Alice,' Shauna said as she carried the cafetiere and milk out to the veranda.

'Oh, that gabby one. I'm not mad about her; she's such a consequence. And the more she drinks the more she twitters on about nothing.' Carrie made a face. 'She's real nosy and cute, isn't she? She'd ask you what you had for your breakfast and tell you nothing. Remember how she had the nerve to ask Maria how often she and Colin had sex?'

330

'Yeah. She was really pissed.' Shauna grinned.

'Listen, she doesn't need to be pissed to be rude. I don't know why you ask her.' Carrie slid some Club Milks onto a plate.

'It would be awkward not to. It's such a small cul-de-sac, it would be seen as a real snub. She informed me she's going on a Caribbean cruise so I want to find out when it's happening and maybe I'll have the lunch then. I don't even want to think about it.' She groaned. 'Honestly, now they've come to expect it. I shouldn't have got into the habit of it. And then they'll all be coming for barbecues when Greg's home. I'm just not in the humour for entertaining this year for some reason or another. I just want to veg.'

'*Don't* entertain then. Tell Greg you're taking it easy this year,' Carrie retorted. 'Here's a treat for you.' She handed her sister a packet of crisps. Chloe and Hannah were playing with a ball on the grass and she opened a packet each for them.

'This is the life.' Shauna sat back and dunked her Club Milk into her tea.

'I've left a note on the office door. I think I'll mitch for the afternoon.' Carrie yawned. 'I forgot when I decided to take this on that I wouldn't be my own boss on hot, sunny days.'

'You're sitting on a sunny veranda dunking Club Milks; not a bad sort of job, all the same,' Shauna teased. 'Poor old Greg's gone to Dubai for a few days. He rang me last night. He's up to his eyes with work. Rather him than me. It's like an oven out there at the moment. Next year I won't be able to come home until later because of Chloe going to school, so I'll have to make the most of this summer.'

'You do that,' Carrie advised. 'Take it easy and do nothing and have the most relaxing summer ever.'

Shauna smiled, raising her face to the sun. 'You know, you're absolutely right. Because next year, if all goes well, I'll either have a new baby or be pregnant. I came off the Pill two weeks ago. Greg's finally agreed to go for it. It's a much bigger gap than I wanted, but better late than never.'

'Ah, Shauna, that's great. I'm delighted for you. And when they're older, five years is nothing in the age difference.' Carrie squeezed her hand.

'Six years. Don't forget I'll be pregnant for nine months,' Shauna pointed out.

'Well, six years then. There's more than six years between Bobby and me and look at us now,' Carrie reminded her.

'True. I'd really love if it was a girl. I'd love Chloe to have a sister,' Shauna said wistfully. 'We're lucky, aren't we?'

'Yeah, we are.' Carrie smiled at her. 'You'd better come home for the birth. You can't be out there on your own without me.'

'I wish we were coming home to live, to be honest with you. Chloe went out the front yesterday and all the kids were playing and she was too shy to join in. My heart went out to her. It's awful to see your child excluded. You know the way they're such tight little groups and a stranger is always an outsider. It's always the same when we come home. And then by the time we're getting ready to go she's finally fitted in and then she has to leave them. It's hard on a child. But Greg doesn't want to leave the Gulf.' Shauna gave a deep sigh.

'Have you said this to Greg?' Carrie asked, looking down at her niece who was chomping on her crisps and licking her fingers. She could only imagine how Shauna felt. There must be nothing worse than seeing your child left out. Her children were lucky. They had a big circle of friends in the village.

'It doesn't seem to bother him. He thinks it's more important to give her a good lifestyle. He feels she's getting plenty of cultural diversity. We don't see it in the same way at all. Don't get me wrong, Greg's a very generous husband. I've never made a wedding dress since we went out to Abu Dhabi. He didn't want me working. He's making pots of money. I can spend what I want and he never queries it. But money's not everything.' She shook her head. 'I can see where he's coming from, in a way. Once you get used to a level of wealth it's hard to let go of the golden goose. He's told me that the job in Dubai is the last one he's doing out there. That's if he gets it. Part of me is hoping that he doesn't. Is that disloyal?' she asked ruefully.

'No! Don't be silly. You're a very loyal wife. He's lucky to have you,' Carrie declared in a very firm tone of voice.

'And you're very loyal to me. Thanks,' Shauna said gratefully.

Carrie's mobile rang. 'Hello?'

'Carrie, it's Vera O'Neill. Your dad's had a little accident. He's dropped a heavy block on his foot and he was only wearing his slippers. I think he might have broken some of his toes. You might need to get his foot X-rayed. Sorry to be the bearer of bad news.'

'For goodness' sake. You never know what he's going to do next. That's OK, Mrs O'Neill. Thanks for ringing.' Carrie threw her eyes up to heaven as she clicked off.

'What's up?' Shauna eyed her warily.

'Dad's let a fucking block fall on his bloody toes. Mrs O'Neill thinks some are broken and he needs to get his foot X-rayed.'

'For crying out loud.' Shauna couldn't hide her exasperation.

'Two weeks ago he nearly took the finger off himself with a knife and I had to bring him in to get stitched. Honest to God, I should put up a bloody tent in the grounds of Our Lady of Lourdes. If I never saw that hospital again I wouldn't be sorry.' Carrie was fit to be tied. 'I'll have to ring Dan. I can't go because Kenny is going to Dublin for a night out with some mates and I

can't ask him to stand in for me again. He did it twice last week.'
Carrie punched in her husband's number.

'I suppose I should go,' Shauna said reluctantly.

Carrie looked at her, finger poised to press the green key.
'Welcome home,' she said dryly. 'I'll mind Chloe for you. The
kids will be home from school in the next twenty minutes.'

'Oh, bugger!' Shauna cursed, taking a last sip of her coffee.
'I'll see you when I see you.'

'Keep in touch,' Carrie murmured.

'Will do. Chloe, be good for Carrie, I've to bring Grandpa
somewhere. I'll be back soon.'

'OK, Mom,' her daughter said unconcernedly as she wandered
into the mobile with Hannah in tow.

Carrie watched her sister stalk out of the enclave, grim-faced.
Guilt and relief and irritation battled for supremacy. She felt
sorry for Shauna, knowing very well what it was like waiting
hour after hour in A and E. She felt relief that she wasn't going.
She'd had more than her share of it and that's where the
irritation crept in. If she hadn't had the excuse of her new job,
she probably would have had to take Noel to the hospital.
Shauna never acknowledged just how much she and Dan did for
Noel and that bugged her.

She had a face on her like thunder, and Carrie knew that she
was put out about it. Tough! Carrie had to carry the can *all* the
time. Shauna could just get on with it. *She* had to do it week in,
week out. She stood up and gathered up the cups and plates.
Trust their father to have one of his dramas. She'd been enjoying
the natter with her sister. The site was peaceful and quiet
because it was a weekday and still termtime, and none of the
families with children were on site. July would be a different
kettle of fish and she might not find it so easy to put her feet up
for an afternoon.

Shauna's life was so complicated compared to her own, she mused as she washed their cups. If she was torn between Dan's needs and what was best for the children she wasn't sure how she'd deal with it. But then Dan was a different kettle of fish from Greg, she acknowledged wryly. There really was no comparison.

Greg gritted his teeth and applied an ice pack to his very, very tender and extremely painful privates. He was in bits. He swallowed another two painkillers even though he wasn't supposed to take them for another hour and a half. He'd ruined himself. He groaned. He'd never be able to have sex again. He'd had a slash and nearly fainted. What was he going to say to Shauna? How was he going to get back to Abu Dhabi in three days' time? He'd never be able to drive that far.

He lay in the darkened hotel room. He had to stay lying down as much as he could for the next twelve to twenty-four hours. That wouldn't be a difficulty. He was shattered. But the urologist had assured him that he'd be able to return to work the day after tomorrow. 'Lying bastard,' he muttered. He'd probably never work again. He could very well die here on his own and no-one would know, he thought gloomily. He was being punished for going behind his wife's back and having a vasectomy when her heart was set on another baby. If anyone was the lying bastard it was he. He'd made a big mistake and now he was rueing it.

Shauna sat beside her father as he sat with his foot up in a wheelchair, waiting to be X-rayed. He was doing his crossword, and not inclined to talk. That suited Shauna. She wasn't in the mood to talk to *anyone*. As his problem wasn't serious they could expect to be waiting for at least three hours, she was told by the triage nurse. What a pain in the butt! She'd been really enjoying herself sitting gabbing with Carrie.

Her sister had been more than happy to pawn their father off on her. She might have given her a bit of leeway. She was hardly in the country forty-eight hours, she thought crabbily.

Her phone vibrated and she saw that she had a message.

Hi where r u? Called 2 c u, will wait until u get home. When will that b? Della x

Shauna's lips thinned. Good enough for her, she thought nastily. She hadn't given her much time to settle in, and how typical of her to arrive unannounced. *Wagon!* she thought crossly as her fingers flew over her keypad. It was almost worth sitting in A and E to be able to write: **Have no idea. In A&E with Dad. Long wait ahead. S.**

She waited for the reply, which wasn't long in coming.

Sorry to hear that. Hope not serious. Will visit again soon. Della x

Would she never learn? Shauna thought irritably as she read the message. **Suggest you ring first. Have a lot on,** she texted back tartly. Unsurprisingly there was no reply.

'Would you like a coffee or tea or a cold drink?' she asked Noel.

'Not for me, thanks, but you go ahead and get something if you want,' her father replied, grimacing in pain as he moved his foot, which was black, blue and very swollen.

'No, I'm fine,' Shauna murmured. They lapsed back into silence and Noel sucked his pen and looked into the distance, trying to work out a particularly difficult clue.

Shauna glanced round her at the crowded A and E waiting room and noticed a heavily pregnant woman sitting beside an elderly lady who was wheezing noisily. The woman shifted uncomfortably in her hard seat, her cheeks red, damp tendrils of hair sticking to her forehead.

Not the place to be if you were well gone in pregnancy. She thought of what it would be like to be pregnant out in Abu Dhabi in the scorching summer temperatures. Perhaps Carrie was right about coming home for the birth. It would all depend when she got pregnant and when her baby was due. That would be another bridge to cross with Greg. She wouldn't think about it until she had to, she decided. The most important thing was getting pregnant. All the other decisions that had to be made would follow on after that. She whiled away the time thinking of names that she'd call her baby. Mostly she concentrated on girls' names, discarding this one and that until it danced in front of her, the perfect name for her new daughter.

Charlotte Anna Cassidy.

That was it. Perfect. If Greg didn't like it he could lump it. He'd kept her waiting long enough for her little Charlotte. Chloe and Charlotte went beautifully together. They would be the best of friends.

A smile flitted across Shauna's face as she daydreamed of her daughters shopping and talking and drinking coffee together in the years to come.

30

'IT'S SUCH A PAIN IN THE ASS. I WAS SUPPOSED TO BE STAYING with Shauna but Dad's on crutches and it would be kind of callous not to stay with him, wouldn't it?' Bobby looked at his partner, half hoping that Anton might disagree with him and tell him to stay at Shauna's anyway. He'd been disappointed that his partner couldn't come on the trip because of his family commitments. Perhaps it was just as well, in the light of his father's accident, he thought ruefully.

'Very callous,' Anton said firmly. 'Heartless even.' He looked at Bobby and grinned. 'Sorry. I know that wasn't what you wanted to hear.'

'You know me so well,' Bobby growled.

'Ah cheer up, at least you're talking to him. That's a big step after all those years of silence. Think positive,' Anton encouraged.

'Talking's different from actually being in his company. It's going to feel strange going home. I'll be on edge. I'm not looking forward to it,' Bobby groaned. 'I didn't feel so bad going to stay with Shauna.'

'I know. It's easy for me to tell you what to do. But it might not be as bad as you think.' Anton gave him a hug. 'Let's sit here and take a breather and we'll walk back to the pub and I'll buy you a pint.'

'OK,' Bobby agreed, flinging himself down on to the grass. They'd gone for a walk on Primrose Hill as they often did in the evenings after work. The city skyline was hazy in the distance and a refreshing breeze whispered through the grass, bringing relief after the heat of the day.

He closed his eyes and let the evening sun warm his face. He liked strolling on Primrose Hill, its trees and greenery and open spaces a reminder of home. He'd made a good life for himself in London. He had a lot of friends. His sexuality wasn't a big deal, and now that he was with Anton he couldn't ever see himself going home to live, but he missed the smell and sounds of the sea and countryside. He slanted a glance at his partner who was sprawled out on the grass, face raised to the sun, totally relaxed.

They'd met at the launch of a mutual friend's art exhibition and liked each other. Anton Kavauna was in his mid-thirties, a little older than Bobby, and he was tall, dark and handsome with silky black hair. A small scar on the side of his cheek, the result of a childhood fall, gave him a slightly rakish air. His amber eyes, fringed by long black lashes, sparked with good humour. He'd give Colin Firth a run for his money for definite, Bobby thought happily, a warm glow of happiness suffusing him. After all the years of loneliness and confusion he'd found who and what he'd been looking for. Anton was a gift from God, sent to teach him what real love truly was, he thought gratefully, sending up a little prayer of thanks.

It had been a friendship first, for which, with hindsight, Bobby was thankful. He'd had flings that had happened quickly and fizzled out. With Anton it had been a slow getting to know each other before romance had entered the equation. They got on very well, they had similar interests and, most important, they made each other laugh. Laughter was a big constant in their relationship. When he was with Anton, he felt perfectly content, happy and peaceful. His partner was a calm, thoughtful, steady type, the perfect foil to his own impulsive, exuberant queeny-ness. Chalk and cheese, but they worked.

He'd love to bring his beloved to Ireland to visit Whiteshells Bay and meet the girls. That was Bobby's dream. It was a pity about Anton's mother's knee replacement. That was crap timing, and unforeseen when they'd made their plans for the visit earlier in the year.

'Shame you can't come. I was looking forward to it,' he said regretfully, gently waving a wasp away from his face.

'It *will* happen,' Anton assured him. 'There'll be plenty of time for me to visit. The important thing is for you to go and get things on an even keel with your dad first. Now that he's written the letter of reconciliation there's no point in upsetting him.'

'I wish he was like your parents. They're so . . . so . . . accepting,' Bobby said longingly.

'He is what he is. You're not going to change him. Accept it, Bobby, and stop banging your head off a brick wall,' Anton retorted matter-of-factly. 'And stop acting like a drama queen about it and wallowing in your so-called sad, hard life while you're at it. Life's what you make it.'

'Bastard.' Bobby pretended annoyance but he knew Anton wasn't fooled.

Anton was such a no-nonsense chap, which was just as well. If his friend was as much of a flibbertigibbet as he was himself it would be a disaster, Bobby admitted, rolling over onto his stomach.

'Shall we head down to the Washington and sink a few pints? I'm going to hit the sack early tonight,' Anton suggested, yawning. He'd been working on a new website until the early hours and he was bushed.

'OK,' Bobby agreed. He was tired himself. He'd worked a double shift the day before and he could do with an early night as he was on a dawn flight the next morning. In less than twenty-four hours he'd be breathing in the rich, tangy air of Whiteshells Bay. He was looking forward to it and dreading it at the same time.

'Did you get my silks?' Della nibbled on a crudité, trying to ignore Ashley, who was pulling the tail of her neighbour's cat. She was sitting on a lounger on her patio talking to Shauna on the phone.

'Yes, I did, but not in the colour you wanted. It's royal blue. It's very nice though,' her sister-in-law informed her.

'Oh!' Della exclaimed, annoyed. 'I suppose that will have to do. I had my heart set on the green one. It would have gone lovely with a cream dress I have.' She scowled. Royal blue wasn't her favourite colour by any manner or means. The green would have suited her far better.

'Well, sorry,' Shauna said, a trifle tartly. 'They had no green left. If you don't want it I'll keep it myself.'

'No, no, I'll take it,' Della said hastily. Shauna had more than enough clothes. Royal blue silk was better than no silk. 'So when are we going to see you? Kathryn and Ashley are longing to see their cousin. How about if we pop up at the weekend?' She hid her annoyance.

'Bobby's coming home and he's staying with me, so could we leave it until after he's gone?' Shauna's voice was so clear down the line she might as well have been next door.

'Why wouldn't he stay with your father? Especially if the poor man's on crutches?' Della quizzed. 'He must find it hard to manage.'

'Well we *will* be spending a lot of time in Whiteshells Bay so

341

I'll be toing and froing.' Shauna's voice had an edge to it and Della knew she was getting the brush-off.

'You're always so hard to pin down, Shauna,' she said acidly. 'It's just a cup of coffee I'm talking about, not a black tie dinner.' She couldn't contain herself.

'Look, Della, I'm only home, Dad's had an accident, I'm having a visitor, but I'm here for three months so we'll sort something, OK? There's no rush,' Shauna retorted acerbically.

'Sure, whatever you say. Tell your father I was asking for him and Bobby too. It's years since I've seen him. The Christmas before you went to Abu Dhabi, actually.' Della rowed back. She didn't want her sister-in-law to get into a snit. She wanted a couple of weekends up in Dublin, with Filomena waiting on her hand and foot, and minding the children to boot. Weekends in Shauna and Greg's meant no cooking, washing or cleaning. She'd managed to have three good ones last summer.

'I'll let you go, and I'll be in touch. Good to talk to you.' She injected a bright, breezy note into her tone, despite the fact that she was seriously pissed off with her sister-in-law.

'Thanks for calling,' Shauna said politely and hung up. Della stared at the phone, disgusted. What a snooty cow Shauna had become over the years. When she'd first known her she'd been friendly and welcoming, but over the last couple of years in particular Della had become aware of an edge of tension between them that was certainly not of her making. Shauna was always making excuses not to have them stay over when she and the children went to visit them in Malahide. And even out in the Gulf Shauna was leaving them to their own devices rather a lot. Della had noticed that particularly during their last trip at Christmas. Shauna had gone off to her various classes and clubs and coffee mornings and hardly included her at all.

'Leave those flowers alone,' she screeched at Ashley, who was now pulling the petals off her roses. Rage bubbled inside her. How dare Shauna McCarthy make her feel like a nuisance? How *dare* she! She was a nothing before she married Greg. A McCarthy from some little hole called Whiteshells Bay. And that Carrie one was as bad. She hadn't even bothered her ass to get her the few things she'd asked for when she was out in the Gulf at Easter. That pair really had notions about themselves, Della fumed. It was because of *her* brother's money that Madam Shauna was where she was today. It was because of marrying into the Cassidy family and raising her social status that she now felt she could turn up her nose at Della and treat her like a country bumpkin. *Big* mistake! There was only so much crap a woman could take from her in-laws. And she had taken more than enough. One of these days Della was going to tell Shauna McCarthy Cassidy *exactly* what she thought of her.

'You'd better put a few hot water bottles in that bed to air it when you've changed the sheets,' Noel said. 'And put a few clean towels on the end of it. He's always showering and washing.'

'Yes, Dad, now would you excuse me, you're in my way,' Carrie said tightly, trying to contain her exasperation. Now that Bobby was coming to stay with their father, Noel had her running around like a lunatic, changing beds, shopping for meals and cleaning and hoovering. She was knackered and annoyed. It wouldn't have killed Shauna to come over for an hour or two to help out. After all, Bobby was supposed to be staying with *her*, she thought resentfully.

Noel was like a cat on a hot tin roof and the more agitated he got the more demands he made on her. She was at her wit's end. Now he hobbled out of the room on his crutches. At least he'd got the hang of them. The first day he was on them he'd kept tripping over them.

Her mobile rang. It was Shauna.

'Hi,' her sister said breezily. 'Are you going to come to the airport with me to collect Bobby tomorrow?'

'No, Shauna, I'm not going to be able to make it,' Carrie said testily.

'Oh! What's up? You don't sound in great form.'

'I'm not. I've taken an hour off to come over to Dad's to change the bed for Bobby and he wants me to dust and hoover not to mention doing the shopping. You'd think it was the Queen that was coming to stay.'

'Well you wouldn't be too far wrong there,' Shauna quipped.

Carrie giggled in spite of herself. 'Very funny, smartass.'

'You change the bed and leave the hoovering, I'll come over and do that,' Shauna offered.

'No, I'll do it.' Carrie sighed.

'Stop acting the martyr, I'll be over in an hour,' Shauna said briskly. 'See you.' She hung up.

'That's a relief,' Carrie muttered, not feeling quite as harassed, as she struggled to fit a clean cover over the duvet. And she *wasn't* acting the martyr, she thought crossly. Or was she? She grimaced as she slid a pillowcase onto the pillow. *Was* she adopting the martyr role? She'd need to nip that in the bud, she decided, but she did feel hard done by sometimes. After all, she was the only one living at home and she was the one who took care of their father in his hour of need. And his hours of need were becoming more frequent. She sighed. Maybe she just wasn't good at coping. Other women seemed to juggle far better than she did. A woman in the village had her mother who was suffering from Alzheimer's disease living with her, *and* she had three teenagers to cope with. 'Get over yourself,' she muttered as she placed two towels neatly on the end of the bed.

'Dad, Shauna's going to dust and hoover; I've got to get back to work,' she said five minutes later once the bedroom was sorted.

'Have a cup of tea before you go,' he invited, leaning on his crutch.

'No, Dad, I'm in a rush. I'm supposed to be at work,' she explained.

'I think you've taken on too much with that caravan park,' Noel grumbled. 'You hardly have time to talk to me these days. Sit down and have a cup of tea with me. It won't take a minute.'

Guilt smote her. Her father was right. She hardly had time to bless herself these days, let alone sit and chat to him. Noel wasn't the only one who was neglected. Poor Dan was getting a droopy vegetable sitting beside him on the sofa in the evenings. Once she'd made the school lunches, prepared the meal for the following day and ironed only what had to be ironed, she'd sit beside him on the sofa yawning her head off. Having a job outside the home was far from easy, she was beginning to realize. But she had to admit she enjoyed the challenge of it. She'd settle into it in time.

'A quick cuppa then.' She relented. 'I'll make it.'

'No, you sit down and relax. *I'll* make it. You look tired,' Noel insisted, hobbling to the sink. 'It's the least I can do for you.'

Her heart sank. She would have been quicker doing it herself but it would have made her father feel bad. He still looked a little shaken after his accident. She knew his foot was very painful. It was all the colours of the rainbow, much to his grandchildren's fascination. They charted its progress every day, noting the changing colours of purple and red, yellow and blue with ghoulish curiosity.

They'd told Shauna at the hospital that there was nothing you could do for broken toes and that they would just heal themselves. But he wasn't able to drive, or come up to her for his dinner, so she was doing the meals on wheels run again and it was time-consuming. And time was something she seemed to have precious little of lately.

She sat on her hands and took a few deep breaths. If she was this whacked and harassed in June, what was it going to be like in July and August when the site was full and buzzing? Maybe she didn't have what it took to be a businesswoman, she thought gloomily. Ruth Conroy, a friend of hers who owned Seashells, the café on the main street, and had two children, never seemed fazed by the demands made on her and she was the epitome of elegance at all times. Carrie sighed deeply. She was wearing a pair of jeans and a cream top and was far from elegant right at this moment. Hannah had given her a big soppy hug earlier, straight after eating a carton of strawberry yoghurt. Carrie had a yoghurt stain on her right shoulder and a tomato ketchup stain on her jeans. Far, far from elegant, she thought with a wry grin. She felt she was juggling dozens of balls and that they were all going to fall down and whack her on the head.

At least Bobby was going to be here for a few days. That would take the pressure off her for a while. She knew he wasn't over the moon about the idea of staying with Noel. He'd have preferred to come and go as it suited him. And he'd be a lot more comfortable in Shauna's guest room.

Tough! She gave a little shrug. Whether he liked it or not, Bobby was part of the family and all that it entailed. It was time he took on some of the responsibilities that came with it.

'Don't tell me you're heading out. I've hardly seen you.' Sylvia Lyons, one of Shauna's neighbours, pouted as she stood at the front door.

'Sorry, Sylvia. Dad had an accident and Bobby's coming to stay so I'm shooting over to Whiteshells Bay to give Carrie a hand.'

'Oh dear. Nothing serious, I hope.'

'Broken toes, bad bruising. Painful, awkward, but not serious,' Shauna assured her.

'So when are we going to have time for a gossip? I met Alice yesterday and she tells me you're organizing the lunch. I'm looking forward to it. She said you're having it before she goes away.' Sylvia arched an eyebrow at her.

'Did she now?' Shauna said tightly. 'She door-stepped me the other day to tell me about her Caribbean cruise. She's such hard going, Sylvia. To tell you the truth, I'm sorely tempted to have it when she's away.'

'Good thinking,' her neighbour approved. 'She's *so* rude, you know.' Sylvia ran her fingers through her mane of blond hair, hooked her thumbs into her jeans and leaned against the porch, all ready for a gossip. 'Paula Weldon had a lunch about a month ago and she had a delicious lamb dish that she served with baby potatoes. And Alice turned round and said to Jill Conroy, "I *hate* those baby potatoes." I'm sure Paula heard her. Jill was mortified.'

'I bet. Typical Alice. Do you know when she's going away?' Shauna probed.

'The last week in June. I think.' Sylvia furrowed her brow trying to remember exactly when their neighbour was heading off.

'I'm waiting until she's gone. The last thing I need is pain-in-the-ass Alice rabbiting on about her holiday. Look, why don't you come in tonight and we'll open a bottle of wine and catch up?' she invited. 'I have to get going, Carrie's waiting on me,' she added hastily, noting that Chloe was starting to look fed up in the back seat of the car.

'Terrific. I'll enjoy that. I could do with a bit of diversion,' Sylvia agreed.

'Right. I'll see you later.' Shauna pulled the door closed and got in to the car and reversed out the drive.

Honestly, her neighbours were gas, she thought with wry amusement. Sylvia had just said *she* needed a bit of diversion. Alice was going round talking about the lunch as if it was a given. It would be nice for a change if one of them organized a lunch for *her*.

Shauna frowned. She didn't know what was wrong with her. She just wasn't in the humour for socializing. She'd done so much of it the past year. She wanted a bit of space. Maybe she was starting the change early or something; she'd read about women having it in their late thirties.

'Oh, don't be ridiculous,' she muttered as she slowed down to allow Orla Jenkins to pass by in her Saab. Orla stopped and rolled down her window.

'Welcome home, Shauna. You look fantastic. How's life?'

'Great, Orla. How are you?'

'Oh, don't talk. I've had a terrible year. Denis and I are having problems. We're going to counselling. He had an affair,' she confided morosely.

'Oh! I'm sorry to hear that,' Shauna murmured.

'Why don't I pop over for coffee in the morning? I'll tell you all about it then. You can advise me.' Orla brightened up.

'Actually, I've got Bobby coming tomorrow and we'll be going to Whiteshells Bay. I'll catch up with you one of the days,' Shauna said, relieved beyond measure that she had Bobby as an excuse. Listening to Orla Jenkins moaning was not for the faint-hearted. She thrived on drama and angst. It was her life's blood.

'Oh! OK then.' Orla was deflated. She was longing to tell Shauna of Denis's callous betrayal and bask in the sympathy that her friend would offer. 'See you whenever.' She drove past and Shauna headed out of their cul-de-sac.

'I can't wait to see Uncle Bobby,' Chloe piped up from the back seat. 'I'm glad we're collecting him 'cos I bet Olivia and Davey wishes that they were.'

'Don't be like that, Chloe,' Shauna chided, wishing Chloe wasn't so prone to triumphalism. It probably stemmed from being an only child and maybe from the fact that she felt she wasn't getting as much parental attention as her cousins did. Daggers of guilt pierced her heart in a thousand cuts. Chloe was left in Filomena's care more than she should be, Shauna acknowledged, and as far as Greg was concerned, there were days when he never saw their child. He'd be gone to work before she was up and often she'd be in bed when he got home if he had a function or business do to attend.

She was glad she was going to Whiteshells Bay for the afternoon. At least Chloe would have her cousins to play with. She'd sat on the low front wall earlier, watching other young children playing together, but not invited to join in, and not brave enough to push herself forward. Shauna's heart stung as she watched her timid daughter. *Go on*, she urged silently. *Be brave.* But Chloe had just sat watching forlornly until Shauna could stand it no longer and had called her in and asked her if she would like to watch a video. This summer she was going to devote a lot of time to her daughter, she vowed, as she picked up speed and headed northwards.

'It's so peaceful here,' she sighed a couple of hours later as she sat on the veranda of a vacant mobile sipping a cup of tea. She could hear the laughter of children up in the playground and was utterly content knowing that Chloe was in the middle of them having a ball.

She'd hoovered and dusted her dad's house and brought him and all the kids to Seashells Café for a meal to save Carrie from cooking. Noel had enjoyed a steak, and the kids, including

349

Hannah, had gobbled up a tasty chicken and pasta dish. She'd dropped her father home and settled him in before strolling down to the caravan park to see how her sister was getting on. Everything was calm and peaceful. Carrie, looking a lot less harassed, informed her proudly that she was finally on top of her paperwork, thanks to the couple of hours of peace and quiet she'd had to work in the office without having to worry about Hannah and the others.

'Let's have a cup of tea on the veranda,' she'd suggested and Shauna was happy to agree. She could hear the shushing of the waves against the shore and it soothed her more than any tranquillizer could. The smell of fresh cut grass was sweeter than any perfume and she inhaled the fragrant scent wafting on the breeze with pleasure.

'I wish I could spend the summer here,' she said casually. 'I had Sylvia asking me when I'm having my lunch, and she's calling in tonight for, as she put it herself, "a bit of diversion". Honest to God, Carrie, sometimes I feel I'm the summer entertainment. Orla Jenkins invited herself over for coffee to whinge about her husband's affair. If I were married to her *I'd* have an affair. She's the pits. I've never known anyone who is so consumed with herself and her problems. And of course, dear Alice no doubt will be annoying me about the lunch as well. I wish they'd all feck off and leave me alone. I don't know what's wrong with me but I just don't want to organize *anything*!'

'I suppose you do so much socializing in Abu Dhabi it's nice just to sit and flop,' Carrie observed, stretching like a cat, warmed by the heat of the late afternoon sun. Bees hummed in the geraniums and a lark sang in the trees opposite them.

'It's great that Chloe's up there playing with the others. She's very timid sometimes. Maybe I should book one of your mobiles for a couple of weeks.' Shauna looked over at her sister questioningly.

'Too late. The rented ones are fully booked from the weekend, unless we get a cancellation. It's a pity I didn't know; it would have been perfect,' Carrie said regretfully.

'Drat!' Shauna muttered. 'I could have sent Filomena home to the Philippines early and Chloe and I could have had a great time.'

'I wonder would the Feeneys rent their mobile out?' Carrie mused. 'They have it up for sale. Mr Feeney had a fall a few days ago and when he was in hospital they found he needed an urgent triple bypass. They've decided to sell up. They're going to move to Cork to be near their daughter. They're from Cork originally.' She sat up straight. 'I could give them a ring and put it to Mrs Feeney.' Her eyes gleamed. 'We'd have great fun, Shauna. We could do barbecues at night and watch the stars and get tiddly when the kids were in bed. Will I ring her?'

'Why bother renting? Why don't I just buy it outright and have it for good?' Shauna exclaimed.

'Crikey, Shauna, they're looking for thirty-two thousand euros. It's practically new. It's only two years old.'

'I'll buy it as an investment. You can rent it out when I'm not using it.' Shauna couldn't disguise her excitement. 'I could move in straight away. I wouldn't have to entertain *anyone*. I wouldn't have to do a ladies' lunch. I'd stay here until August. Oh, Carrie, it's too good to be true. I'm going to ring Greg.' She scrabbled in her bag and found her mobile and scrolled down until she got her husband's number. She dialled it and waited impatiently for him to answer. He might have it on silent, depending on what type of function he was at. He'd hardly be at home.

'Answer! Answer!' she urged.

'Hello!' Greg sounded groggy.

351

'You weren't asleep, were you?' she asked in dismay. 'It's only—' She glanced at her watch.

'No, no, no problem. I'm watching football. How's it going?'

'Great. Will I ring you on the landline?'

'No, I'm still in Dubai. I'll be home tomorrow. I'll ring you on the landline then. Everything OK? Is Chloe OK?'

'Yeah, fine. Listen, it's a long story but what would you think of us buying a mobile home? Carrie and Dan have bought the caravan park down the road from them and there's a mobile home for sale. There's also good investment potential,' she exaggerated, using a phrase that was always music to her husband's ears.

'How much?'

'Thirty-two thousand euros.' Shauna crossed her fingers. 'There's central heating and all mod cons and an en suite in the master bedroom. I'd really like it, and Chloe would be over the moon,' she added.

There was a long pause and then a low whistle. 'That's a lot of money for a caravan,' Greg exclaimed.

'Oh, it's much, much more than a caravan. It's like a small house. Lots of people are actually buying mobile homes to live in because they can't afford houses,' Shauna explained, crossing her fingers again. 'Honestly, they're good investments these days and there's no stamp duty on them and they've a great resale value,' she added, playing her trump card.

'Go for it, then,' her husband instructed. 'I'll get the bank here to transfer the money first thing in the morning.'

'Oh, thanks, Greg, thanks a million. I'll make the call to the vendors to let them know that they've got a sale. Greg, you're going to enjoy it here. I love you so much.' She was nearly crying with gratitude.

'I love you too. Take some photos and email them to me. I'll talk to you tomorrow, OK?'

'OK, Greg. I can't wait to tell Chloe. 'Night.'

''Night, Shauna.'

She heard the dial tone and gave Carrie the thumbs up. 'I can buy it. Quick, ring those people.'

'Way to go, Shauna. Imagine being able to put your hands on thirty-two thousand euros just like that.' Carrie eyed her in amusement.

'Yeah well, working in the Gulf can be very financially rewarding,' Shauna said dryly. 'Greg might not get to see Chloe as much as he'd like but he makes plenty of money.' She shrugged. 'He's not going to change and Chloe and I have to adapt and deal with it or forget it. I don't think we'd last as a couple if I insisted he come home to Ireland now,' she confessed. 'I keep telling myself that it's only for another year or two. That's how I keep going. Eventually, though, we're going to have to come home for Chloe's sake. And with the political situation out there, who knows what's going to happen.'

'That's not easy, Shauna,' Carrie said quietly, shocked at her sister's disclosures. She hadn't quite realized just how difficult things were for her.

'No, it's not. People think I've a great life. They don't see behind the facade. But hell, enough of this. Ring those people and see if they'll sell me their mobile home,' she ordered.

'Yes, boss!' Carrie smiled at her, hardly able to believe what was happening.

Greg looked at the mobile phone and marvelled that moments ago he'd been speaking to his wife on the other side of the world. It was an amazing invention, he reflected despondently. He'd been asleep when she phoned, drugged on painkillers and exhausted after a night tossing and turning. No-one had told him that the discomfort would be so bad. He'd phoned the clinic and

Bob had assured him that everything was normal and that the discomfort would ease as the days went by.

If Shauna had asked him for sixty thousand euros he'd have given it to her. He was crucified with guilt, never having thought that he was capable of such duplicity. Even thinking about it now was enough to bring him out in a sweat.

He'd told Bob that he wanted the vasectomy as a birthday present for Shauna, when the urologist had told him that he needed a form signed by his wife, giving her consent. 'Honestly, Bob, if I told her I was having one, she'd freak. She wouldn't allow it. She'd be too worried about me,' he'd lied. 'She's heading for forty and she's coming off the Pill and she definitely doesn't want to get pregnant again, and to tell the truth I don't want any more children either. We're very happy the way we are.'

'What if you meet someone else and your marriage ends and she wants children?' the urologist pointed out.

'Highly unlikely. And even if Shauna ever left me and I *did* meet someone new, I wouldn't want more kids now. I'm too old for young babies. We had visitors with a toddler at Christmas and more at Easter and I nearly went crazy. They're so *noisy*! They're constantly falling and hurting themselves. Nothing was safe. My sister's kid at Christmas broke a Tiffany lamp, the little bastard.' Greg scowled and Bob laughed.

'Look, are you sure about this? It's a quid pro quo, I do the vasectomy and you do up the plans for my villa in Melbourne and we keep it just between us.' Bob eyeballed him. 'I could get struck off, you know,' he reminded him as he passed him the form to forge Shauna's signature.

'Just between us,' Greg had agreed, signing with a flourish, recognizing a kindred spirit. At the time it had seemed so simple and he'd been completely untroubled by scruples.

He stood up and poured himself a glass of whiskey from a bottle given to him by an appreciative client. He knew that he shouldn't drink with the tablets but he wanted to take the edge off his guilt. It was an emotion he wasn't used to and he didn't like it one bit. He didn't even want to contemplate what would happen if Shauna ever found out. And he was so petrified something had gone badly wrong and that he'd never be the man, physically, he was pre-vasectomy. There was every chance she'd find out something was amiss.

It was all her fault anyway, he thought irrationally. He'd told her over and over that he didn't want another child. Why couldn't she just *listen* to him? Why was she annoying the daylights out of him about having another baby when she knew that in his heart of hearts he was completely against it? 'Is this what you want?' he'd demanded when Ashley had sent a ridiculously expensive Tiffany lamp smashing into smithereens when he'd careered into the small table that held it.

'Every kid's not like him,' she'd raged, furious with Ashley and with Della for not keeping him under control.

When a colleague had told him that he'd had the snip recently, he'd got the name of the surgeon and made an appointment to see him. Now he was bitterly regretting that decision. Bob Kelly had already shown himself to be a bent surgeon; just say he was a *crap* surgeon as well and that Greg was deformed for life. He broke out in a cold sweat, groaning as a burning pain shot through his balls.

'Oh fuck!' he muttered. 'What the hell have I done?'

Half an hour later Shauna, Carrie and Dan were drinking champagne on the deck of Shauna's new mobile. Mrs Feeney had agreed straight away to sell to Shauna and generously told her to start using the mobile as soon as she wanted to when

Shauna assured her that the cheque would be in the post by the end of the week. Her daughters had cleaned it out and closed it up for the rest of the season after their father's hospitalization, so all their personal possessions were gone.

'We've got a mobile home, Mom, this is the best thing ever.' Chloe was dancing up and down with excitement. 'Can we stay tonight?'

'No, not tonight, darling, but maybe tomorrow if you're good,' Shauna promised her, hugging her tightly.

'YIPPEE!!!!!' Her joyous yell could be heard across the park. Dan and Carrie laughed. The children were hyper with delight, exploring the new mobile, which could sleep six comfortably. Great plans were being made for a sleepover and a midnight swim and midnight feasts.

'You've got a great site, too. One of the best in the park. Sea views and the beach just below you. You always land on your feet, Cassidy.' Dan dug her in the ribs.

'Bet you're sorry you didn't marry me,' she grinned.

'Ah I'm happy enough with my old dear here. She's not a bad old doll.' He drew Carrie close to him. 'Here's to happy family times in Shauna's mobile.' He raised his glass.

'To happy family times,' they all chorused as the setting sun cast a pearly glow over them and birdsong and sea music accompanied their light-hearted toast.

31

'I CAN GO HOME TOMORROW?' FILOMENA. LOOKED UTTERLY shocked.

'Yes. If you agree to take six weeks on half pay for June and July, and then full pay for your holiday in August, you can go home tomorrow. I can book tickets from Dublin to Heathrow and Heathrow to Manila on the net. I've checked and there are flights available. Chloe and I are going to Whiteshells Bay until Greg comes home.'

'Oh, ma'am, this is a miracle from God.' Tears welled up in the young woman's eyes.

'I take it that's a yes, then?' Shauna grinned.

'Oh, yes, ma'am! Yes!' Filomena was dazed with joy.

'Go pack,' her employer instructed. 'And when you're packed, pack a case for Chloe. We're going on our holidays to the seaside.' She laughed, feeling more light-hearted and giddy than she'd done in years. 'I'm going to book your tickets and then go and pick up Bobby. We'll be back soon. I'm going to bring him to an art exhibition tonight but we won't be home late because you'll have an early start in the morning.'

'OK, ma'am.' Filomena practically danced out of the room. Shauna was delighted with herself. She often felt sorry for her young au pair, knowing how much she missed her family and homeland. It was a hard life for the young woman. Shauna knew that she sent home half her wages to provide for her family. At least she wasn't married. She'd met many Filipino women who had children back in the Philippines, being raised by family members, while their mothers worked like Trojans to provide an education and a good lifestyle for them. Shauna thought it was heart-rending and truly admired their stoic sacrifice. She knew that she wouldn't be able to do it.

She was glad Filomena would have six extra weeks at home. It would tie her down a little, if she wanted to go out at night, but she'd decided, anyway, that she was going to devote this summer to her daughter and that was what she was going to do.

There was an air of excitement in the house. Filomena was packing, and humming. Chloe was organizing her dolls for their holidays. Shauna felt the stress seep out of her body. She was going to read and swim and spend time with her daughter and sister. She knew it was going to be a wonderful interlude. When Greg came home, she'd entertain their neighbours. Until then, her time was hers to do what she liked. What an unexpected blessing, she reflected as her fingers tapped in the details of her credit card number to book Filomena's flights. It was like *The Great Escape*.

Sylvia had called in around ten the previous night, soon after she and Chloe arrived home tired and exhilarated from Whiteshells Bay. They'd chatted about the neighbours and her friend had brought her up to speed on all the goings-on, including Orla and Denis's drama. 'Don't worry, she'll be over to tell you what a bastard Denis is. We've all had it,' Sylvia assured her, giggling tipsily after her third glass of wine.

As she listened to her friend chattering away, Shauna was even more pleased that she was going away until August. She had enough problems in her own life to try to cope with. She was in no mood to be an agony aunt to the neighbours.

'Actually, Sylvia, I won't be here for a few weeks. Chloe and I are going to Whiteshells Bay to help Carrie out with Dad. I'm letting Filomena go home early and we're heading off the day after tomorrow with Bobby. I'll come back in August when Greg's here. I probably won't have the lunch until them.' She didn't mention the mobile home. She didn't want Sylvia suggesting a visit with her eight-year-old twins. This year she just wanted to be free of friends and acquaintances. She was all entertained out, she thought ruefully. She just wasn't in the humour for any of it.

'Aw, no! I was really looking forward to having you home and having a day away from the cooker. Your lunches are *such* fun. And besides, you'll have to invite Alice in August,' Sylvia protested.

'I'll deal with that when the time comes,' Shauna murmured.

'Well honestly, you're only home a couple of days and you're deserting us already.' Sylvia drained her glass and held it out for a refill.

'These things happen,' Shauna said easily, trying not to yawn. The sea air had knocked her for six and she was longing for bed. Sylvia had stayed drinking until one a.m. before tottering woozily across the road.

It would be her that would be doing the tipsy tottering from now on, Shauna thought happily as she laid out trousers, jeans and an array of pastel cut-offs on the bed. Knowing the vagaries of the Irish weather she took out a selection of sweaters and fleeces. At least her mobile home had central heating. She was beginning to adjust to the cooler climate again but she still found the nights very cold and wore thermals in bed. She pulled out a couple of pairs of warm pjs as well, and a pair of bedsocks. Utterly unsexy but warm.

She felt like a child going on vacation.

'I can't keep up with you,' Bobby laughed from the back seat as he listened to her news several hours later, his arm tucked round Chloe who was revelling in having him all to herself.

'Oh, Bobby, it's going to be fun.' Shauna bubbled. 'We're not going until tomorrow because I've to bring Filomena to the airport. Besides, I thought you'd like one night with us before going home.' She glanced at him in the rear-view mirror.

'It feels a bit weird,' he confessed.

'Dad's fluttering around like a regular Mrs Mop, making sure everything is all right for the "royal visit". I think he's nervous too.' She caught his gaze.

'That makes two of us.'

'Stay calm. We'll have a few barbies and I'll send you home singing every night,' she promised.

'You must be looking forward to Bobby's visit, all the same,' Mrs O'Neill remarked as she poured her neighbour a cup of tea. She'd dropped in a loaf of fresh baked currant soda bread, remembering how much Bobby had loved it as a child.

'I suppose I am. It's been so long since I've seen him, though, and our last words to one another were harsh when he left. I'm a little apprehensive,' Noel admitted. 'This gay thing is difficult to deal with.'

'Don't be fretting about all that now, Noel. That's all in the past. You wrote the letter to him and he responded, so move on from there,' his neighbour advised matter-of-factly. 'And think how lucky you are to have your three children around this summer.'

'I know, Mrs O'Neill. I do give thanks for it,' Noel assured her. 'Will any of yours be home this year?' he asked kindly, feeling very sorry for his friend.

His neighbour brightened and a smile creased her worn face.

'Did I not tell you? Brona is coming home for six weeks at Christmas with the children. I'm delighted, Noel. It can't come quick enough.' Her bright blue eyes, undimmed by age, shone with anticipation.

'That's great news, great news,' Noel said warmly, delighted for her. She was a lovely neighbour, even if she had some very unusual religious beliefs, he acknowledged, as he watched her rinse the teacups and dry them. He felt very comfortable with her, the true sign of a good friendship.

When she was gone, he made his way down to Bobby's bedroom and opened the window to air the room. He really should get a new bed for him, he reflected as he stared out the window. Twiskers came into the room and hopped onto the bed, which was bathed in sunlight.

'Get out of it, you scamp,' he admonished, not wanting cat hairs all over the covers. He gave her a small tap on the rump. Twiskers stared up at him with haughty indignation and stalked out of the room, waving her tail. Noel laughed. That cat was a character. There was no doubt about it.

What would he say to Bobby? he wondered. Should he shake hands? Or should he behave as if nothing had happened between them? He was relieved that his son wasn't coming home until the following day. It meant that he'd only be staying for three nights. That was a terrible thing to think, he acknowledged guiltily, but three nights was enough for this first trip. There was no need for him to come home to look after him. He was managing fine with Carrie's help.

Noel sighed and looked at the bed again. It had a terrible sag in the middle. Maybe Dan might be able to bring him to buy one in Drogheda. He could carry it back in his big delivery van. He limped out to the hall and picked up the phone and dialled Carrie's number.

*   *   *

'I like this one,' Bobby declared, pointing out a particularly colourful abstract in sharp-angled reds and blacks.

'I hate abstract. I'd much prefer that one.' Shauna pointed to a delicate watercolour of autumn trees. They were strolling around the big, high-ceilinged showrooms of the Kennedy Gallery in Harcourt Street, in the city, sipping a glass of wine each and commenting on all the paintings as the artist stood nervously wondering whether there would be any precious red dots placed on his work to indicate a sale.

'Oh, look, look at this one,' Bobby exclaimed, pointing to a small, exquisitely executed watercolour of a field of glorious red and yellow poppies. 'Anton would love that.'

'Let's see how much it is.' Shauna glanced down the list. 'Number twenty-two. Four hundred and fifty euros. Very reasonable for an original.'

'Yes, moneybags,' Bobby riposted. 'I could buy it for his birthday in August. I know he'd love it.'

'Buy it then,' Shauna urged.

'I'd have to write a sterling cheque.'

'Oh, for goodness' sake.' Shauna whipped out her chequebook. 'I'll get it and you can sort me out later.'

'But we've to leave it in the exhibition until the end of the month. I won't be here,' he dithered.

'I'll collect it. Do you want it or not?'

'Right. OK then.' Bobby let himself be bulldozed. Moments later a little red dot reposed discreetly on a corner of the painting and he studied it with pleasure. The perfect present for his beloved, he thought happily.

'Let's go and have some chow,' he suggested after they had perused the paintings several times and clapped politely at the speeches. 'My treat. Anywhere good near by?'

Shauna wrinkled her nose. 'Wagamama's if you feel Japanesy, or Mao's is more Thai oriented,' she suggested.

'Thai sounds good. Lead on, big sis.'

'Less of the big sis, please.' Shauna glanced down at herself, feeling the tightness of the cream linen trousers she was wearing. She'd want to start watching her weight. She was putting it on. It was all those Club Milks and crisps she was devouring at Carrie's. 'We'll walk briskly,' she ordered, striding off ahead of him towards Grafton Street.

'Hold on a minute,' Bobby protested, hurrying to catch up with her. The streets were buzzing at the tail end of the teatime rush. Couples strolled along arm in arm. Businessmen and women hurried along, frowning and preoccupied, talking animatedly into mobile phones as they made their way home from work. Birds sang in the verdant greenery of Stephen's Green. It was a beautiful summer's evening. Shauna was enjoying herself. It was *great* to be home.

'This is nice, having a meal together, isn't it? Pity Carrie's not here,' she remarked, half an hour later, as they tucked into Malaysian chicken for her and sizzling prawns for him. There was a convivial hum of chat and laughter in the restaurant and the food was very tasty. 'You know, I think it's going to be a terrific summer for us all,' she confided, spearing a piece of chicken and dipping it into the creamy coconut sauce.

'It's starting off well,' he agreed. 'So far it's been a good year for the McCarthy clan. We all met out in Abu Dhabi, Dad and I have a truce of sorts and now you've bought your mobile home and Chloe's going to get to spend a lot of time with her cousins. Perhaps you're right. Maybe all our bad times are over.' He offered her a prawn to taste and she reciprocated with a piece of creamy chicken.

'I feel they are, Bobby, I really do,' she said earnestly. 'Let's let go of the past and enjoy being on good terms with Dad. The past has caused us enough misery and he does seem to be making the effort.'

'I'm with you all the way,' Bobby agreed, lifting his glass. 'To Family!' he toasted.

'To Family,' she echoed, hoping that this time next year there'd be a new little member of the clan.

Lucky Bobby and Shauna, Carrie thought enviously, wishing that *she* was gadding about town with her siblings, who had just texted her in riotous good form, full of the joys. Instead, she was stuck in a furniture shop waiting for her father to buy a bed.

'Dad, this one is fine, honestly,' she assured her father as they stood looking at a selection of divan beds in the shop in Drogheda. 'I'll ring Dan and ask him to go to the loading bay and get them to load one into the van. That's if they have one in stock. If it was a double bed, you could forget it. You'd be waiting for weeks.'

'You don't think it's too hard?' Noel thumped it.

'It's fine, Dad. Come on. I don't want to leave the kids with Sadie too long; it's well past Hannah's bedtime.'

'Oh. Oh, right. Sorry, I didn't think,' Noel apologized.

What's new? Carrie thought irritably. She'd been in the middle of cooking dinner when Noel had phoned her and informed her that he wanted to go and buy a new bed for Bobby and asking would Dan be able to bring him in the van.

'I'd like to give him a surprise, and that bed can't be very comfortable. It's donkey's years old.' He cleared his throat. 'I'd like him to know that I went to a bit of effort to welcome him home.'

Carrie's heart had softened. Even if it was truly inconvenient she couldn't refuse him. Not when he put it to her like that.

Now, though, he was starting to get on her nerves with his indecision. They'd have to bring the bed home, strip the other one and take it out the back and set up this one. At least another hour and a half if she was lucky.

'This one so,' Noel said firmly, taking out his wallet. 'Where do I pay?'

'Follow me,' Carrie said.

'Right,' said her father and promptly tripped over his crutch and fell against the bed.

Jesus, Mary and Joseph, please let me get him home in one piece, she prayed silently as she hauled him up.

'These *bloody* things,' he cursed, straightening himself.

'You should be resting like they told you,' she said crossly. It was rare for her father to curse.

'I will tomorrow when Bobby comes home,' Noel said meekly, knowing by her tone that she was getting agitated.

'Sorry! I didn't mean to snap,' Carrie apologized. 'Are you OK?'

'Grand,' he assured her, watching what he was doing this time. He was very pleased. He'd got a new bed and a new bedside locker to go with it. He hoped his son appreciated it.

Bobby licked his lips. His mouth was dry. It was midday of the following day and he, Chloe and Shauna were driving into Whiteshells Bay. It was so strange to be back again, he thought, glancing at the small whitewashed building where he'd gone to school aeons ago. The church had had a new coat of paint and colourful hanging baskets of flowers hung from shopfronts. An Angel gift shop stood where there had once been a fruit and veg shop and Tessa's Hairdressers had been replaced by a trendy new salon called Snips.

'The place looks great. The flowers are a nice touch.'

'Yes, it's for the Tidy Towns competition. The village has been given a makeover. Remember when we used to sneak a smoke down Smuggler's Lane?' she whispered, conscious of Chloe in the back seat. Fortunately, her daughter was engrossed with her Barbie dolls.

'Yeah.' He smiled at the memory. He blessed himself as they passed the cemetery and thought of his mother.

Thanks for sending me Anton, he said silently to her, as his father's bungalow came into view. Great masses of roses tumbled over the doorway and the small herbaceous border was a splash of riotous colour. Anton would love it, Bobby thought ruefully. He adored the country garden look and their great plan was to buy a small cottage in the countryside somewhere and have a massive garden.

'Here we are. Chin up, chest out,' Shauna encouraged as she drove into the drive and switched off the engine. The front door opened and Noel struggled out on his crutches.

'God, he's got old-looking!' Bobby was dismayed in spite of himself.

'I know. I felt that too, but don't forget you haven't seen him in a few years. Carrie said he's eating like a horse and when he's eating his meals OK she doesn't worry too much about him.' Shauna unfastened her seat belt.

'Better get on with it,' Bobby murmured, opening the door. 'Hello, Dad.' He got out of the car.

'Hello, son. Welcome home,' Noel said, his tired grey eyes brightening. He held out his hand, the crutch hanging from his wrist.

How bony and thin it is, Bobby thought in shock as he took his father's hand in his own.

'It's good to see you, son,' Noel said awkwardly. 'It's been too long.'

'I'm sorry for what I said, Dad,' Bobby blurted suddenly, unable to help himself.

'So am I, son, so am I.' Tears came to Noel's eyes and he blinked rapidly.

Bobby felt a lump in his throat. His father, the tyrant of old, was apologizing. Never able to hold a grudge, Bobby clasped his father to him. 'Forget it, Dad. Thanks for the letter,' he murmured, noticing how thin and wispy his father's white hair had got.

'I bought a new bed for you. I thought it would be more comfortable,' Noel managed, smothered against his son's lanky body.

'Thanks, Dad. Let's go have a look.' Bobby smiled down at him as he draped an arm round his father's shoulder and they walked into the hall together.

Shauna bit her lip and kept her head bent as she pretended to struggle with Chloe's seat belt. She hadn't expected to be so moved at the reconciliation between her father and her brother. Maybe she too had finally let go of the past. Noel was elderly now and had no power over her any more. It gave her a great sense of freedom and release. She hoped that Bobby would come to feel the same during this visit. She kissed the top of her daughter's head and tried to compose herself as she helped her out of the car. A plop of rain wet her cheeks. The skies had clouded over and a rumble to the east heralded the sound of a thunderstorm out to sea.

'Quick, Chloe, hurry,' she urged as the plops turned into a steady drizzle. What a shame the weather had turned; she hoped it was only temporary. Still, it was a treat now and again to have rain. She could spend the afternoon on the sofa in her new mobile home, reading. Chloe could play with Olivia and their Barbies, their current craze. She'd settle her brother in, have a cup of tea with them and head off to her little haven.

'Are you sure you won't have something else for your supper?' Noel asked as Bobby took a bite out of a chunk of Mrs O'Neill's currant bread that he had smeared with thick creamy butter.

'This is scrumptious. It brings me right back to when I was a child. It was very kind of her to remember how much I liked it.' He took a drink of hot, sweet tea and wished Anton was with him to share his tasty feast. It was still raining and the grey dusk had turned to darkness. He was tired. There was still an edge of awkwardness between him and his father, although Noel had gone out of his way to make him feel welcome. After lunch he'd driven his father to Shauna's mobile where they'd spent most of the afternoon before coming home after tea. He'd settled his father in front of the TV and told him he was going to unpack. In the privacy of his bedroom he'd phoned Anton and given him all the news.

'So it's not as bad as you'd thought it would be?' Anton's deep voice came down the line. Bobby had felt lonely for him.

'No, it's OK really. It was great being with Shauna and the kids in the mobile; it takes the pressure off. It's a pity it's bloody raining. I'd have gone for a walk on the beach.' Bobby sighed. The night ahead seemed very long. They'd chatted for a while before wishing each other goodnight. Bobby lay on his new bed. It was good and firm, a far better bed than the one he'd slept in on his previous visits home. He yawned. He was tired. It must be the sea air. He took his small photo of Anton, in its silver frame, out of his rucksack and placed it on his bedside locker. He wondered whether Noel would make any comment about it. Was he being provocative by putting it on public view? He stared at the photo of his beloved. Anton would tell him to put it away, he thought with a wry smile. But there was only so much he would do to appease his father. Denying Anton was like a betrayal of who and what he was and he wasn't going to do it. It was Noel's problem if he couldn't deal with it.

That was his last memory. He'd fallen fast asleep and only woken up when Noel had knocked on the door to see whether he wanted a cup of tea and a slice of currant bread.

'Wha . . . what? What time is it?' Bobby jerked up, blinking at the light spilling in from the landing.

'It's almost half ten,' Noel informed him as he made his way into the room and pulled the curtains to shut out the blustery, wet night. Bobby switched on his bedside lamp.

'Sorry, Dad, I fell fast asleep,' he apologized.

'It's the sea air. It's better than any sleeping tablet.' Noel chuckled.

'It's a bit rude to come on a visit and spend it sleeping,' Bobby said ruefully, stretching.

'Who's that?' Noel pointed with his crutch to the photo of Anton.

Bobby took a deep breath. 'That's my best friend, Anton,' he said quietly.

'I see. What does he do?' Noel leaned on his crutch and stared at his son.

'He designs websites for businesses.'

'Oh. That's different, I suppose. Do you share a flat?' Bobby knew his father wanted to know if they lived together. But at least he wasn't being aggressive or disapproving, which was a step forward.

'No, not yet. We might buy a place together sometime. Property is very expensive in London.' He put it in a way that would be more comfortable for his father to deal with. 'I don't think I'd ever be able to buy anywhere on my own and rent really is money down the drain.' He stood up and smoothed the bed cover.

'You're always better to have your own roof over your head,' Noel agreed, as he preceded him out of the room. 'And when I go, there will be a share of this house for the three of you.'

'Ah don't say that, Dad. You're not going anywhere.' Bobby patted him on the shoulder.

'Well I just wanted you to know,' Noel said gruffly.

'Thanks, Dad,' Bobby said appreciatively, knowing that this was his father's way of saying that he hadn't cut him out of the will.

They sat at the kitchen table drinking tea and buttered currant bread as the rain battered the window and Twiskers purred contentedly in her cushioned nest.

'If the weather improves I'll whitewash the back yard for you,' he offered.

'It needs doing. I'd be very happy if you did that, son; I don't like to annoy Dan, he's busy enough. I'd planned to do it myself until I had my accident.'

'I'll do it. Carrie said the weather was only a blip and it should be dry tomorrow.' Bobby buttered himself another slice of bread.

'She knows. She and Dan always watch the weather forecast for his farming.'

Bobby topped up their teacups with more tea and felt himself relax. The worst was definitely over. Anton had been introduced into the frame, and Noel hadn't thrown a wobbly. A miracle in itself. Things had changed and very much for the better. The trip wasn't going to be half the ordeal he'd expected. In fact, he reflected, as he spooned sugar into both their cups, he was actually enjoying himself.

O dear Lord, help me not to judge. Noel lay in bed, praying, wishing that sleep would overtake him. It had been an eventful day. The return of the prodigal son. His heart had lifted at the sight of Bobby, in spite of the blond hair and the red scarf coiled in a flamboyant manner round his neck. His son had been very kind and gracious and apologized for his harsh words at their last parting. It had made it easier for him to apologize also and their hug had been one of awkward forgiveness.

Mrs O'Neill had cautioned him over and over to accept his son as he was. She'd reminded him that he was beloved of God and created by the Divine hand just as he, Noel, was. He was trying to remember that now. It had been all right until he'd seen the photo of the young man beside Bobby's bed. If he had a photo of him they must be very close. A fine, handsome man that should have a wife and children for himself, not another young man who was clearly misguided. Bobby too would make some young woman a good husband. He was good-natured and kind. Why had he turned out the way he had?

Noel sighed. It was hard to understand, very, very hard, but Mrs O'Neill was right, even though it was annoying to admit it. No matter how much he felt he had the right to, he should not judge his son. The Lord himself had said *judge not, lest ye be judged*. Difficult one. Very difficult, he thought solemnly. Mrs O'Neill had told him it was probably a great lesson that Bobby had to teach him. The lesson of not judging. She had some very strange notions, but the thing about it was that when he really thought about it, everything she said was right in a funny sort of way.

Still, it was nice to have all his family around him. Noel turned his thoughts to more pleasant matters. Carrie had said that she and Shauna were going to have a barbecue. He'd never been to a barbecue; it was something to look forward to. Eating out in the open with the children would be fun; they truly were the greatest joys in his life. He'd told Chloe he'd take out his photo album and show her photos of her granny. 'You look very

371

like her,' he'd whispered, anxious that Olivia wouldn't overhear. He didn't want to put her nose out of joint. There was a little bit of 'he's my grandpa too' going on.

Chloe had gone pink with pleasure at his whispered words. He felt sorry for his young granddaughter. There was something lonely about her, and as far as he could make out her father spent precious little time with her. It was just as well that she was spending the summer in Whiteshells Bay. He'd make a great fuss of her, discreetly of course, so the others wouldn't be jealous. She needed to know that her family in Ireland loved her dearly.

The loving thoughts eased his mind and soon Noel's snores rumbled to the ceiling as Twiskers lay asleep at his feet, whiskers twitching, dreaming of plump mice.

Shauna lay snug in her bed as the rain hopped off the roof of the mobile home and the wind rustled through the branches of the fir trees. The sea crooned its rhythmic lullaby, soothing and relaxing her better than any tranquillizer. The lemon and terracotta décor of the room gave it a warm, cosy ambience and the peachy glow from her bedside lamp was reflected in the gleaming mirror on the small wardrobe door. It was a peaceful room and she was delighted with her new purchase.

It had been a dreadful day, weatherwise, but she'd really enjoyed it. She'd read her book lying on the sofa as the girls played with their dolls. She hadn't been so relaxed in years, she decided, as she listened to the cousins chattering happily together. This was just what she needed. The perfect antidote to her hectic social life out in the Gulf. Bobby and Noel had come to visit in the afternoon, then Carrie had called in and they'd spent an enjoyable few hours catching up.

Who would have thought that her father and Bobby would be reconciled after all these years? It was hard to believe, she thought drowsily, as her book slipped from her hand. She switched off the light and burrowed down into the bed, glad of her bedsocks and electric blanket. It was going to be a mega summer, she determined as her eyes closed.

Peace had come to the family at last.

32

'WELL WHAT'S ALL THIS? SHAUNA, YOU DARK HORSE.' DELLA'S brittle accusatory tones rang out along the veranda as she stepped up onto it, followed by a surly Eddie, and their two children.

Shauna's stomach lurched in dismay. She couldn't believe her eyes. Della was marching down her veranda with a sickly-sweet smile on her lips, arms out to greet her.

'What are you doing here?' she asked weakly, handing a glass of chilled white wine to Carrie.

'Oh well, if we weren't going to get to see you in Malahide we thought we'd pop over to Whiteshells Bay to see how you were and how Mr McCarthy was?' She air-kissed her sister-in-law and turned to Noel, all insincere concern, and bent down to give him a kiss. 'How are you, lovey?'

'Ah it's yourself,' Noel exclaimed, quite unaware of the tension rending the air. He was sitting on a cane chair with a plate of steak, baked potato and salad on his knee, thoroughly enjoying himself. Bobby, wearing a chef's apron he'd bought in Drogheda, was barbecuing like a madman. Curlicues of smoke from the grill wafted out to sea. He flipped over two steaks, and a couple of ribs, their juices sizzling onto the hot coals beneath. He was far from pleased to see the interlopers and muttered a greeting.

'So, I met Mr McCarthy's next-door neighbour when I

couldn't find anyone in Carrie's,' Della explained, eyes darting here and there, taking everything in. 'And she told me that you'd bought a mobile home, Shauna. You never said!' Her sly, piggy eyes were cold and accusatory even though she had a smile plastered on her face.

'Any beer there, Bobby?' Eddie asked, plonking down into the white chair Shauna had been sitting on.

'I'll check,' Bobby murmured, knowing that Shauna was furious.

'So, when did you buy and why the big secret?' Della persisted, acerbically.

'No secret. It all happened very quickly. I didn't even know, the last time I was talking to you, that I was going to buy one,' Shauna said tightly. 'I suppose you could call it an impulse buy. That wouldn't be your style, I know.' She couldn't hide her annoyance and she didn't care if Della took umbrage at her tone. She was hopping mad. They were having a lovely, relaxed family lunch, making the most of the returned good weather, and now bloody Della and her gang had gatecrashed it.

'I see. I believe you own this place, Carrie? The gates were closed so we left the car parked outside and came in through the pedestrian gate. How long have you had it?'

'A couple of months,' Carrie said sourly. Raging. They'd been having fun, in a rare light-hearted family gathering, for the first time in years and now the Freeloaders had invaded *yet* again. Shauna was going to have to do something about them, otherwise they'd be dropping in morning, noon and night. She'd noticed Della taking it all in. She'd known her long enough now to guess that the other woman was planning on spending a lot of time in Whiteshells Bay. Shauna was just going to have to put her foot down once and for all. And that wouldn't be easy with a selfish

375

and manipulative woman like Della. The fact that she was Greg's sister made it much more difficult.

'And how many does your mobile sleep, Shauna?' Della strolled into the lounge area and gazed round.

'Six,' Shauna said shortly.

'Four beds, then, for guests, when you and Chloe are here by yourselves. We must come and stay a night or two,' Della challenged.

'That would be nice,' Noel contributed cheerfully. 'It's good for families to spend time together.'

'*Exactly*,' Della agreed from inside the mobile. Shauna could have throttled him. Who was he to talk about what was good for families? For years he'd made his own family's lives miserable, she thought with a surge of the old, familiar resentment.

Della opened press doors and poked around the neat fitted kitchen before wandering into the bedrooms and bathroom. Carrie and Shauna stared at each other in silent dismay. Kathryn was pulling Chloe's dolls out of the toy press in the sitting room and Ashley was throwing twigs onto the barbecue until Bobby got him by the scruff of the neck and dumped him over the veranda rail onto the grass, much to his outrage.

'It's fabulous.' Della emerged onto the veranda moments later. 'It's really modern. How much did it cost?' she asked bluntly.

Shauna ignored the question and took the plate of food Bobby proffered. She'd completely lost her appetite.

'I'm starving,' whined Kathryn, coming out onto the veranda with two of Chloe's dolls. 'Can I have something to eat?'

'Mom, she's got my dolls and she never asked me,' Chloe protested.

'Now don't be mean. It's good to share, Chloe,' Della intervened briskly. 'Isn't that right, Shauna?'

Shauna wanted to slap her. How could she not agree that

sharing was good without seeming churlish? But she wanted to stand up for her daughter too. Della had her backed into a corner and she knew it. She could see the triumphant glint in her sister-in-law's eye. Chloe looked at her anxiously.

'It's good to share but it's manners to ask first, Kathryn. It's rude to go through people's cupboards,' she retorted. 'Isn't that right, Della?' She knew she was being childish but she didn't care. *Ha!* she thought, as Della's lips tightened in annoyance.

'Want some, want some.' Ashley interrupted the tit-for-tatting as he tried to grab the Ribena drink Chloe was sipping.

'Stop that, Ashley,' Carrie ordered.

'Won't! Want some.' The little boy stamped his foot.

'Any spare grub there, Bobby?' Eddie queried.

''Fraid not. If you want to go to the supermarket and get a few burgers and sausages I'll toss them on the barbecue for you,' Bobby offered grudgingly. 'Didn't know you were coming.'

Well done, Bobby, Shauna thought approvingly. She tried to take some control of the situation.

'Della, why don't you go for a walk on the beach? We'll be finished here in an hour and I'll make a nice cup of tea for you when you come back.'

Della's eyes narrowed. 'I don't feel like a walk at the moment. We'll just sit here and relax. Do you have any more chairs?'

'No. I'll get a rug and you can spread it on the grass, if you like,' Carrie said shortly.

'Grand.' Della was defiant.

'I'll go and get it.' Carrie put her plate on the table and stalked off the veranda to go up to the office and get a rug.

'What are you eating?' Kathryn asked Chloe.

'Ribs,' Chloe declared, chomping on a spare rib with gusto.

'Can I have a bite?' her cousin asked hopefully.

Chloe looked at Shauna, uncertain.

'Here, have one of mine.' Bobby stepped in and slapped a rib on a plate and handed it to the little girl.

'Yummy,' Kathryn said triumphantly.

'Want some,' screeched Ashley.

'Give your brother a bite,' Bobby ordered.

'Give me a bite too,' Eddie demanded.

Shauna couldn't believe her ears.

'Have one of mine,' Noel offered kindly. 'I've more than enough food here.'

'Ta.' Eddie didn't need to be asked twice.

'I'll have a bit of the salad there, that will keep me going,' Della piped up. 'Pass me over a plate, Bobby.'

Bobby handed her a plate, gobsmacked. And watched as she helped herself to a large portion of Caesar salad and some tomatoes in basil.

'Is that potato going a-begging?' Eddie motioned to a baked potato wrapped in tinfoil.

'That's Carrie's,' Shauna snapped.

'Ah I'm sure she won't mind giving me a chunk of it.' Eddie stood up and cut the potato in half, helped himself to a spare plate and ladled on some coleslaw.

'Eating outside just adds to the flavour, doesn't it?' Della remarked airily, leaning across Eddie and helping herself to a portion of feta cheese and olives.

'Indeed it does,' Noel agreed. 'I've never eaten at a barbecue before. It's very, very tasty. Thank you for doing the cooking, Bobby,' he said to his son. 'You should have been a chef.'

'No thanks, Dad, I think the hotel chef is the most stressed man in the building.' Bobby shook his head.

By the time Carrie got back with the rug, Della, Eddie, Kathryn and Ashley were eating all round them, Della sitting in the chair Carrie had vacated, Eddie seated in Shauna's.

'Mam, I'll sit on the rug,' Davey offered, as Carrie shook it out.

'Good idea. You kids go and sit on the rug and let us grown-ups have the chairs,' Della approved. 'Let Shauna sit on your chair, Olivia, and go down on the rug,' she added bossily.

Olivia threw her a filthy look and sat where she was.

'Stay where you are, Olivia, I'll sit on the step.' Shauna hunkered down on the step of the veranda and Chloe came and sat beside her. Carrie sat in Davey's chair.

'So, tell us all the news,' Della said gaily. 'How's Greg? When's he coming home? When can I collect my silk?' She settled back, ready to be entertained.

Shauna could hardly eat she was so angry. 'He's fine, he'll be home in August,' she muttered, thoroughly pissed off. Couldn't Della see how unwelcome she was? The only one of the family who was being any way nice to her was Noel. How could she sit there, brazen-faced, pretending everything was hunky-dory? What did it take? Did Shauna have to stand up and tell her bluntly to get lost? Was that what it was going to take to get some respite from the in-laws from hell? They made Shauna feel so *helpless*. It was infuriating.

It was many hours later before the Keegans finally left. Carrie had eventually excused herself and gone back to the office. Noel had been quite happy to sit and chat to Della. Eddie had snored his head off; the children had gone up to the playground accompanied by Shauna, who had slipped her paperback into her bag. She was damned if she was going to sit entertaining Della for the afternoon.

'How will we get rid of them? Can you believe how cheeky they are?' Carrie asked irritably as she joined her sister on the bench at the side of the playground.

'Could we say we were going over to Sadie's for tea?' Shauna suggested.

'I could give her a ring and tell her what's going on,' Carrie agreed.

'Don't. There's no point. Della would probably say they'd come too. Or else she'll tell us to go and they'll stay at the mobile. And when we get back she'll have Ashley in bed or something and tell us that they're all staying the night,' Shauna said despondently.

'True. Nix that.' Carrie gave a sigh that came from her toes.

Shauna chewed her lip. 'This is the pits, Carrie. She's never going to leave us alone now. I can see her plotting and planning already. Did you hear her going on about the four beds for guests? She'll be down for weekends and then, when the kids are off school in July, she'll be here for a week at least. It's not fucking fair.'

'You'll just have to have it out with her. Lay down your boundaries, Shauna, and nip it in the bud now or you'll be stuck with her. *Don't* let her ruin your summer,' Carrie warned.

'I know, I know,' Shauna groaned. The phone in the office rang.

'I'd better go and answer that. I'll come down with you in a little while and we'll see if we can put the skids under them.' Carrie stood up to go.

'Thanks,' Shauna said distractedly, picking up her book. It was pointless trying to read. She could feel her tension levels rising. She saw Ashley pulling Chloe off the swing. She jumped up. 'Ashley Keegan, you stop that right now or I'll send you back to your mother,' she warned. Ashley stuck his tongue out at her. 'You little brat. Go down to your mother this minute,' she ordered.

'Will not.' He ran round to the slide.

'He never does what he's told,' Kathryn informed Shauna matter-of-factly.

'Well, you go down and tell your mother that he's being a very bold boy,' Shauna clipped.

'Do I have to?' her niece pouted.

'Yes, this minute.' Shauna felt she was losing control of the situation fast. What would she do if Kathryn refused? She could hardly manhandle the pair of them off the play area.

'OK,' the young girl said sulkily. She marched off in high dudgeon. Shauna waited for Della to appear . . . and waited.

Kathryn arrived back. Eventually. 'She'll be up in a minute,' she said. 'And she wants to know if I can have a pair of Chloe's togs to go swimming in? Except she'll have to tie the straps in a knot 'cos Chloe's so fat and I'm not,' Kathryn said artlessly.

Chloe burst into tears. 'I'm not fat. Sure I'm not, Mom.'

'No, darling, you're not.' Shauna was horrified as she hugged her daughter. 'That's a very unkind thing to say, Kathryn.'

'Well that's what Mommy said.' Kathryn shrugged.

I'll swing for that bitch, Shauna swore silently as she dried her daughter's tears. Kathryn was a skinny little stick because she wasn't half fed. She and Chloe were completely different builds. She felt a frisson of inadequacy. If Chloe *was* a little chunky it was her fault for letting Filomena take her to the Pizza Hut so often. She was going to have to start watching what Chloe ate and take more of an interest in her nutrition, she acknowledged guiltily. This only deepened her resentment of Della and co. Carrie was right. She was going to have to put her foot down or else the summer was going to be ruined.

Bobby slipped home after the lunch on the pretext of collecting his iPod. He phoned Anton and acted out the whole scenario over the phone, much to his partner's amusement.

'They can't be that bad.' He chuckled.

'They are and worse. The Simpsons aren't even in the race when the Keegans are around,' Bobby assured him.

'Poor Shauna,' Anton murmured. 'She's never going to get rid of them.'

381

'I know. It's a real problem.'

'How's it going otherwise?'

'Not bad at all, surprisingly,' Bobby informed him. 'The few days went very fast. Dad's making a big effort. I think he likes it that I'm cooking for him and fussing over him and cleaning the house. I whitewashed the yard this morning. He's content to sit and read his paper and potter in his glasshouse. I suppose it's lonely for him living on his own. He seems to like it that I'm around. How's your mum?'

'Coming on well but in a lot of pain. Dad's really missing her. Just as well I stayed. He's not great at looking after himself.' Anton sighed. 'Something else we have in common, elderly parents.'

'Yeah. I guess we just have to muddle along and do the best we can for them. I'm glad I came home. All in all it's been a good trip, but I'm longing to see you,' Bobby confessed.

'Me, too,' Anton assured him. 'I'll have a meal ready for you when you get home.'

'Great. Any chance of your beef stir-fry with noodles?' Bobby asked hopefully.

'If beef stir-fry with noodles is what your little heart desires, that's what you'll have,' Anton assured him. 'Now go and rescue your sisters.'

'I suppose I'd better,' Bobby agreed. 'That lot are heading for trouble, though. I think this time they've pushed Shauna too far,' he predicted cheerfully. 'I'd like to be there when they get their comeuppance.'

'It would be nice to stay the night,' Della remarked casually as the sun began to set behind them in the west and the sea turned from blue grey to pearly.

'Not tonight, if you don't mind, Della,' Shauna said curtly.

'It's Bobby's last night and we wanted to spend time together as a family. It's a long time since he's been home.'

'But we *are* family.' Della was not to be put off.

'Not tonight. The kids have planned a sleepover and there won't be enough room.' Shauna was adamant and her face was like thunder. Even Della knew she'd pushed too far.

'OK, some other time then,' she said sulkily.

'Actually, Della, would you mind heading off now? I'd like to start getting Chloe to bed and she won't go when her cousins are here. It's long past her bedtime.' Shauna stood up briskly and began to clear away teacups and saucers.

'Good thinking, Shauna. I'd want to get my lot ready for bed too. Hannah's wall falling. She'll be like a bag of cats tomorrow if I don't put her to bed soon.' Carrie jumped up to help her.

Della made no move to go. Carrie eyeballed her. 'I'll call the kids so you can get them ready,' she said firmly. She marched off the veranda and headed for the playground, fuming. That woman wouldn't even take a blatant hint. She was the absolute pits.

'Ashley, Kathryn, it's time to go. Say goodbye to your cousins,' she instructed crisply from the edge of the playground. 'And you guys,' she turned to the others, 'come on down to Shauna's and get into your pyjamas. It's getting late.'

'Aw, Mam,' protested Olivia. 'You said we could stay up late for a special occasion.'

'You can. I just need to get Hannah to bed, so come down now anyway and play around Shauna's mobile. It's getting late and people want a bit of peace and quiet in the park,' she said firmly.

Grumbling, the others did as they were told. Ashley stayed on the swing. 'No way,' he declared, swinging faster. Carrie's lips thinned. She strode round to the back of the swing and hoisted him off by the scruff of the neck, much to his annoyance.

'When I tell you to do something, you do it, and don't give me any of your lip,' she snapped.

'You're not my mommy,' he retorted cheekily, kicking at the bark under the swing.

'Thank God,' Carrie growled. 'Now get going or I'll give you a good clatter.'

Even Ashley Keegan would not defy Carrie when she spoke in that tone and he marched along in front of her, glowering at her every so often. All he got were glowers back in return.

With many whinges and moans, and great reluctance on Della's part, the Keegans finally said goodnight. Carrie, Shauna and Bobby watched them go, not even making the effort to wave. Noel was at a parish meeting and had said his goodbyes earlier.

'Right. I'm putting Hannah to bed,' Carrie declared, kissing her exhausted toddler.

'What a perfectly lovely day ruined.' Shauna scowled.

'Not quite,' Bobby interjected mischievously. 'I've three bottles of Cloudy Bay and a big dish of fresh prawns and scallops that I got off the boats earlier today chilling in Dad's fridge. I had no intention of producing them when the Freeloaders were here.' He grinned. 'Let's have a midnight feast.'

Dan guffawed. 'Way to go, Bobby. I think Della's finally met her match.' He'd arrived from work to find his wife and sister-in-law with faces on them that would curdle milk.

'She needn't think she's going to pull stunts like she did today for the rest of the summer.' Shauna grimaced.

'Forget her. She's gone. Plonk your ass in the chair there and prepare to eat, drink and be merry. I'll pop up to Dad's and get the goodies,' Bobby ordered, throwing a few more coals on the barbecue to ward off the chill of evening.

'I love when you boss me around, Bobby.' Shauna grinned, sinking into a white chair. Now that Della and co. were gone she was beginning to relax again. It was Bobby's last evening at home, and she intended to make the most of it. And Cloudy Bay was her absolute favourite wine.

Cloudy Bay, prawns and scallops, and the gang ensconced on the veranda beside the glowing barbecue coals with a silver moon shining on a silver sea. What more could she want?

'They are the rudest, most ignorant and inhospitable family I've ever had the misfortune to encounter. What Greg was doing marrying into them, I'll never know. Did you see the way they practically threw us out?' Della was incandescent with rage as she drove out of Whiteshells Bay.

Eddie, slumped in the front seat beside her, grunted something unintelligible.

'Don't wanna go home,' wailed Kathryn. 'I want to sleep in the caravan.'

'I'm hungry,' whined Ashley.

'I'm hungry too,' Kathryn snivelled.

'Be quiet,' hissed Della as she spun round a corner on two wheels, brakes squealing.

'Mind your driving,' her husband growled.

Della ignored him. 'That Shauna one is as cute as a fox. She wasn't even going to mention anything about buying that mobile home. If we hadn't gone visiting to Whiteshells Bay we'd have known nothing about it. How mean can you get? Well, she doesn't own it, it's Greg's too and I'm going to ask him if we can have it when that one's not here,' Della informed her husband as she drove over a ramp at speed and nearly decapitated him.

He was definitely not feeling as sore, Greg decided as he gingerly inspected his wounded manhood. The phone rang and he pulled up his shorts and went to answer it. He was back in Abu Dhabi

385

and for the first time since the vasectomy he was envisaging the possibility that all would be well.

'Well, brother, how are you?' His younger sister's voice floated down the line.

'Fine. What's up?' he asked, surprised to hear from her. They weren't great ones for keeping in touch.

'Nothing,' Della assured him. 'Just ringing to see how you were. We had a barbecue with your nearest and dearest yesterday in your new mobile home. Congratulations; it's a great buy. You certainly know how to relax and enjoy yourselves. You have it down to a fine art. Shauna has, anyway,' Della remarked sweetly.

'Do you think so?' Greg raised his eyebrows. Della wasn't usually so effusive.

'I do, and you both deserve it. But listen, you and Shauna will only use it for a couple of months and then it will be empty. I'm sure you'd have no objections to myself, Eddie and the kids using it the odd weekend?'

'Sort it with Shauna. I'm sure she won't mind.' Greg poured himself a Scotch. His mobile phone erupted into Mozart 40 on the coffee table.

'Have to go, Della, my mobile's ringing. See you in August,' he said hastily.

'Great, and we can definitely use your caravan?' Della pressed.

'Sure. 'Bye,' Greg agreed, wishing she'd get off the line. The number coming up on his mobile belonged to his boss and he wanted to take the call.

''Bye.' Della sounded as though she was smiling even though he was rushing her off the phone. That was a relief. No-one could get into a snit like his sister. He took the call from his boss and was immediately engrossed in plans for a two-day trip to Kuwait. By the time he had everything sorted to both their satisfaction his conversation with Della was totally forgotten.

33

'THERE'S NOTHING LIKE A PICNIC ON THE BEACH, SURE THERE isn't?' Shauna said to Carrie as they spread out a tartan rug and laid out an array of plastic beakers and saucers. Carrie opened a parcel of tinfoil-wrapped egg and onion sandwiches. Shauna inhaled appreciatively.

'Egg and onion. Delicious. And I've made some banana sangers. Just smell them, Carrie. I'm eight years old again. Remember when we used to come to the beach with Mam?'

'Yeah, she always made a picnic such an event. She'd love this with the grandchildren,' Carrie said, sadness darkening her eyes momentarily.

'I know. Look at Dad, can you believe him? He's very good with the kids. He was so different with us.' Shauna watched as Noel stood paddling with Hannah while Chloe, Davey and Olivia squealed and shrieked as they danced up and down in the foamy white waves.

'I think Mam's death, as well as knocking the stuffing out of him, softened him and made him realize he's not in control of everything. Mind you, some things never change. I heard him the other day telling Davey that *The Da Vinci Code* was a tool of the devil and that he was *never* to read it.'

Shauna laughed heartily. 'You're joking!'

'Honestly. The sad thing is that he really believes it. You should hear himself and Mrs O'Neill arguing the toss. It's hilarious.'

Shauna shook some packets of crisps out onto the rug. 'Will I call them? I'm ravenous.'

'Me too,' Carrie agreed. 'I made a big bowl of fruit salad and frozen yoghurt for dessert.'

'How healthy,' Shauna teased.

'I've got Soleros in the freezer bag as well,' her sister confessed.

'Excellent!' Shauna stood up and yelled at the children. 'Come and get it.'

A mad race ensued as the youngsters dashed out of the water and arrived at the picnic rug, dripping wet and spraying drops of water all over the place.

'Wrap yourselves in towels and don't dare step on the rug with your wet, sandy feet,' Carrie warned as she poured tea out of a flask into a plastic cup for Noel.

'Tuck in, and eat your crusts.' Shauna handed round the sandwiches as they all settled themselves down on the sand.

'Phew, I needed this.' Davey bit into his egg and onion sandwich with relish.

'What is it about tea out of a flask? It's *so* satisfying.' Carrie drank her tea appreciatively.

'Can I have crisps, please?' Chloe asked. 'I want to make a crisp sandwich.'

'Brill idea,' enthused Olivia.

'Very tasty, girls.' Noel sat like Neptune on his throne on a small deckchair.

This is the life. Shauna raised her face to the sun, utterly relaxed. The past ten days had slipped away so easily and all traces of tension had left her as she and Chloe had settled into

388

days of ease and relaxation. She and Carrie had settled into their old familiar companionship, helping each other out, gossiping, taking the odd jaunt to Dundalk to stroll around the shops. Chloe was having the time of her life.

'Aren't you bored after all your socializing? Don't you miss it?' Carrie had asked her one day when Carrie had an hour to spare as they sat in Hughes & Hughes sipping coffee, having restocked their book supplies. But she wasn't at all bored and, to her surprise, she didn't miss it.

'Amazingly, not in the slightest. It must be the onset of middle age!' She grinned. If someone had told her ten years ago that she'd spend a summer in a mobile home in Whiteshells Bay enjoying herself immensely, she would have told them they were mad.

It was such liberation not having to worry about her clothes and what she was going to wear to a function. Not having to be made up to the nines, not having to worry about entertaining or being entertained. Solitude was a gift that she was savouring. She was changing, becoming calmer, quieter. It felt very good. She bit into a banana sandwich and felt the grit of sand between her teeth and took a drink of hot strong tea and wouldn't have swapped it for the poshest restaurant in any of the capitals of the world.

An hour later she was drowsing on the rug, with the sound of the children playing in the distance. Carrie was snoring, delicate little cucking snores that rippled in the breeze. A great sense of well-being enveloped her and she lay in a drowsy stupor listening to the sea. Noel had gone home to go bowling with Mrs O'Neill. He was off the crutches and making good progress.

'Oh no!' she heard Olivia exclaim crossly.

'What's wrong, Olivia?' she asked drowsily, without opening

her eyes, thinking that her niece had knocked down the sand village she was laboriously building with Chloe and Davey's help.

'It's those people again. I don't like them. That boy is very bold,' she said in disgust.

'What people, darling?' Shauna yawned. Carrie snored on serenely, oblivious.

'Chloe's cousins. Look, they're waving at us! I'm glad we finished our picnic before *they* came.'

Shauna jerked up into a sitting position and squinted in the direction her niece was pointing. Rage suffused her as she saw Della, Ashley and Kathryn advancing along the beach. 'I don't believe it,' she muttered.

'Hi, you lucky beggars. You're so blessed having a beach on your doorstep. We decided to come and spend the day with you,' Della trilled.

'We brought buns for tea,' Kathryn boasted.

Carrie woke up and gazed up at the other woman in dismay.

'You lazy thing, snoring on the beach. Some people have all the luck. You pair have the life of Riley. Is that a flask? Any chance of a cuppa?'

'There's none left,' Shauna said shortly.

'Ah sure we'll pop up to the mobile in a while and have some there. Any chance we could stay the night? I told Eddie to drive down later. He had to go to a funeral,' Della informed her casually.

'Actually, Shauna and I were going out for a meal tonight,' Carrie interjected.

'Great. I'll come with you. We can have a girls' night out. I'd enjoy that. I haven't had one for ages,' Della suggested. 'I'll get Eddie to mind the kids.' She turned to Shauna. 'I was talking to Greg and he was saying it would be OK for us to use the mobile when you're not here in the autumn. We'll look after it for you and keep an eye on it over the winter.' She smiled a saccharine smile at her sister-in-law.

'*Excuse me?*' Shauna couldn't believe her ears.

'Greg said we could use the mobile home when you're not using it,' Della explained sweetly.

'I don't think so,' Shauna said icily, her eyes flashing dangerously.

'Right, you guys, come on. We're going to go for a walk as far as the rocks. Shauna and Della need some privacy for a few moments,' Carrie said calmly, standing up.

'There's no need for that, Carrie,' Della blustered.

'Oh I think there is, Della. I think Shauna would like to talk to you on your own and not in front of the children,' Carrie said coldly.

'Thanks, Carrie. It won't take long.' Shauna tried to keep the tremor of anger out of her voice. This was it. The long-promised showdown had come at last. Her stomach clenched in knots. She felt sick. She wasn't great at confrontation. Altercations reminded her of bad times with her father and she tried to avoid them.

'Quick march, first to the rocks gets a euro,' Carrie said gaily. The children took to their heels in an avalanche of flying sand, Hannah's skinny little legs carrying her like a baby ballerina across the beach.

'There's no need to be dramatic,' Della exclaimed defensively. 'Do you have a problem with me using the mobile or something?'

'Yes I *do*, Della. How *dare* you go behind my back to Greg? How dare you! And not only do I have a problem with you using my mobile, I have a problem with *you*, Della. I'm sick to the back teeth of you arriving whenever you feel like it, unannounced. I'm sick of you eating and drinking us out of house and home. I'm

391

sick of you coming out to stay with us in Abu Dhabi with one arm longer than the other and treating Filomena like a servant. You're mean and manipulative and you take advantage like no-one else I've ever met. You know what we call you?' She stared at the other woman, who was rigid with shock at this unexpected onslaught. 'We call you the Freeloaders, because that's exactly what you are.'

It was pouring out of her, years of pent-up resentment and dislike erupting like a lava flow. She took a breath and continued, feeling strangely exhilarated. She couldn't believe that she was letting rip. She wasn't going to hold back one little thing. She was on a roll and Della was stunned into silence, her sullen face as red as a beet. For the first time ever in their relationship Shauna felt in control, and she continued her tirade with vigour.

'How *dare* you think that you can come onto Carrie's caravan park without a by your leave—'

'Now hold on a minute. You can't talk to *me* like that,' Della retorted angrily, thrusting her face aggressively close to Shauna's. 'Just who exactly do you think you are, you little jumped-up, snooty, snobby show-off? If it weren't for *my* brother you wouldn't have the life you've got and all the luxuries that go with it. You knew what you were doing when you married into our family. If you hadn't married Greg you'd be stuck in your dull little village with your stuck-up sister and your poncy nancy boy brother and your pain-in-the-ass auld fella going on about his precious church. And as for that spoilt little brat of yours—'

That was as far as she got. Shauna, white with fury, raised her hand and slapped her sister-in-law across the cheek.

'*Oh!*' Della was stunned. 'You vicious *bitch*!' She held her hand to her cheek, utterly shocked.

'You get the hell out of here! I don't want to see you or that big, lazy slob of a husband of yours ever again,' Shauna spat. 'If you want to keep in touch with Greg, fine. You can even visit him out in the Gulf in the summer when I'm here. I don't care, but I don't want to see you ever again, Della Keegan. Do you hear me?'

'That was an assault!' Della screeched.

'Fine, sue me,' Shauna challenged. 'Now you go and get Ashley and Kathryn and get out of my sight. I've put up with you and Eddies' freeloading for too long and I've had enough of it. It ends here. Now. No more, Della. No more.'

'I'm telling Greg about this,' Della threatened, nursing her reddened cheek.

'You do that. I couldn't care less.' Shauna was trembling. She felt sick. She couldn't believe that she'd slapped Della. She couldn't believe that she'd finally had it out with her sister-in-law. She took a deep breath. 'This is a public beach. Stay here if you want but I don't want to see you up in the park or in Malahide again. Do you hear me?'

'Fuck off,' Della muttered.

'With pleasure,' Shauna retorted coldly and turned on her heel and strode down the beach towards Carrie, who had been keeping a weather eye on proceedings and now drew away from the children, who were scrambling over the rocks, and walked towards Shauna.

'Well?' she asked grimly.

'I gave her a smack in the chops.' Shauna bit her lip and looked at Carrie warily.

'Did you?' Carrie gave a horrified giggle. 'Good for you,' she added stoutly.

'She really pushed me too far. She called Chloe a spoilt little brat. And you're stuck-up and I'm a snobby, snooty show-off and Bobby's a poncy nancy boy. And Dad's a pain in the ass.'

'Jeepers. Let me at her. I'll whack her one myself. The *cheek* of her.' Carrie glowered in Della's direction.

'Well I've told her not to set foot in the park, or in my house, again. I told her that she could visit Greg in the Gulf in the summer if she wants to keep in touch.'

'Well done, Shauna. She's had that coming for years. That's why I left you to it. If you didn't do it today you were going to be stuck with her *every* summer. She's no loss. You did the right thing. What do you want to do now?'

'I could do with a drink,' Shauna said shakily.

'Right! Let's get our stuff and get out of here. We'll bring the kids for afternoon tea in the hotel in Bettystown and you can have a G and T.'

'Sounds good to me.' Shauna managed a weak grin.

'You did great. She's a sponger and a manipulative cow. Don't feel bad. You needed to stand up for yourself and you did,' Carrie said firmly.

'Greg will probably go ballistic,' her sister responded glumly.

'Let him. You're his wife; he should stand up for you,' Carrie answered as she beckoned to the kids to come to her.

'Say goodbye to Kathryn and Ashley. We're going out for a spin in the car,' she instructed.

'Where are we going, Mam?'

'You'll see,' Carrie said brightly. 'Now collect up the stuff and let's go.'

'We want to come too,' Kathryn demanded.

'Not today, Kathryn,' Carrie said firmly over her shoulder as she walked back with Shauna to where they'd been sitting.

Della glared at them when they reached their belongings but moved away from the rug and the windbreak.

'They're going somewhere, Mommy, and they won't bring us,' Kathryn raged.

Ashley kicked Hannah's sandcastle apart.

'Mammy, did you see—'

'Don't worry about it, Olivia, just get your sandals and towel and head up to the mobile,' Carrie said briskly, ignoring her daughter's outrage. 'Davey, take the buckets and spades, please.'

'Why can't we go with you? Mom said we're staying the night in your caravan,' Kathryn protested.

'Mom made a mistake, Kathryn. We had arrangements made and it doesn't suit,' Shauna said evenly.

'It's not fair! You have all the good things and we have *nothing*.' Kathryn stomped off along the beach.

'Hope you're happy now,' Della said nastily. 'Come on, Ashley, we won't stay where we're not wanted.' She stalked off, indignation emanating from every pore.

'Oh, crikey,' muttered Shauna. 'Now she's going to start the emotional blackmail.'

'Ignore it,' Carrie instructed. 'She's manipulated you enough over the years. Don't buy into that stuff. It's her own fault, Shauna. Let's take the short cut so that we don't have to pass her on the way out.'

'Yeah, let's. I never want to see her again,' Shauna whispered.

'Short cut over the dunes, kids,' Carrie called to the children, who had started to walk after Della.

'Oh, Mam, I can't carry all this stuff up the dunes,' Olivia complained.

'Give it to me,' Carrie ordered. 'And call me Dee Dee the Mule while you're at it.'

'Stop, Mam.' Olivia giggled.

'Come on, make the effort,' her mother urged, taking a run at the dunes and getting halfway up. They struggled up against the sliding sand, groaning and laughing. Shauna got to the top first and held her hand out to haul Chloe and Olivia up. Carrie panted up beside her. 'Best foot forward and no looking back,' she murmured.

Shauna smiled at her. A reckless exhilaration enveloped her. She felt free. She'd finally sorted Della out. Once and for all. If Greg didn't like it, he could lump it. Let him entertain his family. She hoped never to see them again.

'I'm buying a bottle of champagne for tonight. We've a lot to celebrate.' She tucked her arm into Carrie's.

'You bet we have,' Carrie agreed. 'Pity Bobby's not here to enjoy our freedom.'

'We'll just have to drink enough for him.' Shauna smiled. 'Hell, after what we've been through with the Freeloaders, we deserve a bottle each.'

'A bottle! Don't you mean a magnum?' Carrie retorted.

Shauna laughed. This summer was getting better and better!

Della felt tears prick her eyelids. She was trembling. Fury, hate and humiliation juggled for dominance. That reckoning had been a long time coming and she'd told that little tart what she thought of her, but somehow she felt she'd come off second best. And had her face slapped into the bargain. Vicious cow!

There was no going back after this. It was a final reckoning, she admitted. The bombs had been dropped. All that remained was the wreckage. It didn't bother her that she wouldn't ever see Shauna again. That was no hardship. But it was the added extras that went with the relationship that she'd really miss.

How dare Shauna call her a freeloader? She and Greg were wealthy. How mean of them to expect her and Eddie to arrive laden down with gifts. God Almighty, if they couldn't share their good fortune with their immediate family, who could they share it with?

'Why aren't we going with them?' Kathryn whinged.

'Because we're not and I don't want to hear any more about it,' she snapped.

Kathryn burst into tears. Della felt like bursting into tears herself. Those bitches had got the better of her and she was going to pay them back one way or another.

'Hold on a minute, Della. What are you saying?' Greg's fingers paused over the calculator where he'd been adding figures to see what his rental income would be from the new apartment he'd bought in Dubai.

'I said your wife not only insulted me but she slapped me in the face and I could sue her for assault if I was that way inclined.' His sister's agitated tones came across the airwaves.

'Shauna slapped you in the face! For what?' Greg demanded irritably. What the hell was going on with the pair of them?

'She was very rude. She told me she doesn't ever want to see my family or me again and that if I want to keep in touch with you I can come and visit you in the summer when she's in Ireland. She's an almighty bitch, Greg.' Della burst into tears.

'Oh, for crying out loud, you women. Have you nothing better to be doing than fighting and arguing? Look, I'm up to my eyes here, you better sort it out between you,' he said harshly.

'There's no sorting; she's a bitch and I don't want to have anything to do with her. But I want you to tell her that we can have that mobile when you aren't using it. It's the least you can do for your family. She called us freeloaders; I've never been so insulted in my life. How would she like it if you spoke about her precious Carrie like that, Greg?'

'I'll talk to her,' Greg snapped. ''Bye.' He didn't give her a chance to respond but hung up in a foul humour. What the hell was going on? The last thing he needed was a family row. He dialled Shauna's mobile number.

'Hi, Greg,' she answered after a few rings, sounding surprisingly cheerful.

'What's going on with you and Della? She says you slapped her in the face,' he demanded.

'Yeah and it wasn't hard enough,' Shauna riposted coldly. 'So little tattle-tale couldn't wait to get on the phone to you.'

'Shauna, what the hell are you doing slapping her across the face? Kids do that, not adults.'

'Listen, Greg, I'm not getting involved in the ins and outs of it. Suffice it to say we had a row, I told her a few home truths, and as far as I'm concerned I don't want to see her again. There's no need for you to get involved.'

'Well, she wants to use the mobile when we're not using it,' Greg said, taken aback by his wife's unyielding position.

'What she wants and what she gets are two different things, Greg, and she can go and fuck off for herself. She's not setting foot in Carrie's park after the way she insulted her—'

'God Almighty, Shauna, I've enough on my plate without this crap,' Greg raged.

'Me too. Deal with it,' Shauna retorted and hung up.

Greg stared at the phone. Shauna *never* spoke to him like that. What had got into her? He knew Della was no angel but whatever had gone on between them was clearly heavy-duty stuff. He shook his head and stared at the figures in front of him. Let them get on with it and sort it. He hadn't time for women's petty catfights.

Shauna sat curled up on the sofa, looking out to sea. She could hardly make out the horizon. A dank mist hung like a shroud on the caravan park. It was a grey, cold, dismal day. The weather had changed overnight but she didn't mind. The gas fire flickered merrily, Chloe and Olivia were playing with their dolls, Hannah was having her nap in Shauna's bed and Davey had gone to a scouting meeting.

She'd taken Greg's phone call in the bathroom so that the

children wouldn't hear the exchange. She was glad in a way that Della had phoned Greg; it let her off the hook about telling him that she wouldn't be having anything to do with that bitch again. And she was extremely pleased with the way she'd handled her husband. She hadn't got into any long, involved explanations and had just told him to deal with it.

She smiled, imagining him sitting in his office wondering what had got into her. He had sounded very taken aback by her attitude. Usually she was the pacifier in their relationship. Well, not any more. This summer she was coming into her own. She was doing what *she* wanted, when she wanted, and she wasn't feeling one bit guilty. It was a tremendous feeling.

What an unexpectedly interesting summer she was having, she mused as she watched a fishing boat bob up and down like a cork on the cloudy, wind-tossed sea. She'd put herself first and had set her boundaries about entertaining the neighbours in Malahide. There'd been a family reconciliation, which made life much less stressful, and she'd finally dealt with the Freeloaders so decisively that she might never have to see them again, with any luck. *And* she'd taken no nonsense from Greg about it, after years of swallowing down her annoyance and resentment just so he could feel good about his appalling family. The icing on the cake would be getting pregnant, and then she could truly say that it had been the best summer of her life.

She stretched out and picked up her book and opened it at the page she'd been reading. The rain began to batter against the window and thrum in a steady downpour against the roof. Most people in the park hated to see it raining. She didn't mind it. She liked the sounds of angry, insistent drumming on roof and window; it made her feel snug. It gave her an excuse to do nothing but laze on her sofa and read. Stretching like a cat, Shauna settled in for an afternoon of total relaxation.

34

'NOW BE A GOOD GIRL FOR CARRIE AND WE'LL BE HOME AT THE weekend. Daddy is dying to see you and he's got a present for you.' Shauna hugged Chloe tightly. Her daughter looked the picture of health from a summer spent in the fresh sea air. Her eyes were glowing, her skin was lightly tanned, and her hair shone, streaked with silky blond highlights where it had been kissed by the sun. Greg would surely be delighted to see how well she was looking.

She straightened up and gave Carrie a hug. 'Thanks a million for looking after her. I'll call you from Paris,' she promised.

'You look terrific,' her sister complimented her. 'He'll jump on you.'

'He'd better. He's not getting out of bed for the four days.' Shauna grinned. She was wearing a tangerine linen trouser suit with a cream camisole and cream high-heel sandals. Her hair was swept up in a chignon. Her tan gave her a healthy, vibrant luminescence and she was fizzing with anticipation. June and July had whizzed by in a blur of lazy, relaxed days that had slipped away in easy passage, especially since her showdown with Della.

The more she thought about it, the more pleased she was that she had finally confronted her sister-in-law with her unacceptable behaviour. She had endured it for too long because of her reluctance to rock the boat and make a stand. She hadn't wanted to upset Greg. He got on with her family; she'd wanted to get on with his. She'd tried, hard. But she had to acknowledge that at the end of the day she couldn't stand Greg's sister and her husband, and when she finally admitted it out loud it was as if a huge burden had lifted off her shoulders. Knowing that Della, Eddie and the kids would not be dropping in uninvited had given her such a sense of relief that she had thoroughly enjoyed the weeks following the bust-up.

Greg had phoned her and asked whether she had sorted things out with his sister and she'd told him in no uncertain terms that *yes* she had sorted things with his sister and she *wouldn't* be seeing her again. *And* she had no intention of discussing the matter further. To her surprise he'd let it go and hadn't raised the question again. Satisfied that that was the end of it, Shauna was really looking forward to their reunion in Paris. Having had almost two months of R&R she was even looking forward to hosting a barbecue or two in Malahide. She was determined to make the most of the month of August; next year she'd have less time at home because Chloe would be at school.

She gave her daughter another hug. She had spent a lot of time with her this summer and it had paid off. Chloe had begun to come out of her shell and the whinging and clinginess had lessened enormously. It was heartening to see.

'Here's your taxi,' Carrie said. She had driven over to Malahide with Shauna, who had arranged for the mini-maids to come and give the house the once-over in preparation for Greg's homecoming.

Shauna left in a flurry of hugs and kisses, relieved beyond measure that Chloe showed no sign of distress. That was the wonderful thing about being so close to her aunt and cousins.

Carrie was like another mother to her and her cousins were as close as siblings. A smile came to her lips as she sat back in the taxi. If God was good to her, Chloe might have that much longed-for brother or sister sooner rather than later.

Carrie waved after her sister, thinking that she had never seen her looking so well or relaxed. It had been a good summer for all of them, she thought as she closed the door and went into the kitchen to wash up the coffee mugs. Getting rid of the Freeloaders had been an added bonus. Greg hadn't seemed too pissed off about it, according to Shauna. That was good news; she'd worried that it might affect their reunion.

Carrie gazed out at the perfectly manicured lawn in the back garden and thought how different her marriage was from her sister's. If she thought she was going to be parted from Dan for two months she'd freak. She'd miss him so terribly she didn't think she could bear it. Yet Shauna hadn't seemed to miss Greg much at all and seemed perfectly content on her own with Chloe in the mobile home.

They spoke every couple of days on the phone but Carrie had often been there during the conversations and not once had Shauna told Greg that she missed him. Still, it seemed to work for them, and it really was none of her business, she told herself. Perhaps the reunions made up for the time spent apart.

'Come on, you guys, time to get going,' she called to the kids, who were playing in Chloe's state-of-the-art tree house. She looked out the window at her niece laughing her head off with Davey. She'd hardly mentioned Greg over the summer. Even the fact that he was coming home wasn't a big deal to her. All she was interested in was her present. That was sad, Carrie reflected. She might have everything money could buy, but Olivia, Hannah and Davey had far more than the poor little mite had or ever would have, unless Greg came to the realization that there was a lot more to life than work and making money. Somehow Carrie didn't think that that was ever going to happen.

Greg stood on the balcony of his hotel room, looking out at the skyline of Paris. The Eiffel Tower pierced the cobalt sky in the distance, and a pigeon cooed on the crumbling grey parapet of the building opposite. The heat rose and shimmered from the pavements. But even though Paris was hot, it was a damn sight cooler than the oven-blast heat he'd left behind him. He strolled back into the bedroom and ate a couple of grapes from the dish of fruit that lay on the coffee table. He was weary from the long flight and the interminable hot summer he'd endured in the Gulf. This was a badly needed holiday.

He towelled his hair dry and lay on the bed and flicked on the sports channel. He could have gone to the airport to meet Shauna but he was so tired after travelling that he'd phoned her and asked would she mind if they rendezvoused at the hotel. He glanced at his watch. Her flight would be landing shortly; it was too late to change his mind.

Greg sighed. He'd sensed that she was disappointed. Part of him was dreading meeting his wife. He didn't regret having the vasectomy, he assured himself, especially since he'd recovered so well from it. In fact he was *totally* recovered. He'd found that out when he'd bedded one of the company secretaries at her farewell party just ten days previously. He was in perfect working order. If only he could get rid of the niggle of guilt that wouldn't go away. He'd never been unfaithful to Shauna before. But it wasn't as if he was having a full-blown affair. It had only been a one-night stand and he'd never see Avril Kowloski again. She had flown home to the US to get married.

The closer he'd got to his reunion with Shauna, the more

guilty he'd become. He knew that she was hoping to get pregnant and now it was never going to happen. She'd never know the reason why and would possibly end up blaming herself. That wasn't a very fair thing to put her through, and he'd been toying with the idea of telling her straight out. She might be frosty for a month or two but that would pass and at least the baby thing would be sorted once and for all.

If he could get his nerve up he'd tell her, he decided. It might be the easiest thing to get it out of the way and over and done with. The little interlude between him and Avril would remain his secret. Shauna would definitely *not* forgive him for that.

His chin drooped onto his terry robe. Guilt was a wearisome thing, he thought before he nodded off to sleep.

He woke to find Shauna smiling down at him. A porter had let her into their room.

'Hello, babe,' he said drowsily, thinking how relaxed and healthy she looked.

'Hello, Greg.' She leaned down and kissed him and the familiar scent of her Nina Ricci perfume wafted past his nostrils and a hunger for her enveloped him. He pulled her to him and kissed her passionately, all notion of telling her about his vasectomy instantly dismissed.

Shauna lay in the crook of her husband's arm, her head resting on his shoulder. She felt perfectly content as he slept beside her, his breathing deep and rhythmic. They had spent the afternoon in bed, making love, and then ordered a room service dinner. They'd bathed together in a scented bubble bath and gone back to bed and made love again as dusky pinks and purples turned to darkness and lights sparkled across the city.

The breeze made by the air-conditioning cooled her naked body and she lay drowsily replete. She'd been thrilled to discover how alive and responsive her body had become, having been liberated from the libido-reducing effects of the Pill. The love-making had been wonderful. So wonderful that she was sure she could easily have got pregnant, she thought happily. It was perfect timing, right in the middle of her cycle.

She'd never forget this summer, she thought as she drifted off into sleep. It had been the best time she could remember in a long, long while.

'Hello, Daddy,' Chloe said shyly as her father got out of the car.

'Hello, Chloe. You've got tall. Look at you.' Greg bent down and kissed the top of his daughter's blond head.

'This is my daddy,' Chloe said proudly to her cousins. 'And he's brought me a present. Haven't you, Daddy?' she said anxiously.

'Indeed I have. Hello, kids.' He waved at his nieces and nephew and followed Shauna into the house.

'What did you get me, Daddy, what did you get?' Chloe was dancing up and down with excitement.

'In a minute, Chloe. Have patience,' Shauna chided.

Chloe pouted sulkily. 'I want my present,' she muttered. Shauna sighed. Greg had only been home five minutes and Chloe was pouting and sulking.

Greg rooted in his travel case and took out a gift-wrapped rectangular box. 'There you go.' He handed it to her. Chloe grabbed it and began to tear away the paper. The others looked on with anticipation.

'Say thank you,' Shauna reminded her.

'Thanks, Daddy.' She pulled at the paper impatiently until a polished, intricately painted box was revealed.

'What is it?' she demanded, disappointed.

'Open it.' Greg laughed.

405

Olivia opened the little clip for her and when the lid was raised a dainty, pink-tutued ballerina spun slowly round on a mirrored lake to the sounds of *Swan Lake*.

'Ooohhhh, Chloe, it's gorgeous! You lucky sucker,' Olivia said enviously.

Chloe's face lit up as she watched the little dancer move gracefully in front of her to the tinkling music. This was a great present. Olivia thought so, and she didn't have one. Only *she* had one because her daddy was very rich and had lots of money. Her daddy was the best daddy in the whole wide world.

AUTUMN
(a year later)

35

'THEY'RE A WEIRD FAMILY, CARRIE. EVEN THOUGH SHE KNEW HER mother was very poorly, Greg's mother went off on a trip to Rome and the poor old dear died on her own in the nursing home. They're waiting for Joanna to get a flight back. Greg's going mad. We should have been back in Abu Dhabi two days ago.' Shauna shook her head. 'I know this is an awful thing to say, but I'm delighted to have a few days extra here, and needless to say Chloe's thrilled to be missing school.'

Carrie laughed. 'It's even sweeter for her that my lot are back since Monday.' She glanced over at Chloe, who was pushing Hannah backwards and forwards on the swing in the otherwise deserted playground. 'Isn't the place so empty compared to last week? September is always quiet here,' Carrie observed as she filed the chit for a delivery of gas cylinders.

'Do you want a cup of tea?' Shauna asked.

'Why not? I'm sorted here. I'll go to the funeral with you, if you like. As soon as you know when it is, let me know so I can make arrangements about the kids.'

'There's no need, Carrie. It won't bother Greg if you don't go. You know them, they've a different way of looking at family than we have.'

'Even so, you're not going to face the Freeloaders alone. I'll be right beside you,' Carrie assured her.

'Thanks, Carrie, but they don't really bother me any more. Honestly, I never give them a thought.' Shauna dropped two tea bags into the teapot. 'Imagine, it's over a year since we saw them last.'

'I know. It flew, didn't it?' Carrie said ruefully.

'You're telling me. I can't believe Chloe's starting her second year at school. She hates the thought of going back to Abu Dhabi.' Shauna sighed as she poured the tea into mugs and opened a packet of chocolate goldgrain biscuits.

'Well, at least you didn't have to move to Dubai so she didn't have to go and make new friends,' Carrie comforted her.

'True, but Greg spends three days a week there now, so we see even less of him. This year's going to be tough for Chloe, though,' Shauna predicted glumly. 'Filomena's not coming back from the Philippines. Her father's not well so I'm going to have to get a new au pair and Chloe's going to have to get used to her. And her best friend, Carly, has gone back to the States. Brett didn't get the Dubai job and he's had enough of Pierre. I'm really going to miss him and Jenna; they were my great buddies out there. So all in all Chloe's not the only one not looking forward to going back.'

'And there's no way that Greg will come home?' Carrie dunked her biscuit into her tea and licked the melted chocolate with pleasure.

Shauna shook her head. 'Nope. I'd hoped that I might have got pregnant and that would have given me some leverage but it hasn't happened yet and I don't know if it will.' An expression of sadness crossed her face.

'Did you ask the doctor about it?' Carrie probed gently. She knew that Shauna's lack of success in conceiving was a cause of great distress to her sister. She'd seen how down she got every time she got a period.

'She says I'm fine and to relax. Easier said than done when you're hitting forty,' Shauna said ruefully. Her mobile phone shrilled.

'Hi, Greg,' she answered, seeing her husband's name come up on the screen. 'What's happening?'

'Gran's going directly to the crematorium on Thursday. Mother's decided against a religious service, as Gran didn't bother about that kind of thing.'

'No, she was definitely a free spirit,' Shauna agreed with a smile.

'Mother just wants to get the funeral over and done with,' her husband informed her. 'She's coming directly to the crematorium from the airport. Glasnevin's only about a fifteen-minute drive from there. If you don't feel like coming to the funeral home, don't bother. You can meet us at the crematorium that morning,' Greg said matter-of-factly.

'That's a bit casual, Greg. She *was* your grandmother,' Shauna murmured.

'I was only thinking of you,' he said. 'What's the point in driving all the way to Enfield to have to drive back again?'

'Hmm. Would you like me to collect your mother from the airport?' she offered.

'No. Wendy, the woman she went away with, is organizing a lift. I think her husband's collecting them.'

'I see. Are you coming home now that you've made all the arrangements?'

'No, I'm going to have a bite to eat with Della and Eddie and our cousin Billy and his wife Gwen. You've met them. I'll give you a call when I'm leaving. Will you get a wreath?'

'OK,' Shauna agreed. 'Talk to you later.' She finished the call

411

and reached for the teapot. 'I'm telling you, Carrie, they're awful,' she reiterated as she poured herself another cup of tea. 'Greg's just told me not to bother coming to the funeral parlour. Just to meet the funeral in Glasnevin. There's no religious ceremony, only a cremation. The mother wants it over fast. She's coming directly from the airport. She's a cold fish. No wonder Della's the way she is.'

And Greg, Carrie thought privately. 'So what are you going to do? Just going to the crematorium would be handy, wouldn't it?'

'I know.' Shauna made a face. 'But I wouldn't like to give Della an opportunity to say that I didn't give their grandmother and Chloe's great-grandmother the respect she deserves or that I'm not a supportive wife.'

'I thought you didn't give them a thought,' Carrie said dryly.

'I don't, but you know what I mean,' Shauna said exasperatedly.

'Hmmm. True. I'll come with you. I'll ask Sadie to collect the kids from school. Do you want me to ask her to mind Chloe or do you want to bring her with you?'

'She didn't know the woman. I'll ask Greg what he thinks. I suppose it's up to him. I'd prefer to leave her here, if that was OK. If Sadie can't do it, I'll ask Dad.'

'Fine, just let me know.' Carrie waved at Hannah, who was sliding down the slide.

'I'll bring the two of them for a jaunt into Drogheda, if you like. I'd better organize a wreath.'

'OK, just take Hannah's fleece with you. There's a nip in the breeze today. It will be cold in the shade.' Carrie went into the back room and found the little jacket.

'Do you need anything?' Shauna applied some lipstick and a dust of bronzer.

'Not a thing, thanks. I'll stick your dinner in the pot. I'm making a chicken and pasta dish.'

'Sounds good. Thanks, Carrie. See you later.' Shauna headed out into the breezy September day, trying to decide whether or not to go to the funeral parlour and have to endure an added encounter with her detested in-laws.

'Go on, have a drop, it's the best of stuff,' Billy Allen urged his cousin, proffering a bottle of poitin. 'I've been saving it for a special occasion.'

'I can't drink that, I've to drive back to Dublin,' Greg exclaimed.

'What are you going home for, to have to drive back down again in the morning? Can't you stay the night? Come on, we should give Edith a decent send-off,' Bill urged, pouring a generous amount of the explosive drink into two glasses. He took a slug and grimaced as he swallowed. 'Cripes, that's strong. Phew!'

'I haven't tasted poitin in years.' Greg grinned as his cousin's eyes watered.

'Try this, go on. It'll blow your head off.' He thrust a glass at Greg.

Greg sniffed it and eyed it warily. He wouldn't mind getting tanked. He hadn't been on the razz in ages and perhaps Billy was right. What was the point in driving back to Dublin to have to drive back in the morning? Recklessly, he took a gulp. The alcohol burned the back of his throat and made him choke. 'You're right, that *is* strong,' he gasped.

'I'll have a drop of that.' Eddie walked into the room.

'You will if you're offered,' Billy retorted. 'What did you bring to the party?'

'I didn't know you were going drinking,' Eddie muttered.

'As good an excuse as any, I suppose, and you're good at excuses,' Billy said, but he handed the other man a glass and poured a measure of the precious liquid into it.

An hour later the three men were feeling no pain. Greg hadn't laughed so much in a long time. He was totally relaxed and very pissed.

'Come on, Eddie, I want to get home. I didn't think I was going to have to drive.' Della marched into the room with a face like thunder.

'Ah don't be giving out,' her husband muttered.

'Well, you'd be giving out if you were seven months pregnant and had sciatica,' Della snapped.

'I'm telling ya, boys, I'm having the snip. I'm not going through this again,' Eddie grumbled, hauling himself to his feet.

'You wouldn't have the snip. You'd be afraid for your life,' Della jeered. 'You faint at the sight of a needle.'

'Nothing to it, mate. I had it. It's a doddle,' Greg slurred. 'It's sore for a while afterwards but it's worth it.'

Della shot him a look, surprised. 'You had the snip! Shauna never said.'

'It's no big deal,' Greg mumbled. 'You two should make up at Gran's funeral.'

'Yeah.' Eddie giggled. 'I wish they would. The only place I ever got a decent feed was in your house. All I get at home is fuckin' rabbit food.'

'Shut up, Eddie, and get out to the car,' Della exploded, furious at her husband's disloyalty.

'G'bye, lads. Aren't you the lucky ones? I'll be gettin' an earbashing all the way home. See yiz tomorrow.' He stumbled out the door after his wife, throwing his eyes up to heaven.

'Have another drink there, Greg,' Billy encouraged.

'I don't mind if I do.' Greg held out his glass with a very unsteady hand.

'Did you mean it about the snip being a doddle?'

'Yeah, but it was bloody sore afterwards, I thought I'd ruined myself for life. I was running scared for a couple of weeks. Are you thinking of having it?'

'I think I'd have to be a lot drunker than this if I was going to do it.' Billy guffawed, and raised his glass.

Della drove towards Cavan seething with anger. Eddie was such a bastard, making a show of her in front of Greg and Billy. How dare he say he was only fed rabbit food? He was fed the best of organic wholesome fare. Greg would probably blab it to Shauna. Della's lip curled at the thought of her sister-in-law. They'd be seeing each other tomorrow and she was not looking forward to it. Shauna would probably be dressed up to the nines and be as slim and slender as ever, while she'd be looking like a beached whale in black trousers and a maternity top that looked like a tent.

She'd probably forced Greg to have the snip so that her fabulous figure would never again be endangered by pregnancy. How vain could you get? Della thought furiously as Eddie snored loudly beside her. What bad timing for Gran to die, when she was looking like a great fat dumpling. If she had hung on for another week the Cassidys would have been back in the Gulf and would not have flown back for the funeral.

There was no point in wearing a corset, she mused. She was too far gone. Her hair had become dreadfully greasy, too, over the past month. Maybe she'd wear a hat, she decided, as she rattled over a pothole and groaned as her sciatic nerve throbbed in protest. She wouldn't let on that she was feeling less than good about herself, Della decided. She'd apply some fake tan and wear

415

her highest heels and put on the performance of a lifetime. She wondered if that other bitch, Carrie, would be coming. Her heart sank. The thought of seeing those two snooty cows was enough to give her a dose of serious heartburn.

Eddie gave a belch and alcohol fumes wafted across the seat. He could sleep in the boxroom from now on; she'd had more than enough of him. It would be a *pleasure* to have the marital bed all to herself.

'Shauna, it's Gwen, Billy's wife. If you were expecting Greg home, he won't be coming. Himself and Billy are asleep on the couch. They imbibed a drop too much alcohol. Poitin, to be exact. I wouldn't like to be them in the morning.'

'Oh . . . oh. Right! Thanks for ringing me. I was going to give him a call to see what was happening.'

'Nothing much,' laughed Gwen. 'I think they've shot their bolt. When he sobers up I'll tell him I called you.'

'Thanks, Gwen. I'll see you tomorrow.' Shauna smiled. She'd only met the other woman a couple of times but she'd liked her.

She didn't mind that Greg was pissed. She liked the idea of him staying over with his cousin. He rarely saw his extended family. It was good for him to make a connection with them. It also meant that she could drive to Enfield with Carrie and have a laugh. It wasn't a funeral where she'd feel great grief, as she'd hardly known the deceased woman, and she might as well make the most of her time with Carrie, and she wouldn't have to face Della on her own.

'Oh Lord! Enfield's the last place I want to go to tomorrow but I can't let Shauna go on her own.' Carrie yawned and snuggled in against Dan.

'You might knock a laugh out of it. Surely Della will have

something outrageous to say or do. You can tell me all about it tomorrow night.' Dan smiled down at her. 'At least it's not a funeral that you're involved in, if you know what I mean.'

'I know. Dad felt he should come but I persuaded him not to. He doesn't know about the bust-up with Della and Shauna doesn't want him to know. I wouldn't put it past Della to insult him. I'd say Shauna and I will be lucky to escape without a barb or two.'

'Look on it as a girls' day out,' he teased, and she thumped him with her pillow. He grabbed her and kissed her and Carrie forgot her tiredness and kissed him back with passion. She was so lucky to have a husband like Dan, she thought gratefully, knowing she'd never cope with a husband like Greg. She felt sorry for Shauna having to go back to the Gulf when she didn't want to.

Dan ran his fingers along the curve of her waist and down over her hips and she forgot about Shauna and her troubles and turned her thoughts to pleasuring her husband. Sliding her hand gently down the flat, taut plane of his stomach, she smiled with satisfaction as she heard him groan with pleasure and murmur her name as her hand explored further. They could still turn each other on. Not bad for a pair of old marrieds, she thought happily as he drew her closer and kissed her hungrily.

The traffic on the M50 was bumper to bumper from the Blanchardstown slip road and Shauna cursed as they slowed to a five-mile-an-hour crawl. 'This is ridiculous. We'll be all hours getting to Enfield. So much for the plan to have brekkie in Mother Hubbard's,' she moaned.

'Stay calm. We'll be fine once we get through the toll bridge,' Carrie assured her. 'We've loads of time. Were you talking to Greg?'

'Is he one sorry boyo. He's in bits.' Shauna grinned. 'He said he's never had a hangover like it.'

'Poitin's not for the faint hearted.' Carrie laughed as she sorted out her coins for the West Link.

'I wouldn't like to be going to a funeral with a hangover. He'll probably look like the wreck of the *Hesperus*.'

'Well you look fantastic, if that's any comfort,' Carrie assured her, glancing at her sister, who was dressed in a superbly cut black trouser suit and a cerise camisole which showed off her tan to perfection. The neat clutch bag she carried was an exact match to the camisole. She wore a small gold cross at her throat and a single gold bangle on her wrist. She looked the height of elegance. Carrie wore a long, straight black skirt and a cream boxy jacket. She knew she looked smart but she could never aspire to her sister's effortless elegance.

Her prediction proved right and once they'd gone through the toll bridge and taken the first exit off to join the N4 they speeded up. They were sitting tucking into a tasty breakfast in the well-known restaurant in just over an hour.

Della gazed at her reflection in dismay. Her fake tan had streaked and looked rather on the orange side.

'Bloody hell!' she muttered as she turned this way and that, examining her reflection. She felt like bursting into tears. Shauna was always effortlessly chic, and she'd badly wanted to present an appearance of glowing radiance. She was glowing all right but in completely the wrong shade. She saw her hands and gave a squawk of dismay. The sides of her fingers and wrists were white and the rest was orange. Why oh why had she done it? Why hadn't she gone to a salon and had her tanning done professionally, instead of relying on her amateurish ham-fisted efforts? She'd made a complete hames of it.

She rooted in a drawer and found a pair of black leather gloves. She'd wear them to disguise her disastrous efforts at fake tanning.

'You'd want to get a move on,' Eddie roared up the stairs. He'd brought the children to school and crèche and was nursing the mother and father of a headache. Della had no sympathy for him whatsoever.

She studied her hair critically. It was limp and lacklustre. She'd have to wear the hat she'd borrowed from a friend. It was black with a large brim that would hide her face, so she could pretend to play the grieving granddaughter.

A thought struck her. Had Gran left a will, and if so, what was in it? Would she have any money left in her savings, having paid a fortune to the nursing home where she'd spent her last year? She'd sold a big house. Surely there had to be some money left over from the sale. Della would very likely be a beneficiary. There was only Greg and their mother to divide the estate between. Perhaps because Greg was so wealthy their grandmother might have bequeathed his portion to her, Della fantasized as she fastened a string of pearls round her neck. Pearls were so elegant, so *Sex and the City*. She'd bought them cheap in a Spanish market, but no-one would know the difference.

Feeling marginally better, she adjusted the brim of her hat and waddled down the stairs.

'You never told me that Della was pregnant,' Shauna whispered crossly to Greg, as they stood behind the coffin in the funeral parlour, waiting for the undertakers to carry it to the hearse.

'What difference does it make?' Greg muttered uncomfortably.

Shauna wanted to shout, 'Because it's not fair! She'll have

419

three children and I only have one.' She swallowed down her bitterness and couldn't give him an answer.

'Crikey, look at the colour of her. She could give a Jaffa orange a run for its money,' Carrie whispered, catching sight of Della's startling tan under the brim of her hat.

Shauna giggled despite herself, suddenly very glad that Carrie was by her side. She was sorry now that she'd made the effort to drive all the way to Enfield, especially when she'd seen Della like a ship in full sail, heavily pregnant and playing the grieving granddaughter to the hilt. The other woman had hardly acknowledged her and that suited Shauna just fine.

Greg was ashen-faced, squinting painfully against the glare when they emerged into the sunlight. He and Billy were truly the worse for wear after their night on the tiles and Shauna was glad she'd insisted on taking her car instead of Carrie's. At least she wouldn't have to drive back to Dublin with a surly, grumpy, hungover husband.

Ten minutes later they were on the road again. 'Thank God we had breakfast,' Shauna remarked as she slid into the funeral cortege. 'They never even offered us a cup of tea. They haven't a clue.'

'Are they having a meal after the cremation?' Carrie yawned. She and Dan had made love twice last night and talked until all hours, and after her early start she was ready to fall asleep.

'Don't you dare go asleep on me,' Shauna warned. 'Greg does that all the time when I'm driving and I hate it.'

'Yes, boss!' Carrie said dryly.

'I think there's something laid on in a local pub. I'll be surprised if it's a full meal,' Shauna said as they slowed down to let an ambulance pass by.

'Very warm welcome from Della. She was shooting daggers at

us from under the Hat. It looks more like a flying saucer,' Carrie observed with a grin.

'You're awful.' Shauna laughed. 'God, Carrie, I never hated her as much as I did when I saw that she was pregnant,' she confessed. 'It's so unfair. I'm horrible, aren't I?' She glanced ruefully at her sister.

'No you're not,' Carrie assured her. 'It's a bit like when someone you really don't like loses loads of weight and it really gets to you . . . only worse.'

'*Exactly*.' Shauna nodded. 'At least she looks like a blimp!'

'A big *orange* blimp,' Carrie emphasized and the pair of them guffawed.

Greg drove over a pothole and cursed long and loudly as his head took off like a rocket. Little red devils danced behind his eyelids and he felt decidedly queasy. What on earth had possessed him to drink poitin? He wished this damn funeral was over and he could get out to the Gulf and back to work.

What bloody bad luck that his grandmother's timing was lousy, he thought sourly. He'd been riddled with guilt when Shauna had laid eyes on Della and seen that she was heavily pregnant. He could well imagine how his wife was feeling. Every time she got her period there were tears. It was doing his head in. Why the hell hadn't he confessed to her in Paris that he'd had the vasectomy? They'd have got over it and moved on. But he could never tell her now. She'd never forgive him for the misery she'd endured this past year.

Greg glanced in his rear-view mirror and saw that Carrie and Shauna were laughing. That was a relief. He was glad that she was driving with her sister. It took the pressure off him.

*   *   *

'You look very nice, Shauna,' Joanna Cassidy murmured as she air-kissed her daughter-in-law outside the crematorium. 'Thank you for staying for the funeral. I know that Greg's anxious to get back to the Gulf. Mother mucked us all up. I was having a great time in Rome.'

'That's unfortunate,' Shauna murmured, amazed at her mother-in-law's lack of emotion as she stood watching her mother's coffin being lifted from the hearse. Joanna Cassidy really *was* a cool customer. No wonder Della and Greg were so self-obsessed. Joanna had no time for her children just as she'd no time for her mother. The only person Joanna was interested in was herself. She was a slender twig of a woman with chestnut hair liberally streaked with grey, which she wore in a plait. She favoured floaty chiffons and today was dressed in a long, flowing, mint green dress with a white crochet cardigan and cloche cap. She didn't believe in wearing black to funerals. It wasn't her colour.

Shauna watched her flitting here and there, between the mourners, and thought of her own warm-hearted, cuddly mother who had enveloped her children in an endless flow of love and tenderness. She felt a sudden pang for Greg. He'd never known a mother's love as she had. She tucked her arm in his and smiled at him. He managed a small smile back and squeezed her hand. It was obvious he was still under the weather. The sooner they got home the sooner he could go for a sleep and recover, she thought kindly.

'Sorry for your trouble,' she heard a familiar, deep voice say and looked up to see Dan, hand outstretched, in front of them.

'Thanks, Dan,' Greg mumbled, shaking hands.

'You're very good for coming, Dan,' Shauna said warmly. 'We weren't expecting you.'

'No problem.' Dan smiled at her as he dropped an arm round

Carrie's shoulder and followed the rest of the mourners into the crematorium.

'There's something comforting about a church funeral. The crematorium's a bit clinical, isn't it?' Gwen remarked an hour later as they sat in a local pub, eating limp ham sandwiches and drinking watery, lumpy tomato soup.

'I suppose it depends on what you like personally. Carrie's going to fling me onto the compost heap in Five Acre Field and say a few prayers over me,' Dan teased.

'You'll be lucky to get the prayers,' Carrie retorted fondly.

'How's the head?' Gwen asked Greg, who was sipping a spritzer.

'Improving,' he said dryly.

'That will teach the pair of you,' she chuckled, winking at her husband.

'It was good while it lasted,' Billy informed her. 'Wasn't it, Greg?'

'I mightn't go that far,' the other man grimaced and they all laughed.

Della glanced over to the corner where Shauna and her gang were sitting laughing. The cheek of them, she thought furiously. Laughing at her grandmother's funeral. Had they no sense of decorum?

She'd felt the old familiar envy, bitterness and intense dislike when she'd seen Shauna looking like a Paris model at the funeral parlour. Even Carrie looked smart. How she'd cursed her bulk, which couldn't have been disguised no matter what she'd worn. The gloves were making her hands sweat and the hat was giving her a headache but they were staying firmly in place, even in the dark pub.

'Everything seems to be going fine, doesn't it?' her mother

murmured, nibbling a ham sandwich that was curling at the edges.

'Yeah,' Della said heavily. Her feet were killing her in her high heels and her sciatic nerve was giving her hell. She wished it was all over and she was at home. She felt very down in the dumps.

'Shauna looks very well as usual,' Joanna remarked, looking over to where her son and daughter-in-law sat.

'Why wouldn't she, with all her money?' Della snapped.

'Don't be like that, Della. Money isn't everything,' her mother reproached her. 'She probably looks at you with envy.'

'Me!' Della snorted. 'Don't be *ridiculous.*'

'I'm not being ridiculous,' her mother said hotly, annoyed at her daughter's derisive tone. 'There you are, seven months gone with your third child and she's been trying for over a year to get pregnant, so she told me during the summer, when they called to visit.'

'What!' Della's nose wrinkled in disbelief. 'I'm afraid you're barking up the wrong tree there, Mum. Greg's had the snip. He said so last night.'

'Impossible,' Joanna retorted. 'I caught Shauna crying in the garden because her period had arrived. That's when she told me they were trying for another baby. Maybe he had it reversed or something.'

Della's brow furrowed in a frown.

'Oh look, there's Frannie Williams, Mother's last home help. How nice of her to come. She even used to visit her in the nursing home. I should go and say hello.' Joanna stood up and drifted off in a cloud of floating layers, leaving Della staring after her.

Greg had *definitely* said that he'd had the snip and that it was a doddle. She'd heard him with her own two ears. Now her mother was telling her that she'd caught Shauna bawling because her

424

period had arrived. How could that be? She looked over at her brother, deep in conversation with Billy. Greg made no secret of his dislike of kids. She vaguely remembered him once saying that one was more than enough. Her eyes widened. He hadn't had the snip without telling Shauna, surely? Or had he?

It was *exactly* the kind of thing her darling brother would do, she thought with a sudden sure knowledge. Excitement raced through her. She'd always sworn that she'd get even with those bitches. Maybe the moment was at hand. What was the old saying about revenge being a dish best served cold? This dish was so cold it was icy, she thought malevolently as she stood up from the table and moved with heavy, determined steps and a bright gleam of anticipation in her beady little eyes to where Shauna and Carrie were sitting.

36

'THANK YOU ALL SO MUCH FOR COMING TO GRAN'S FUNERAL. WE appreciate it, don't we, Greg?' Della cooed sweetly to the group sitting round the table.

'You're welcome,' Carrie murmured. Shauna remained silent. She was family. She didn't need her sister-in-law thanking her for coming to Greg's grandmother's funeral.

'I hope we didn't put you out, having to stay the few days extra.' Della turned to Shauna as though nothing untoward had ever happened between them. Shauna was gobsmacked. She wasn't expecting this friendly display at all.

'It's fine,' she said politely. 'Chloe's delighted to be off school for a few more days.'

'I decided to leave Kathryn in school today. I don't think funerals are any place for children. Unfortunately I had to bring this one,' she chuckled, patting her bump.

'When's the baby due?' Carrie asked, feeling she had to make some effort.

'Late November, just in time for Christmas.' Della's heart was thumping. This was her chance. She took a deep breath and turned to Greg. 'And after that, I think I'll be trying to persuade Eddie to get the snip, like you did. How did you persuade him to have a vasectomy, Shauna? Give me a few tips.' She smirked at her sister-in-law.

'*Sorry?*' Shauna looked flummoxed.

'The snip. How did you persuade Gr—'

'Shut up, Della, and don't be talking nonsense!' Greg snapped, his eyes registering dismay at her words.

'What do you mean, don't be talking nonsense? *You* were telling us about it yesterday.' Della pretended puzzlement.

'I vaguely remember you saying something about running scared – or was it *scarred* – for a few weeks afterwards. I'm surprised you were able to run at all,' Billy chortled, highly amused at his little joke.

Shauna looked stricken, but no-one except Della was looking at her. They were all looking at Greg, who had gone a dull red from his neck to his hairline.

Bingo! Good enough for you, Della thought triumphantly as she saw her sister-in-law swallow hard and turn pale under her tan. An uneasy silence descended on the group as they looked at each other, wondering if this was a joke.

'I should circulate,' Della said airily. 'Nice talking to you all.' She directed a malevolent gaze at Shauna. 'Safe journey back to the Emirates.' She moved away, absolutely satisfied that she had dropped a bombshell from which Shauna might never recover.

Shauna felt as though she was hearing Della's voice from a long distance. She couldn't take her eyes off Greg. He wouldn't look at her. Fear engulfed her. Her stomach twisted in knots. Della was right. Greg had had a vasectomy and she'd found out about it and had deliberately come over to them and manipulated the conversation so that she could reveal his secret. She *knew* that Shauna didn't know. She *knew* that this would destroy Shauna's marriage. Della had got her own back in the vilest way possible.

427

She took a deep breath. 'It's true, Greg, isn't it? You had a vasectomy,' she said quietly. Billy and Gwen looked horrified. Dan was stony-faced. Carrie was stunned. Shauna didn't even notice them. All she could see was Greg and how he wouldn't meet her gaze.

'We'll talk about it later,' he muttered.

'When?' she demanded. 'When did you have it?'

'Last year when you came home,' he growled.

'You *bastard*, Greg.' Carrie couldn't contain herself. 'How *could* you? Have you any idea what you've put Shauna through?'

Shauna stood up. 'Carrie, let's go home,' she said shakily. She walked out of the pub, trembling, followed by her sister.

Della watched her go, well pleased. If Greg tackled her about it she'd plead innocence. How was she to know that he'd gone behind Shauna's back and had the operation? He wouldn't be able to argue with that. Win win! she thought viciously, feeling not the slightest twinge of regret or guilt for the anguish she had caused.

'That was low, Greg,' Dan said grimly as he stood up to leave.

'Mind your own business,' Greg retorted angrily.

'Shauna *is* my business and I should knock your block off,' Dan said tersely. He strode out of the pub leaving Greg sitting with Billy and Gwen.

'I think it's time we left too,' Gwen said icily.

'Sorry, mate,' Billy muttered uncomfortably, knowing his big mouth had got Greg deeper in trouble. He had a sneaking sympathy for him. He got up and followed his wife.

Greg gulped his drink, sitting alone at the table. It seemed he was a pariah. Even if it meant the end of his marriage, it was a massive relief to have his secret out in the open. It had been a heavy burden to carry all these months. He cringed as he remembered the way Shauna had looked at him, wounded to her core.

His head throbbed. He stood up and went over to where his mother was talking to one of his aunts. 'I'm heading off. I'll talk to you soon,' he said briskly, pretending nothing was amiss.

'Fine, dear.' Joanna proffered a cool cheek. He kissed her and turned to search for Della. She was sitting with Eddie, watching him like the cat that got the cream.

He walked over to her and put his face close against hers. 'Everything Shauna said about you was right, Della. You're a horrible person,' he said flatly.

Della flushed, taken aback at his words. 'It takes one to know one,' she retorted, stung.

'I can't argue with that. Good luck with the baby. It's got a cold bitch for a mother.' He didn't wait for her response but hurried out of the pub, anxious to put as much distance as possible between them.

Shauna, Carrie and Dan were gone. He was on his own.

Shauna felt completely numb and very cold. She'd been reading a book of short stories called *Moments*, whose theme was how life could change in the blink of an eye. In a 'moment', literally. Well, her life had just changed in a moment. All she had built her marriage on was gone in an instant. Her security, her life plan, such as it was, vanished. Her foundations were rubble under her feet.

It was over between her and Greg. She could never be with him again. He had no love for her. If you loved someone you'd never wound them so deeply that they felt destroyed. Tears welled in her eyes and dropped silently down her cheeks. A muffled sob escaped her.

'Oh, Shauna, don't!' Carrie exclaimed helplessly from the driver's seat, as she heard her sister cry. She'd insisted on driving them home.

'How could he do it to me, Carrie? Has he no feelings for me? Has he no respect for me? How could he let me go through abject misery, month after month, knowing that he was the cause of it? How could he be so devious? How could he make love to me knowing that he'd betrayed me in the cruellest possible way?' The questions poured out of her as she sought answers that might take the crucifying pain away.

'I don't know,' Carrie said miserably. 'Look, you said it yourself, Shauna, they're a weird family. They only ever consider themselves, because that's the way that they've been brought up. So even though he's done this terrible thing to you, sometimes I think he acts the way he does because he knows no better,' she added lamely.

'That's not good enough. Anyone with any morals would know that what he did was an appalling breach of trust. He robbed me of my chance to have another baby, and you know the worst thing? I let him. I stayed on the Pill for at least three years even though I didn't want to.' She was crying and talking at the same time, her face a mess of streaked make-up and mascara.

'All my life I've let men bully me. First Dad, then Greg. Never again, Carrie. Never again! I'll never give my power away to a man again,' she vowed bitterly.

'What are you going to do?' Carrie asked hesitantly as she drove back onto the M50 and headed north.

'One thing's for sure, I'm not going back to Abu Dhabi,' Shauna said grimly, taking a tissue out of her bag. 'I'm staying at home and I'm going to make a life for myself on my terms.'

'You'll have to get Chloe into a school,' Carrie pointed out.

'I know. But I think we're better off here. I couldn't bear to live with Greg, not even for Chloe's sake.' She started to cry again.

'Look, give yourself a week or two. You don't have to make a decision immediately,' Carrie advised.

Shauna's phone rang. She took it out of her bag and saw that it was Greg. 'Go to hell,' she muttered and let it ring out.

They drove on in silence. Carrie turned off the busy motor-way onto the relative calm of the M1. Shauna gazed at tilting fields full of massive golden bales of hay that lined either side of the dual carriageway. Cattle grazed contentedly in a field of emerald green. A tractor and a combine harvester worked together, harvesting a field of rippling corn in perfect precision, moving slowly in great wide arcs to gather the precious grain. Smoke curled from the chimney of a small cottage, drifting into a copse of russet-tipped trees that swayed idly in the autumn breeze. The calm, indolent rhythm of the September afternoon was a complete contrast to her own turmoil.

'Della took great pleasure in letting me know about it, didn't she?' Shauna said a little later as they turned onto the slip road that led to Whiteshells Bay.

'She's a vindictive cow,' Carrie declared vehemently.

'I think she's sad,' Shauna said reflectively. 'If that's what it takes to make her happy and feel superior, who'd want to be her?'

'Well, you know what they say, what goes around comes around, and what we put into the lives of others comes back into our own. She'll never have any luck for what she's done today, and neither will Greg.'

'Is that supposed to make me feel better?' Shauna managed a small smile.

'Yeah, but it's true. "Do unto others . . ." and all of that, as Dad used to say when we were naughty.'

Shauna groaned. 'Oh Lord, what's *he* going to say when I tell him that I've left Greg? I'll never hear the end of it.'

'Let that be the least of your worries,' Carrie counselled. 'The important thing is to do what's right for you and Chloe.'

'What am I going to tell *her*?' Shauna burst into fresh tears.

'I don't know how to advise you, Shauna. Sleep on it tonight. You'll have to talk to Greg at some stage. See what comes out of that,' her sister suggested. 'Do you think that you could get beyond it?' she probed delicately.

'Could you?' Shauna retorted.

'No,' Carrie said quietly. 'I'd die if Dan did that to me.'

'Dan would never do anything like that. Dan's a real man in every sense of the word. Morally and physically. He *knows* how to treat people. You've a great marriage, Carrie,' she said wistfully.

'I know,' her sister agreed.

'I don't respect Greg now. And I hate him for what he's done to us. To our family, to the family we could have had, and could have been.' She cried bitter tears and Carrie let her alone, knowing that there were a lot more tears to come in the weeks ahead.

'You'll stay with us tonight, won't you?' she said as they drove into her driveway.

'I don't know. Maybe I should go home and get it over and done with.'

'Not tonight. Stay tonight,' Carrie urged. 'And Shauna, when you go to meet Greg, leave Chloe here. She doesn't need to hear you fighting.'

'OK,' her sister agreed wearily.

Dan, who had got home just before them, had the kettle boiling when they went into the kitchen. 'If there's anything you need or there's anything you want me to do, you only have to ask,' he said sympathetically, drawing Shauna to him in a bear hug.

'Thanks, Dan,' she murmured against his chest, thinking how solid and strong and dependable he was.

'Sit down and have a cup of tea here with Carrie. I'll go over to Sadie's to collect the kids.'

'OK.' She sank tiredly onto the comfy, fat-cushioned sofa and felt a little of the tension seep out of her.

They had just finished their tea, and Dan had left to collect the children, when Noel arrived. 'Are you all right? You look shook. Was it a very sad funeral?' he asked as he noticed his younger daughter's ravaged face.

'You could say that, Dad,' Shauna murmured.

'But she was a good age. I'm sure it was a happy release. Wasn't she ailing for a while?' Noel sat beside her and patted her arm.

'Oh, Dad, it wasn't that. I found out something terrible today. Greg did an awful thing to me,' she blurted, starting to cry.

Noel looked at Carrie in horror; he found tears hard to cope with. 'What did he do?' he asked hesitantly.

'He . . . he . . .' Shauna swallowed and buried her head in her hands, distraught.

'What? What happened, Carrie?' Noel demanded anxiously.

'Greg had a vasectomy and never told Shauna,' Carrie explained, handing her sister a wad of tissues.

'May God forgive him!' Noel exclaimed, aghast. 'That's a terrible thing to do. Wait until I see him, he'll get a good talking to from me. To treat my daughter like that . . . I . . . I don't know what to say.' He put his arm round her and tried in vain to comfort her, but Shauna cried with abandon, as years of pent-up sorrow and grief poured out of the depths of her until she could cry no more. Noel and Carrie watched helplessly.

'Sorry,' she murmured eventually.

'Why don't you go and lie down for a while?' Carrie suggested gently.

'Yeah, I think I will. I've got an awful headache,' Shauna said shakily as she struggled to her feet.

'I'll light a candle for you,' Noel said awkwardly.

'Thanks, Dad.' She managed a wobbly smile and gave him a quick hug.

'Go into the spare room. It's nice and quiet at the back of the house, and the sheets are fresh on the bed,' Carrie told her.

'Right,' Shauna said tiredly. 'I'll be down in a while.'

'Stay there as long as you like. I'll bring you up your dinner, if you want.'

'I don't think I could eat any, Carrie. There's a lump like a golf ball in my throat.'

'That's understandable. See how you feel later,' Carrie said firmly. 'Now go on before the kids get home.'

'Bossyboots,' her sister said affectionately, but her lip wobbled as she left the room and Carrie could hear her crying again.

'This is a terrible state of affairs.' Noel shook his head worriedly as he paced up and down. 'I'll have to speak to Greg. They'll have to go and have counselling.'

'Dad, stay out of it. They have to work it out for themselves. It's not our place to interfere,' Carrie said as she put the mugs into the dishwasher.

'I know, but there are services for marriages in distress,' Noel pointed out earnestly.

'Dad, Shauna has every right to leave Greg after what he's done to her, and don't you make her feel bad about it if she does,' she warned.

'Now Carrie, what God has joined together let no man put asunder,' Noel said sternly.

'Dad, stop it. Greg had a vasectomy behind Shauna's back and let her think they were trying for a baby. How could she live with him after that? If there's no love and respect there's no true marriage.'

'But—'

'But *nothing*, Dad. Don't you dare go adding to Shauna's burdens with all that religious stuff,' Carrie said crossly.

'Now, miss, I don't like your tone,' Noel said with some of his old authority. 'The Church says—'

'Tough, if you don't like my tone, Dad. I'm not interested in what the Church says. You gave Bobby a hard enough time; I won't let you do it to Shauna. It's not up to you to judge. You haven't walked in her shoes. You don't know what it's like.' Carrie's tone brooked no argument. 'Greg's deprived her of the chance to have a baby, he's lied to her, and treated her abominably. Why would anyone want her to stay in a marriage like that with a man like that? That's not marriage, that's abuse,' she exploded, wishing she could get her hands on Greg Cassidy.

'Hmmm, you have a point.' Noel backed down, unused to Carrie lecturing him so vehemently. 'She has grounds for annulment there, I think. After all, because of what he's had done, he's a eunuch,' he pronounced solemnly. Carrie, who had her back to him, spluttered and managed to turn it into a cough. She had a hysterical desire to laugh, but Noel would not be amused. He took his theological matters very seriously. As far as he was concerned, Greg was now officially a eunuch in the eyes of the Church. Trust her father to come up with a gem like that.

'Go and light a candle for her. I'll have the dinner ready in another hour,' she suggested, thinking that it was all very surreal. If only she could wake up and find it was just a bad dream.

Shauna lay curled up in a ball in the comfortable double bed in Carrie's guest room. She felt sick and cold. Her stomach was tied up in knots. She'd never felt so alone in her life. Why had Greg done this to her? Did she mean so little to him? Was she, or her needs, of no consequence? Did he not see her as equal in their marriage? Obviously not, she thought forlornly as she switched on the electric blanket.

But then, had she ever been his equal? she wondered. It had

always been about him and what he wanted. She'd never *really* asserted herself. The thoughts raced around in her head. It was her own fault. Knowing that made it all the worse. She buried her aching head under her pillow.

She was going to have to meet Greg and confront him about what he'd done. She couldn't run away from this one. This time she was going to have to make the decisions as to what she wanted to do with her life. The thought frightened her to her core. Did she have the strength to stand on her own two feet? She'd never done it before and right now the thought of it enveloped her in dread.

Greg poured himself a stiff whiskey and lay down on the couch. He'd phoned Shauna twice. The first time the phone had rung out. The second time it had been switched off. He wanted to book flights back to Abu Dhabi. Would he be booking for three or one? What would she decide?

He wished he could fly out tonight and get back to work and bury himself in it. Work was his solace. It made him feel good about himself. It was the *only* thing that made him feel good about himself, he thought glumly. Ever since Shauna had got the bee in her bonnet about having kids, he'd come second in her life. How was that supposed to make a man feel? It was *all* her fault that they were in this mess, anyway. And he was going to tell her so if she started giving him a hard time. Angry and embittered, he went into their bedroom and began to pack the remainder of his gear. He'd left a message on his wife's phone telling her to get in touch. He'd give her until midday tomorrow. If not, he was going to book a ticket for himself and she could do what she bloody well liked. She always did, anyway.

37

'ARE YOU SURE YOU DON'T MIND IF CHLOE STAYS HERE?' SHAUNA said to Carrie as she carefully made up her face in preparation for her encounter with Greg.

'Of course not. She's better off here,' Carrie assured her.

'Imagine being nervous going to meet your own husband,' Shauna said wryly. 'My stomach is in a heap.'

'That's natural. There's a lot at stake,' Carrie said quietly.

'I know. I was awake all night trying to decide what to do,' Shauna confessed.

'Look, I'll go down to the school tomorrow and see if they could take Chloe for a couple of weeks. That would give you time to think. And give you and Greg some space,' Carrie offered.

'That's a good idea. Thanks, Carrie. I might take you up on that,' Shauna said gratefully. 'It would give me a bit of leeway.' She kissed her sister. 'I'll see you later. Wish me luck.'

'Just don't let him persuade you to do anything you don't want to do or feel uncomfortable with,' Carrie advised.

'You know Greg. He's good at getting his own way.'

'Shauna, this isn't about Greg or what he wants. It's about you and don't forget that,' Carrie said firmly.

'I won't. But thanks for the advice.' Shauna picked up her bag and car keys and walked slowly downstairs. She was sick to her stomach and had only managed to eat a slice of toast for her breakfast. Butterflies as big as bats fluttered inside her. She felt more lonely, apprehensive and unsure than she ever had in her entire life. But she couldn't fall apart. She needed to be strong for herself and Chloe.

The Friday traffic was heavy. Greg had sent her a terse text telling her to get in touch by midday or he was booking his flight. She'd sent an equally terse text back telling him that she'd see him at two o'clock in Malahide.

By the time she pulled up into her own driveway she had managed to regain some of her poise. Why should *she* be nervous? It was Greg who should be shaking in his boots after what he'd done, she told herself grimly as she inserted her key in the front door.

Greg was in the kitchen eating a mushroom and cheese omelette that he'd cooked for his lunch. The sight of it infuriated her. How dare he be able to eat after what he'd done? Didn't it bother him in the slightest?

'What sort of bollox are you?' she demanded. 'How can you even think of eating? Aren't you sick to your stomach like I am or do you not give a damn?'

'For fuck's sake, Shauna, don't start,' Greg blustered, taken aback by her onslaught.

'What do you mean, don't start? I've every right to start. Why did you do that to me? Have you no feelings for me? Have you no respect for me? Didn't I count for anything? Why did you let me go through torment month after month? How could you watch me in tears when I'd get my period when you knew there was no chance of me conceiving?' She was shouting at him. She wanted to batter him.

'I wanted to tell you,' he muttered. 'I wanted to tell you in Paris but I lost my nerve.'

'How could you do it, Greg? How could you go behind my back like that?' She stared at him, trying to find some hint of regret in his eyes that would give her some crumb of comfort.

'Because you wouldn't *listen* to me,' he roared. 'I told you over and *over* that I didn't want another baby but you kept on and *on* at me. You talk about counting for anything. Well, *I* counted for nothing. *My* wishes counted for nothing. *You* wanted a baby come hell or high water, no matter what I said. How do you think that made *me* feel?'

'I wanted a brother or sister for Chloe,' she shrieked. 'I didn't want her to be an only child. I wanted us to be a proper family like Carrie and Dan's.'

'Aw yeah, throw the bloody Waltons in my face again. I'm fed up to the back teeth hearing how perfect they are. Do you know how hard it is to live with someone you can't satisfy no matter what you do? Do you have any idea how hard I work? And why do I kill myself working? I kill myself working trying to provide a better than average lifestyle for you and Chloe. But do I get any thanks for it? No bloody way. I just get the fucking Waltons thrown up in my face. Sometimes I wonder why the hell you married me.' Greg was puce with anger.

'Stop using work as an excuse,' she raged, incensed. 'That's *your* choice, not Chloe's or mine. She hardly sees you anyway; it won't make much difference to her whether we split or not.'

'Well then, I might as well go back to Abu Dhabi and get on with my life. You two don't need me,' he said sulkily.

'Oh, typical, feel sorry for yourself now. You've no business feeling sorry for yourself. *I'm* the one who should be feeling sorry for herself, you bastard.'

'Is that so?' he sneered. 'You've a big apartment in the Gulf. A big detached house in Dublin. Your *caravan*. More jewellery and clothes than any other woman I know. Your own credit card. Oh yes . . . you've a lot to feel sorry about.'

Her slap reddened his jaw and brought a flash of temper to his eyes. He grabbed her wrist. 'Don't ever do that again or you might get one back,' he said furiously.

She pulled her wrist away. 'You go back to Abu Dhabi. I'm staying here with Chloe for a while until I decide what I want to do.'

'What about school?' he snapped.

'Oh, don't pretend you're concerned about her schooling,' she scoffed. 'That's never worried you before.'

'She's my daughter. I have a right to make decisions concerning her,' Greg retorted.

'If I bring you to court after what you've done to me you'll have no bloody rights at all, mister,' Shauna shot back.

Greg paled. He didn't like the sound of that.

'Oh yes, I could play very dirty, Greg Cassidy. I know you've got your little secret accounts stashed away here and there. You probably even have properties that I don't know about, but Gina Andrews hired a very *thorough* forensic accountant for her divorce and she took Walter to the cleaners. He hadn't a chance by the time that accountant had gone through his cash and assets with a fine-tooth comb. Fortunately Gina and I have kept in touch . . .' She stared him down.

'What do you want to do?' He scowled.

'Carrie's going to see if she can get Chloe into the village school. I think it's best for her. She needs some stability in her life. Filomena's gone, Carly's gone, we're the way we are. At least she'll have her cousins.'

'I want to see her before I go,' he muttered.

'Fine. I'll bring her over. Text me and let me know when

you're leaving.' She turned on her heel and left him staring after her in fury.

She was on a high as she drove out of the cul-de-sac. She'd said her piece and taken control. She'd told him what to do for a change. She smiled grimly, remembering how he had paled at her threat to bring him to court. She'd use that to keep him in check. If he could play dirty having a vasectomy behind her back, she could play dirty too. The knowledge gave her strength. In the next few weeks . . . or months . . . she'd make a decision about her future. And this time it would be on her terms.

Greg sat at the computer checking out flights to the Emirates. He was completely rattled. He wasn't used to Shauna being assertive. It was extremely disconcerting. Her threat to go to court was hugely unnerving. Forensic accountants were seriously lethal and seriously expensive. She had him by the balls. She could possibly sue him for lessening her chances of having a baby, or some such charge, as well. His photograph would be plastered all over the papers. He'd never be able to hold his head up in Ireland again. He'd be a laughing stock among his Irish business colleagues. *And* she really could take him to the cleaners. He'd better tread warily and not antagonize her, he decided morosely, as he keyed in his credit card number and booked the first available flight he could find. The sooner he got out of this bloody country the better.

'How would you like to stay in Ireland for a while and go to Olivia and Davey's school?' Shauna slipped her arm round her daughter's waist and drew her close.

Chloe looked at her, puzzled.

'Well, you know the way Filomena isn't coming back to us any more and Carly's gone to live in America? Wouldn't it be nice to stay here with Carrie and your cousins just to see how it goes, and maybe live in Ireland all the time?' Shauna explained patiently.

'Can we live in the mobile?'

'Well, for a little while, anyway, until I sort things out.' Shauna smiled.

'Wow, Mom, that would be cool. I really like this place. I don't want to go back to Abu Dhabi,' her daughter enthused.

'Dad will have to go back to work,' Shauna said hesitantly.

'Poor Dad,' Chloe said matter-of-factly. 'Will I be getting a new school uniform like Olivia's?'

'Yes.' Shauna nodded, relieved but saddened at her daughter's lack of concern for Greg.

'Great. I *loovve* the red dickie bow. It's cool.' Chloe was thrilled. 'When can I go?'

'Tomorrow. Carrie checked it out for me this morning. Would you like to start tomorrow?'

'You bet, Mom. They play great games in the yard,' Chloe confided.

'Do they?'

'Yeah. They play Queenie I O Who Has The Ball, and everything.'

'That sounds fantastic.' Shauna hugged her. 'Now listen. We've to go to Malahide and say goodbye to Dad and get some clothes and things.'

'OK. Can I bring my music box back? I want to show it to my new teacher.'

'Sure,' Shauna agreed. 'Let's get ready to go.'

We're on our way. Act normally, she texted Greg.

I will if you will, came the curt response.

*   *   *

'Daddy, Daddy, I'm going to Olivia's school and I'm getting a new uniform.' Chloe raced in the front door half an hour later, full of her news.

'Are you?' He swept her up in his arms.

'I'm getting a dickie bow,' she informed him proudly.

'Well you'll just have to get Mom to take some photos and email them to me,' he said, kissing the top of her head and looking at Shauna.

'We'll do that,' Shauna said lightly. 'Won't we, Chloe? And we'll email every week.'

'Better than nothing, I suppose,' Greg said bitterly.

Shauna flashed him a warning look. 'Have you called a taxi?'

'Yes. I'm flying to Heathrow and getting the red-eye from there. What will I tell people when I get home?'

'Darling, run up and get your music box.' Shauna smiled at their daughter. 'Tell them whatever you want, I don't care,' she said tonelessly when Chloe was gone from the room.

'Are you sure this is what you want?' he demanded.

'I don't know what I want. But I know I need time to think and I need time away from you,' Shauna said curtly.

'Fine.' Greg flicked a piece of lint off his expensive grey suit. 'I'll be in touch.'

Shauna said nothing.

'I'm going up to say goodbye to Chloe,' he said brusquely, brushing past her.

'Right.'

She heard him run up the stairs and tried not to feel guilty. Was she being totally selfish? she wondered. Would it not have been better to go back with Greg and get Chloe settled back in school and try to work things out in Abu Dhabi?

You're only staying for a while until you get over the shock and sort things out in your head, she argued with herself as the taxi beeped outside.

'The taxi's here,' she called.

Moments later Greg came down the stairs followed by Chloe, clutching her music box.

''Bye, honeybunch,' he said gruffly. 'Be a good girl for Mom.'

'I will, Dad,' she assured him, looking up at him with her big blue eyes.

'See you,' he said to Shauna.

''Bye,' she murmured, stepping aside to let him out the door.

'Dad, Dad.' Chloe ran after him. 'I forgot. I brought you this. It's a stone with an angel in it. Carrie bought it for me but you can have it to mind you.' She thrust a grey stone with the shape of a small white angel imprinted in it into his hand.

'That's really kind, darling. Thank you.' Greg took it from her and slipped it into his pocket. He couldn't believe how touched he felt by her little act of kindness. 'I love you, Chloe,' he said. 'And Shauna . . . I'm sorry.' He climbed into the taxi and closed the door.

Shauna watched it leave and didn't know whether she was on her head or her heels.

38

SHAUNA WATCHED THE FOR SALE SIGN BEING ERECTED BESIDE HER big wooden electronic gates and felt a huge sense of relief. The past weeks had been a nightmare. She'd been commuting between Whiteshells Bay and Malahide and feeling ever more unsettled as the days went by. The only positive aspect to the whole sorry situation was how well Chloe had settled into her new school. She was making new friends and really coming out of her shell, and the security of having her cousins near was a huge plus for her.

Shauna felt like a nomad. She'd hated going back to the house in Malahide. She knew she was going to have to tell the neighbours about her split with Greg. She'd told them that she was staying in Ireland until after Christmas. She'd used Noel's health as an excuse. They expected her to be her usual, social, bubbly self, and she was finding it hard going keeping up the facade.

She knew she couldn't keep going in the limbo she was in. It wasn't feasible to spend the winter in the mobile home and the thought of driving to and fro up the M1 daunted her. One morning she'd woken up and decided enough was enough. She needed to move nearer to Whiteshells Bay and she wanted to leave her house in Malahide and get away from the claustrophobia she was feeling surrounded by her neighbours in the cul-de-sac. They were always popping in for coffee, or inviting her into their houses, and she just wanted to be on her own.

She'd seen new apartments nearing the end of construction along the coast road at the edge of Whiteshells Bay and had gone to view them when they were launched. Without even asking Greg, she'd impulsively paid a booking deposit for the penthouse. It was even bigger than the apartment in Abu Dhabi and had huge wraparound balconies that gave panoramic views all along the east coast. It had three bedrooms, two with en suite, two reception rooms and a study, and a state-of-the-art kitchen that had Carrie pea green with envy.

'I'll move in with you,' she'd teased as she wandered around the light-filled airy rooms with her sister.

'Do you think I should buy?' Shauna felt strangely exhilarated at the prospect of a fresh start.

'I think it would be a good move for you,' Carrie said slowly. 'If you and Greg do get back together, you still have a home in Ireland. And if you don't, it will be your and Chloe's home for as long as you decide to live here.'

'We're staying here until she's finished primary school at least. She deserves that much stability,' Shauna had said firmly, taking out her chequebook.

'Aren't you going to ring Greg and discuss it with him?' Carrie asked hesitantly.

'Did he ring me to discuss it when he was going for a vasectomy?' Shauna retorted tartly, pen poised.

'Oh . . . OK . . .' Carrie had murmured.

Shauna smiled as she remembered the look on her sister's face. She imagined it was nothing compared to the look on Greg's face when she'd phoned him and told him of her plans.

'Hey, steady on. We need to discuss this,' he'd blustered.

'No we don't,' Shauna had snapped coldly. 'I'm moving nearer to Chloe's school. I'm selling the house in Malahide, which I might remind you is in my name, and you have no say in the matter, just as I had no say in the matter when you went off and had your vasectomy. End of conversation!'

'Do what you want, Shauna,' Greg gritted and hung up.

'Don't you worry, I will,' Shauna retorted as she replaced the receiver.

She had her husband worried. The threat of a forensic accountant had been a masterstroke and she didn't even know where it had come from. For the first time in ages she felt she was starting to control her own life again. It felt good. She watched as the last nail was hammered into the sign and prepared for the knocks on the door.

She'd ordered a selection of canapés and a cold buffet from her caterer, and a dozen bottles of champagne. And then she'd asked her neighbours to come to lunch. It would be her last ladies' lunch in Malahide and that too was a liberation of sorts.

'You're selling up! You never said. How much are you looking for?' Alice shrieked when Shauna opened the door to her twenty minutes later. Sylvia Lyons arrived on her heels.

'What's going on? You're putting the house up for sale? You can't do that.'

Shauna saw Maria strolling up the path just as Hilary, her next-door neighbour, emerged through her front door and another trio of neighbours hastened across the road.

'Ladies, let's have a glass of champagne and I'll tell you all together,' Shauna said calmly, ushering them all in. They clip-clopped across the wooden floor into the lounge, agog. 'Tuck into the champers, girls.' Shauna handed out slim flutes of sparkling Moët.

'Aren't you having some?' Hilary asked.

'Can't, have to drive over to Whiteshells Bay to collect Chloe. That's why I'm moving. It's too much of a commute.'

'But why didn't you put her into a school here?' Maria asked. 'Surely it would have made more sense.'

Shauna took a deep breath. 'Because Greg and I are separated at the moment and she needs the security of her family around her, as I do myself,' she said crisply.

Alice spluttered her champagne, and coughed as tears came to her eyes when it went against her breath. This *was* gossip! Gossip of the highest order. She couldn't *wait* to tell her cronies.

'That's terrible!'

'How sad.'

Hilary and Maria moved to Shauna's side, concerned for her. She liked them both and planned to keep in touch with them, but the rest of her neighbours were not what she'd call friends.

'I wanted to come home for Chloe; I wanted her to go to school here. Greg doesn't want to settle in Ireland. He loves it out in the Gulf. It's all quite amicable,' she fibbed. That was all they needed to know. She wouldn't dream of telling them about the real reason for their split.

'That's such a shame,' murmured Maria.

'Where are you moving to?' Alice demanded, having recovered her equilibrium.

'Whiteshells Bay,' Shauna said cheerfully.

'The *sticks*!' Alice's nose wrinkled. 'How provincial.'

'Alice!' hissed Hilary.

'Well it *is* the sticks, Hilary,' Shauna murmured, amused in spite of herself. 'Don't worry, Alice, I won't expect you to visit,' she said sweetly, and then excused herself to go and answer the phone. It was another neighbour saying that she couldn't make the lunch, and as she listened to the babble and buzz of chattering coming from her lounge she felt a huge sense of relief that her news was out in the open and she'd be gone to her new penthouse in plenty of time for Christmas.

WINTER
(the same year)

39

'GOD ABOVE, IT'S FREEZING,' SHAUNA COMPLAINED AS SHE trudged across the beach with Carrie. 'I'd forgotten how cold it gets in the winter,' she added as she pulled her scarf tighter round her face so that all that was showing was her nose.

'Stop moaning, you wimp.' Carrie grinned. She was walking bare-headed, letting the wind whip her auburn hair around her face. It was a Sunday afternoon on the last day of November. They were walking off the big roast dinner they had eaten in Carrie's an hour previously.

'Greg wants to come home for Christmas,' Shauna said slowly as she kicked a piece of driftwood out of her way.

'And what do you want?'

Shauna sighed. 'I don't know. I'm trying to think of Chloe and what's best for her.'

'Well if he doesn't come home you're more than welcome to come to us on Christmas Day, you know that,' Carrie said warmly.

'Or we could have it in my new pad,' Shauna suggested.

'That sounds good, but would you be up to it?'

'I'm not an invalid, Carrie,' Shauna said dryly.

'I know that. Are you sorry that you sold the house in Malahide?' Carrie asked.

'God no! I couldn't bear all the nosy patronizing once they

451

found out Greg and I had split. I'd never be free of it. At least this way it's a fresh start with new neighbours. And an apartment is much more practical for us.'

'Apartment,' snorted Carrie. 'It's a penthouse.'

'True.' Shauna grinned. 'It was such a pain in the ass having to come over from Malahide every day, anyway. It was driving me nuts. I got nothing done. Those apartments are perfect for us.' She squinted along the shore to where she could see the elegant sandstone and glass building that housed their new home. She and Chloe had moved in a week ago. 'They came on the market at just at the right time for me.'

'They're ideal for you,' Carrie agreed. 'I wonder what will Greg think when he sees it.'

Shauna shrugged. 'Who cares what he thinks? If he comes to visit he can sleep in the third bedroom. And if he comes to visit in the summer I'll be in the mobile. That's why I kept it.'

'Doesn't sound as if you're planning to get back together,' Carrie murmured.

'Just let's say I'm keeping my options open,' Shauna said grimly. 'You know, it's ironic. Greg's never had so much communication with Chloe. He emails her most days and phones three or four times a week. When he got the Dubai job last year he could go three or four days on the trot without ever seeing or talking to her.'

'Well at least he's making the effort to keep in touch,' Carrie commented.

'I suppose so.' Shauna frowned. 'She's really happy at school here, isn't she?' She glanced down to the shore where the four children were dancing in the foamy wash of the waves in their bright red wellingtons.

'She's thriving.' Carrie threw a stick for a dog that bounded along the beach, tail wagging.

'She's even going to be in the Christmas play. Remember the

last play we were at on the Christmas morning before we went to Abu Dhabi? Two of the angels had a fight?'

'Yeah, and remember Olivia singing "Little Donkey" at Mam's grave? And Chloe singing "BimBamBom"!' Carrie smiled at the memory.

'Hannah wasn't even born. Can you believe it? Look at them all now,' Shauna marvelled.

'That was the year the Freeloaders invited themselves.' Carrie made a face. 'I wonder has Della had the baby yet?'

'I don't know and I don't care and I certainly won't be asking Greg about her.'

'I suppose we can be thankful for small mercies that you're not involved with them any more. Could you imagine Della, Eddie and *three* kids? The mind boggles.' Carrie laughed.

'I'm not even going there,' Shauna retorted. 'Can you imagine another Ashley?'

'Let's change the subject,' Carrie said hastily.

Please don't let it be another boy, Della prayed as her labour pains intensified and she groaned in agony. Her epidural hadn't taken and she was in the throes of labour. She wished Eddie were here so she could hurl abuse at him, but he never came to the delivery ward with her. Not after he'd fainted the first time with Kathryn and broken his nose.

This was definitely the last time she was getting pregnant. Shauna was crazy to want to. If Eddie had gone and had the snip behind her back she'd have given him a medal. He was going to have to do something, because she wasn't letting him near her again unless she was absolutely certain there was no chance of her getting pregnant. She didn't mind a life of celibacy. Sex wasn't all it was cracked up to be, anyway. Well, certainly not with Eddie, she thought crabbily.

453

'Come on, Mrs Keegan, one last push,' the midwife urged.

'I can't,' she whimpered.

'You can. Push.'

'Uuugggg,' groaned Della as a pain that nearly split her in two creased her body and the baby shot out of her.

'Well done, well done,' she heard the midwife say from far away. 'You've got a lovely baby boy.'

Oh no! she thought before she fainted clean away.

'Bobby, I was just thinking, maybe you and I could cook Christmas dinner this year. You know the way the girls are so good to me. I'd like to repay them somehow. And it's been such a rough year for Shauna, it might be nice for her to have all her family around her at a difficult time.' Noel's voice came excitedly down the phone.

Bobby's jaw dropped. He hadn't planned on going home for Christmas. He and Anton had planned on going to Anton's folks for the festive season. 'I'm not sure if I'm off this Christmas,' he fibbed. 'I'll have to check it out and get back to you.'

'Oh! I hadn't thought of that.' Noel sounded deflated.

'How are things otherwise?' Bobby asked guiltily.

'Not bad. Shauna moved into her new apartment last week. It's got a great view. They're built at the edge of the village. It's very handy for young Chloe going to school. I was hoping they'd move in with me,' he confided.

'They're probably better off to have a place of their own,' Bobby said diplomatically.

Noel chuckled. 'Shauna said we wouldn't last a week. She's a bit more excitable than Carrie, you know.'

Bobby laughed. 'That's putting it mildly. I'll get back to you about Christmas, Dad.'

'All right, son. It was just a thought. I wouldn't manage it on my own. I'm not the world's greatest cook but you're pretty nifty in the kitchen.'

'I'll get back to you soon. See you, Dad. Take care.' He hung up and turned to Anton, who was sprawled on the sofa watching an old black and white Bette Davis film. 'You'll never believe what Dad's concocted. He wants him and me to cook for the gang in his house on Christmas Day. Oh, can you believe it?' he groaned. 'I had to lie and say I thought I might be working. If I told him I was going to your parents for Christmas he'd take it badly. Especially when he wants to cook dinner for the girls so that he can do something for all their kindness to him. Oohhh, I feel such a heel.'

'Oh dear,' Anton murmured. 'Dilemma, dilemma.'

'No dilemma. I've made my arrangements with you,' Bobby said grumpily.

'Your dad's getting old. You can always come to us for New Year,' Anton suggested.

'How come you're much nicer than me?' Bobby grumbled.

'You haven't been home for Christmas for a long time. Since before you met me, actually,' Anton pointed out.

'I was working last year,' Bobby retorted.

'I think you should go.'

'If you were able to come with me I wouldn't give a toss. It would be a hoot,' he moaned, looking hopefully at his partner.

'Not for your father,' Anton said gently. 'He'd be very uncomfortable. He's not going to change. It wouldn't work. Be realistic. I *can't* come. It would be terrible if everything you've both achieved fell apart.'

'Why does it have to be all about him? Don't you *want* to spend Christmas with me? Aren't you disappointed that we're not going to be together? Do you love me at all? You're making me feel very rejected,' Bobby said petulantly.

Anton laughed. 'And what drama are we enacting today? The paranoid lover? Of course I love you. Of course I'm disappointed, you idiot. Of course I'd love to go to Ireland with you. Of course I want to spend Christmas with you, but the fact that your dad has asked you to come home and cook Christmas dinner with him is almost a miracle. Isn't it?'

'I suppose you're right,' sighed Bobby. 'As usual!'

'Go on. You'll be glad you did. Your sister could do with some TLC. This is her first Christmas on her own. It won't be easy for her.'

'Enough of the guilt trips!' Bobby threw a cushion at his partner. 'I'll go. I'll be a shoulder for Shauna to cry on and I'll cook the friggin' Christmas dinner.'

'And I'll cook you the best New Year dinner you ever tasted,' Anton promised, laughing heartily at his beloved's theatrics.

'Now, girls, I've a proposal to put to the pair of you and I hope you'll say yes,' Noel said to his daughters as they sat in his kitchen having a cup of tea with him. His eyes were gleaming with anticipation.

'What's that, Dad?' Carrie couldn't hide her curiosity. It was unusual for Noel to be so animated.

'Well, Bobby and I would like to have you all come here for Christmas dinner. It's our turn to put on a feast for you,' he informed them earnestly.

'Oh! I was planning on having Christmas in my place,' Shauna said in surprise. Noel held up his hand.

'No, Shauna. I insist. It's *our* turn and we'd be delighted to do it. You've had a tough time. Bobby and I would like to be the hosts this year.'

'It sounds great, Dad.' Carrie leaned back in her chair. 'I'll go anywhere I'm invited.'

'Now, the only thing is, I might need to borrow cutlery and plates. But Bobby can sort that out, he'll know better than me. We'll use your mother's good linen tablecloth and napkins, and maybe one of you might do a centrepiece for the table the way she used to. I think I might get the dining room painted. And I'll have to get the chimney swept so that we can light a fire in it. I haven't used that room in so long. It will be nice to have a Christmas dinner in it.' He was delighted. 'Wait until I tell Mrs O'Neill. She's having her daughter and son-in-law and three grandchildren over from Australia for Christmas, so the two houses will be full on Christmas Day.'

'Fantastic, Dad.' Carrie smiled at him, pleased to see him so lively.

'I'll paint the room for you,' Shauna offered. 'I like painting. I'll get a colour chart from the hardware shop.'

'Would you do that? Good girl,' he said rubbing his hands together. 'I'll organize the chimney sweep.' He became absorbed in happy plans.

'Well, it's either going to be brilliant or a disaster,' Carrie said wryly as she and Shauna walked down the village later on to collect the colour chart. 'There could be fireworks in the kitchen.'

'And queeny tantrums. Oh dear.' Shauna grinned. 'The family peace and quiet could be in for a dramatic turn for the worse.'

'Don't say that even in a joke,' Carrie warned as a flurry of snowflakes began to swirl and dance around them.

Just to let you know my plans for Christmas in case you want to make ones of your own. Will be going to Dad's for a family Christmas so if you intend coming to Ireland and staying with us, I'd prefer if you could wait until the day after St Stephen's Day. Also if you could let me

457

know how long you intend to stay, as I'd like to be able
to plan a party or two myself.

    S

Greg read his wife's email and felt disheartened. It was cold
and to the point, like an email to a stranger. She seemed to be
getting on fine without him and she certainly didn't want him at
her father's house for Christmas dinner. She wasn't letting the
grass grow under her feet. The house was sold. She had a new
apartment. Hell, for all he knew she had a new man.

She'd made a killing on the house. He could have objected to
the sale and said it was the family home, but he'd figured it was
better to keep her sweet by letting her sell it to buy the apartment and hope that time would heal and absence make the heart
grow fonder. Although it didn't seem to be working out that way,
he thought despondently. The threat of a forensic accountant
hung large. She was really playing dirty. He never thought she
had it in her. He should have known. She was a woman; they
were all the same, he thought bitterly. He deleted her email and
went to take a shower before heading off to a function in the
Hilton.

As he lay in bed later that night, he had to admit that he
missed Shauna and Chloe. He'd observed the other couples at
the do and missed knowing that Shauna was there, sparkling and
animated and dressed to kill. They'd been a good team. He
hadn't appreciated how good until they'd split. He'd taken her
very much for granted, he supposed. And when he got Chloe's
innocent emails telling him all about school and her cousins, he
felt darts of sadness that astonished him. She was quite an
interesting little character, he was discovering. His work wasn't
satisfying him as it once had, either, which surprised him.

He sighed and thumped his pillow into a more comfortable

458

shape. He knew what was wrong with him. He was consumed with guilt. He was working like a Trojan to block it out but it wouldn't go away. He needed to talk to Shauna, to try to persuade her to come back to him and make a go of it. But there was no point in trying to do that in Ireland. All her family were against him now. They'd put pressure on her not to be reconciled with him, he was sure of that. They needed to meet on neutral territory.

Paris would be perfect, he decided with a surge of hope. They'd meet in Paris and he'd persuade her to come back to him and everything would be fine. Delighted that he had come up with a great plan, he fell asleep and had the best night's sleep since his grandmother's disastrous funeral.

Carrie unlocked the office door and hurried into the building to turn on the heater. It was still snowing and already the grass was hidden under a white mantle. The kids would be thrilled. She made herself a cup of tea, attended to the post and switched on the computer to read her emails. There was only one, a regular customer wanting to book one of the mobiles for the St Patrick's weekend. She dealt with it, paid an ESB bill out of her twenty-four-hour banking account and switched off her computer. It was such an easy job in the winter months, she acknowledged, as she washed up her cup, switched off the heater and locked the door after her. She'd do a quick walk round in the evening to make sure everything was OK, and that was her work done for the day. Often when she'd been tempted to give up the site during the summer madness she'd reminded herself that for three months of stress and hard work she had nine months of relative ease.

Sharp needles of sleety snow stung her face and she pulled up the hood of her parka. Head down, she hurried home to cook the children's dinner. She'd been really surprised by her father's invitation to Christmas dinner, cooked by himself and Bobby. In theory it sounded good. She hoped against hope that nothing would go wrong. The past two years had been good for them as a family compared to the turmoil that had gone before. She prayed it would stay that way.

Shauna seemed happy enough with the plan. It meant she had a legitimate excuse not to invite Greg until after Christmas Day. If it wasn't for Chloe, Carrie felt she wouldn't want to see him at all. It was difficult for her sister, and lonely. Christmas would probably be an ordeal for her. Carrie sighed as she inserted her key in the lock and let herself in to her warm, welcoming house.

'Stop feeling guilty, woman,' Dan said to her that night as they lay in bed discussing the events of the day.

'I'm not,' she said defensively. Trust Dan. He knew her better than she knew herself.

'You are. You're feeling guilty because we're contented and happy and Shauna's on her own with a broken marriage. That's not your fault, Carrie. You can't fix everything. You're doing a very good job of being there for her. That's all you can do. And if your father and Bobby come to blows . . . so what! We'll grab the turkey and run.'

She giggled at the notion as she curled in against him and his arms tightened round her.

It was a long time since she'd seen snowflakes dancing on the sea, Shauna mused as she drew the heavy gold brocade curtains and shut out the dark night. The flames of the gas fire flickered in the grate and a soothing piano concerto played on the stereo. She lay down on the sofa and picked up her book. Chloe was fast asleep, exhausted after an afternoon spent playing with her cousins in the snow. It was the first time that she had seen it since she'd been a toddler, and she was enthralled. The snowman that now resided in her grandfather's garden was a work of art.

She was asking about putting up a Christmas tree already. Shauna sighed. Chloe had settled down far better than she could have wished for. That was a huge relief to her. She herself, however, felt terribly lonely. Here she was, a single parent, with her fortieth birthday looming. That wasn't much to boast about, she thought glumly. Jenna and Brett had invited her and Chloe to come and visit them in the States but she'd hedged. It was different now that she was separated. She was in a financial limbo. To be fair to Greg, he hadn't put any obstacles in her path when she was selling the house and she still had a joint current account with him. But it was unsettling and she was going to have to make up her mind whether she wanted to try to make a go of things with him again or plough her own furrow.

His betrayal had cut her deep. She couldn't imagine making love to him again. It would be impossible. All she'd be able to think about was that because of him she would never have another child. A tear trickled down her cheek.

He'd asked her why she had married him. If she were honest, she'd have to admit that she'd married him because he was good-looking and fun to be with and he offered an escape from her father's control. That was no reason to marry anyone, she admitted, cringing, as she looked deep into her soul and realized that she too must share the blame for their mistakes. It wasn't fair to blame Greg for everything that had gone wrong between them. He was right when he'd accused her of not listening to him. He'd said from the start that he didn't want another child, and she'd kept on and on at him. If she really loved him would she not have respected his wishes?

'And if he really loved me, would he not have respected mine?'

461

she muttered angrily, wiping her tears away. Each of them felt hard done by. Each of them was bitter. What a sad legacy to leave behind them from their marriage. At least Chloe was happy, she comforted herself. And right now that was the most important thing of all.

The following morning she checked her emails and her heart did a triple somersault when she saw one from Greg.

Please, please, meet me in Paris so that we can talk. Please give our marriage another chance, if not for our sake, then for Chloe's.

I'm sorry. I love you and I really miss you and Chloe. What I did was unforgivable. I know that. If you can put the past behind us it would be wonderful but at least let's talk. Chloe deserves that much.

I love you,

Greg

Shauna felt myriad emotions as she read the email. Rage, loneliness, guilt, sadness. It was too late to be laying a guilt trip on her about Chloe. His daughter had not been a priority when they'd lived together. It was manipulative and mean of him to use her as a carrot to get them back together.

But he was right, even though it angered her to admit it. They owed it to Chloe to talk. Would it be possible to overcome what had happened, for their daughter's sake? A meeting might ease her pain. It would certainly help her to decide her future one way or another. Anything was better than the lonely limbo she was in at the moment.

She sat with her fingers poised over the keyboard. Then: OK. I'll meet you in Paris next Saturday. Separate rooms wherever we're staying. Shauna, she typed, and clicked on send.

She sat staring at the screen for a long time. She knew it would be up to her. Greg wanted her back. He wanted them to be a family again. But what did she want? She just didn't know, she thought forlornly. She was lonely. The thought of being a single mother was daunting. What was the best thing for Chloe?

Her daughter padded into the room wrapped in a warm, fluffy dressing gown.

'Morning, darling.' Shauna inclined her cheek for a kiss.

'Hi, Mom. I've to go to rehearsals for my school play, don't forget.'

'I know. Would I forget something so important?' Shauna teased. 'Listen, Dad wants us to go back to Abu Dhabi. What do you think about that?' She studied her daughter intently. Chloe's big blue eyes registered dismay.

'Oh, no, Mom! I don't want to go back *there*!' She wrinkled her nose in disgust. 'I love living here. I love my teacher and my school and all my friends and Olivia and Hannah and Davey and Grandpa and Carrie and Dan,' she reeled off breathlessly. 'Grandpa and I are going to grow marrows next year. I *can't* go back there. I'm a Wise Man in the play. That's a very important part. Tell Dad to come and live here,' she urged plaintively.

'Maybe I will,' Shauna said slowly. 'That's exactly what I'll do and we'll see what he says.'

'So we're not going back to Abu Dhabi?' Chloe queried anxiously.

'No.' Shauna shook her head.

'Brill! Mom, can I have Frosties for breakfast?'

'Absolutely not,' Shauna said firmly, getting up from the computer. 'Come on and we'll make your porridge.'

'Aw, Mom.' Chloe pouted, but she skipped out of the room, blond pigtail flying, and Shauna realized that her daughter had provided the solution to her problem. If Greg wanted them to be together as a family he was going to have to come back to Ireland. Chloe didn't want to go back to the Gulf and, to be honest, neither did she. That life was behind her. She wanted to put down her roots and make a life for herself at home, with or without him.

She'd know how he felt about it soon enough. Did he really mean it when he said he loved her and Chloe? It was time to put his protestations of love to the test.

Greg read Shauna's email with a sense of elation. Great! She hadn't shot him down out of hand. He'd woo her in Paris. It would be like a second honeymoon. By the time he was through there'd be no need for separate bedrooms. He lifted the phone and called his secretary in the outer office.

'Book me a flight to Paris and a suite in the Ritz for next Saturday and Sunday,' he instructed crisply, wishing that he could have gone on the Thursday so that he wouldn't miss so many days' work. Still, it was worth it if it gave him a chance to have his family back with him. He'd told everyone in Abu Dhabi that Shauna had stayed at home because her father wasn't well. That excuse wouldn't last for ever.

He wouldn't need it soon, he thought confidently. Things were going to get back to normal. His phone rang. It was Pierre. The company were expanding their operations into Hong Kong. He was on the team. They were flying out early in the New Year to meet with builders and developers. He wondered what Shauna would think about moving to Hong Kong. It was a brilliant, life-enhancing opportunity for them. But he wouldn't say anything about it until the New Year, he decided. There was no point in complicating things. That was for another day.

* * *

464

'Greg, I'm not sharing a room with you,' Shauna said angrily as she walked around the sumptuous suite he had laid on for them in the Ritz. She'd been sick with nerves flying to Paris to meet him but now she was feeling downright mad.

'You don't have to,' he said, disappointed. 'It's got two bedrooms.'

'Oh . . . oh . . . OK,' she said, slightly mollified. She felt up in a heap. She'd thought that she might feel a surge of affection, at least, when she saw her husband, but she just felt flat. All she could think about when she looked at him was that he had made her life a misery for the past year with his selfishness. How could she possibly get back with him feeling like this? Would the pain, anger and resentment ever go away?

'I got you this,' he said hesitantly, handing her a box.

'No!' She pushed it away.

'Please, Shauna, open it,' he urged.

Reluctantly she took the red velvet box from him and opened it, to find a ring and earrings of diamonds and rubies. They were beautiful. He knew her tastes so well, she thought sadly. But how typical of him to think that expensive jewellery would make everything all right.

'I can't take this.' She handed it back to him.

'Please, don't be like that. Let's try again,' Greg pleaded. He shoved it back to her. He looked tired and worn and he was a lot greyer at his temples than before.

Shauna took a deep breath and placed the box on the sofa. 'Greg, it's like this. If you want us to get back together you've got to come home. Chloe doesn't want to go back to the Gulf and neither do I,' she said flatly.

'We don't have to stay in the Gulf,' he said excitedly. 'I've been offered a job in Hong Kong! We're expanding out there. I've great news for you.' His brown eyes were sparkling. 'I was supposed to be going out early in the New Year but Pierre wants me to go next week. I know it's Christmas but he's offered us a week at the company's expense in any hotel of our choice. Just imagine it, Shauna. Christmas in Hong Kong. Chloe would love it!'

'Are you mad!' Shauna exclaimed, horrified. 'She'd hate it. She'd be afraid Santa wouldn't come. She'd have to try and make friends with whatever kids were in the hotel. For God's sake, Greg, use your head. What child wants to spend Christmas in a hotel?'

'Aw, Shauna. It's a great opportunity. How many children have the chance to travel the world and soak up new cultures like she's had?'

'She loves it at home,' Shauna said exasperatedly. 'Do you not realize that? She has what she's always wanted. Family.'

'Ah family . . . fucking family . . . there's more to life than family,' he said resentfully.

'Actually there isn't, Greg,' she said quietly. 'Family is what it's all about and you never gave ours a chance,' she added bitterly.

He flushed. 'I suppose you'll hold that against me for the rest of my life,' he taunted.

'I don't know,' Shauna said wearily, sitting down. Deep down she knew they were finished. Greg was never going to change. The fact that he was so excited about going to Hong Kong proved that to her. He'd *never* settle in Ireland. 'I think we have to be realistic,' she said slowly. 'It's clear you don't want to come home and settle down and I don't want to live abroad any more. Maybe it's time to call it a day.'

Greg sat on the sofa opposite her. 'I don't want to call it a day,' he exclaimed, staring at her in dismay.

'You know what you have to do, then,' she said, amazed at

how calm she sounded. She stood up. 'Greg, I'm not going to stay. I'm going to go back to the airport and try to get a flight home. You need to think about things and I have our daughter's play rehearsals to attend. We could sit here all night talking and get nowhere. The options are quite simple. You decide.'

Greg said nothing. He looked bleak and miserable and she felt a pang of pity for him. She bent and kissed him on the cheek, glad that all her anger seemed to have momentarily evaporated. He was never going to change. There was no point in denying that reality. She walked across the thickly carpeted floor and let herself out and never looked back. The red velvet box rested on the sofa where she'd left it.

CHRISTMAS DAY

40

'OH, SHAUNA, THE ROOM'S ABSOLUTELY GORGEOUS!' CARRIE
exclaimed as she stood at the door of her father's dining room
and gazed in admiration at the change her sister had wrought.
The old décor had been insipid: peach floral wallpaper and peach
curtains that had long faded. Shauna had scraped and sanded the
walls and painted them a rich burgundy and cream. She'd
bought new cream curtains and two burgundy and cream lamps
that threw a warm glow around the firelit room. It was intimate
and inviting, especially on the grey, gloomy, cold day that they'd
all woken to. The table was dressed in Anna's best linen tablecloth and Bobby had decorated it with a simple arrangement of
holly and red carnations around a wide red candle.

'Champagne in the sitting room,' Bobby announced gaily, his
barbecue apron protecting his mauve shirt and black trousers.

'How are things in the kitchen?' Carrie asked as she divested
herself of her coat and hat and bent down to help Hannah with
hers.

'To be honest, I'd be better off on my own. Dad's got very
slow, hasn't he? He keeps getting in my way,' Bobby whispered.

'Do you want me to come out and help?' she offered good-
naturedly.

'He won't have it. Do or die, he's going to repay you and Shauna for all the meals you've cooked for him. He'll do and *I'll* die,' Bobby said dramatically, speeding back to the kitchen.

'Mom, this is a *great* Christmas,' Chloe announced as she shrugged out of her new red coat with the soft furry collar. 'Grandpa said that I could sit beside him,' she added happily as she pranced into the sitting room to join her cousins.

The doorbell rang and Noel called out, 'I'll get that.' He hurried out to the hall with the tea towel over his shoulder. 'Come in, Mrs O'Neill, and you're very welcome,' he said warmly to his neighbour, who stood at his front door with a huge pudding on a plate. It smelt divine.

'Is that for us?' Davey's eyes widened.

'It certainly is, love,' she laughed.

'We've *loads* of puddings,' Davey announced gleefully to the others. Christmas pudding was his absolute favourite food after roast potatoes.

'There was no need for that now, Mrs O'Neill. We're delighted to have you here,' Noel said warmly, ushering her into the hall and taking the pudding from her.

Bobby came out to greet her with a kiss. 'Hi, hon, get in there and have a glass of champers and that will fix you,' he ordered and she hugged him tightly. When her daughter had phoned to say that they wouldn't be coming until New Year because the youngest child had measles, she'd been devastated. She'd cried telling Noel the news, much to his dismay.

'You'll come and have dinner with us,' he'd said firmly.

'I couldn't do that. You'll just want to have all your family around you,' she'd demurred.

'Mrs O'Neill, you're as dear to me as family. You've been a great friend to me. *And* given me sound advice,' he added with an uncharacteristic twinkle in his eye. 'We'd be honoured if you'd dine with us.'

'No, Noel, but thank you for asking,' she'd said, to his disappointment.

'Leave it to me,' Bobby had said when his father informed him of the state of affairs, a week before he was due to fly home. He'd phoned Mrs O'Neill immediately. 'Do you think I'm going to poison you, is that it?' he demanded when she'd answered the phone. She burst out laughing.

'Go on, ya little rip,' she exclaimed.

'*Please* have Christmas dinner with us?' he begged. 'We're all so grateful to you for the kindness you've shown us all over the years. And you introduced Dad to bowling. That alone deserves a nosh-up. Please, please come. Or have you a secret lover you want to spend Christmas with?' he teased.

'Now that you mention it,' she responded, 'when are we going to meet *your* young man?' Bobby had told her all about Anton in the summer.

'Sooner rather than later, I hope, but we'll get Christmas out of the way first. If Dad and I survive cooking a Christmas meal together, we'll survive anything. So won't you come to us for dinner?' he urged.

'All right then,' she agreed. 'If you're *sure* that I won't be intruding.'

'Don't be silly,' Bobby had chided, delighted that she'd agreed. Now, a week later, he shooed her into the sitting room.

'Go and put your feet up by the fire. Dad and I are coming in to have a drink in a minute. We just have a few more little chores to do. Carrie, look after our special guest,' Bobby ordered, following his father back into the kitchen.

'I just need you to spoon the oil over the parboiled potatoes for me,' he explained to Noel. 'They're the last to go into the oven, then we can have a quick drink, take the turkey out of the oven to rest, steam the veg nicely al dente, serve the starters and we're away on a hack.'

'Right you are,' said Noel, who was thoroughly enjoying himself despite being a tad flustered.

Bobby heated the butter and oil in the microwave he'd insisted on buying, until it was boiling and showed his father how to dip the floury spuds into it with a slotted spoon before placing them on the roasting tray. The smells emanating from the oven were tantalizing and Noel was looking forward to his dinner. While he did the potatoes, Bobby put the finishing touches to his starter of roasted peppers, olives and feta cheese. He was very good under pressure, Noel acknowledged as he watched him garnish the dish with fresh basil. They were working very well as a team. They had shared the preparation of the vegetables and the stuffing the night before and Bobby had got up early to dress the turkey while Noel had set out their breakfast. Then they'd joined the rest of the family for Mass and the visit to the grave.

Noel felt a rare sense of contentment as he worked with his son in the kitchen. He'd never dreamed that they would prepare a family Christmas meal together. If he hadn't been so bitter and foolish in the past it could have happened long ago, he thought with a pang of guilt. *Forget about it now*, he told himself as he oiled the last potato. The past was the past; it was time to let go of it.

'There you go, chef. Potatoes are ready,' he said with satisfaction.

'So's the starter. Let's go and have that drink,' Bobby said, taking the roasting tray from him and sliding it onto the lower shelf of the oven. When he took out the turkey he'd move them up to the top shelf to crisp them golden.

There was a happy buzz in the sitting room when they joined

their guests. Mrs O'Neill was sitting, pink-cheeked from her champagne, beside the fire, with Chloe perched on the arm of her chair showing her the new Barbie Bride doll that Santa had brought her. It was just like the one that Olivia had. She was thrilled with it. Shauna was cuddling Hannah who was ready to fall asleep after her early start and Carrie, Dan and Olivia were watching Davey do magic card tricks with great panache.

'Let's toast the chefs,' Carrie proposed gaily, raising her glass. 'Dinner smells divine.'

'He should have been a chef,' Noel said proudly. 'He's as good as any of those fellas on the TV.'

'Say that after you've had the dinner,' Bobby grinned, his face flushed and his hair dishevelled from the heat of the kitchen.

Twenty minutes later they were tucking into his starter with hearty appetites and murmurs of appreciation.

'That went down well enough,' Bobby murmured to his father as they carried the dirty plates back into the kitchen.

'It was very tasty,' approved Noel.

'Oh my *God*! Look at the fucking cat, Dad!' Bobby yelped as he opened the kitchen door and saw Twiskers on the table, where the turkey steamed succulently, with her nose stuck in the stuffing.

'Ya brat of hell,' Noel exclaimed, swatting the culprit with his tea towel. Twiskers jumped off the table and meowed indignantly as Noel gave her another whack of the towel, and then she escaped into the safety of the hall.

'What are we going to do?' Noel whispered, looking over his shoulder to make sure no-one had followed them into the kitchen. He gazed at the turkey, horrified. 'We'll just have to serve the ham on its own.'

'Stay calm.' Bobby put the plates down and ran his fingers through his hair. He inspected the turkey. Twiskers had taken a bite out of a leg, as well as sampling the stuffing.

'Look, if no-one knows, it won't bother them. I'll say nothing if you don't,' he proposed.

'Would they get food poisoning?' Noel asked doubtfully.

'No. Not at all.' Bobby hoped he sounded convincing. He wasn't quite sure, to tell the truth, but he wasn't going to let on to his father. 'Look, I'll carve away the bits that Twiskers was at and we'll put them in a dish for her, even though the little brat doesn't deserve it, and I'll do the same with the stuffing. I'll carve from the other side for the dinner and we'll forget about it. OK?'

'If you think it's all right, then we'll do what you say,' Noel agreed, relieved. 'You couldn't have a Christmas dinner without turkey, sure you couldn't?'

'Absolutely not,' Bobby agreed as he began to carve away the offending bits of the bird.

Fifteen minutes later the guests were demolishing their Christmas feast with much praise and many compliments to the chefs, oblivious of the drama in the kitchen earlier.

Bobby raised his glass. 'To Dad,' he said, with a little conspiratorial wink at his father.

A beam of pleasure crossed Noel's face. He felt strangely happy. In spite of the disaster in the kitchen his family meal was a success. He had them all around him and even though some things caused him concern, like Bobby's . . . problem . . . and Shauna's broken marriage, they didn't seem to matter right now.

'To the best grandpa in the universe and outer space even,' Davey toasted.

'To a great neighbour.' Mrs O'Neill smiled at him.

'To a sound father-in-law,' Dan said firmly.

'To Dad.' Shauna and Carrie lifted their glasses.

Twiskers came and rubbed her face against his leg. He leaned down and patted her forgivingly. His little companion deserved a Christmas banquet the same as the rest of them.

It was the best Christmas he'd had in many, many years. God had been very good to him, he reflected as he stroked the linen tablecloth gently. He felt very close to his wife today. He knew that she'd be very happy to see them all like this, and that was the greatest gift of all.

'I'm bushed.' Bobby was yawning as he lay sprawled in front of the fire in Carrie's sitting room.

'I'm pissed.' Carrie grinned as she took a slug of her brandy Alexander.

'And I'm off to bed.' Dan uncoiled himself from the sofa where he'd been sitting with his arm round Carrie. ''Night, you guys.'

'You mean you're not going to walk me home?' Bobby demanded, horrified.

'You can take your chances.' Dan laughed. 'It was a great meal. Thanks a lot.'

'You're welcome,' Bobby said warmly. 'It was long overdue.'

'Better late than never.' Dan bent down and kissed the top of his wife's head. 'I'll warm the bed for you.'

'I won't be long,' she assured him.

'Do you know what I'd love?' Bobby said dreamily a little while later.

'What? You couldn't possibly eat anything else.' Shauna eyed him in amazement.

'I'd like a mug of hot chocolate.'

'Oohh, that sounds nice.' Carrie perked up. 'I'll make us some.'

Ten minutes later the three of them were sitting in the firelight under the glow of the Christmas tree, sipping steaming hot chocolate and nibbling mince pies.

'It was a great day, wasn't it?' Carrie said appreciatively.

'Poor Dad. The snores out of him before I even left the house, and it was only half nine. He was wrecked.' Bobby blew bubbles in his froth.

'Chloe had a great time. She can't remember the last Christmas we had at home,' Shauna said. 'This one was so different,' she added dryly. 'No Greg and no Freeloaders.'

'How did you feel? Were you very lonely?' Bobby sat on the edge of her armchair and dropped an arm round her shoulder.

'Sometimes. But not as much as I thought I'd be. It really helped that we spent last night and tonight here. Poor old Chloe was very apprehensive that Santa wouldn't realize that she was here. There's notes everywhere in the apartment and Greg was instructed to leave notes all over the one in Abu Dhabi before he went to Hong Kong. She was ecstatic when she found her toys on the end of her bed this morning. That was hard to beat.'

'Stay as long as you like,' Carrie invited.

'Thanks, but it's great that I'm only down the road. I might take you up on it when Greg comes to visit at the end of January.'

'How do you feel about that?' Bobby asked.

Shauna shrugged. 'I'm glad for Chloe's sake. And I want him to see her whenever he wants. I'll even take her out to Hong Kong at Easter if he wants me to, but that's it. I've decided to ask him for a divorce,' she said quietly.

'Have you?' Carrie looked startled.

'When he took the job in Hong Kong, and I knew that he would, that was the end of it. I might have muddled along with him if he'd come home to live with us. At least I would have known we were important enough for him to make the effort. But that's not Greg.' She sighed.

'Bastard!' Carrie said hotly.

'Ah, no, Carrie, it's not all his fault and I don't want him to take all the blame,' she said firmly. 'I was as much to blame in some ways as he was. I married him because I thought he was so different from Dad, but in his own way he was just as controlling. And I didn't listen to him when he said that he didn't want any more children. So I have to accept some responsibility for the mess we're in. But I don't want to live with him again, not after what he did to me. And I certainly don't want to live in Hong Kong.' She shuddered. 'I need to make a fresh start. Chloe's settled in well here. All her toys and stuff have been freighted home from Abu Dhabi, so now it's time for me to decide what I'm going to do with myself. I want to get a job and earn my own money. I want to put down roots,' she told her siblings.

'Wow. A divorcee *and* a homosexual in the family! Poor, poor Dad,' Bobby said wickedly.

Shauna giggled. 'You're awful.' She dug him in the ribs.

'No, hold on, you might be entitled to a Church annulment, according to Dad. I didn't tell you this before, I didn't think you were ready for it, but to all intents and purposes poor old Greg's now become a eunuch,' Carrie informed them, straight-faced.

Bobby nearly choked on his hot chocolate as he guffawed. 'Oh, my God, that's the *best* I ever heard. Oh, he's *priceless*,' he said fondly, tears of mirth streaming down his cheeks.

Shauna started to giggle and then she was rolling around in the chair, splitting her sides laughing. Carrie joined in and they laughed their heads off, happy to be in each other's company again.

'Oh, that *was* a tonic,' Bobby declared as he wiped his eyes.

'Are all families like us or are we unique?' Carrie demanded.

'Oh, I think we're unique. Let's face it, who else has a eunuch for a brother-in-law?' Bobby hooted and they all started laughing again.

'Well I'd rather be us than anyone else,' Carrie said tipsily, raising her mug. 'To Family,' she toasted.

Shauna and Bobby leaned over and clinked their mugs to hers. 'To Family,' they echoed, smiling at each other, as the wind howled outside and the rain lashed against the windowpanes.